"*Never Let Go* is a unique and intriguing romantic suspense that will have your heart racing. Goddard's fast-paced storytelling combined with emotional depth will keep you guessing until the very end."

Rachel Dylan, bestselling author of the Atlanta Justice series

"From the riveting opening to the satisfying conclusion, *Never Let Go* is a stellar beginning to what promises to be a thrilling romantic suspense series."

Susan Sleeman, bestselling and award-winning author of the White Knights series

"Fast-paced and suspenseful, *Never Let Go* lives up to its name. It grabs you by the throat from the first page, takes you through riveting twists and turns, and doesn't let go until a powerhouse ending. Goddard has a lethal way with words and characters. She's an author to watch—and love!"

Ronie Kendig, bestselling author of The Tox Files series

"A twenty-one-year-old cold case, arson, murder, romance . . . I couldn't put *Never Let Go* down until 'The End,' and then I wished for more."

Patricia Bradley, winner of the Inspirational Readers Choice Award

"Wow! *Never Let Go* has everything I want in a romantic suspense novel. Heart-pounding action, a second-chance romance, and a frightening cold case that won't let you put the book down until the very last page."

Lisa Harris, bestselling author

"With deception at every turn, danger behind every door, and a romance that was and could be again, Goddard has crafted an edge-of-your-seat experience with *Never Let Go* that hooks readers from the first page and holds them tight until the satisfying and surprising conclusion."

Lynn H. Blackburn, award-winning and bestselling author of the Dive Team Investigations series

NEVER LET GO

ELIZABETH GODDARD

Revell

a division of Baker Publishing Group
Grand Rapids, Michigan

© 2019 by Elizabeth Goddard

Published by Revell
a division of Baker Publishing Group
PO Box 6287, Grand Rapids, MI 49516-6287
www.revellbooks.com

Printed in the United States of America

Library of Congress Cataloging-in-Publication Data
Names: Goddard, Elizabeth, author.
Title: Never let go / Elizabeth Goddard.
Description: Grand Rapids, MI : Revell, a division of Baker Publishing Group,
    [2019] | Series: Uncommon justice ; 1
Identifiers: LCCN 2018026773 | ISBN 9780800729844 (paper : alk. paper)
Subjects: | GSAFD: Christian fiction. | Love stories. | Mystery fiction.
Classification: LCC PS3607.O324 N48 2019 | DDC 813/.6—dc23
LC record available at https://lccn.loc.gov/2018026773

19 20 21 22 23 24 25   7 6 5 4 3 2 1

Mom, you taught me to love books.
Inspired me to write them.
More importantly, you showed me the way to Christ
by walking with him every day of your life on this earth.
Because of him, we'll be together again!

PROLOGUE

WEDNESDAY, 12:30 P.M.
TWENTY-ONE YEARS AGO
HOUSTON, TEXAS

Nursing scrubs? Check. White sneakers? Check. Keycard? Check.
Calm, even breathing? Nope.

She had everything she needed to get in and out quickly. The plan seemed so easy. Too easy. Then why did her heart pound against her rib cage until it ached? Why did her pulse roar in her ears as she walked the sterile hallway, heading for the maternity ward?

Palms sweating, she pushed through double doors into a wide corridor. Almost there.

Everything inside screamed for her to keep her head down. But that might give the wrong impression.

Forcing her chin high, she carried the file folders with purpose as her sneakers squeaked down the long white hallway. She made it to the wing where mothers and their newborn babies rested until released and found it busy with food service workers, janitorial personnel, and other hospital staff. Good. She'd been right to carefully calculate her arrival for the lunch hour.

Without missing a step, she traded the folders for a food tray sitting on a cart against the wall and then counted down the rooms, twenty-three forty-two, twenty-three forty . . .

Twenty-three thirty-eight.

Her heart palpitated. She slowly drew in a calming breath. It was now or never. She had no choice, really. This was better for everyone.

Please don't let hospital staff be in the room . . .

With forced confidence, she shoved open the door and entered. "Lunchtime," she proclaimed in what she hoped was a pleasant, singsong voice, but instead the word sounded hoarse and gravelly to her pulse-buzzing ears. There was no turning back now.

A nurse glanced up from a hospital bassinet where she was changing the baby's diaper. The woman in the bed pulled her gaze from her infant and offered a puzzled smile at the lunch tray.

What do I do? What do I do?

When the nurse paid her no attention, she snapped out of her panic and moved forward as if she had every right to be in the room. Another tray of food already sat on the bedside table, untouched. No wonder the woman had given her a funny look. Her breath hitched. She'd fooled herself into thinking this had been too easy. The plan was far from easy. It had only been easy before she entered the room where she had to engage with others.

She smiled at the mother—a fortyish-looking woman with dark circles under her eyes. "Oh, they already brought you lunch. I'll just return this tray."

She pivoted, but the mother called out to her. "Wait, what did you bring? The other lady brought me ham and it doesn't look good. I have no appetite as it is, so I'm hoping for something at least palatable."

She turned to face the mother. The nurse exited the room without comment. Perfect. It was all working out. She lifted the domed cover from the plate. "Looks like turkey and dressing."

The mother shifted to sit up higher on her bed. "My favorite."

"Wonderful." After removing the plate with ham, she set the new tray before the woman, then without another word glided over to the pink newborn in the nearby mobile bassinet. "While you enjoy your meal, I'll take this little princess to the nursery and return her in a bit."

She didn't dare look into the woman's eyes. She had to flee the room before the mother registered she was gone or thought to ask any questions. Besides, another glance into the sad eyes of the mother dying of cancer might thwart her resolve to see this through. She had a heart, after all. And she knew what this was going to do to this woman—kill her faster than any disease. But the mother wouldn't be able to care for the baby for very long anyway. This was all for the best. And she needed this baby more than the dying mother needed her.

Shoving through the door, she pushed the bassinet as if she belonged.

This would be the hard part.

She lifted the baby.

Yes, definitely the moment of truth. Could she do this? Could she really take this baby, who would become her daughter, and walk right out of the hospital without anyone noticing her? She realized she could, in fact, carry through with the plan. A satisfied smile lifted her lips as she cooed to another woman's baby in her arms.

CHAPTER ONE

A family tree can wither if nobody tends its roots.

—Unknown

MONDAY, 8:31 P.M., PRESENT DAY
ANDERSON CONSULTING OFFICES
SEATTLE, WASHINGTON

While death was no stranger to her, a courteous knock on the door to give warning this time would have been appreciated.

Willow Anderson had been blindsided. Hadn't seen it coming. Everyone faced death sooner or later. Reading obituaries and looking at tombstones were a part of her job, after all. Her life. So why had it come as such a surprise? Either way—warning or no warning—she had to face what had been left behind. There was no point in putting things off.

She stood at the edge of a cluttered desk and stared blurry-eyed at the stack of mail piled high. A fluorescent light in the corner of the office that had been converted from a warehouse flickered and buzzed, then dimmed, leaving her with less-than-adequate lighting. But she wouldn't be deterred and riffled through the envelopes in a daze, dropping each one on JT's desk as she went. Electricity.

11

Water. Something from the appraisal district? Oh, look, JT won a free Caribbean cruise. Junk mail. More bills.

The next one looked like a check. She ripped it open. Sure enough, a check had been made out to Anderson Consulting for services rendered. Willow hung her head. Wait. Not Anderson Consulting. In her grief-stricken state, she'd read that wrong. The check had been made out to James T. Anderson, her grandfather.

Everyone had called him JT. Anguish gripped her. Had he really been gone two weeks? He'd been the lifeblood of this forensic genealogy business. How could she keep it going without him?

She let the remaining envelopes fall back to the desk, where they fanned out.

A stupid tear escaped. Raced down her cheek. Tonight she'd mustered the courage to return to the office and face what JT had left behind when he'd been killed. Willow could have let Dana Cooper, JT's assistant, take care of some of it, but she'd told Dana to leave the office alone. They both needed time to mourn. Besides, Willow wanted to be the one to go through his things, including the mail.

She crumpled a piece of junk mail in her fist. Maybe she'd feel less fragile if she waited a few more days. Except the bills couldn't wait until Willow had finished grieving. Nor could clients in any outstanding cases on which he'd worked.

I can do this. I have to do this.

What choice did she have?

The heat kicked on, reminding her of the chill in the air. She rubbed her arms. Only a corner of the warehouse had been renovated into offices for Anderson Consulting. The rest seemed like a waste to Willow, but JT had thought he'd gotten a great deal on real estate at the time. The vaulted space had given them room to spread out, but now it felt far too . . . empty. Willow would have to figure out what she would do with the business and the real estate it occupied.

With the mail spread out, an envelope from the Washington State Department of Health caught her attention. She tugged it from the pile. Hands shaking, she carefully slit the envelope with a letter opener and pulled out the official document.

Her grandfather's death certificate.

Air whooshed from her lungs. Willow sank into a chair.

He's gone. Really gone. She wouldn't hear his words of wisdom. His jokes and boisterous laughter, or warm and friendly banter. At least not in this life.

JT had been one of a kind.

She touched his name on the certificate and, for good measure, let the shock of his death roll over her again. That moment she'd first heard the news.

JT had been killed riding his bike. To think he'd taken up the hobby as a way of extending his life after being diagnosed with cardiovascular disease. No plan had ever backfired so completely.

Why, why, why? You weren't supposed to die yet.

Tension corded her neck. A sliver of anger cut through her that he'd died when he'd had so much life left in him. But trying to come up with answers when there were none was a futile endeavor. Willow forced herself to focus on the task at hand. At this rate, it was going to be a long night. She rolled her neck around to ease the stiffness.

The outer office door opened and closed. "Willow? You in there?" Dana called.

Great. She'd wanted time alone. "Yep. JT's office."

A few seconds later, Dana appeared at the door. Willow masked her irritation. The woman meant well. "You didn't have to come."

Dana dropped her designer bag in a chair and frowned. She shrugged out of her sparkly jean jacket and stepped closer. "You didn't think I'd let you go through this alone, did you?"

"It's late. Don't you have a husband or something?" Willow forced warmth into her voice and then a half smile slid onto her lips. She was glad to see Dana after all. The woman knew what Willow needed. No wonder JT had leaned on Dana all these years.

"Stan is fine. On his laptop and watching television. He won't miss me." Dana leaned over the desk to look at the certificate. "Besides, he wanted me to make sure you were all right."

She slowly slipped the certificate from Willow's hands and studied it. "Are you sure you're ready to go through his things here? I can do this for you."

Willow covered her eyes. "I thought I'd accepted he was gone, but seeing his death certificate . . . it's so final."

"Oh, honey. I know it's hard." Dana rushed around the desk. After offering a comforting squeeze, she handed Willow a tissue, then snatched another from the box.

Willow wiped her eyes and blew her nose. "It's okay. I'm okay. I have to do this."

"I wish I hadn't told you about Mrs. Mason's call. But it was the only case he was actively working. You really don't have to get back to business so soon after your grandfather's death."

"I appreciate your concern." Willow touched Dana's arm. The woman had held her hand over the last two weeks—through the tragic news of JT's death, selecting a casket, and seeing him buried. In her fifties, Dana was more like an older sister or a best friend than a mother figure despite being two decades older than Willow. She was practically part of the family, though she had one of her own—a doting husband, two grown children, and four grandchildren who kept her busy outside of work.

Willow tossed the tissue into the wastebasket. "Decisions have to be made, and I'm the one to make them now. I need to call Mrs. Mason back and tell her that JT's gone. But I have to know what the case is about first. Maybe I can finish it up for him." If Mrs. Mason would allow her, and if Willow had the required skills.

Her grandfather was the talent behind their consulting business. Willow didn't want to ruin the reputation he'd garnered. She hadn't mentioned it to Dana yet, but she was seriously thinking about closing up Anderson Consulting.

"Dig into a new project." Dana gathered the scattered mail into a pile again. "It might help take your mind off things if you get busy again."

"Can you get her file?"

"I can do better." Dana smiled. "He videoed their conversation."

"What? When did he start doing that?"

"With Mrs. Mason. You were traveling, looking for the lost heir for that law firm. He came into the office one day with a GoPro camcorder, more than pleased with himself and anxious to try it on the next client."

Willow had missed spending the last few weeks of JT's life with him. She wanted more time.

While Dana sat down and started the desktop computer to bring up the video, Willow looked at the framed photographs on the walls. The floor-to-ceiling shelves filled with history books and dusty old journals. Curio cabinets showcasing collectibles and souvenirs. Her grandfather had provided an adventure as they traveled around the world conducting research about people's pasts. She'd watched as he'd used DNA and genealogy techniques for solving mysteries, such as identifying remains of World War, Korean War, and Vietnam War servicemen. Even law enforcement entities had often contacted him for assistance. The list went on and on.

"Okay, here it is." Dana grabbed another chair.

Willow sat next to her friend. The video started up on the computer screen. Her grandfather's voice boomed loud and confident. His boisterous laughter and warmth made the slender, sixtyish woman smile in return.

JT offered Mrs. Mason coffee and made her feel right at home. He had a way about him that made him personable. Everyone responded to his warmth.

He didn't have any enemies.

Or so she believed.

Willow paused the video. "He never met a man, woman, or child he didn't like." The words rasped out past the lump in her throat.

Dana sighed. "I'm sorry. I didn't realize that JT took up such a big part of the video. You don't have to do this tonight. We can tackle it later."

Shaking her head, Willow pressed play. "Tackling it later isn't going to make it easier for me."

As they continued watching the video, Willow smiled, her love for JT swelling in her heart. He propped his ankle up on his knee in a relaxed pose. His blue eyes were bright and intelligent. He acted like a man in the prime of his life, not someone in his late sixties, as he told a few jokes that made Mrs. Mason genuinely laugh. In fact, both Willow and Dana joined in the laughter, adding a few sniffles. Her grandfather was a force to be reckoned with. A pleasant, jovial force that the world would miss.

Then Katelyn Mason leaned forward and began her tale.

"I came all the way from Texas to speak to you about taking on a project for me," she said.

"A Texan, huh?" JT chuckled and winked. "I never would have guessed by your accent."

The woman actually blushed and smoothed out her collar. Was JT flirting?

"Let me ask you a question," he said. "Why Anderson Consulting?"

"I read an article about what you've accomplished. You've done the impossible."

Though JT kept a straight face, amusement and satisfaction glimmered in his eyes. "Tell me your story."

"Twenty-one years ago my baby girl, Jamie, was taken from me in the hospital. She was only a few hours old." Mrs. Mason

16

hung her head for a moment, then raised her quivering chin to pin her gaze on JT.

Lines in his forehead deepened with his frown. "And the FBI? The police?"

"Failed to find her. It's a cold case now. Through the years I've hired private investigators. They have all failed."

"And why are you just now coming to me?"

"As I said before, I read that you can do miracles. I have . . . I have less than three months to live, so the doctors tell me." Her voice hitched. "I believe with every fiber of my being that she is still alive out there, and I desperately want to say goodbye to her. I want her to know how much I love her. How much I have always loved her. And I never stopped praying for her. I believe you, Mr. Anderson, are the one to finally bring my baby home."

JT cleared his throat. His tender heart must have flooded with compassion. Willow wanted to reach through the screen and comfort him. He got up and fiddled with the GoPro, his anguished face filling the screen. He understood the pain of losing a child. His daughter, Willow's mother, had been killed in a car accident along with Willow's father.

Mind racing, Willow shut the video off.

Less than three months to live. "When was this interview?"

"A month ago."

Mrs. Mason had less than two months to live then, if her prognosis was accurate.

But a baby stolen twenty-one years ago? How had JT thought he could help? He'd never done this kind of project, especially one with such a short deadline. Still, Mrs. Mason's desperate plea for help must have compelled him to take action. Willow understood why he hadn't been able to say no. She had to think, so she got up and paced the room.

"You should finish this one. Find that woman's daughter." Dana's voice broke the silence. "It would keep your mind off losing him."

"Mrs. Mason believed JT was the one to finally bring home her baby girl. That's what she said. JT was the one with the skills—the genius behind solving impossible mysteries."

"You're every bit as brilliant." Dana sighed. "Look, he's been training you since you were just a kid. Since your parents died. You know he meant for you to take over."

"Maybe so, but I don't have his knack for uncovering clues. Knowing which ones to follow."

Dana vehemently shook her head. "You're too hard on yourself."

She flipped through the manila file folder she'd retrieved from the desk drawer. Something flickered in her eyes. What was it? Worry? Frustration?

"Okay, what *aren't* you telling me?" Willow asked.

A smile quickly replaced the frown on Dana's face. "No clue what you're talking about."

"Right. I know you well enough to see something else is on your mind." Willow tried to snatch the file away, but Dana was quicker and held it close.

"Now I'm sure you're hiding something."

The woman buried the file back in the desk drawer already crammed with folders, then riffled through the same stack of mail Willow had been through minutes ago. "I can take care of these for you. You didn't have to come in tonight."

Willow crossed her arms. "You can't put me off forever."

"Okay, okay." Dana rolled her head back and groaned. "Before he died, JT called Austin McKade to ask for his help on the Mason case."

Willow's stomach coiled. She pressed her hand against her midsection. She'd had a hard enough time getting over Austin without having to see him again.

"He did? But . . . why?" Did Austin even know about JT's death?

"It's an FBI cold case. JT had hoped Austin could get information so he wouldn't have to reinvent the wheel, so to speak."

Willow sank into a chair. "That makes sense. Total sense."

But she wouldn't put it past JT to have wanted to use the Mason case to his advantage.

This case might have been the excuse he'd needed to call Austin when he had other motives. He had an uncanny ability to convince people to go along with his wishes or what he believed was best for them. He had believed that Willow and Austin should be together. He just wouldn't let go of it. But JT couldn't have been more wrong.

Willow and Austin McKade had already crashed and burned, and those ashes would never be resurrected.

CHAPTER TWO

Austin McKade waited next to his gate in the terminal at Denver International Airport. Outside the window that overlooked the runways and grounded jets, lightning flashed and rain pummeled the asphalt. The storm had delayed his flight to Seattle. All he wanted to do was get home and into his bed. He couldn't wait for that moment when his head hit the pillow.

He slumped into one of the uncomfortable seats and dropped his carry-on next to him. The last few days had drained him.

Nothing like walking in on law enforcement processing a crime scene and seeing your client murdered on the floor. Well, technically, Michael Croft had no longer been a client. He'd fired Austin two days earlier. Michael had believed he was safe after they'd returned from a trip abroad. Who was Austin to tell him otherwise?

Except Austin had gone back to do just that. He had gone to see Michael one last time to explain that the danger wasn't over yet. But he had been too late.

Austin had informed the authorities of his position working with Michael and would likely be contacted to answer additional questions. Though Austin was no longer an FBI agent, he worked

20

with a group of ex-agents termed *independent special agents*. A laugh escaped.

A man in a suit across from him glanced up at him, then back to his iPad.

Independent special agent. Right. Austin still had all the necessary skills to conduct an investigation, but he couldn't arrest anyone. He was nothing more than a private investigator with the skills and credentials to work as a bodyguard if allowed to do his job. Michael Croft had been safe while Austin had protected him. So why did guilt leave a sick feeling in the pit of Austin's stomach? He sent up a prayer that the authorities would catch the thugs who killed Michael.

Austin pulled out his cell phone and scrolled through his messages. When he read the email from his assistant, Emma, he frowned. Austin called her. "Hey, Emma, why the cryptic message?"

"I left you a message to call me. What's cryptic about that?"

"Details. I want details." Austin stood and moved to the window, wishing the storm would subside. In the meantime, at least the lightning flashing in the clouds put on a show for those waiting.

"Okay, giving you the details now. Your brother called."

What? His brother? "Which one?"

"You have more than one? You never said."

No, he hadn't. Wasn't like he shared a lot of personal information with Emma. Maybe he should have. "It doesn't matter. So who called?"

"Heath. Does that ring a bell?"

Sarcasm? To be fair, he probably deserved it. "Did he say what he wanted?"

"Yes. Your cell number."

Palms moist, he gripped his phone. "He didn't say why?"

"Nope. He didn't give any details either. I assumed it was okay to share your cell with him. Kind of strange he didn't already have it since he's your brother."

Okay, Emma, you're stepping over the line. Austin reeled in his retort. Emma cared about people, a positive trait he valued. Besides, he liked her spunky personality. He appreciated that she fielded his calls—a refreshing personal touch in this digital age—and assisted with the massive paperwork and research side of this business while he worked in the field with clients, even when a client like Michael Croft took all his time. But he really didn't feel like sharing his tumultuous personal life with her. She might want to offer her version of therapy. It wouldn't be the first time someone thought he needed help.

"Anything else?"

"Yeah. He wanted me to pass on a message. He wants you to call him. Also, Dana Cooper called to let you know since JT Anderson has died, your services will no longer be needed."

Austin pressed his hand against the glass and leaned into it. That sick feeling in his stomach progressed to full-on nausea.

"Is that it?" He'd heard about JT's death. The accident had happened while he was out of the country with Michael.

"Yes," Emma said. "Are you okay?"

"I'm fine. I'll talk to you soon." *Over and out.*

A guy could only take so much in one day. He would call Heath back tomorrow. Michael's death, so sudden and brutal, cracked the Kevlar shell he'd put in place. He'd thought about calling his brothers—Heath and Liam. People could leave this earth suddenly. It shouldn't be so hard to make a simple phone call. So what if they'd had a rough childhood. They'd been close growing up, battling their demons together.

Their father had been the one to nearly destroy them all.

Austin hadn't spoken to his brothers since Dad had gotten himself killed four years ago. Since the funeral. Or maybe he had that backward. His brothers hadn't spoken to *him*. Austin was the reason Dad was dead, after all. Not something he should think about tonight, at this moment. He was an expert at compartmentalizing.

Tomorrow, he'd think about Heath.

Tonight, while he waited for his flight to Seattle, he'd think about JT.

He still couldn't accept that JT was gone. His death was a great loss to so many people, including Austin, though he hadn't seen the man since Austin and Willow had parted ways two years ago. That JT had called Austin, wanting to involve him in a project, had surprised him. What had Willow thought about that? Or had she even known? Austin hadn't exactly had a chance to appropriately respond to JT's request other than to let him know he would talk to his FBI contacts. First he would have to find out the details, but JT had died before he'd gotten the opportunity.

And Willow. What was she going to do without her grand-father? At the very least, he wanted to offer his condolences for her loss. But he figured she didn't want to hear from him. Anything less than a personal visit seemed completely inadequate. What should he do? He rubbed the back of his neck, then flinched when lightning flashed brilliant and blinding.

His pounding heart slowly calmed. He knew what to do, then, and hoped his appearance wouldn't upset Willow, because he had every intention of offering his condolences in person.

CHAPTER THREE

Willow would take tonight to think about Mrs. Mason's case. The woman didn't have much time left. But seeing JT on the video had left Willow unsettled. She and Dana had locked up the office and headed to their respective homes. Willow clomped up the steps and onto the porch of the cottage-style house she'd shared with JT. Somehow she would have to move on. Life wouldn't come to a stop for her to catch her breath or give her another choice, except to go forward.

At the dark walnut door, she slipped the key into the hole. The door creaked open with barely a touch. Had she been in such a hurry she hadn't even secured the lock? Entering the foyer, she flipped on the Tiffany lamp that illuminated the portrait-lined hallway and dining area to her left.

She set the file folder containing her grandfather's notes on the dining room table, unsure if she had the ability to read through his messy scrawl regarding Mrs. Mason's impossible-to-solve case.

Something shifted at the edge of her vision. A shadowy silhouette. She strode to the window and glanced out. Probably a neighbor walking the dog before the clouds released their payload.

24

Exhaustion crept into her bones. She headed upstairs to her bedroom. She would attempt to read through the notes tomorrow before she made the final decision to dash Mrs. Mason's hopes. Despite Dana's encouragement to the contrary, Willow couldn't do the impossible. Not like her grandfather.

She hardly had the clarity of mind or heart to take on the case. Even the FBI hadn't been able to locate the child back when the evidence remained fresh. Her grandfather possibly would have succeeded in finding the abducted baby—now a young woman— had he lived.

With fatigue from the last two weeks finally taking its toll, she fell into bed, leaving her window open so the night sounds could lull her to sleep.

TUESDAY, 2:36 A.M.

Willow coughed and wheezed in a state of half consciousness until she finally woke up to an overpowering stench. Thick black smoke accosted her in the four-poster bed. Her throat grew raw, her eyes burned. The smoke alarm blared. How long had it been going off? Why hadn't she heard it earlier? Flames licked the bedroom around her.

And panic stole the last of her breath.

Her limbs froze.

Please help me, Lord!

Willing herself to move, she rolled out of bed and onto the floor, jamming her shoulder. She ignored the pain and sucked in a breath. The air grew hotter with each second. She was moments away from being overcome by either noxious gas or explosive flames.

How would she get out of this alive?

She glanced at bright-gold fingers dancing wildly at the window, engulfing the curtains. Could she do it? Could she push through the blazing curtains and out the second-story window? Screams erupted from her throat.

Is this a dream? A nightmare?

Except she knew it wasn't. She wasn't ready to die. Not yet.

Willow crawled to the end of the bed.

There were only two ways out. The door? Or the window? Neither looked promising.

"Help me!" Her shouts brought on another fit of coughing and she collapsed.

Paint bubbled on the walls. Black smoke billowed and spilled out the door and window. The stairwell creaked.

As if conjured by the sheer force of her will to live, a bulky silhouette appeared in the doorway, wearing a face mask and breathing apparatus. He marched through the flames while water dripped from the ceiling and burst through the bedroom window.

He snatched a blanket from the bed, covered her, and then lifted her into his arms. She braced herself to be dropped out the window and caught by firemen below. Instead, he trudged through the torrid heat toward the stairs.

Squeezing her eyes shut, she prayed they would make it out alive. Then she opened her eyes and tugged aside the corner of the blanket. She had to witness what the inferno looked like before it destroyed everything. Portraits and mementos of her travels and adventures with JT crumbled and fell from the mantel as they passed the living room. She was losing her precious memories on the heels of his death.

A crash resounded behind them and the fireman picked up his speed, lunging through the front door. She thought he would tumble forward and slam with her against the ground, but he found his footing and kept on running. Cheers erupted around her.

Voices spoke to her as the EMTs appeared in her line of sight, gripping her, lifting her to a gurney. Someone placed a mask over her face, allowing her to breathe pure oxygen and clear the noxious smoke from her lungs more quickly. The hiss of water conquering the flames brought no comfort. The fire had consumed the house.

A female paramedic appeared at her side. "You're going to be all right."

Shaking her head, Willow pushed up on her elbows and tugged the mask out of the way. Her throat raw, she struggled to speak. "No, I'm not. I've lost everything."

"Not everything." The dying flames glinted off the woman's shoulders. "You still have your life. That's all that really matters. But we need to get you to the hospital now for treatment."

Treatment. What was wrong with her? Had she been burned? Exhaustion and grief overwhelmed her, and she rested back on the gurney.

Nearby, two firemen spoke in quiet tones, and she heard their words just before the EMTs closed the ambulance doors. "You thinking what I'm thinking?"

"Maybe. Are you thinking there's no way this was an accident?"

"Yeah. The way that fire took over so fast."

CHAPTER FOUR

TUESDAY, 4:19 A.M.
AIRSPACE OVER WASHINGTON
SEA-TAC APPROACH

Austin sensed when the Boeing 737 began its descent on the red-eye from Denver. Delayed flights were the nature of the travel beast. He should be accustomed to it by now and shouldn't complain about the hours he'd waited for the flight to Seattle. Why today of all days? He really wanted to grumble, but nobody wanted to listen.

Still, he was almost home. Spread out, maybe thirty souls occupied the dark, stuffy cabin, most of them sleeping. The fuselage creaked and shook with the expected turbulence upon descent into cloud cover over Puget Sound. Pressure in his sinuses built up. Awakened from her slumber, the woman in the aisle seat across from him gasped and squeezed the armrests.

As a former fighter pilot, he shouldn't be bothered by a little turbulence, but back then, he'd been the one in control. Even after logging too many miles as a passenger on commercial flights, he still hated the takeoffs and landings, the most dangerous parts of any flight. The hazards were relative since, statistically speaking, flying was the safest mode of travel.

Still, the ascent demanded the most from the plane, and landing demanded the most from the pilot. Like the woman across the aisle, Austin gripped the armrests, only he didn't cling to them as if they could save his life. Pressing his head against the seat back, he closed his eyes, willing away his own private terror as memories hounded him from his crash in a foreign desert.

His heart rate jacked up when the shaking increased. The descent seemed to take forever as the 737 approached the runway, dipped to the right, and overcorrected to the left. The landing gear touched the asphalt, bumped and skipped, then settled onto the runway. The pilot slowed the aircraft and taxied toward the terminal. Austin released the armrests and noticed the woman breathing a sigh of relief. He smiled.

When he turned on his cell, a text immediately came through from Zena Helms, a friend and someone he'd worked with at the FBI.

Anderson home in flames. Thought you'd want to know.

His pulse quickened.

Willow!

He scrolled to the next text.

Willow's status is unknown. I'll try to find out more.

Then nothing. No more texts. Zena probably thought he'd ignored her, but he'd been in the air. His heart thrashed against his rib cage and his breath hitched. Sweaty palms and trembling fingers affected his ability to return Zena's text asking for more information. He tried to explain he'd been on a flight from Denver, and autocorrect wreaked havoc on his text.

As the plane taxied, he searched the internet for any news of the fire, but the loading pages took much too long. His patience ran out. He had to get off this plane—now.

Every minute counted.

After the aircraft was secured at the gate, the passengers stood, grabbed their things from the overhead bins, and prepared to disembark. Austin quickly reached for his carry-on and excused himself, pushing past the people in the aisle. One largish fellow refused to budge and remained in Austin's way.

"Look, it's an emergency. I need off this plane—now."

"Wait your turn. We're all in a hurry."

Fuming, he bit back the angry response that entered his mind. That would only cause him more trouble, and he didn't have the patience to disentangle himself. He'd bide his time and make a mad dash around the man when he could. His phone signaled another text.

Zena again.

She's at Northwest Medical Center. Condition unknown.

Austin silently prayed for Willow. He would go straight to the hospital. On the ramp, he rushed around the large man who'd stood in his way earlier. The guy actually moved to the center as if he would stand in Austin's way again. Jerk. But Austin was more agile and quickly skirted the man. He rushed by the few families, couples, men, and women who'd taken the red-eye, apologizing as he pushed his way past. Then he ran through the terminal and outside to the parking garage.

Brisk morning air greeted him, his light jacket feeble protection against the temperature in the fifties and the damp Seattle morning.

Inside his silver Acura, he peeled out of the Sea-Tac long-term parking and headed north toward the hospital. He drove as fast as the speed limit allowed, maybe a little more. He tried to call for an update or to be connected to Willow's room but couldn't get through.

He steered through the hospital parking garage, tires squealing, until he found a spot. Easy enough at this hour. He couldn't care less that he'd taken up two spots.

If Willow had been hurt . . .

He hadn't seen her in two years. Still, concern lashed through him. At the information desk, he stood in line behind grandparents who comforted a coughing, whining little boy. Austin took in his surroundings, making note of all the exits in the waiting room. A couple of guys wearing leather and sporting tattoos sat in the corner, waiting to learn their buddy's fate, he presumed. Several family members huddled together with grim expressions.

The grandparents shuffled the child away and Austin faced the plump woman sitting at the desk. Willow was still in the ER, but in an observation room. He released a pent-up breath. Tension eased from his shoulders.

She'll be all right.

Still, he rushed down the hall searching for her room.

As he neared the observation wing, something suddenly hit him. What if Willow didn't want to see him? She might not like the intrusion. Someone else might be there to comfort and reassure her. Who did he think he was? He'd planned to try to see her tomorrow and offer his condolences for JT's death, but now wasn't the right time for that.

Regardless, he had to see for himself that she was okay. He found her room and hesitated. Through a crack in the door, he watched her. At that moment he wasn't much different from a stalker. She focused on a television in the corner depicting images of the house fire. Tears pooled in her somber eyes.

Her sadness nearly undid him. Yes. She'd survived the fire. Physically, she would be fine. But psychologically? Not so much. Especially with the fire happening so soon after JT's death.

He leaned against the wall and allowed his heart rate to normalize. Now that he'd seen for himself that she had survived, he should go.

But that was Willow in there. He could feel the draw of her presence from where he stood.

CHAPTER FIVE

From her bed in the ER wing, Willow watched the early morning news coverage of her burning house. Though beyond exhausted, she was still unable to sleep after the trauma.

Dana had stayed with her for several hours but had left to grab Willow some clothes. She had also promised to purchase greasy comfort food. If she were still here, she would have insisted on changing the channel, but Willow couldn't stop staring at the news.

Someone knocked on the half-opened door.

She started to tease Dana for taking so long, but in he walked, like a specter from a forgotten past.

Six foot one, dark haired, and gorgeous. Willow gulped air, then stifled the cough itching to get out. Why had he stepped back into her life? JT had wanted his help before he died, but that didn't explain what Austin was doing here now in her hospital room.

She caught her breath. "Austin?" Then cleared her throat. "I mean, Special Agent McKade. What are you doing here?"

He closed the distance but remained at a couple of feet from her bed and crossed his arms. "It's ex, actually."

"Ex as in—"

"I'm no longer with the bureau."

"Oh."

But he still hadn't answered her question. Why had he come? The usual awkwardness hovered between them, and she doubted he would. His gunmetal grays studied Willow but remained guarded. Secretive. He hadn't changed much in that regard. He'd always been sophisticated. A company man. The perfect agent. What had happened to change that? Behind his dimpled grin she'd caught the edge of something feral—it had been the very thing to draw her to him. A challenge maybe? But she'd never been able to crack the shell and see what was beneath.

Saying nothing, he worked his jaw. He was agitated, definitely agitated. "I heard about what happened. I had to see for myself that you're all right. I'm sorry about the house. But thank God you're alive."

Did he mean those words? The pain flooding his eyes confirmed that he did. "Thank you for coming. And, yes, thank God I survived." A pang hit her—the images from the inferno remained too vivid and raw.

As if sensing her pain, he stepped closer.

But when he said nothing more, Willow had to ask. "You heard JT died, didn't you?"

His features were somber. He hesitated, then said, "I'm sorry I wasn't able to attend his funeral."

"It was a private graveside service. I didn't expect you to be there."

Hurt flickered in his eyes before he shuttered it away. "I know how much you must miss him."

Averting her eyes, she nodded.

Miss him? She had yet to comprehend he was gone. Willow

struggled with putting her feelings into words. That would be difficult on a normal day without Austin McKade taking up space in her personal bubble. His sudden appearance had thrown off her equilibrium—something she'd only recently found again after they'd gone their separate ways two years ago. And in that time, he'd resigned from the FBI. Wow. Or had he been fired?

Why had he waltzed into her room and clouded her thinking? When they'd been an item before, the intensity of his presence could sometimes become too much. This was one of those moments. She stared at her hands resting against the bleached-white bedsheet and fidgeted, wishing he would go away and give her space so she could think. But then when he left, he would suck all the oxygen out of the room and take it with him like he always did. Willow could still vividly remember what it felt like to be deprived of oxygen. Had that only been a few hours ago?

She wanted him to go.

She wanted him to stay.

"I can see the wheels in your head are spinning too fast for either of us," he said. "I was out of the country, Willow, or I would have been at JT's service even uninvited. I could have hung back in the shadows, but I wanted to be there to show my support. I still care, you know."

That jerked Willow's attention back to his rugged face. Her gaze lingered there too long, taking in his strong jaw, his five-o'clock shadow, and his broad shoulders. The thick dark hair she used to run her fingers through.

Stop it. Just stop it. What was taking Dana so long?

"I had planned to come see you in person tomorrow to give my condolences. Then I heard about the fire when my flight landed, so I came directly to the hospital. I've never been so relieved in my life. When I heard the news, I feared the worst." His voice cracked on his last words.

And the sound pinged against her heart. He *did* still care.

His transparency, unusual for such a guarded person, could break her. She fought the stupid tears, but they spilled onto her cheeks anyway. And Austin rushed to her and pulled her into his arms.

Oh no, not this.

It was just what she wanted. Just what she needed, and yet she shouldn't want the comfort he offered. She couldn't afford to let herself be vulnerable.

She sucked in a calming breath. If only she could push away the sturdy form that now held her. After she'd found the words and thought things through, she'd planned to tell Dana, but instead Austin had showed up and Willow needed to tell someone the suspicions burning through her mind. Except this man had too many secrets himself.

Still, protection poured off him as if he wore armor and held up a shield to defend her. She was absolutely certain he hid a fiery sword somewhere.

The words boiled up inside until she couldn't control the eruption. "I think someone started the fire on purpose."

CHAPTER SIX

He bristled at her words. Had the trauma made her paranoid? He almost pulled away to look into her eyes and make sure they weren't wild or irrational, but he couldn't let go of her. Not yet. The Willow he'd known before was solid and levelheaded. No, he'd need to take her seriously.

Footfalls announced someone's approach, and Willow stiffened against him. He sensed the instant she disconnected, so he released her and took a step back to see Dana standing in the room with her mouth hanging open. She was holding up a couple of sacks from McDonald's. His mouth watered. Unfortunately, he doubted he would be invited to share. But after learning about the fire that had destroyed JT and Willow's home, and her near death, he could use the comfort too.

"I brought fast food just like you asked, and grabbed cheesecake from the all-night supermarket." Dana had finally composed herself and lifted the bags high. She placed the paper sacks on the bedside table pushed out of the way against the far wall. "And I brought you some extra clothes for when they let you out of this place. They're mine and too big but will do for now."

"Thanks, Dana." Willow sat up straighter and appeared to put her suspicions about the fire aside for the moment. She also looked eager to get out of there as soon as possible.

He didn't blame her but focused his attention now on the assistant, who ignored him.

"Good to see you again, Dana," he said.

The look Dana flashed him was clear. *The feeling isn't mutual.* She likely blamed him for breaking Willow's heart before. How could she know that Willow had been the one to break his? Did Willow know about Dana's call to Emma, his assistant, letting him know his help was no longer needed? He had a feeling she didn't. Then again, maybe that call had been Willow's idea.

"And it's good to see you, too, Special Agent McKade."

"Ex." Both he and Willow spoke the word simultaneously. He caught the edge of her tenuous grin. He wished he could see her flash her thousand-watt smile, but under the circumstances, that might be too much for either of them.

"I'd like to hear the story behind that." Willow adjusted her pillow.

He studied her, trying to read a meaning behind her words that probably wasn't there. "Some other time maybe."

"Well, sounds like you two have been catching up," Dana said, "but I think Willow needs her rest now." She gave him a look that warned him to stay away.

What are you, her mother? He kept the words to himself.

He couldn't blame her for attempting to protect Willow. He felt the same way. Except did she know that Willow suspected someone had committed arson? If so, she should be grateful for his presence. After all, he'd been a top cop. He still had skills and would use them when allowed.

"Well, I have to eat first," Willow said. Was that her way of saying she wanted him to stay? He couldn't be sure.

Dana busied herself with laying out the food, and Austin hung back.

He still hadn't gotten over JT's death, and now Willow's near death . . . was there any merit to her comment about the house fire? If he wanted to think it through with any clarity, he needed sustenance after his long flight.

The smell of greasy food wafted up to him. Yeah. He definitely needed comfort too.

In fact, if he were being honest, he'd needed to hold Willow in his arms again to reassure himself that she was alive and he wasn't dreaming. He still had his share of bad dreams after his on-the-job experience with the FBI.

He was grateful for Dana's interruption and shouldn't have let Willow affect him that way. He hadn't thought that seeing her after two years would bowl him over like this. Maybe it had everything to do with the fact that she rested in a hospital bed with an IV tube coming out of her arm and an oxygen-level monitor on her finger.

Though her expression appeared haggard, she remained beautiful with her long, shiny black hair spilling over her shoulders and those sensitive, compassionate hazel eyes that could hold him captive. She was more stunning than he remembered, even with the deep pain of loss etched into her features and that hollow look in her eyes. A look that disturbed him in ways he couldn't begin to comprehend.

I shouldn't have come back.

He could have sent a sympathy card for JT's death instead. She would have preferred that, he was sure.

Except if someone had burned down her house with her inside . . . if someone had actually tried to kill Willow, Austin was in the right place at the right time. And when had that ever happened? He might have stayed with the FBI if he'd been at the right place at the right time before.

Approaching the table, he hoped Dana would be generous and offer him something from the display of greasy comfort food, which would give him an excuse to hang out. Otherwise, he would have to insist on staying long enough to get some answers. Better that she offered than he demanded. The woman frowned up at him, but with one glance at Willow, her expression softened. Clearly, she loved Willow and realized that Willow wanted him to stay.

He breathed easier.

She held out a sack to Austin. "Egg McMuffin and hashbrowns? Sorry, no cheeseburgers. They only serve breakfast this early."

"Thanks." He grabbed it and dug out the breakfast sandwich. "I don't think I've eaten McDonald's in, oh, maybe a decade."

"No way." Willow's laugh morphed into hacking again.

Abandoning the sandwich, he rushed to one side of the bed as Dana hurried to the other side. After the coughing subsided, Willow rested her head against the pillow, exhausted. Seeing her like this felt like a dull-bladed knife was cutting open his insides.

What was he doing here? He wasn't in her life anymore. She didn't need him messing her up again. He had to get his own head straight first, if he ever could. But he couldn't leave her. Not until he found out what had happened and made sure Willow was safe. If he left now and something happened to her, he would never forgive himself.

Dana disappeared into the restroom. Maybe she'd decided it was best to let Austin have his time with Willow, but he doubted that would last long.

He moved to the table again and retrieved a cup with a straw, then brought it back to the bed. "I assume Dana got your favorite. Want some?"

Willow's eyelids fluttered open to reveal her luminous hazel eyes again. She lifted her hand and took the soda from him. He helped her sit up to drink.

Watching Willow, he considered his next words. He didn't want this to be real. "Why do you say someone started the fire?" he whispered.

Dana washed her hands at the sink against the wall and grabbed a paper towel, then approached the bed. "Wait. You think someone started the fire?"

She had good hearing.

Willow shut her eyes and breathed slowly.

Then she opened them again. "I overheard the firemen. They said no way the fire was an accident with the way it took over so fast."

"So the firemen suspect arson," Austin said.

Dana looked at him. He really wanted to like the woman, but he wasn't sure he could get past the fact that she couldn't stand *him*.

"Arson? Don't you think you're getting ahead of yourselves, the both of you?" Dana left the bed and munched on a hashbrown, like any good nervous eater.

He paced the room and rubbed his neck. Unlike Dana, he'd lost his appetite. "The fire chief will conduct an investigation and we'll find out soon enough." Austin would do his best to learn the truth even sooner. But it didn't make a whole lot of sense. "Can you think of any reason why someone would want to burn down the house?"

Austin hadn't heard about any random arsons in the area, but he would check on that too.

"No. None." Willow shook her head. "This is just too much. Maybe I heard the firemen wrong."

He hoped that was the case. Austin ignored Dana's piercing stare. This wasn't an issue to dance around or pretend wasn't happening. Then again, maybe he was getting ahead of himself, like Dana had said. His world had been wrapped up for many years with the criminal element, so he was quick to jump on Willow's suspicions, and maybe even conclusions. Still . . . if the house fire had been arson and hadn't been random, there had to be a reason. Motive was everything. He drew on his law enforcement experience and asked the next logical question. "You might have heard them wrong, and let's hope so, but humor me—are there any cases you're working on? Something someone might be willing to kill over?"

"There was only one project JT was working on when he died, and I took his notes home tonight."

Her words could mean nothing or they could mean everything. But Austin had every intention of taking Willow seriously.

CHAPTER SEVEN

I took *his notes home tonight. They're gone now. Turned to ash. I really have lost everything.*

She pressed her face into her hands. But she'd already cried all the tears she had, and she hated crying. Anguish engulfed her. How much more could she take? For the first time in her life, she wondered if she would recover. Her heart and mind had been crushed in every way possible.

"Willow." Austin gently touched her arm. "Are you okay?"

Oh, why did he have to be so gentle? Why did he have to care? Or even be here? Yet, that he was here meant the world to her. She didn't want his presence, his caring touch to mean anything. At the very least, she shouldn't let herself count on him too much.

Except for Dana and her family, Willow was all alone now, and she had to be strong. But that wasn't entirely true.

Somewhere out there, she had a half uncle. He probably didn't even know she existed. Her parents had been researching her father's side of the family when they had come across her grandfather's indiscretion that had resulted in a child. A half brother Dad hadn't known about. The news revealed the big family secret. A discovery that happened more often in this day and age of DNA testing through genealogy sites than two decades ago when it first became available to genealogy enthusiasts. Though Grandpa Paul had known about the child, he had taken that secret with him to his grave. Of course, the child's mother knew and the secret had eventually been shared because someone began making connections via genealogy sites for a complete medical history regarding some rare, genetic disease. That's all Willow knew about it. She'd been young when it happened. JT had shared a few details later. Mom and Dad had been traveling to try to connect with Dad's half brother when they'd died in a car accident.

How did that make any kind of sense?

Add to that all the years she'd worked with JT visiting cemeteries and reading headstones to connect the living with their ancestors. All the dead people she'd "reunited" with families, and Willow found herself alone. That was downright ironic.

She pushed away the dark thought.

JT's whisper to her after her parents' death drifted through her mind.

"You're not alone. God is always with you."

God would never leave her nor forsake her. But she couldn't sense him with her. With everything that had happened, Willow felt like God was far from her.

Then there was Austin . . .

"Willow," Austin said again. The bed shifted. The guy had actually sat on the bed, albeit near her feet, waiting for her answer.

She lifted her head, wishing that he didn't have to see her like this. She must look like an absolute wreck. "No. I'm not okay. You're scaring me."

"Why? Because I'm taking you seriously?" His expression pinched, he scraped a hand down his handsome face. "You're the one who said you overheard the firemen. Seems to me you were scared before I got here."

"I was more in shock than anything."

"Understandable."

"What the firemen said got lost in the trauma of the night, and then you showed up and I had someone other than Dana to tell. I was kind of hoping you would tell me that I'd heard wrong."

"For your sake I hope you did."

Her grandfather's death was bad enough. Losing the house to a fire, losing everything was beyond comprehension. But . . . arson? She thought about the firemen's words but still struggled to truly believe them.

Austin punched in numbers on his cell, then held it to his ear, his gaze holding her prisoner.

"Who are you calling?"

"Someone who can give me answers."

"Why? Austin, what are you doing?" Willow wasn't sure why he would entangle himself with her again. Hadn't they both been shattered enough before? Then again, she wasn't sorry he had showed up, as long as he was only here to help.

"I'm going to do what I do best"—he shot her a grin—"and get to the bottom of this. That is, if it's okay with you."

The truth would put her mind at ease. But she gave him no definitive answer. Instead, she threw her legs over the side of the bed, ready to get out of there. And go where?

The room tilted.

Austin had never taken his eyes off her. Frowning, he ended the call, then stood. "You should get back in bed."

Willow appreciated his concern and the gentleness in his tone. She realized, too, with a little humiliation, that she was in a hospital gown.

She glanced around the small room for Dana as though she could have somehow missed her. The bathroom door was wide open, so she wasn't in there. "Dana? Where'd she go?"

One minute she'd been eating and the next minute she'd disappeared.

With the lines in his forehead deepening, Austin strode across the room and looked out the door. "She's talking to a nurse."

He crossed his arms and remained by the door, his features taut.

"What's wrong?" Willow asked.

"She doesn't look happy. If I had to guess, I'd say she's asking the nurse to remove me because I'm upsetting you. Am I upsetting you, Willow? Do you want me to leave?"

How should she answer that? With his presence, her pulse had kicked up and stayed too high for comfort.

"That's just Dana. She's protective of me." She hadn't exactly answered him, because she wasn't sure what she wanted. But had she seen hurt in his gaze? If she were in his shoes, she'd probably feel the same way. After all, it took some nerve for him to show up here. Willow had to give him credit for walking in here without knowing how he would be received. She and Dana hadn't exactly welcomed him with open arms.

His expression turned contemplative. "Willow, can you tell me about the case your grandfather was working on? You said you'd taken his notes home. Then I want to know everything that happened tonight."

"I appreciate what you're trying to do, but you aren't with the FBI anymore, remember?" Ouch. She hadn't meant it the way it sounded. "What I mean is—"

"I'm not sure it would be a case for the FBI, but you should definitely talk to the police if you're concerned." His lips flattened. "I work with a network of ex-FBI agents in an organization called Ex-Agents International. I'm in the private sector now, instead of working for the government, that's all. I'm still an investigator and I can help."

"You're a private investigator then."

"Yes. JT had asked for my help on a cold case. He probably thought I was still with the FBI. Is that the case you're talking about? The notes you took home? Or is it something else?"

She nodded. "I didn't mean to sound like I don't want your help. I just don't want to presume." Getting tangled up with Austin, whether he helped with the cold case or investigated her suspicions about the house fire being arson, might not be the best idea. But what did she know except that her head was pounding and she couldn't think straight.

"Nor do I. If you'd rather work with someone else, I understand. I was already set to contact JT for the details and then try to get information for him."

Though since he was no longer FBI, she guessed he couldn't just walk into the federal building and get it.

"I can look into the possible arson too," he said. "I'm concerned—"

"You really think that someone burning the house down last night has something to do with what JT was working on? That's too farfetched."

"Willow, I'm concerned about you. Please let me help, giving you the same help JT had wanted on the case. We'll know sooner or later if it was arson, and if it was, whether it was connected or not. But if someone did commit arson tonight, I want to be there to keep you safe." His forehead crinkled with hesitation. "Just to be clear, I want to do this as a friend, not as a hired investigator."

His eyes said what his lips would not. *It's what JT would have wanted*.

Far be it from her to deny JT—his persuasive ways still reaching her from the grave.

She searched Austin's gaze, warning signals going off in her head. *What are you doing, Willow Anderson?* Why was she so indecisive when it came to this man? "Last night I decided I would wait until morning to read through his notes, but I had pretty much already decided I would call Mrs. Mason in the morning to tell her I couldn't take her case. That I'm lacking in the skills my grandfather had, though I wouldn't have worded it like that.

But I can't think straight since he died. I don't know what I want to do now."

Hands in his pockets, he hung his head, let a few seconds pass, then lifted his chin and shoulders.

"You're right, of course. I'm pushing you. You've just been through two tragedies. You need time to recover. Time to make decisions." His broad shoulders shifted lower as a deep sadness filled his eyes.

A nurse entered the room, followed by Dana—fierce, protective friend that she was—and asked him to leave.

"Take care, Willow." Austin nodded and sent her a dejected grin before he exited the room—walking out on her just like he had two years ago.

CHAPTER EIGHT

At his car, Austin unlocked the door and got in. Heart still hammering, he remained in his seat and stared, unseeing.

One decision on his part could have the potential to turn his life upside down. He'd only meant to check on JT's granddaughter to make sure she was okay. He clenched his fists. Come on. Couldn't he at least be honest with himself? Willow had been much more to him than simply JT's granddaughter. How did he go back to thinking of her as such? If she let him work with her, he'd have to find a way to bury for good that rush of emotion, that burn of attraction that came over him when he was near her.

Pure torture.

Facing the demons head-on wasn't always easy. He already knew that from experience—that's why he kept running from them and had previously let his past come between Willow and him. What was done was done. There would be no going back with her.

That's why he never should have stepped foot in her hospital room. Seeing her up close and personal had his head swimming.

But he would never forgive himself if he walked away from this, walked away from her, and harm came to her. No, he'd have to see it through for JT . . . for Willow. And for himself.

For all his lamenting, he might put it all to rest—say goodbye to Willow, this time for good—after a little digging. He'd investigate the question of arson, then if it turned out the fire hadn't been deliberately started, he would walk away. He wouldn't see her again. Besides, she had wavered far too much on whether she wanted his help, wanted him there or not.

He pulled out his tablet and searched for information on the specific fire crew. Easy enough. The fire had been covered by the local news. He looked at his cell and started to call, then decided against it and entered the address of the fire station into the GPS. Better to show up and ask questions. It could take the fire chief days—and more investigators could be called in, adding weeks—before an assessment of arson was officially given. Austin could possibly find out all he needed to know today.

Putting his cell away, he remembered that he still hadn't returned Heath's call. Emma had given Austin's number to Heath, and his brother still hadn't called him either. Or maybe Heath had suddenly had his world turned upside down too. Nah. What could go wrong at Emerald M Guest Ranch?

Looked like reaching out, connecting again, was too much trouble. Maybe it was more that it opened too many old wounds.

But he was wasting time sitting there reflecting on his mistakes. He started the car and tuned in Sirius Satellite Radio to an '80s station, hoping it would yank him out from under the sudden heaviness that had come when the forces of the universe had conspired against him, throwing everything at him at once.

He steered from the parking lot. Twenty minutes later he pulled up to the curb next to the fire station—Engine Co. 45. One of the newer stations, it appeared. He got out and hung by his car, studying the facility before he approached. Here's where he would feel the big difference between his past job as an FBI agent and his current job as, well, without the glorified name of independent agent, simply a private investigator, as Willow had pointed out.

If he were still an FBI agent, he wouldn't be the one to investigate this fire unless it fell within federal jurisdiction, but if he were, then he'd walk in and show his badge and ask his questions. In his capacity now as a private investigator or bodyguard or whatever his previous FBI experience could afford him, showing his credentials didn't give him the same power. He was no longer a Fed.

But he knew more ways to find the truth than wielding a badge with the force of the US government behind it. Austin had to become . . . well . . . personable. Likable. People would rather open up to someone they connected with. That didn't always come naturally to him, but it should be easy enough in this situation.

He'd come to thank the guy who'd carried Willow out of the house and saved her life. He'd seen that much on the news. Austin approached the large station with a reserve engine parked in the garage and another in the drive. Only one garage door stood open. These guys worked twenty-four-hour shifts, so Austin could find the fireman he'd come to talk to at the station, though he might be getting his rest after last night.

God, please let me find the answers.

A short and stocky fireman wore boots with blue slacks and suspenders over a red T-shirt as he wiped and polished the side of Engine 45. Another guy, taller and skinnier than the first but dressed similarly, stood on the front bumper and squeegeed the windows. He approached the firemen. Short and Stocky glanced away from his task to acknowledge Austin's presence, but his focus remained on cleaning the fire engine.

"Can we help you?" he asked.

"Sure. I'm looking for the guys who showed up at the Anderson home fire. I wanted to thank them, and especially the fireman who carried Willow out of the house and saved her life. I know it can be a sacrificial, thankless job. She's very important to me." All true, but he didn't want to lay it on too thick.

He held out his hand, hoping to make friends. Both men jumped from the engine and walked over and shook Austin's hand. "How's she doing?" the taller, dark-haired man asked.

"She's better, but still has a nasty cough. They're releasing her this morning." Austin had overheard the nurse reveal this detail as he left Willow's room. "Thank you for all you did to save her."

"You're welcome. All part of a day's work." Shorty grinned, then said, "Hey, Tim!" He called out toward the open garage. "Tim, somebody's here to see you."

Tim didn't appear.

"Go on in and ask for Tim," Tall and Skinny said. "I'm sure he'll appreciate it. Your friend is fortunate to be alive. That was one hot fire."

That's exactly what Austin wanted to find out about. He wouldn't go into the station for Tim yet if he could keep these guys talking. "Why do you say that? Was it hotter than other fires?" *Why was it distinctive?* He pursed his lips to keep from asking too many questions and spooking them.

The two guys eyed each other. Short and Stocky was the one to speak. "The chief's investigating. He's at the house now. You should talk to him. The police could already be there too."

So the firemen decided to clam up. Too bad. But the fact that the fire chief was investigating told him enough. These guys, the first responders, had seen enough to raise their suspicions.

"If you hurry, you could catch him there." Tall and Skinny climbed back onto the bumper and started wiping the windows again, finishing what Austin had interrupted.

The chief might be even less willing than these guys to share what he had found if this had officially become a criminal investigation.

"Thanks, guys. I think I'll go find Tim now to thank him

personally, then I'll be on my way. I know Willow will thank you as soon as she's feeling better."

Austin entered the garage, passed the reserve engine, and walked through a door into the facilities. Down a hallway, he stopped at the kitchen and found a muscled guy, gray at the temples. "I'm looking for Tim."

"You're looking *at* Tim. What can I do for you?"

"They tell me you're the one who carried Willow out of that burning house."

"She's one lucky woman. We almost didn't make it in time. A few more seconds and it would have been too late for her."

Austin thrust out his hand. The guy took it. "My name's Austin McKade. I'm here to thank you for your courage."

"I'm Tim Colton."

Austin released his hand. "She's very important to me. And without you, she wouldn't be here today." He wasn't sure he enjoyed repeating the words—it just drove home the point of what she still meant to him after two years. Maybe it would always be that way. Why had he let her go in the first place? He swallowed against the sudden thickness in his throat.

Tim studied him. "You're welcome. It's just part of the job."

"Oh, come on, it's more than a job to you. It's in your blood." It was worth the guess to get him talking.

Tim smiled, his eyes warming. "Yeah, my dad and his dad before him were firemen. Both retired now. How did you know?"

"It takes a special person to do what you do. My dad was a firefighter." Though only part-time and until Mom died in a fire. Then his drinking ramped up. Austin thought he was stronger than his father, but he'd left his job with the FBI because he couldn't get over his own failure. He had the same weakness in his blood. Stuff like that—the good and the bad—it ran in the blood.

"Where about?"

"Grayback, Wyoming, up around Bridger-Teton National Forest.

Jackson Hole area. He died four years ago, but I understand the sacrifice it takes. I guess I can recognize when something runs deep."

"But fighting fires is not in *your* blood," Tim said matter-of-factly.

Sharp man. "You're right. I didn't follow in my father's footsteps. I served in the air force." That's all he wanted to say. His story was long and complicated, and not easy for him to tell.

Respect shone in Tim's eyes. "Then you've made your sacrifice, and now let me thank you."

He shook Austin's hand again. The man seemed to understand Austin didn't want to say more about his own life. Tim was on the clock anyway. Austin would draw this conversation to a conclusion. Get the information he needed. "I know Willow will want to thank you when she's feeling better."

Tim's expression turned serious. "I'm glad we could help."

"Listen." Austin scratched his nose. "She overheard some of the guys talking just before they put her in the ambulance. Someone said something about arson. She's kind of freaked out over that. I told her I would come over and thank you but also find out if it was arson or not. If it wasn't, then I can give her that peace of mind, and if it was, then I want to keep her safe from whoever did this. Understand?" He counted on the connection he had made with Tim.

Tim stiffened. He might clam up too.

"She's scared, and, frankly, so am I," Austin continued. "Should she be worried that someone burned down her house and almost killed her?"

Tim appeared to measure his words, then something behind his eyes shifted. Austin had made a friend. The man would tell him what he needed to know.

"It didn't act like a normal house fire. Far from it. As first responders, it's our job to notice these things and report them. So the chief is over there now. He'll call in additional arson investigators if necessary. Some of the evidence of arson could have burned up in the fire, but what we saw made us suspicious."

"Why do you say it didn't burn like a normal fire?"

"It burned much faster. Flashes and explosions almost kept us from getting in to search. A neighbor told us they'd seen the woman come home and believed she was still inside."

Austin would talk to the neighbors and ask if they'd seen anyone skulking around the house. He cleared his throat. Nodded. Tried not to get thrown from the roller coaster.

"Some of the flames were white. They put off thick black smoke."

"What does that mean?" he asked.

"Gasoline could have been the accelerant."

Okay. He'd heard enough. Why hadn't Willow smelled gasoline? Or maybe she'd been sound asleep when the arsonist had done his work, which could mean the person was inside her house while she slept. The thought slammed into his gut. Austin thanked Tim again and headed back to his car.

Inside the vehicle he thought through their conversation. Looked like he wasn't going to walk away from Willow after all, no matter that Dana didn't want him near her friend. Even if Willow agreed with Dana, Austin would at least share the information he'd found out so she would be warned. He wanted to help her, to protect her. JT would ask that of him if he were still alive. However, it would be much better if someone else took his place protecting Willow.

The police would investigate the arson. But would they keep Willow safe? Believe that someone had tried to kill her? Austin didn't know. He couldn't count on them.

And something equally ominous gnawed at the back of his mind. JT had died in a hit-and-run. Now his house had been burned down. Had his death truly been an accident?

CHAPTER NINE

Willow stared at the new clothes hanging in the closet. While she had slept in the guest bedroom in Dana's bungalow-style home, Dana had purchased pretty T-shirts, relaxed-fit jeans, and comfy shorts and sweats for Willow at the nearest discount department store. Willow chose a white T-shirt and gray sweats to go with her mood and changed out of Dana's too-big clothes. Who would go to the trouble to buy her a selection of new clothes except a close friend or relative—a mom or a sister? No doubt about it. Dana was much more than her late grandfather's assistant. The woman really was a friend to take Willow into her home for the time being until she could get her head together. Call the insurance company and figure out where she would live. What she would do with her life. She almost felt like a Phoenix at the moment, with so much of her life taken from her, burned up with the house. This was her chance to start afresh if she would take it. But not yet.

No. Not yet.

JT's words, hidden in some distant moment from the past, floated through her mind now.

"You're alive, Willow, and that counts for something. Use the time and the gifts God gave you."

She could hear his voice in her head as if he were standing right behind her. That was both a blessing and a curse.

Somehow she would gather her strength and hold it together.

She wasn't alone in this house and would *not* let herself crumble repeatedly in front of Dana and her family, though deep inside she wanted to. Oh, she really wanted to let herself fall apart. But she was JT's granddaughter, and she would inevitably pull herself together and move forward. The man had modeled that for her all her life.

But she hadn't imagined it would be so hard. Losing JT was one thing, but losing the house—all her belongings and memories—in one fell swoop? All the times she'd heard about a family losing their home to a fire, she'd never understood the soul-piercing, utter devastation. From now on, she'd be more deliberate about finding a way to give back to those who'd lived through a catastrophic fire. But one step, one day at a time. For now she'd face what was left of her own tragedy.

Nothing.

Everything was gone.

Including Austin. Once again he'd walked out of her life. She wished he hadn't come to her hospital room to begin with. Her throat constricted. Even in the aftermath of her near-death experience, his presence had sparked embers she'd believed were long cold. His offer of assistance had merely kindled false hope. No. She couldn't count on his help or seeing him again. That was for the best. Time to ignore the way her heart beat when she was near him. She wouldn't think about him. She couldn't afford to. It would destroy her resolve to pick up the pieces.

Besides, she wasn't the only person to ever lose something precious. Mrs. Mason had lost her daughter the day she'd been born. Willow's first step would be to climb out of the despondency she was quickly sinking into. She could do that by focusing on helping someone else. In this case, she wouldn't actually be helping Mrs. Mason but freeing her to find another investigator. Willow couldn't search for her daughter.

A soft knock came at the door. "Willow, it's me. Can I come in?" Dana asked.

Willow opened the door and let her friend in.

Dana's eyes flashed over Willow and she smiled. "They fit you perfectly."

Just sweats and a T-shirt. What could go wrong? "I can't thank you enough"—Willow gestured at her clothes and the bedroom— "for this, for everything."

"Oh, please stop." Dana hugged her. "We're practically family. In fact, I want you to think of us as your family if you don't already. No need to thank me as though I'm doing anything more than I would do for my own daughter or little sis. You're welcome here as long as you need." Dana handed over a box. "Stan stopped home at lunch. He got you a cheap cell phone to use just until you can replace your iPhone."

Willow took the box and held it against her chest. *Do not cry. Do not cry.* "That was thoughtful. Please thank him for me."

"You're very welcome." Dana lingered at the door. "Why don't you get some rest? I'll start working on dinner. Stan should be home from work in a bit."

"I've been resting all day. I think I'm done for now."

"Oh?"

On the one hand, she appreciated Dana opening up her home more than anything in the world, but on the other hand, she didn't want to be treated like a child. Willow sagged. Dana was only trying to help. "I was thinking about Mrs. Mason. I need to call her and let her know what's happened."

"Oh, honey, are you sure you want to do that right now? The fire was just last night."

"She's on borrowed time, with what, less than two months to

live now if her doctors can be believed. I need to tell her so she can find someone else to continue the search for her daughter before it's too late."

The doorbell rang. "I'll leave you to it then. Let me know if you need anything at all. Oh, don't you need her number?"

"That would be nice."

"I'm sure I have it on my computer downstairs. I'll just get that for you after I see who's at the door."

Dana left Willow. When she opened the box, she saw that Stan had gone to the trouble to charge the phone. What would she do without Dana and Stan?

"Use the time and the gifts God gave you."

Willow gathered her composure, pushed aside the trauma of last night to the best of her ability, and opened the door. She headed downstairs. Maybe she could work on Dana's computer and log in to the Anderson Consulting system.

Working would do her soul good, and closing down Anderson Consulting might be even better. She would start over, and slowly time would heal these deep wounds. Willow was a survivor. JT had made sure of that.

Voices spoke in low tones and drifted up the staircase. Dana's voice along with a man's. Recognizing the voice, Willow slowed on the last step.

Austin. She hadn't expected to see him again. She'd read his exit from her hospital room completely wrong. Now what should she do? A vortex of conflicting emotions swirled inside.

"She's resting right now." Dana's tone held firm, her intention clear.

"Please have her call me as soon as possible. It's important." Unease edged his voice.

Willow crept forward to stand behind Dana. His attention shifted from the sentinel barring the monster's entrance to Willow. An unreadable emotion flashed in his eyes.

58

"It's okay, Dana," Willow said. "I can talk to Austin."

Dana turned to look at Willow, disapproval apparent in her features.

"That is, if it's okay with you if he comes in." Willow offered her a teasing grin.

Soft worry lines grew in Dana's forehead. "Of course it's okay. I can't make your decisions for you."

Glad you understand that. Dana was only trying to protect her, but she might need to have a talk with her about her attitude toward Austin. What had happened between them before hadn't been Austin's fault alone.

"Come on in." Dana opened the door wide.

When he stepped into the foyer, his well-toned form and broad shoulders made the entrance feel much smaller. A hint of his familiar woodsy cologne wafted around her. Her heart tried to jump free though she held it firmly in place. She wanted to reconsider her decision to let him in.

"Why don't you talk in the living room?" Dana led them deeper into her eclectic arts-and-crafts-decorated home. "Would you like something to drink, Austin? Willow?"

"No, I'm fine." He never took his eyes from Willow.

"I'm good, Dana, thanks."

"I'll give you two some privacy." She disappeared.

"What is it?" Willow asked.

"Why don't you sit?" He gestured to the sofa, then took a seat in the closest plush chair, drumming his fingers on the armrests.

Willow eased onto the edge of the sofa. "Okay, I'm sitting. What did you find out?" The last time she'd seen him, before he'd walked out of her room and, she'd thought, out of her life again, he'd been planning to make a call and ask about the fire. Was it arson? She'd left those worries behind for another day. Let the firefighters and police officers figure it out. What could she do about it if someone had deliberately burned down her house?

"I stopped by and talked to the firemen who were at the house last night. I thanked them for you. I hope that's okay. Thanked Tim, the fireman who carried you out of the house."

"That was thoughtful of you." She ran a hand over her hair and realized that, once again, she probably looked like a wreck. Then again, why did she care how Austin saw her? "I appreciate it. I need to write them a thank-you note. Did they tell you anything?"

"They didn't specifically tell me it was arson. It's not their place to say one way or another. But what they said confirmed to me that it was. The way the fire burned. The color of the smoke. The fire chief is investigating now. The police are on the scene too. I stopped by the house, or what was left of it." Though he kept his tone gentle, she didn't miss the rage he contained.

Willow eased back on the sofa. "Why would someone intentionally burn down JT's house?" She had enough to deal with without heaping this on top.

Austin sighed. "There's more."

Please, no. I can't take any more.

Dana entered the living room and set a tray on the coffee table. "I brought some coffee and scones." She took one look at Willow's face. "What's happened? Willow, what is it?"

Then glared at Austin as if to ask . . . *What did you do?* Willow grabbed Dana's hand and pulled her down onto the sofa next to her, mostly for support, but also because she feared Dana might actually kick the man out of her house. That talk would have to come soon. "Austin spoke to the firemen and confirmed they believe it was arson."

Dana drew in a breath to speak, but Willow interrupted her.

"You said there's more, Austin. I want to hear it."

He hung his head.

What? What could be so bad? Her pulse kicked up.

"It's about JT's hit-and-run. The so-called accident."

Dread crept up her spine. "What about it?"

"After stopping at the house and getting rebuffed by law enforcement there, I canvassed the neighborhood to ask if anyone saw someone skulking around last night. I ended up talking to your neighbor at the end of the street. She saw the accident. She saw everything."

"What did she see?" Willow held her breath.

"She was taking video of her terrier chasing a duck near the pond. Heard a car revving its engine, accelerating too fast for the neighborhood. She whirled around to capture the offender on camera and caught the car swerving toward your grandfather."

Oh, that. "I know about the video. I didn't want to see it. Couldn't watch."

"She believes the driver deliberately swerved toward your grand-father." His words came out in even, measured tones, but that didn't hide his struggle to speak them.

Willow hadn't heard that part. Why hadn't she been told? "Do the police know?"

"I called a friend I've worked with in the Seattle PD. I asked him to keep me updated on the arson status, and I also asked about the hit-and-run. If they had any leads on the vehicle or the driver. As of this morning, they had recovered the vehicle. It had been stolen, which makes JT's death suspect."

Willow stood up and rubbed her arms. "Are you saying someone stole a car and then deliberately hit my grandfather? That he was killed on purpose? He was mur . . . murdered?" Without waiting for his answer, she paced the room. "Someone murdered JT. It was deliberate." The words wouldn't sink in. How could that be? Fury exploded in the tears she'd held back but now let free. "I want justice. Do you hear me, Austin? I want this person found. Why don't the police do something?"

"They are. The police initially disagreed with the witness's as-sessment of the accident. They're still looking for the driver. I'm sure a detective will be by to ask you questions about why someone would want to kill JT."

"You've been busy today." Dana rose from the sofa. "Are you trying to make a case? Give yourself a reason to stay in Willow's life? Nobody asked you to do this."

"Dana, please," Willow said.

"I can't listen to this." Dana fled the room.

"I'm sorry about Dana," Willow said. "She means well. I think she might be under pressure because she feels responsible for me somehow. Protective."

"I know." His gray eyes never missed a thing.

"I appreciate all the legwork you've done. But I have no idea what to do with this information. What should I do, Austin?"

He pushed himself from the chair and approached until he stood entirely too close. He lifted his hand and gently swiped a stray hair from her face, touching her skin in the process. Willow ignored the tingling sensation his touch created. The way her breath caught in her throat.

"You can close the case JT was working on, for starters."

His words surprised her, breaking the spell his nearness cast, and she took the chance to move away from him. She walked the room and studied Dana's decorating skills without actually seeing. She retrieved the cell from her pocket and stared at it. "I was going to call Mrs. Mason before you came by. Dana was getting me her number. I was going to tell her about everything and that I couldn't do this. But this news changes everything. If this is at all related to Mrs. Mason's case and this person wanted to stop Anderson Consulting, if they thought burning down the house would stop me, then they're dead wrong. I'm going to call her and tell her what's happened, and that I'll do everything in my power to find her daughter."

Austin closed the distance. She couldn't escape him. Unfortunately, she wasn't sure she wanted to.

"You can't know for sure that his last case is the reason for any of this. But it's not worth the risk. I'm merely suggesting that you drop it for now until the police figure out who burned the house and find the hit-and-run driver who killed JT." His face contorted as if saying the words were painful for him too. She understood that completely.

"I haven't told you about the case yet. You should know the woman has less than two months to live. She doesn't have time to wait for the police to investigate the fire and JT's death."

"Even so, continuing with the case could be dangerous. I don't . . ." His brows furrowed. "I don't want you to get hurt. We can talk to the police about all of it. Tell them everything. In the meantime, I'll investigate too. I'll find out who is behind this and why."

He was moving too fast. Pushing himself into her life when she'd already decided it was best if he stayed away. "*You'll* find out, Austin?"

CHAPTER TEN

Her question startled him. Didn't she understand he was in this with her? That is, if she wanted him to be. Or was she questioning how far he would go with her in this quest for answers? They didn't have a great track record together. She wanted to know up front his level of commitment. Austin studied Willow's beautiful eyes—what had drawn him to her the day they'd met. She'd been working with Zena Helms's grandmother to connect the missing pieces of a genealogical puzzle. He'd gone with Zena to stop in and check on her ailing grandmother and met Willow. One look into her eyes and Austin wanted to know more about her. A person could see deep into her heart through her compassionate, loving eyes. Willow had been transparent, willing to open up and share her life with others.

In that way, she'd been the complete opposite of Austin, who'd carefully protected everything about himself. She'd been an anomaly in the world in which he'd worked and lived. A beautiful anomaly, at that, both inside and out.

But now the world's corruption and ugliness closed in on her, and instead of open compassion, a storm brewed in her eyes. She fought to outrun it by questioning his involvement in her life. She didn't trust him. He didn't blame her. Maybe he'd been presumptuous in thinking she wanted his help. It was too much too fast, but as she'd explained, someone was already running out of time.

This couldn't be about their past.

Still, what exactly was she asking him? To explain what he was doing here at Dana's house? What he was doing sticking his nose into any of this? He hadn't even figured that out himself, so he couldn't exactly explain it. But it all boiled down to one thing.

Fear. The healthy kind.

He had enough experience—though it didn't take much in this case—to read well enough that something criminal was happening. And this time, it was happening to Willow.

Austin scraped both hands down his face. He didn't want to argue. This wasn't the time or the situation. "I'm concerned for you. No, I'm being too gentle. I'm scared for you, Willow. JT called me in to help with a project. An FBI cold case, but he gave me no details. I don't even know what this is about. Maybe we should start with that. Tell me what is going on. Maybe that will give me a lead into if this could possibly be connected to what happened to you and JT. I can talk to the FBI then. Who knows, maybe they'll inject warmth into this woman's cold case."

"I think Dana called you to cancel your services." Willow stared right through him. "At least that's what she told me."

What was she doing? Trying to get rid of him now? Maybe he'd been much too forward, too personal when he'd touched her hair, her cheek. He couldn't deny feeling her soft skin against his fingers had stirred longing in him. He wanted to feel all that was Willow, her goodness and her softness, in his arms again. But he couldn't have a future with her. This was about keeping her safe, not reviving what they once had—it had been a dead end anyway. Still, she was someone he cherished. He couldn't stand by and let her remain in danger.

Come on, man, why are you still here? "Just humor me. Tell me what's going on."

"Mrs. Mason contacted JT about a month ago. At that time, she said she had less than three months to live and wanted to find her daughter who was taken from her hospital room just hours after her birth. Twenty-one years ago."

His gut clenched. Not what he'd expected to hear. Not the kind of case he wanted to get involved in or even think about.

Was that why JT had wanted Austin's help? Because of his experience on the CARD team—Child Abduction Rapid Deployment team? At one time, he'd had a unique set of skills, honed to find children before it was too late.

When every minute counts. That had been their mantra.

But twenty-one years? Austin walked to the window and stared out. A gentle rain had started falling—droplets clung to the window and slid down like huge tears.

He'd left the FBI because he'd failed miserably. More often than not, children were found safe. But Austin's last case had left him physically, emotionally, and mentally depleted. He hadn't been able to pick himself up and go back. He'd thought he was stronger than his father and would never let tragedy take him down, but he'd been wrong. He'd been taken down and out, all right.

Like he'd told the fireman—it was in his blood.

Now what? He thought he could help Willow, but he'd been wrong. Except walking away now would be the hardest thing he'd ever done.

"Austin . . ." Willow's tone was gentle as she approached from behind. Warmth emanated from her body. *Please don't stand so close.* He swallowed, unwilling to face her yet.

"Are you okay?" she asked.

They'd ended their relationship before he'd left the FBI, so she couldn't know what had happened. And now he was pushing her, trying to influence her decisions. Who did he think he was?

No, I'm not okay. But this wasn't about him. This was about helping Willow and keeping her safe, except he couldn't help her with this. She wouldn't want him to if he told her what had happened. And if he knew anything about her, it was that she would be furious he hadn't already shared with her why he'd left the FBI. He'd been such an idiot to hide his pain, the pathetic broken soul he really was, from her.

Now it was time to suck it up.

He turned to face her. *Willow* . . . The storm in her eyes had settled to a misty rain and the compassion had returned. He missed her. Would he ever get over her? "Please tell me you're not going to dig into this. And that you're going to tell the police. Tell the FBI even that there could be a connection between what's happened to you and the Mason case." He gripped her shoulders. "You have to understand that this could be a lost cause. You could be putting yourself in danger for nothing. What do you think you're going to find? What if Mrs. Mason's daughter is dead? Do *you* want to be the one to tell her?" But he was getting ahead of himself. "Tell the authorities and let them investigate. In the meantime, take a trip. Get out of Seattle, if you can, until this is over."

"What? *You* came to me. You're the one who came to the house today to tell me about the arson and that JT's death was no accident. So to me that says your assessment—that this could be related to Mrs. Mason's abduction case—is right on. If I take the case and find Mrs. Mason's daughter—now a twenty-one-year-old woman—maybe that will lead me to JT's killer. And if it doesn't, then at least I will have done my best to solve this for Mrs. Mason. The FBI failed to find her child twenty-one years ago. They could fail again, no disrespect intended."

Her words stabbed him to the core. Still, he set his tragic experience to the side.

"And this time, Mrs. Mason doesn't have time on her side."

He stepped away from the window in their dance around Dana's living room, putting some distance between them. Now he could breathe. Now he could think clearly. "Promise me you'll consider everything I've told you. I only meant to warn you that someone could have targeted Anderson Consulting. Not draw you to the flame. So I'll leave you to think about it."

He headed to the door. He needed some fresh air. Talking to her hadn't gone as he'd planned. Trying to protect and warn her, he'd only made the situation worse. Why couldn't he just walk away from this? From her?

"Austin, wait."

He'd already opened the front door and should've kept walking but turned to face her instead. She slowly approached. "I promise I'll think about what you've said."

That surprised him. In fact, it left him speechless.

"But if I decide to pursue this, I want your help. I want to hire you to help me find Mrs. Mason's missing daughter."

He shifted on his feet, again surprised. He should be glad to hear those words. So why wasn't he?

"Fair enough." He nodded and left the house. He hoped his services wouldn't be needed, but that would mean he had no reason to see Willow again.

Though he shouldn't feel this way, Austin wanted nothing more in the world than a reason to see her again.

CHAPTER ELEVEN

Willow stared through the open door, a perfect frame for the picture before her—Austin walking away from her on the sidewalk that cut through the groomed lawn. A hazy mist nurtured the trees, mums, late-blooming roses, and dahlias lining the path. A Salvador Dali couldn't have been more surreal to her. She could hardly believe she was once again watching him leave, only to wonder if he would come back. At least she'd made an effort to hold on to him this time. The rest was up to him. She sure hoped it was for the right reason—to help her find Katelyn's daughter, Jamie Mason. How sad it was that she couldn't even trust her own heart.

"Willow," Dana said from behind. "You're not actually thinking of hiring him."

She turned around and looked at Dana. "I know you don't like him because you believe he hurt me, but I hurt him too, Dana. That happens in relationships. There are no guarantees. But that was in the past. We have to rise above what happened before and focus on Mrs. Mason's case and find out if someone killed JT because of it." Fury boiled in her veins. She couldn't afford to let the news Austin had brought cripple her. "We have to find out if someone tried to kill me in the fire last night. Despite what happened between us before, Austin just happens to be one of the only people I trust, besides you, of course. Don't you agree we could use his help? We have to put the past behind us."

"Just so you remember that and don't fall for him again."

"Don't worry. Never going to happen." That should be the least of her worries.

"He's not for you, Willow."

JT would disagree. "Look, there's no point in talking about this. So let's just move on."

"You're right. I'm sorry if I sound like a nosy friend. A manipulating mother. I don't mean to be. I'm just worried about you."

Willow gave Dana a quick hug. "I'm glad I have someone who cares." Melancholy threatened to grip her, but she focused on Mrs. Mason's case. "If only I hadn't lost JT's notes in the fire."

"You know . . . there are more of JT's notes at the warehouse," Dana said. "In fact, we should get what we can and put it in a safer place. I can hardly believe any of this has happened. *Is* happening."

"We should hire someone to put in a security system too. Someone burned down our house, and they might go after the warehouse next." How quickly she'd gone from considering closing the business to wanting to fight for it. But solving Mrs. Mason's case would be telling. Was Willow as talented as her grandfather had been at solving the insolvable?

"We have a friend in the security business. I'll see if Stan can get something done tonight." Dana hesitated. "I have to say I agree with Austin on one thing. I wish you wouldn't pursue finding her daughter now, if that would mean putting you in more danger."

Too late. "I can't turn back." Whoever was behind this would regret targeting Willow or her grandfather. They'd created a resolve in her to find Jamie she hadn't had before. She hoped her bravado held up. Fear might paralyze her if she stood still too long.

To hide her shaking hands, she said, "I'll go up and grab my—" Oh yeah. She'd lost her purse containing her identification in the fire. It reminded her of everything she needed to replace in order to exist in this world. Fortunately, her passport should still be in the safe at Anderson Consulting, along with JT's. She still needed to contact her insurance agency about the house. There was so much to do. The weight of it could overwhelm her. She rubbed her head. "Okay, let's get to the warehouse first and gather all the pertinent files. While we wait there for security, I can call the insurance company and Mrs. Mason."

"Sounds like a plan. We'll pick up something to eat on the way. Stan can grab his own dinner and contact our security system friend to meet us there." Dana touched Willow's arm. "Even though I'd prefer you didn't work on the Mason case, I'm glad you're picking up the pieces to move forward. But don't push yourself, please."

"I'll be fine." At some point the police should contact her about what happened to JT, and at that time she would tell them everything she knew about this open case, but she preferred to get her hands on the rest of his notes about Mrs. Mason before she spoke to them.

"I'll get my purse and car keys. We can ride together." Dana disappeared up the stairs.

Stan had moved Willow's vehicle to their home and parked it in the garage in lieu of his own vehicle. Hiding it? Smart man.

CHAPTER TWELVE

Willow sat at JT's desk at the Anderson Consulting office in the too-big warehouse, copying files from his computer onto a thumb drive she could keep close. Images of the notes she'd taken home, now turned to ash, accosted her. Instead of keeping the drive close, she would put it in a safety deposit box in a bank. JT always backed up his computer to a hard drive and to the cloud, but she wanted an additional copy of anything to do with Mrs. Mason that no one knew about or could access. It seemed strange that he'd completed his other projects and was working on only the Mason case. It was almost as if he knew his time was short—just like Mrs. Mason's time. Could that be why he took on this seemingly impossible task for a desperate and dying woman? His one last chance to solve the impossible? Again. He would go out with a bang. If that was true, JT hadn't known just how short his time was.

Willow fought the sudden nausea. Refocused her attention on the work at hand. Exhaustion threatened—the sooner she finished this, the sooner she could climb into bed and sleep for a decade.

Still, she probably should also make sure to get additional copies of all their clients' files, including the hard-copy files and the boxed archives. But that could take hours, if not days. Anderson Consulting's primary source of income came from the forensic genealogy side of their business used more in cases of the dead searching for the living, or rather, the search for a lost heir—the deceased had bequeathed property and the heir must be located. The living searching for the dead was a close second in terms of sources of income. With so many genealogist hobbyists out there, people were often surprised that anyone would have need for a professional genealogist. But it was specifically because of the hobbyists and people's enormous interest in learning where they came from—their family history—that professionals were needed.

Often a hobbyist created a family tree by gathering primary source documents—birth, marriage, and death certificates, which were easily found online through genealogy sites or the states where the event occurred—to prove dates. Online groups were populated with professionals who offered free advice. It was the "brick walls," as they were called, when someone was stuck and couldn't go any further in their search, that motivated people to hire a professional genealogist.

Sometimes records were accessible only through state or county archives or historical societies. Other times a person might discover through DNA testing that they weren't who they thought they were.

Maybe they didn't have the time, the expertise, or even the desire to search, but they had money to hire someone.

Like ninety-seven-year-old Albert Schmidt, a holocaust survivor who was separated from his family as a child and as an adult desperately searched for his roots. He hadn't even known who his family was. JT had spent months working for him, traveling to Germany and Poland, scouring museums, digging for answers. Thanks to JT, Albert found and met his family two months before he died, his story just one of so many.

Thoughts of Albert and his history gave her pause. Willow

should make the effort to better preserve *all* the information they'd gathered over the years so this maniac couldn't destroy anything more in their attempt to prevent Willow from discovering the truth, if that's what was going on.

In Mrs. Mason's case, it wasn't the living searching for the dead, or vice versa, but the living searching for the living. Willow hoped. She'd called Mrs. Mason on the drive over to the warehouse and left a voicemail asking for a call back. She wanted to inform her of JT's death, which would come as a shock, as it had to anyone who had known him. The man had so much life left in him. The jolt of his unexpected death rolled through her anew. People told her time would heal the pain, but she hoped she never grew numb to it.

She dreaded Mrs. Mason's reaction—that might do Willow in for the day. It was obvious from the video session that Mrs. Mason clearly liked JT, as did everyone—except for the person driving the car that hit him on his bike that day.

Don't even go there. Thinking about the video of the instant someone hit him would distract Willow from her purpose. She could lie in bed and let the pain destroy her, the bruises to her mind and soul keep her debilitated for days and weeks, maybe even months. Or she could pick herself up and work through it, maybe even accomplish something in the end, such as finding Jamie Mason. Getting to the bottom of JT's murder and the arson, though, that side of things she'd leave to the actual authorities. Still, the two were connected. Her instincts told her that much. Despite his vast experience as a board-certified genealogist and licensed attorney, JT was all about listening to his intuition. He tried to instill that same sense in Willow.

Dana entered the office carrying a box of files and plopped it on the desk.

"What's that?"

"First thing JT did after talking to Mrs. Mason was file an

FOIPA request—Freedom of Information/Privacy Act request—with the FBI regarding her missing child's case. This is a box with a hard copy of everything to do with her case, but it has only a few files from the FBI. I think he wanted Austin to speak with the caseworker and see if he could find out more."

Willow had already taken home JT's notes reflecting his thoughts—everything she would have needed to move forward. She hadn't even taken the time to read them before they were lost in the fire. A pang stabbed through her. "So you're saying there's not much useful in those files?"

"I didn't say that. In fact—"

Willow's cell phone rang. "It's Mrs. Mason!" She snatched up the call.

"Willow Anderson speaking."

"Miss Anderson, this is Katelyn Mason. I'm returning your call."

"Thanks, Mrs. Mason. Please, call me Willow." She squeezed her eyes shut. *Breathe steady now.* "We haven't found your daughter yet. That's not why I'm calling." Willow hesitated. "Though I do have some news to share with you." She let the tone in her voice prepare Mrs. Mason.

"Oh?"

"I wanted you to know that my grandfather, JT, has"—she swallowed the unshed tears—"he's gone."

"Gone. What do you mean?"

"He was killed." In an accident, she'd almost added, but that likely wasn't true anymore.

"Oh dear, I'm so terribly sorry to hear this news. So sorry for your loss."

"Thank you. Please know that I will do everything in my power to continue the search for your missing daughter. That is, if you'll allow Anderson Consulting to continue with the case."

A brief silence met the line before Mrs. Mason answered. "He spoke very highly of you, Willow. I know you'll do him proud. I don't mean to be insensitive, but may I ask what happened?"

Willow hung her head. How much should she tell the woman? "He was on his bike. It was a hit-and-run."

Mrs. Mason gasped. "Again, I can't tell you how sorry I am. In the short time I knew him, I'd grown quite fond of him. I know he will be greatly missed."

"Mrs. Mason—"

"Katelyn, please."

"All right. Katelyn, there's more." *Should I do this?*

"What is it?"

"I can't be sure, and because of that I don't know if I should even say anything, but last night someone burned down the house I shared with JT."

"I'm listening."

"And I've been told the police now consider his death suspicious."

"You mean they think someone tried to run him over on purpose? That it wasn't an accident?"

"Yes, I think so. They found the car that hit him. It had been stolen." Willow calmed her breathing. Steadied herself for what she had to ask Katelyn. "Do you think JT's death could be related to his search for your missing daughter?"

The woman released a heavy sigh. "That just seems impossible. Someone would have to know that Anderson Consulting was searching. How would the abductor even find out? Besides, it's been so long since the actual abduction that they must believe they will never be caught. The FBI looked at every possible connection to me years ago. I'd come into some money, but there was no ransom note. You can read about that in the files, I'm sure. Money wasn't the reason for her abduction. Besides, Anderson Consulting isn't the first company I've hired to investigate. No one has ever been attacked or killed for it.

"Ultimately, the FBI determined the woman who walked out

with Jamie was a stranger. The abduction was random. She posed as a nurse, which isn't uncommon when someone wants to snatch a baby from a hospital. At the time, I thought I was dying from leukemia. The doctors hadn't given me any hope of living much longer, especially since I refused treatment while pregnant with Jamie, but then my leukemia went into remission. If only my baby hadn't been stolen, I could have spent the time that was given back to me with her. Raising her. Loving her. Her father, my husband, Cliff, had died before she was born, so it would have been just the two of us. As it was, such a significant loss should have killed me, but instead it fueled my resolve to find her. But then . . . nothing. I've spent a lot of money over the years hiring investigators, and each of them left me more discouraged. Then I read the article about JT finding Albert Schmidt's family, and about some of JT's other cases, and I hoped he was the one." She sniffed, clearly upset by the turn of events. "I believe JT was able to get some of the information about that cold case to start. Do you have it?"

"Yes, but I haven't had a chance to look at it. I wanted to call you first to tell you what's happened. And maybe you should speak to the FBI about reopening the case. Tell them you've hired a private investigative group to find your daughter and you suspect someone is trying to prevent that from happening. I'd be happy to talk to them."

"Do you have proof of this, Willow?"

Willow cleared her throat. "Not yet. It's all circumstantial, if that's what you're getting at. I don't know that any of what's happened is tied to finding Jamie, but the police will ask why someone would want to burn down the house. Why someone would want to kill JT. I want you to know that I'm going to suggest to them that this could be related to your daughter's case."

"I understand, and you're being smart about it. I'll call the FBI after I'm off the phone with you to share what's happened and to see if I can get movement on my end. Wait. No. Oh no. I just remembered." Katelyn breathed heavily. "Oh, Willow, it's . . . it's all my fault."

"What are you talking about? What's your fault?"

"I can't believe it."

"Katelyn, please tell me."

"A couple of weeks after I hired JT, a reporter approached me from the *Houston Sun*. He was writing an article on abducted babies. There had been a string of abductions in the area—black-market babies, they call them. It just breaks my heart. So the reporter looked me up and asked me about my story—because my baby was never found. I told them I had hired your grandfather to find who stole my baby even though it had happened over two decades ago. The article was featured on the national news. I'm surprised you didn't see it, but then again, there are too many distractions these days." She sighed. "This could be all my fault."

"I don't see how it can possibly be your fault."

"Don't you? Whoever took Jamie saw the story on the news. They don't want you to find her. Like me, they believe Anderson Consulting is up to the task. In light of all this, I'm sorry, but I'd like to cancel my request that you investigate."

"What? Oh, Katelyn, please don't do this. Please give me the chance to find your daughter. The same chance you gave my grandfather. There's no reason why the FBI can't reexamine the case too, if they will even consider it. In the meantime, I'll look into things following the same methods my grandfather taught me. Remember why you hired him—you said he could do miracles."

"Yes. I remember. I just don't want you to get hurt."

"I don't think it will matter if I stop searching. The person responsible has no way of knowing my plans, one way or another. Quitting now won't change anything. I had planned to call you last night and tell you I couldn't continue the search for Jamie. In other words, I had planned to drop the case. What did it matter? The house was burned anyway. See what I'm saying? I almost died.

I believe finding Jamie is the only way I'll reveal the truth about what happened to JT. What happened to the house. If the fire and his death have nothing to do with Jamie, then it doesn't matter. At least I will have continued to search for her. I hope to find her. Please let me continue." Willow held her breath.

"Okay. You're right. Maybe I'm making a mistake, but I feel I have to try this one last time to find her," Katelyn said.

Willow slowly released the breath, unsure if it was relief that surged through her. "That's all I can ask. I'll let you know something as soon as there's anything to tell."

"Be careful, Willow."

She ended the call. Wide-eyed, Dana sat across from her.

"That was intense." Willow steepled her hands and pressed them against her nose. "I'm really doing this, aren't I?"

"Yes, you are. When I encouraged you to take on this project, I didn't know about the danger."

All the more reason to call Austin. She had told him if she decided to take the case, she wanted his help. Maybe having him along as protection would be a good idea too. She should have called him sooner, but she hadn't known what Katelyn would say.

A loud pop resounded in the warehouse. Willow stiffened. Shared a look with Dana. "What was that?"

"I don't know." Dana slowly rose from her chair and rubbed her arms. "I wish Stan would hurry up and get here with Phil."

Willow stood too and crept from JT's office. She wished there wasn't so much empty space in the warehouse. The back part of the building remained dark. Why pay to light the whole thing when they used only the front renovated portion? Maybe she should flip on those lights, but the switch was in the back.

Something moved in the shadows. Or . . . someone.

CHAPTER THIRTEEN

Austin sat in his Acura across the street from the Anderson Consulting office. Uninvited, of course. If she didn't want him to help her investigate or even protect her, then she could hire someone else. He kept thinking of Michael Croft. Maybe he should have shared that grisly story with her before he'd walked out like an idiot, resolving to wait for her to contact him this time.

In the meantime, he would be her shadow.

Just call me, Willow.

Eight o'clock had bled into well after nine, and with the time, his resolution slowly drained into the night. He'd had no intention of barging in on her again or trying to force his way into her life to assist. Unfortunately, too much had already gone wrong for him to walk away and never look back. But what if she didn't call? Would that mean she wasn't going to investigate the missing girl? Or that she simply didn't want to see him?

Man, he hated this kind of torture.

The lights went out. Not just the office lights, but the security light as well.

Tension jolted through his already taut muscles. Grabbing his

80

Glock and flashlight, he slowly opened the door and slid out of the car.

The darkness could mean nothing more than that the ladies were exiting the office to head home. That is, if it weren't for the security light. That was suspicious. His sudden appearance might startle them, but that was a reasonable price to pay. Crossing the street, he crept closer, grateful for the city lights reflecting off the clouds in the night sky. He wouldn't use his flashlight yet. He didn't want to draw unwanted attention to himself.

He waited at the glass door and windows that made up the office portion of the industrial-sized warehouse and peered inside. His attempt to see anything in the darkness was fruitless.

As the seconds passed, fear rippled through him. The women hadn't come out. They wouldn't remain inside in the dark without a good reason, and all of the reasons crossing his mind were bad. He tried the door. Locked.

"Willow!" he called.

Austin broke through the glass door entrance to the office, sending huge shards to the carpeted foyer. Then he faced off with another locked door, this one steel.

"Willow, it's me. Are you all right?" he called while kicking the steel door. It didn't budge. The adrenaline rush minimized the pain shooting through his leg. Willow hadn't responded to his calls. His heart jackhammered.

She was in danger.

"I'm going to shoot the lock. Stay back." He had no way of knowing what he would face on the other side, but he had to give fair warning.

He fired his gun twice. With the doorjamb and lock obliterated, now was his chance. He pushed the door open. Darkness engulfed him. Shining his flashlight now could make him an easy target, so he slid to the right and pressed against the wall. Waited for his eyes to adjust, if possible, in the total blackness.

And listened.

His own too-heavy breathing resounded. Letting his military training kick in, he forced a calm into his body that he didn't feel.

Footfalls approached to his left. His pulse ratcheted up. Was it Willow or Dana? His gut told him neither. He resisted turning on his flashlight. Not yet. Did whoever approached know he stood in their path? Were they coming for him? Or were they headed for the open door to escape?

He fired his weapon into the ground to warn them to back off. "Stop or I'll shoot!"

Tingles ran over his arms. Instinct took over and he ducked. Air whooshed over his head as something large and deadly drove past him and then clanged to the floor. He lunged low to launch into the assailant but missed. Austin whipped around. The shadowy silhouette of a man dashed through the open door. Glass crunched underfoot as the man fled.

Austin's attention returned to finding Willow. He hoped that had been the only assailant. He flicked on his flashlight to search for her while he called 9-1-1.

The assailant was getting away, but Austin couldn't follow. He had to look for Willow. She and Dana could be hurt.

Or worse . . .

"Are you okay? Willow? Where are you?" *Please, say something.*

His heart in his throat, Austin battled through his fear.

The warehouse creaked, but Willow didn't answer.

A pungent odor overwhelmed him the deeper he went into the building. Gasoline.

CHAPTER FOURTEEN

"Sh. I hear something." Crouched between dusty cardboard boxes, Willow gripped Dana's moist hand as they huddled in the dark closet.

When she'd realized someone was in the warehouse with obviously nefarious intentions, Willow had wanted to go for the lights to chase away the shadows and reveal their uninvited guest's identity, but he'd already found the breaker box and put them all in the dark.

Dana had screamed.

Without hesitation, Willow had grabbed Dana's hand and pulled the woman with her as she blindly made her way down the short hallway, back to JT's office. She'd shut and locked the door so it looked like all the other doors, then they'd gone into the closet to hide. If she'd had a weapon, maybe she could have used it to protect them. She would never go anywhere without a gun again. The one she owned had been tucked in a drawer in the bedside table at the house.

In the closet, she'd tried to call 9–1–1.

Before the call had connected, a noise resounded at the office door. If they kept quiet, maybe he would move to the next door. She feared speaking into the phone would give them away. So she'd put off making that call.

Seconds later someone called her name.

"I think it's Austin!" She stood to open the closet door, but Dana snatched her back.

"Wait, you don't know that," she whispered.

"Willow." His familiar voice wrapped her with relief.

"Listen, don't you hear that? It's Austin."

"Willow!" Louder now.

She thrust open the closet door. "We're in here!"

A crash reverberated and the office door jarred wide open. Light beamed into her eyes.

"Willow!" His pure electrified relief shot through her like a thousand bolts of lightning as he pulled her into his arms.

She buried her face into his neck. Drew in the musky smell of his cologne, never so glad to see another person. "Austin." She breathed against his skin. Right there in his arms. Right there she was safe.

For a few heartbeats, she soaked up the essence that was Austin. In another world—another time and place, a life that didn't exist—she could remain in his arms forever.

She eased out of his embrace. "Thanks for finding us." She could guess why he was here—he'd hadn't stopped watching out for her. Any other time she might be frustrated with him. "There was someone in the warehouse. Is he gone?"

"Yes. He got away." Austin shined the light over her face and body and then Dana's. "Are you all right? Did he hurt you?"

Willow shook her head. "No, we hid in the closet. I was about to call 9–1–1."

"I already did. But we need to get out of here. I smell gasoline. I think he intended to light another fire."

"Oh no." Willow looked at Dana. "We haven't finished here. We need to get all these files out before someone tries to destroy them."

Austin glanced at his watch. "Can't move anything until we get the go-ahead. We don't want to mess with any evidence that could lead us to this guy. But we don't want files destroyed either. Let me make sure the premises are safe first."

Willow allowed Austin to take her hand and lead her through the splintered door, revealing his desperation to find her. The image acted like a gentle breath on the spark in her heart.

"Stand right here. After I make sure it's safe to do so—I don't want to start a fire—I'm going to turn on the breaker, along with all the lights both outside and inside." What would have happened to them if he hadn't shown up? Would the warehouse be burning now? She and Dana trapped inside awaiting their fate?

The fluorescent lighting flickered back to life in the main office, and the back portion of the warehouse lit up as well. Since Willow never turned on those lights, the man could have been hiding back there for who knew how long. They'd locked the doors when they arrived to prevent unwanted guests. Had he been there when they arrived, surprised at their sudden appearance but waiting for his chance to burn the place down and escape? She shuddered.

Austin jogged back to them, then led them through the steel door to the outer foyer. "Watch for the glass in here. I'm sorry I had to destroy so many doors to get inside."

They carefully picked their way around the shards as they stepped through what remained of the glass door.

Once outside, he gripped Willow's shoulders. "Let me make sure it's safe for you. Just stay right here near the doorway. I figure this guy is long gone by now, but I don't want to take any chances. Stay alert." He held his gun at low ready as he disappeared around the side of the building.

At least the lights cast away the darkness. Like Austin had said, the guy was probably gone. Who was he?

Next to her, Dana still shook. Willow grabbed Dana's arm and held her close. "It's going to be okay. Austin's here."

"I hate to say this, but I was glad to see him. I just wonder where my Stan is." Irritation mingled with worry in her tone. "If he and

Phil had been here installing the security system, this wouldn't have happened."

Austin returned, giving them a start. "Let's go."

"Where are we going?" Willow asked.

"To wait inside my car until the police arrive." He led them past Dana's vehicle and across the street to his car, where he helped them get inside.

Austin climbed in as well and locked the doors. He started the car.

"Wait. What about the gasoline? We need to move the files. What if he planted a bomb or something to ignite a fire?"

"They're not worth your life." The look in his gray eyes turned dark. "You're not going back in there. The police will be here soon. And when they get here, you need to tell them everything. I asked for the detective who will be investigating JT's death. This has to be involved with his death and the house fire. We'll get the files when they tell us we're free to do so."

Dana sighed heavily from the back seat. "Finally, Stan is texting me. I told him what happened. They're on their way. Phil just had to show him his new boat."

"Don't blame him, Dana. We had no idea someone would be so bold as to attack while we were both there. But I'm thinking that we surprised the guy. He was there when we got there. Maybe planned to burn it down, but then we showed up. He was trying to make a silent escape when he knocked something over and we heard it."

"I don't get it. If he wanted to destroy the files, why not burn the warehouse down last night on the same night as the house. Why wait?" Dana asked.

"That's easy." Austin shifted to peer down the street. Hoping for the police? "He thought he could end the search for Jamie with Willow's death."

He looked at Willow, his meaning drilling down into her. She hugged herself, wishing the nightmare would end.

"That makes some kind of sick sense," Dana said. "It scares

me. If you hadn't shown up tonight, he might have succeeded in burning the warehouse down, with us inside. That brings me to my question. Why *were* you there, Austin?" Dana asked.

"Willow isn't safe until this is over. I kept hoping she would call me, but until she did, I planned to watch over her anyway."

Willow couldn't have been more grateful. How could she ever thank the guy?

"I was sitting in the car tonight watching and waiting. I didn't see anyone go inside, so I think Willow is on to something. He was already here when you arrived."

"We'll know better next time," Willow said. "So what happened? What made you come looking for us?"

"The lights went out. Not just the lights but the security light too. When you didn't come out, I knew something was wrong. I broke through the doors. Whoever was in there came running toward the door. Before he got away, he tried to take me out. I would have gone after him, but I had to find you first. You could have been seriously injured. I couldn't live with myself if something happened to you, Willow. You either, Dana."

"Neither could I." Dana spoke from the back seat. "That's why I'm hiring you to protect Willow. You're doing the work anyway, aren't you?"

Willow had considered hiring him to assist in the investigation. Coming from Dana, the decision to hire him for protection surprised her. "Don't I have a say in this?"

"Of course you do." Austin opened the car door and held her with a look. "The police are coming. Stay here."

Without waiting for her reply, he got out and shut the door. She remembered he hadn't wanted to be hired, but, rather, he wanted to help her as a friend. But Willow had made it clear that she would hire him—to keep their relationship purely professional. However, her reaction to him when he'd found them in the warehouse said otherwise.

"Looks like he's taking the job," Dana said.

Willow crossed her arms. "First you don't like him and do everything to nudge him away, and now you want to hire him?"

"Maybe if he'd been with us tonight in the warehouse, this wouldn't have happened in the first place. It's obvious he still cares about you, and I'm not sure I trust anyone else to protect you." Dana chuckled. "I can't believe I'm saying any of this. But you're family to me. I care about you. You need someone who cares as much as Austin does and has the skills to protect you. He came through for you tonight. For us, Willow."

Yes. Yes, he did.

Had JT ever been involved in anything so utterly dangerous before? What would he want her to do? She honestly didn't know. He might want something different for his granddaughter—like safety and security. But as for JT, if he were still alive, he would see this through to the end. She could think of no better example in life or in this specialty consulting business.

The night before, she'd cowered as flames engulfed the house around her. Tonight, she'd hidden in a closet fearing for her life.

She was done cowering. Done hiding. This experience had messed with her psyche, but she would find the strength to keep going.

Uniformed officers searched the warehouse, both inside and out. Austin stood by a police cruiser and talked with an officer in plain clothes—a detective—as if he'd known the guy for years. Austin had a friendly way about him—just like JT. He gestured back toward his car, and to them. Two more vehicles approached—a fire department patrol truck and a blue Silverado.

"Stan's here," Willow said.

"Oh, thank God." Dana fled the car and rushed to her husband.

Willow squeezed the door handle and mumbled to herself. "It's time to talk to the police."

Feeling the weariness of the last forty-eight hours in her bones, she approached Austin and the detective and introduced herself.

He shook her hand. "I'm Detective Murdoch. Can you tell me what happened, Miss Anderson?"

Nodding, Willow composed herself. "Dana and I were here gathering information about a project we're working on. Downloading information from the computer. We were afraid the same person who burned down my house, who killed JT, might come for the warehouse next."

Officer Murdoch shared a look with Austin.

She hesitated before continuing.

"It's okay, Willow. I told him this could be a part of the larger case, and linked to JT's death. Just tell him what happened here tonight." Willow appreciated Austin talking to him first. She didn't relish repeating the whole story, and shared her part.

"Let me make sure I understand. You think he was already in the warehouse when you arrived and surprised him. You believe this is part of the FBI cold case your grandfather was working on." Detective Murdoch wrote in his notepad.

"Yes," Willow said.

Stan approached with Dana, though they stood back a few feet from Willow, Austin, and the detective.

"But you said it sounded like he was searching for you."

"He could have wanted to hurt us or tie us up or something and take the files. I don't know."

His eyes dark, Austin crossed his arms.

"Okay, thank you, Miss Anderson. I'd like to talk to the woman who was with you."

"That's me," Dana said. "I'm Dana Cooper."

The detective stepped aside, away from Austin and Willow, to speak with Dana.

Willow tried to catch her breath. Two nights in a row she'd found herself in a precarious situation. Austin remained close, protection emanating from him. What she could really use right now was a good, long hug. But she refused to give in to that desire.

"I keep wondering what would have happened tonight if JT hadn't called you to begin with. If you hadn't . . ." She couldn't say it. Couldn't finish the sentence. *Come back into my life.*

"The outcome would be the same." He kept his voice low.

She lifted her eyes to study his strong jaw. Lips that had called her name tonight, infusing her with hope and something entirely forbidden. She'd kissed those lips before. "What do you mean?"

"Zena Helms texted me about the fire. You worked on a project for her grandmother, remember? I came to check on you in the hospital. That had nothing at all to do with JT's call. Once I knew you were in danger, well, you couldn't get rid of me so easily."

Austin's strength drew her closer. She couldn't help herself. She leaned into him, and he wrapped his arms around her as if he'd known what she'd wanted all along. As if he'd wanted the same thing.

"Now we need to get you someplace safe."

Which meant she couldn't stay with Dana and her family. Though she'd already put Dana in harm's way, she wouldn't put her or her family in more danger. Willow hoped she hadn't already done just that.

"I'm not sure any place will be safe until we find who's responsible," she said.

"Let the police do their jobs."

"Sure, they can do their jobs, but in the meantime, I'm doing mine and I'm searching for Katelyn's missing child. I'm going to find her, Austin. I'm going to find Jamie Mason, and I need you to help. It's what JT would have wanted."

She saw the question in Austin's eyes.

But is it what you want, Willow?

That shouldn't matter to either of them. Maybe she'd always have a thing for Austin. But she'd spent her life uncovering the past, metaphorically digging up dead people and sometimes their secrets too. Austin had gone to great pains to hide his past and secrets, and that had caused conflict between them before. Her digging into his life, her curiosity about his history had only pushed him away.

CHAPTER FIFTEEN

Austin hiked up the steps, lugging the box of files to his second-floor apartment located in a gated community in northeast Seattle. Despite the cool mist of a gray-skied Seattle day, sweat beaded his brow. He'd moved here when he'd taken the position with the FBI as a field agent. A new lease on life, as it were. The only hiccup in that plan happened a year later. He'd gone to see his father, and after a heated argument, the man had died in a car accident. Austin couldn't even remember what they'd argued about.

At the memory, he nearly stumbled on the steps but caught himself in time.

Willow trudged behind him, carrying one of her own boxes—the last one that contained information regarding their search for Jamie Mason.

The police had finished processing the warehouse scene, looking for prints and other evidence that might lead them to the person who had burned down Willow's house or driven the car that killed JT. This morning, Willow had been allowed to retrieve the office files for safekeeping. He'd helped her move all the other client files to a secure storage facility while Dana waited with Stan for the security system to finally be installed at the warehouse. Too little too late, if they asked Austin. Security could have prevented last night's debacle.

They'd spent the morning deep in manual labor because Willow couldn't bear to part with JT's forensic genealogy work or allow someone to destroy it. Everything of value was being removed.

He didn't blame her. Besides, someone might request additional information in the future. Once the police put this criminal behind bars, if Willow chose to move everything back and work from the warehouse office, the security system would be in place.

Exhaustion from the last two grueling days clawed at him as he peered over his shoulder. "Just one more step."

He took the last one, then hefted the boxed files to his side as he approached the maroon door and opened it for Willow. He stood to the side and waited. She'd pulled her long, dark tangles into a ponytail that swung as she carried the box through the door ahead of him, her hazel eyes sliding to him as she passed. In his apartment, she hefted the box onto the dining table next to a couple of others. Austin closed the door and unloaded his haul next to hers.

He knew that look in her eyes. She was on a mission, albeit a dangerous one. Better that look than the haunted look of defeat he'd seen on her face in the hospital after the fire.

She tried opening the taped box with her fingers. "Got a box cutter?"

"No, but I have Dr Pepper." *Your favorite.* How crazy was it that he'd stocked up on it yesterday? He couldn't have known she would be here with him. His subconscious gave away what he thought he'd buried.

Her eyes brightened with appreciation. That worked for him.

"Let's take a five-minute break." He wished they could have two weeks to rest up before diving in, but time was a luxury.

"All right."

In the rarely used kitchen, he grabbed the scissors in lieu of a box cutter. Took a couple of sodas from the fridge, then opened them, trying not to think about the last time Willow had been here with him in this apartment. So much had happened since then. The memories pricked him. He headed back into the living room, though it was an open floor plan—the kitchen, living, and dining rooms all part of one big space. With her back to him and her hands on her hips, she eyed his unintentionally minimalist apartment.

He paused, taking her in—running shoes and a bright blue hoodie over form-fitting jeans, ready to tackle the world. Where did she get her energy, especially after all she'd been through? Like JT, Willow was a force to be reckoned with. It would take any normal person a week—no, a month or more—to rest and get over what had happened, but not Willow. Her presence, her inner strength, had him wishing for more with her.

Had him reaching for the past.

He'd honed his skills at compartmentalizing everything, including the past, which he slung away to be dealt with never. But being so near Willow, involved in her life like this, could dismantle the carefully placed cubicles.

She yanked the band out of her silky hair, letting it fall to her midback, and weaved her fingers through, then secured it into the ponytail again. His pulse inched up.

Unable to speak, he cleared his throat. She whipped around in surprise and smiled. He held out the Dr. Pepper, which she quickly took from his hand. After a swig, she returned her attention to the paintings he'd snagged from starving artist sales. Grand Teton. Didn't every dentist office in the country feature that one? Another of the Yellowstone River. Nothing so personal as a family photograph lying around to reveal his past. Yet with those paintings, he'd managed to give himself away.

"You never were much for decorating, but I'm glad you finally put something up."

"Yeah, something. Other than the DP, my refrigerator is empty. If you want lunch, we'll have to order takeout or grab some fast food."

"All that work this morning gave me an appetite. Let's order in. We can dig through the files while we eat."

He'd hoped to distract her from the paintings, but she lingered. He knew exactly what she was thinking.

Why did Austin pick these paintings?

Studying photographs remained an important part of her work as a genealogist, and somehow after years of it, she might even fancy herself being able to profile people. There was no doubt one could learn a lot about a person from their photographs, but he hadn't put any on his walls. Certain aspects of his life he wanted to forget or, at the very least, keep private, and yet he'd been drawn to those paintings. Reminders. What had he been thinking? He hadn't.

Nor had he expected his paintings to bring them full circle, back to their relationship issues. But maybe he was completely wrong and Willow wasn't thinking about that. After all, she hadn't asked him about the paintings, and that wasn't her usual M.O.

"How about Chinese?" he asked.

"Perfect."

He pulled out his cell to make the call.

She gave up on the paintings and took the scissors he'd found to cut open a box. "The sooner I figure this out, the better." She blinked up at him. "I mean, the sooner *we* figure it out, the better."

Austin called the number for Ming's Chinese Delivery, one of his staple takeout places. Willow's box cutting made too much noise, so he moved into the kitchen to place his order, then back to the small dining area.

The box open, she removed files and sat at the table to leaf through pages. "This is like nothing I've ever done before."

He grabbed his laptop and pulled up a chair next to her. "What do you mean?" he asked as he sat down.

"I'm usually either connecting the dead with the living or the living with the dead. But Katelyn is hoping I'll find her daughter alive. It's like you said before, what if she's not? What if she died a long time ago?"

"Then Katelyn needs that closure." Still, having to be the one to break that news was something to consider. They were in too far to go back now. He started to place his hand on her shoulder to comfort her but thought it best to keep his distance for both their sakes. "You're not alone." *I'm here with you.* "You can and will do this."

"Thanks." The word was barely a whisper as she stared at him with eyes that might see right through him if he'd let her.

"For what?"

"For your encouragement. For sticking with me to help. For coming to my rescue last night."

"You're welcome." He couldn't have done anything less.

They shared a look that lasted a few seconds longer than necessary, then she returned her attention to the file on the table. "I hope Dana gets here soon. She might be able to tell me more about what JT has already done. I found out last night that he'd requested the FBI files. So I have those." When her eyes shot to him, then back to the file before her, he hadn't missed the question in her eyes.

Why had JT needed his help? Now it was his turn to second-guess what he was doing. If he told her how he'd failed while working on the CARD team, would she still want his help? Thinking about that failure could cripple him enough that he wouldn't be able to help Willow. But if he could help Willow find Jamie, maybe he could set things right—make peace with himself. If he told Willow about what had happened before, she might no longer want his help. And he needed this. He needed to help.

"So, Austin, you were working with the CARD team, right?" *Uh-oh.* "Yeah, why?"

"What can you tell me about the stats on abducted babies?"

At least she hadn't asked him why he was no longer with the FBI. On his laptop he pulled up statistics compiled from law enforcement agencies, including the FBI. She could have done that but might not have known exactly where to look. He skimmed the information to jar his memory, but not too much. He read from the website. "Of the nonfamily member newborns that have been abducted since 1965, most were taken from health-care facilities. Most were taken directly from the mother's room."

"Most. How many are we talking about?"

"Just over three hundred babies have been abducted since 1965."

"How many have been found?"

His throat constricted. "Most of them. Fifteen are still missing. One of those is Jamie Mason. Nine of them died at the hands of their abductor, either directly or indirectly." A few rocks closing off the cavern holding his pain fell away. No, no. He didn't want to feel that again.

"Are you okay?"

He shook it off. "Yeah. I'm sure we'll read about this in the FBI files, but to give you an overview of what the profile of a typical infant abductor looks like—again, I'm talking a nonfamily member, a stranger—"

"Wait. Why are you focusing on a nonfamily member?"

"I suspect that's what we're talking about here. The FBI would have already looked into anyone close to the mother who could have been involved in the abduction, since family abductions are the most frequent. If a family member had taken her, Jamie would have most likely been found not long after her abduction, but she wasn't."

"That makes sense."

"But I'm speculating. Best if we just read the files. Things have changed a lot in twenty years. Now we have radio-frequency identification tags for babies. The tag is secured to the baby's ankle with a band and makes it difficult to walk out without authorization.

An alarm is triggered if the baby is taken outside of a designated area or the band is cut."

"Like walking out of a department store with a stolen shirt. Only it's a baby."

"Exactly. Another big difference is that social media connects people and opens up the door for would-be abductors to befriend mothers on Facebook and other sites." Social media hadn't had anything to do with the child abduction case that still haunted him. The abductor had come right through the front door without an invitation because they hadn't needed one. He needed to shut his memories down or else he'd be telling her all about his last child abduction case and the reason he'd left the FBI.

Austin shoved away his past failures one more time. He'd better get good at it, considering their focus here. But dread filled him that Jamie Mason wouldn't be found alive. Wouldn't be found at all. And Willow might remain in danger.

She handed him the file and grabbed a new one for herself, then quickly skimmed the documents.

"Oh." Her brows lifted. "Katelyn provided her DNA to JT for testing just in case Jamie's shows up on a database somewhere. No hits on any of that as far as we know."

Austin read through the contents of the files from the FBI cold case, looking for anything that could help them. "Says here the authorities had an image from a hospital security camera, but it was grainy. Katelyn even had a conversation with her." He frowned. A pang hit his gut. "The woman pretended to be a nurse and brought her a lunch plate. They had a short, friendly conversation. Makes me sick."

He read further. "Back to the image. The authorities distributed the image in a massive investigation and search for the baby in Houston and all of Texas. The FBI and police pursued hundreds of leads. Searching for a woman who fit the profile of an infant abductor, they actively searched the community where Katelyn lived and around the hospital. The abductor might have visited nurseries and maternity units around the city. Looks like they did everything they could." Nausea began a slow churn in his gut. He rubbed his eyes. Could he do this? Could he follow through? He really didn't want to be like his father, who'd thrown his life away because of tragedy. He needed to make a change. See this through to the end.

"Even with all their efforts they came up empty-handed." Willow yawned, then peered at the copy of the grainy image. "Frankly, this could be anyone. Anyone at all."

Willow, like her grandfather, was more determined than most, but even Austin saw how completely hopeless this was. Why had JT thought he could solve this? They needed something. Even the smallest tidbit of information could encourage them and open doors. They would keep searching, but this could take much too long. "She appeared to be in her late twenties. Maybe early thirties, so she'd be in her late forties, early fifties, now. We could get a forensic artist involved."

"JT had someone he used. A friend who does age progression. Dana could contact her."

That gave Austin pause. "Why would JT need someone to do age progression? It's used to help find a missing person. Children who've been missing for years."

"JT used her on a specific project to help a woman to know if an ancestor as a child in a photograph was the same person as an older adult in another photograph."

Austin had spent time with Willow and JT and still he could be surprised at the lengths to which people would go for their genealogy research.

"It wasn't all that successful," she said. "She couldn't make a definite match between the child and adult in the photographs."

"If we used JT's forensic artist friend," he said, "she could only do this with any accuracy for the missing person, the baby, not the abductor. She would need photographs of relatives, and since we don't know who the abductor is, we don't have her relatives. As for age progression of Jamie, those images have already been created and put on milk cartons and databases all over the country, I can assure you."

"Right." Willow flipped her file closed. "Chances are the image of the abductor is too rough for use in facial recognition software. But I'd still like to try."

"I don't disagree." Maybe he could use the wealth of connections at Ex-Agents International to process the photo and get somewhere with it. That is, if it wasn't too grainy.

Sometimes having a photograph made no difference. Sometimes a psychopath came right through the front door to take what they wanted.

When a knock came at Austin's door, he brandished his weapon without conscious thought.

Willow stood. "What are you doing?"

Maybe he was entirely too edgy, but he didn't think so. "Who is it?"

"It's Dana. And looks like Chinese takeout."

Still, Austin kept the weapon ready as he opened the door.

Liu Ming wore his usual painted-on smile, and Austin put away his weapon.

"You teach me shoot." It wasn't a question.

CHAPTER SIXTEEN

The Chinese delivery guy wanted Austin to teach him to shoot? While Austin paid Liu Ming, Willow untangled herself from the conversation and scraped off the table, clearing it for a working lunch, but kept the two files they'd been reading. He grabbed the sacks of food and shut the door behind him, barricading them in with the aroma of fried food, greasy chicken loaded with sugar and salt. Her stomach rumbled.

She stepped into the kitchen in search of dishes.

Across the room, Dana dropped her bright coral Coach purse on the sofa. "The security system is installed, so that's out of the way."

"And the archived files are all put away at Puget Sound Security Storage, thanks to Austin's help. You're welcome to join us," Willow said. "You must be hungry."

"No, actually. I ate with Stan at the office. But you go ahead. We can talk while you eat."

Willow returned to the table with two plates, along with utensils, and sat down at the table.

The only two she'd found in Austin's kitchen—the two she'd bought him before so they could eat. Not a whole set for him. No. Only two. He said he never wanted to wash more than two at a time. He hadn't been into entertaining then and nothing much had changed. But if it had, why should she care? Although, the thought of him eating with another woman sent a sliver of jealousy through her. *Utterly ridiculous.* She corrected her sudden severe frown before anyone could notice.

Austin opened the red takeout boxes. Sweet and sour chicken. Fried rice. Egg foo yung. Egg rolls and . . .

"Cheesecake? They sell cheesecake?"

"No. I asked him to find and bring cheesecake. He said he would if I taught him to shoot."

Willow eyed the cheese, eggs, and sugar creamed together on a graham-cracker crust. He'd done this for her. This and the Dr. Pepper. She wasn't sure how she felt about that. They were working together, nothing more. Right? He was putting a saucy glob of the chicken on his plate, pretending he wasn't watching her reaction.

"I think I'll eat dessert first, if that's all right."

His dimpled grin told her he'd gotten his thank-you.

Dana shouldered her bag, signaling an early departure. What? She couldn't stomach watching Willow and Austin eating? And together, no less. Or was it more that she couldn't stomach the chemistry between them? Why couldn't they shut it down? A question for another time.

Dana approached the table. "Something you won't find in the files is that JT had planned to travel to Jackson, Wyoming."

Austin dropped his chopsticks on the floor and bent down to pick them up.

"Jackson, Wyoming?" Willow twisted her fork around. She'd never been able to use chopsticks.

Dana nodded. "I had planned to get the ticket for him the day he died."

"What on earth for?" Willow eyed Dana while gauging Austin's reaction.

"The woman in the picture. The abductor. If you look closely at the image, you'll see she was wearing a pendant necklace. That necklace was found in the parking lot. Mrs. Mason identified it as the one the abductor wore. But that's as far as it went."

"What am I missing?" Willow's heart skipped a beat as her confidence slid. She should see the connection already if she had JT's gift. But she didn't.

Dana snatched up the FBI file and thumbed through until she found the information. "Here. This identifies the necklace as silver and manufactured by the—"

"Wyoming Silversmith Company," Austin said. Dana gave him an inquisitive look. "It was in the file. Why would he go to the place the necklace was manufactured?"

Willow peered at the image of a bucking horse pendant. "How do we know they made the necklace, and why couldn't she have bought that anywhere?"

Dana shifted her bag. "The back is stamped with *Handmade by Wyoming Silversmith Company*. Back then you could only get their items in Jackson, Wyoming. Now you can order online. The stuff isn't cheap. I'm not sure if this information helps. The investigators had the same information back then."

"Someone could have given it to her," Austin said. "I'm sure all those leads have already been followed."

Willow squeezed her eyes shut as if cutting off her vision would send more power to her brain. "Have they? Do we know if the FBI went to the actual place where the necklace was made?"

"Possibly, but we'd have to find out for sure. What are you getting at?" he asked.

Opening her eyes, she shared a look with Dana. "People tend to look for a needle in a haystack—"

"When all they need is one good thread," Dana said, finishing her sentence.

"What does that even mean?" Austin wiped off his chopsticks and chased a chicken chunk around his plate.

Willow tried not to laugh at his efforts. She handed him a fork. "JT used to say it. It means people often search for something that might be impossible to find or focus on obscure information instead of following the obvious threads."

"Okay. I'm just going to be honest here. I still don't know what that means."

"It means that looking deeper into the Wyoming Silversmith Company is a good thread." Willow shrugged. "It's one thread. A lead. He was going to follow it. I can't say that I would have done the same. But if it's as you say and the FBI and police have already followed the obvious leads, and even some of the less than obvious ones, then it's worth a try. JT believed that following every such lead, or hunch even, had the potential to open up new doors. I've seen it happen too often to ignore his methods."

"Okay, wait, so maybe what you mean is that he just starts threading every needle, right? Maybe that's what he should have said." He grinned.

Willow choked on her Dr. Pepper.

Dana's cell phone rang and she took the call, a frown quickly developing on her face. "I'll be right there." She ended the call, worry and an apology in her eyes. "Layne fell, and Shari thinks he broke his arm. She needs me to watch the baby. I'm so sorry."

"Oh, don't be. Go see to your grandbaby. I hope Layne is okay. Tell Shari I said hi." Willow rose from the table and ushered Dana out the door. It felt strange doing so because this wasn't her home. Right now, she had no home.

Dana hung back. "Are you sure you're okay after everything that's happened?"

"Not much I can do about it except finish JT's last project for him. We'll get answers that way."

Dana leaned in, dropping her voice to a whisper. "Was I presumptuous in saying that Austin should work with you?"

"Of course not. Now go see your family." Willow hugged her

for good measure. Dana gave her a tenuous smile, then headed down the steps.

Willow closed the door and sat at the table again, her cheesecake only half eaten. It didn't appear as appetizing as it had before. Especially since it looked like a trip to Wyoming was in order. Austin used a fork to finish off the pile of Chinese delight on his plate. He didn't look particularly excited about the new information. Willow wished she didn't know why. What would he think of her when he found out what she'd done?

Dread prickled through her. She had to remain focused on finding Jamie Mason. Dead or alive. They finished eating in silence. She forced herself to finish the cheesecake, hoping it would bring comfort. Besides, Austin had to teach Ming to shoot now. The least she could do was finish eating his thoughtful gift. She stifled a sigh—she'd missed him. Then she stood to clear away the mess. "I keep wondering about her name."

"What do you mean?"

"If Jamie survived and she's still alive out there somewhere, the abductor or whoever raised her would have given her a new name."

And if so, what was her name?

CHAPTER SEVENTEEN

Even though the town square boardwalk under her feet brought a sense of rightness, Charlie Clemmons could never be too careful. She had to be quick. In and out. Get what she needed in town and leave. Life was always like this now. She hoped it wouldn't stay that way forever. She couldn't keep this up for an extended amount of time. If she could stay under the radar and off the grid until she learned the truth, that would be long enough.

Except today she'd taken a risk. A detour. She'd strayed from her tried and true routine. What did one deviation from her plan hurt?

Maybe she should have run from all of it. Fled to the other side of the country. But *he* would expect that.

By staying here, Charlie was doing the unexpected.

She credited the weather for her decision. In Jackson Hole— the small valley carved out of the Teton and Gross Ventre mountain ranges where she grew up—she might dress for a sunny day in the midseventies, like today. But in mid-September, the weather could shift by the afternoon and turn cold, making her wish for her fringe leather jacket and Double D cowgirl boots

106

Momma had given her five years ago when she'd turned sixteen. Silver studded. Turquoise and coffee leather. In fact, she wished for them now.

Except she couldn't wear them. They would be a dead giveaway.

She walked along the boardwalk until the smell of leather wafted out of a western wear shop and her feet slowed. As if conjured by her thoughts, cowboy boots filled the window display. A whole rack of them were on clearance. The reflection in the glass gave her pause. Who was that looking at her? Fear smothered her. Her heart pounded.

Realization dawned. Oxygen flooded her lungs, calming her heart. She was the stranger in the reflection. She hadn't recognized herself. Good. That was exactly what she was going for with her closely cropped bleached hair, spiked at the top, but not too much—the complete opposite of the thick brown mane she'd had her entire life. Sneakers instead of boots. A plain gray hoodie and faded jeans completed the costume.

Though she'd stood staring for far too long, others walked by or stopped to admire the western wear in the window, apparently unaware that Charlie had been staring at herself. She should be grateful the tourists had thinned out by this time of year. The way Grayback had been growing—adding art galleries, eateries, and all manner of gift shops—the town was modeling itself after Jackson.

Even so, she couldn't linger too long or she *would* draw unwanted attention to herself. She forced her sneakered feet along the boardwalk, past the thirteen-foot-tall grizzly bear carved out of lodgepole pine, taking in the aroma of barbecue pulled pork and the sounds of boots clomping along the boardwalk and traffic on the square. Charlie wasn't sure why she'd taken this detour today, but sometimes a girl had to window-shop. This reminded her of her sweet Momma and the day she bought her those particular boots. Momma loved shoes and lavished Charlie with more than she had a need for.

Charlie regretted coming. Wished she had someone else to share her secret with besides Mack.

No offense, Mack.

A cool mountain breeze drifting off the Teton Range wrapped around her, bringing the promise of a change, a shift in the atmosphere. A shudder ran over her. She hoped she hadn't exposed herself today by coming here. She shouldn't have taken the risk of walking beyond the stores where she bought much-needed supplies and groceries. Mack had assured her he would do it for her, but she couldn't ask more of him. Holding her sack of groceries, she pulled her gray hoodie over her head until it hung forward like she was a devoted monk on the way to evening prayers. She wished she could lift her head high and let the sun warm her cheeks. Maybe someday soon, but not today.

A sheriff's department vehicle eased down the street until it became stuck in traffic and came to a stop right next to Charlie.

Steady, now . . . act normal.

The hoodie hid her face, but it could also make her stand out as someone who didn't want to be identified.

Her breathing spiked. Sweat beaded on her neck and dripped down her back. The world around her disappeared as her vision tunneled and her pulse roared in her ears.

Fall apart now and it's all over.

One . . . foot . . . in front . . . of the other . . .

One foot . . . in front of the . . . other.

One foot in front of the other . . .

The world around her normalized. She breathed easier now. Heard soft conversations as couples and families passed by. Charlie would be okay. She had to make it back to freedom, if she could call hiding in a cabin freedom. She would make sure to kick herself for good measure when she got there. Not nearly soon enough she approached her indistinguishable junker truck she called Bronc and climbed in with her groceries.

After the panic attack, her purchases and going to town to be around others hardly seemed worth it.

If only the masked man hadn't said he would kill her that night.

Right after he'd shot and killed her mother.

CHAPTER EIGHTEEN

The moment Dana had detonated the explosive news about the case's connection to Wyoming, the sour had overpowered the sweet. He might never be able to enjoy Chinese food again, and he'd *still* have to teach the guy to shoot at the range.

He'd done his best to maintain his composure. Arms crossed, he propped his feet on the coffee table. Willow was on her cell, pacing his living room as she argued with the insurance company about the house fire. He kicked away the sandbags around his heart and allowed the angst and confusion to rush over him like floodwaters too long held back—those starving artist paintings staring back at him, mocking him.

At least he had an answer now. He hadn't been sure it was a question until he'd heard the words *Jackson, Wyoming*. He thought JT had contacted him because of his work in the FBI, and then he thought it had to do with his experience working on the CARD team. But it was all so clear now—JT had contacted him because he must have known that Austin had grown up in Grayback, near

110

Jackson. He might have merely wanted to question Austin about the area or ask him to travel with him.

He bolted from the sofa. He'd kick the coffee table if Willow wasn't here. Austin had been out of the country and hadn't immediately responded to JT, who'd been preparing to travel to Jackson.

Someone had gotten to him before he could get there.

Why?

Maybe the police would figure it out. Maybe they wouldn't. But Austin was in the thick of it now, one way or another.

When he'd been honorably discharged from the air force, he'd gone to school for his degree so he could work with the FBI, his every intention to make a life as far away from Wyoming as possible. He'd landed in Seattle. But it could have been anywhere. Now his new freelance job allowed him to travel extensively, so he wasn't home much. All he knew was that he didn't want to go back to Wyoming. He'd tried to push it all out of his mind.

Nothing but bad memories were left for him there.

Even so, he'd felt the past pulling, sucking him back. He could never completely forget. A part of him had left reminders hanging on the wall to be sure he didn't.

And now this thing with Willow was somehow connected to Wyoming? Austin was nothing more than a seed caught in the rush of an unseen wind and he couldn't get out now.

Wouldn't leave Willow to travel there alone. He'd thought she would be safe here in his apartment. He could stay somewhere else or protect her here. That's what he got for making plans.

What are you doing, God? Are you forcing me back? Forcing me to face what I left behind?

And what would he find there? With everything happening with Willow, he hadn't returned Heath's call—he only had enough energy for one major crisis at a time. Willow had officially accepted his help, but even if she hadn't, he would have unofficially protected her. He eased back onto the sofa and kept his hands in his pockets with his legs sprawled out, listening to her call finally start to come to an end.

Soon the moment he dreaded most would be on him. He had hoped they could work together on this without the reason they'd gone their separate ways roaring to life and burning them. He braced himself. The next few minutes would be telling.

She ended the call and stared at the phone like she wanted to throw it.

"Didn't go well, huh?" Stupid. He'd heard enough of her side of the conversation to know.

"They aren't going to pay anything until the investigation into the arson has been resolved. It isn't bad enough that I'm utterly emotionally devastated. That I have no place to live. No clothes or furniture or my own space to decompress. My favorite sandals. I guess that isn't entirely true. Dana bought me clothes. But I can't stay with her. It isn't safe for her family." Her shoulders slumped. "I just talked JT into that fancy, ridiculously expensive refrigerator a few weeks ago. But no, they'll have to conduct their own investigation once the local investigators are done. This could take weeks, Austin. Weeks of my life put on hold."

She covered her face, then pushed her hands up, weaving her fingers through her hair—the picture of frustration.

"Think of it this way. Your life isn't put on hold waiting for them. You'll be busy searching for answers elsewhere." In Wyoming.

If arson was suspected, they would try to blame Willow. Look into her background. Try to make the case that she was desperate for money. But he wouldn't bring any of that up now and add to her troubles. It was all the more reason they had to follow through with JT's project so they could learn who the arsonist was.

Except Austin wasn't entirely sure Willow would want him to

help her once he shared about his life in Grayback—something he'd never done before.

"I don't have time for this. I don't even want to think about it. You're right though. It's a good thing I'm going to Wyoming." She stared down at her cell, ran her finger over the screen, then lifted her face.

Her hazel eyes studied him. Fear ghosted over him. Would she make him reveal himself completely before this was over? Lay it all out there—everything he'd kept inside and buried that had cost him a relationship with her?

"What's wrong?" she asked.

"I hate seeing you like this. That's all." Liar. Seeing her like this was enough on its own, but there was more, much more, and Willow could read that. She'd always been good at sensing his consternation even when he'd gone to great lengths to hide it. And the fact that he wanted to hide anything from her had been the catalyst for their relationship's implosion.

She sat on the edge of the sofa and removed her hoodie, revealing a turquoise T-shirt. "Are you going with me to Wyoming? I don't want to presume that you'll go with me everywhere."

"So you've decided to follow in JT's tracks no matter where they take you?" Dangerous tracks, those. But Austin agreed—it was their only real path.

"Do you have another suggestion?"

"No."

"So you're going with me?"

He toyed with the plaid couch pillow that had come with the sofa. "Do you even have to ask?"

Relief softened the worry lines in her face. He wanted to reach out and cup her cheek. Totally inappropriate.

He should tell her right here and right now. But that would only put those lines right back into her face, turning it from open and transparent to hard and unreadable. They would argue over the fact that the whole time they'd dated, he'd never once told her about his family or his life—his brothers or what happened to his mother and then his father. Or that he'd grown up in Grayback. No. Even Willow Anderson, with all her forensic genealogy investigative skills, hadn't been able to pry that out of him. He'd always managed to evade her questions. Redirect the conversation. But she was a woman who made her living unearthing people's ancestry, and Austin-in-the-present hadn't been enough.

Why had it been so hard to share his past with her? Maybe he should see a therapist after all.

"Are you sure you're okay?" She reached over and put her hand on his. His breath hitched. He hoped she didn't notice his reaction.

"Sure. No need to worry about me. You're the one in the line of fire." How much did she know, anyway? Just because JT had known he was from Wyoming didn't mean Willow knew—she hadn't known much about the case JT had been working on. But Austin wouldn't put it past her to look up his life on her own. Still, he doubted—no, make that prayed—the internet had revealed little of his life. His past. Even if his tragic life in Wyoming was plastered for all to read, she couldn't understand the depth of his pain.

She'd believed Austin couldn't open up to her. How could they have possibly deepened their relationship when he couldn't share the most basic facts about his life—his family? Well, shoot, he was still trying to come to grips with his family history—even years after escaping home. Maybe he didn't feel like sharing. Was that so wrong?

Would his telling her now, bringing it all up at this moment, put a strain on their relationship? But what relationship? They weren't dating or romantically involved.

No.

Instead, right or wrong, Austin would simply keep his past to himself for now. He'd go with her to Jackson. Then while they were there, he'd tell her about his home and his brothers.

In fact, he'd go so far as to call Heath too.

Hey, bro, I was just in the neighborhood . . .

Willow might be furious with his timing. But then again, they would already be where JT had been headed before his untimely death and their focus would be on the case. There would be less chance of their past together sidetracking their mission in Wyoming.

They had a thread, and maybe it was linked to that elusive needle in a haystack.

CHAPTER NINETEEN

The Boeing 737 took a deep dive for the short runway at the Jackson Hole Airport, set right in the middle of Grand Teton National Park and at the base of the Teton Range, no less. Willow chose to ignore the vibrating fuselage. Easy enough to do when she allowed the stunning mountains to absorb her full attention. Though she'd grown up in the shadow of Mount Rainier, the jagged peak of Grand Teton—the tallest peak in the range—took her breath away.

Austin's hand bumped hers on the armrest and she shifted away from him, closer to the window. He'd seemed aloof for most of the flight. Distant. Willow suspected she knew why, but she would give him the time and space he needed. Deep down, she admitted this was as much a test as anything—would Austin tell her about his home and family? Or pretend he hadn't grown up here? Staying silent on the subject took all her willpower. She wasn't ready to tell Austin that she had looked into his background after he hadn't been willing to share it with her.

On the flight, Willow had watched a video Dana had sent her. She'd interviewed Katelyn over video chat and asked her about her interests because Jamie could very well have those same interests. Every detail counted. Katelyn had grown up in a middle-class family in San Augustine, Texas. Her daddy had worked as a roughneck in the oil fields, and her mother had been a bank teller. They'd inherited land from her grandparents. Land that included full mineral rights.

Katelyn had always fancied herself owning a big spread with horses. A pipe dream, she'd thought. After her parents died, the property was divided between their two children—Katelyn and her brother, Shane. When Katelyn was in her midthirties, oil was discovered on the property. Both Katelyn and Shane became overnight millionaires. It was almost too much to grasp. Her dream came true when she bought a ranch with horses. Then she turned forty. She and her husband, Cliff, were finally able to conceive a baby. So many dreams came true all at once.

Then just as fast as heaven had rained down on them, tragedy struck and stole them all away. First, Cliff's sister, Jennifer, died in a plane crash. Maybe the news was just too much for him, but Cliff died of a heart attack—much too young—and Katelyn learned she had leukemia while pregnant with Jamie. Everything had been taken from her, except for the money. But what did money matter when she'd lost her health and everyone she loved?

The worst of it was that Katelyn's last hope, the one thing she could cling to, was ripped from her when the baby was stolen hours after she was born.

Willow's shoulders hunched forward and she shook her head. So much tragedy for one person to endure.

"What's the matter?" Austin asked.

"I was thinking about the video. What did you think?"

Austin had watched it on his own laptop. "She's one strong lady, I'll give her that. Determined, like someone else I know." Brows lifted, he flashed her a wry grin. His attempt to cheer her up.

Leaning over her, he looked out the window, his broad shoulders much too close. Willow studied the mountain range so she wouldn't think about Austin's nearness. His musky scent messed with her focus on the stunning view. She took in the Snake River flowing around the range and the clearly demarcated treeless ski slopes that would soon turn white with the first snowfall. The amazing scenery couldn't block her thoughts of Austin though. Part of her wished she hadn't invited him along, but she'd had no real choice if she wanted to solve this case quickly and safely.

When Grand Teton slipped from view, she shifted away from the window, hoping he would put space between them instead of leaning over her.

"Do you want to review what we have so far?" she asked.

"I think JT is thorough, which I would expect considering the success he's had in solving the obscure. As thorough as the FBI and local police in Texas had been, I can see where they could have done more. But hindsight is twenty-twenty, they say."

"I'm not sure that normal genealogical techniques are going to help much. It's not like I'm trying to find the history of her ancestry or build her family tree. But then, that's why Katelyn approached Anderson Consulting."

His gunmetal-gray gaze held hers. "If JT thought he could do this, there must be a reason. Just trust your instincts, Willow. I can tell you have his gift. He wouldn't have bothered pouring so much into you if he didn't believe that."

The compliment boosted her. "I guess we'll find out."

"Tell me how you typically handle a case. Let's say Katelyn hired you to find an ancestor she couldn't find."

"Normally we would start with Katelyn's full name, Katelyn Jacoby Mason. We'd take her name and start with birth, death, marriage, and military records, then tax documents, court deeds, and other legal records. Census records. Public directories, school records. Newspaper archives. That's not an exhaustive list." She grinned.

"Sounds like a lot of work."

She nodded. "You find a lot of extraneous but interesting information too. JT found out who had murdered someone's great-grandfather through the newspaper archives. So, in effect, he solved a very cold case."

"Let's call that a frozen case."

Willow chuckled. "Nowadays, though, there's so much information available online, much of which we would have had to do in person before. Still, even today, we might travel to Salt Lake City to look at the Family History Library. Add to all of that, now we can use DNA as a search tool. Katelyn already gave her DNA to JT for analysis, but that can take weeks. It's worth a shot in case Jamie's DNA shows up on a database somewhere—law enforcement or various genealogy databases. She might have suspected something about herself and taken a test."

Detailing the process to Austin left her overwhelmed. Squeezing her eyes shut, she pressed her head against the seat back as the plane began to land.

God, I don't know what I'm doing.

When the jet touched the runway, she opened her eyes.

Austin rubbed his jaw. "In this case, I'm not sure it matters what we know about Katelyn. We're looking for Jamie's abductor. A random stranger. Law enforcement already looked at everyone close to Katelyn, including her late brother, Shane, and Cliff's brother-in-law, John Houser."

"I'm not ready to give up on the possibility of a connection. That it wasn't random. On the other hand, maybe we can't find Jamie, and it's a mistake to even try."

"We won't know unless we see this through. We have a thread." Amusement danced in his eyes.

A small thrill shot through her. *Focus, Willow.* "Yes. The Wyoming Silversmith Company. I'm not sure what to ask them. They might not tell us anything."

Why were you really going to Wyoming, JT? She sensed that there was something more.

"Didn't you tell me JT said that in following the threads, other doors will open? That's why we're going. We can walk in a direction and hope it will lead us somewhere. When I was in the FBI, I learned to canvass a neighborhood. Just get out there and walk door-to-door to meet the neighbors. You'd be surprised what talking to people reveals."

"That's how you learned about the neighbor who took the video of JT's so-called accident."

Could she ever think about that without getting a lump in her throat? "I know you're right. I've spent hours talking to people. Listening to their family stories. That usually results in revealing things previously hidden." Oh, now why had she said that? She was getting off track. The fact that Austin was still hiding things from her shouldn't matter. It didn't matter. Not one bit. She didn't care . . .

The plane taxied along the runway toward the terminal at the small airport. This was meant to be a quick trip. In and out. They'd spend the night in a local hotel, just two professionals working together to find answers for a client. They would leave tomorrow. If they didn't find anything definitive by then, she wasn't sure what to do next. At least Dana had already commissioned the forensic artist to rework the age progression of the baby and the abductor, based on what could be seen in the grainy image from the hospital security camera.

Chin resting on his palm, Austin edged closer and spoke in low tones. "In addition to finding Jamie, let's not forget there's another investigation. One involving the attacks on your life and property."

"I haven't forgotten." She was glad to get out of town for a couple of days. The detective had all he needed from her at the moment in their search for the person responsible for JT's death, the house fire, and the warehouse break-in. He'd even suggested she leave for a few days if she could. The trip to Wyoming couldn't have come at a better time.

At the airport they rented a four-wheel-drive Jeep Wrangler and Austin drove, steering them out of the airport parking lot and toward town without punching information into the GPS or looking at a map. Did he think she wouldn't notice? Still, there was only one road out, and the obvious sign directing the way. GPS wasn't exactly required. Austin headed toward Jackson, named after Jackson Hole, the valley where it sprawled, and Willow took in the sights, a thousand thoughts swirling in her mind all at once.

They passed a sign for a wildlife sanctuary. "An elk refuge? I'd love to see them." What was she thinking? They weren't on a vacation together.

He remained silent. She tried not to glance his way but caught his controlled frown. He didn't like being back here, did he? She should divert his attention to the reason they'd come. "Have you thought of anything else that could help us while we're here?"

His shoulders eased back. "Why don't we run through what we know again. Two decades ago the authorities were looking for a woman who posed as a nurse. And a few weeks ago Mrs. Mason had the interview that was shown nationally. JT was killed and your home was burned down. You barely escaped with your life. Your warehouse was set to be burned down. It seems our female abductor has the ability to hire someone, considering a man was at the warehouse, and she is determined to keep the truth hidden."

"Could it be her husband? He loves her. Learned the truth about the child. Doesn't want her to go to prison."

"Or he doesn't want to lose his daughter."

It was the first time he'd injected anything resembling hope about Jamie's current status. "You think she's still alive?"

"I hope so, for everyone's sake."

"Whoever was behind this must believe we can learn the truth." This thought only served to propel Willow forward. With so many failed searches, Katelyn must have remained strong for so long because she truly believed her child was alive.

Austin steered them through the busy town of Jackson—a modernized western town with a rich history she would love to explore on her own outside of looking for clues. He parked the Jeep against the curb near the town square. Wyoming Silversmith Company was nestled between a T-shirt shop and a cafe boasting the best bagels this side of the continental divide. A big stuffed moose stood in front.

Willow couldn't help but stop and stare at the empty-eyed beast that stood two feet taller than her at its shoulders. "It's ginormous!"

Austin gently grabbed her arm and pulled her away from the taxidermied creature. "Stay on track, Willow." At the entrance he paused. "You ready?"

She nodded. "Here goes nothing." *God, please let it be something.* She had a copy of the photograph of the necklace with her, just in case.

Austin opened the door and allowed her to enter first. The odd scent of leather mingled with mossy stone met her. Display cases presented all manner of silver jewelry under lights, as if incubating the cold silver could somehow hatch a sale. Gorgeous western-styled necklaces, earrings, and bracelets hung on open display racks. Belt buckles covered one wall, and silver-studded saddles and cowboy hats another. Customers perused the display cases and examined the saddles.

She and Austin split up to search the small store. She looked for jewelry that was similar to the pendant necklace, but nothing quite fit the description. Finally, she stopped at a display case and admired a western-styled pendant necklace. She wasn't normally a jewelry person, but the appealing presentation worked its magic, and she considered buying something. Only for a split second. It seemed heartless under the circumstances of her search for a dying woman's missing child.

Willow sensed the instant Austin approached from behind. She tensed. Then he peered over her shoulder. She wanted to lean into him. Why did his nearness do such crazy things to her insides?

"I don't see the necklace anywhere, do you?" she asked.

"You didn't know what to ask them, but now you do. You can ask them when they made the necklace in question. It could have been a commissioned piece since it's handmade. Says on the wall they do custom belt buckles and more."

"Like we could get that lucky. The authorities would have found the abductor long ago."

"But they didn't. They missed something before. Something we're hoping to find. It's still worth a try."

Willow approached the petite girl at the cash register who didn't look a day over seventeen.

"Can I help you?"

"You sure can," Willow said. "My name's Willow Anderson, and this is Austin McKade. We're wondering if you can tell us about this particular necklace." She placed the photograph on the counter. "This picture was taken around twenty-one years ago. We want to know if it's one of a kind and who commissioned it."

"Well, I'm only nineteen, so I wasn't around if it's as old as you say. We don't make anything here, but let me ask if there's someone who can help."

The girl disappeared through a door for employees.

The minutes ticked by and Willow tried to be patient. Austin had wandered off and studied a saddle as he spoke to another employee. When the cashier returned, her expression answered Willow's question. It was a dead end for now. She hadn't expected much.

"I'm sorry. Anyone who could answer your question isn't around. Like I said, we don't make them here, especially if they're one of a kind. There's a catalog that features all the old pieces we've made. But I don't know where it is. Hank's one of the owners and would probably know, but he's not here. Can I make a copy of this picture?"

"Sure—"

"No." Austin interrupted Willow. "We'll hold on to it and show Hank ourselves."

"I'll leave a message for him to call you."

Austin nodded. "Fair enough." He wrote his name and cell number down on the back of a Wyoming Silversmith Company card he had grabbed from the counter, then handed it to the young woman.

"We appreciate your help. Oh, and I'd like to buy this." Austin dangled a pendant necklace. The same one Willow had admired. Her throat constricted. Emotion welled thick, slowing her response. "What are you doing?"

"What does it look like? I'm buying some jewelry." He winked.

Seriously? She didn't want to assume he was buying it for her, and if he wasn't, then it hurt. Why had he picked the one she'd considered getting?

His purchase complete, he ushered her through the store and out the door. "Just trying to get on her good side."

So you spent two hundred bucks?

"Give me a sec." He left her waiting next to the moose while he put his packaged purchase in the Jeep. Maybe he checked his cell, too, because he took longer than he should have. Just as well. She needed the time to compose herself.

She didn't believe the excuse he had given her for buying the necklace, but it wasn't her business. Had she read the current between them wrong? A romantic current she had no business considering. Was he involved with someone else? Hard as it was, she turned her thoughts to Katelyn's missing daughter. That was far more important than her own issues.

Austin returned, his smile disarming her.

"I don't understand. Why didn't you just let her take the photograph or make a copy? That would save time."

"We want to see Hank's reaction when he first sees it. I didn't give my card either, because I didn't want to alert him that we're investigating something. Just in case. You never know. It could be that any question over an old necklace will alert him. But, on the other hand, Hank might have no information for us."

"Good thinking, but now what? We can't wait forever. We're leaving tomorrow."

"Now we grab some lunch." His thick dark hair ruffled in the breeze. Hands in his pockets, he projected the air of a young boy guilty of mischief, especially with those sunglasses hiding his eyes. He peered up at the sun. "I need to talk to you about something."

His serious tone gave her pause. Would he finally tell her?

About Wyoming and the fact you grew up here? About the necklace? What? Willow held back her questions. If she'd learned anything from their breakup, it was that Austin didn't want to be the subject of an inquisition. She hoped he would tell her about his life here. She'd waited for this moment for so long. The moment when she would hear Austin's story. He hadn't wanted his life's story unraveled by her or anyone else.

And for them, that had been the end of the story.

CHAPTER TWENTY

Uneasiness swept over Austin with the sudden chill in the breeze. He had nothing to attribute the sensation to, and that bothered him. He had a well-honed skill set. Awareness that went beyond the five senses. Had too much time with Willow distorted his abilities? Whatever. He couldn't take any chances and was in the process of putting extra security measures in place.

Even though they'd left Washington, Austin was watching, always watching. It would help if he had a better handle on who was behind the attacks on Willow. He had to remain vigilant.

Someone could be following them.

Like that black Suburban. Or the red Ford pickup. Maybe the silver Acadia. They'd all been behind him on the road to Jackson. Now were they just like everyone else, tourists circling the town square, looking for parking? He couldn't be too careful.

But here in Jackson, he was distracted. Here in Jackson, he had the sudden desire to show Willow around town. Take her to his favorite places. See where he grew up through her eyes as she saw it for the first time. Maybe that could wipe away the tarnish on his memories.

What was he doing even thinking that way? He and Willow were far from a couple. He couldn't share his past with her like that. Not until he was sure he wanted to be here himself. He had to hold it together long enough to tell her what he hadn't been willing to talk about before.

He'd always wondered why she'd been attracted to him in the first place.

Maybe he'd been an enigma to her. A mystery to solve.

But right now he needed her to trust him. His past—that he'd opened up about it or not—shouldn't matter.

Million Dollar Cowboy Steakhouse called to him from across the road, but he wasn't in the mood for a crowd today. "Let's grab some fast food and find a picnic table. The weather's great. What do you say?"

"I'd love that."

Those simple words took him back in time. The way she had looked at him then, how her dark hair fell over her shoulders, when their relationship was new and fresh and all the baggage he'd brought with him didn't hang over them. His fault, of course, for not having worked through his issues long ago.

They got back into the Jeep. He drove them around the square, through a McDonald's drive-through, then north out of Jackson. Twenty minutes later he steered into a small roadside park on the way to his hometown—Grayback. "I hope the food isn't cold."

"It's worth it for the view," she said. She eyed the Teton Range on the one side, then the Gros Ventre Range on the other.

They carried their sacks and sodas to a picnic table. The wind picked up and blew napkins off the table, which Austin quickly recovered. Sitting across from him, Willow ate her burger, neither of them talking. It was a comfortable silence and yet he sensed Willow was waiting to hear from him.

She knew. Of course, she had to know . . .

He hadn't wanted to admit to himself that she already knew his secret. Her straw sputtered as she sucked the last of her soda from the cup. Time was up.

She eyed him, then pulled her sunglasses down to shield her eyes from a burst of sunlight breaking through a puffball cloud. "So what did you want to talk to me about? You made it sound important. But you're taking your sweet time getting there."

"And you're done waiting." He wadded up the trash and stuck it in the sacks.

She shrugged. "Maybe."

"I think I know why JT called me and wanted my help."

"Because you were in the FBI before. Worked with the CARD team. This is an FBI cold case."

He shook his head. A hawk screeched above them, then swooped down after a rabbit not far from the picnic table. Beyond that was an old cemetery. "He already has everything even I could get from them now."

"Okay, then why did he call you?"

"Because he was coming to Jackson. He must have learned that I'm from the area."

She didn't flinch. Didn't react. She remained focused on him from behind the sunglasses. When she didn't speak, he continued, finally able to share his story for the first time. Or at least some of it.

"I grew up on a ranch in Grayback. Me and my two brothers. My father started drinking heavily when my mother died in a fire. Became more brutal. Was hard on us. An embarrassment." This shouldn't affect him so much. "Each of us found our way out, our escape. I went into the air force. From that experience . . ." Not now. He couldn't tell her that story now. "Let's just say I knew I wanted to join the FBI. I went back to school for the required degree. I focused on helping people find their kids." Entirely too much emotion cracked through his voice. He struggled to compose himself.

"I hadn't seen my brothers since leaving until I came home for a short visit four years ago . . . as it turned out, I was here the week

Dad died. Haven't seen them since the funeral. When he died"—and took another family with him . . . *steady, now, you can do this*—"Heath got the ranch. He turned it into a guest ranch, popular in these parts."

That was it. That was all he could give at this juncture. Other people wouldn't find it so hard to share such details about themselves, but Austin didn't want to go there, so why take someone else to a place he never wanted to go?

Willow said nothing but, instead, stared off into the distance. What was she thinking? He didn't want this to take a dive and be about their breakup. But how could it not?

"Why are you telling me this *now*?"

This was his chance to steer the conversation where it needed to go. "Because we're here and maybe it's time for me to face a few of my demons." He injected a grin, hoping to bring levity. "And my brother Heath called me a few days ago. I need to return that call."

"I'm so sorry about your father, but I don't understand why you didn't tell me this before. Things might have . . ." Tears choked her words.

"Oh, come on, Willow, we don't have to dig up our past." Besides, he had no answers for her.

She sat taller and lifted her chin. "Maybe JT called you because he wanted just that."

"What are you talking about?"

"He wanted us to do this. He knew how much you hurt me, and I hurt you. But he wanted you to go back to Wyoming to face things."

"That's absurd. JT couldn't know the depth of my—" Regrets. He couldn't have known. "It was only about this case for him. That's what we both need to focus on now for your sake, and safety, and for Katelyn Mason's sake. Finding her daughter. If she's even alive. And if she is, she could be in danger too."

She nodded. "Just tell me this one thing. Tell me why you felt like you couldn't be open with me before."

"Maybe I was still trying to come to grips with it all. Maybe I still am. It's not something I want to talk about, okay? Can't you just be good with that? Can't you understand?"

He watched that same black Suburban he'd already seen twice since their arrival in Jackson Hole, now park next to the picnic tables. Maybe his sixth sense hadn't led him astray after all.

CHAPTER TWENTY-ONE

Maybe their relationship had just been too much and too fast before. Why had she asked so much when he clearly couldn't give? "I can be good with it, Austin, because you don't owe me an explanation. You never did. We should keep our focus on finding Jamie."

I haven't been completely honest with you. Willow sucked in a breath to tell him she'd already known where he'd grown up, because when he hadn't wanted to talk about it, she'd done her own digging. He wouldn't be happy, but maybe he already suspected. After all, if JT had called him because of his connection to this town, then JT had known.

Was it so wrong that she'd wanted to know more about Austin when he hadn't been forthcoming? People hired investigators to do that sort of thing, didn't they? All the online dating sites and identity theft—it was hard to trust someone completely.

A relationship that wasn't built on trust didn't have a strong foundation. She and Austin had been a dysfunctional couple from the start. His unwillingness to talk about his deepest darkest secrets or even his family, and her going behind his back to find out about his family. Their relationship had crumbled before either of them had invested much more than their hearts. Still, that had been enough to be devastating.

Willow opened her mouth to tell him she'd already known, but Austin slowly rose from the table. His gaze grew pensive. Searching.

"What's the matter?" she asked.

"I think we've been in one place too long."

"You don't really think we were followed here, do you?"

"I can't be sure. But if we were, that would tell us something, wouldn't it?"

She slowly nodded. "It could tell us we're getting closer, but not necessarily." And if they'd been followed, she was more than glad Austin had accompanied her.

Austin's lips flattened. "Maybe we should return to the silversmith store and see if Hank's back."

"You think he forgot to call?" She rose and brushed off her slacks.

"Or the cashier forgot to tell him. That reminds me." He dug in his pocket and pulled out the necklace. It dangled from his fingers.

A hundred questions flashed through her mind, but she was speechless as he walked around behind her, lifted the necklace over her head, and clasped it at the base of her neck. His warm breath made her skin tingle. Then he came around to stand in front of her. After a quick glance in her eyes—what was he hoping to see there?—his gaze swept down to the necklace. "Looks good on you."

She pressed her fingers against the pendant. "What are you doing? Why did you buy this?" *Not for me. It can't be for me.*

"Don't look so panicked. There's a method to my madness. I saw you admiring it. I thought making a purchase might encourage the cashier to follow through."

"I don't know if I can accept it."

Hurt flashed in his eyes, but he quickly shuttered them. "Well, I'm not taking it back. Give it away if you want. But we should get out of here."

Unshed tears swelled in her throat—along with a hefty dose of anger. What was the matter with her? She grabbed his arm. "I . . . thank you. It was sweet of you."

He nodded, lines etching his features.

Willow eyed the cemetery just beyond the park. "Before we head out, I'd like to look at tombstones."

Austin scrunched his face. "What?"

"The cemetery." She pointed. "You didn't think I could pass that up, did you?"

He shrugged, but his eyes remained on the parking lot. "I suppose it should be included in the tourist package."

Willow almost laughed at his words. "I'm a genealogist. It's what I do. If we come up with another thread or even that elusive needle, I'll want to visit all the necessary places that offer public records too. You know, the historical society and courthouse for starters."

"I guess that makes sense." Together they strolled through the park toward the Grayback Cemetery. Austin walked close to her.

"When I was growing up, JT would take me to every cemetery in every town we visited. We were always on a quest. He thought we'd find something to answer our questions. And sometimes we did. But other times he said it was because every person buried had a story. Some stories were never told. Never shared. Maybe it had been a kind of weird ode to the dead."

"*Follow the clues, Willow.*" Her memories of him so vivid in her mind, she could hear his voice as if he stood right next to her. As if he'd come on this trip with her. His training definitely guided her.

I miss you, JT.

She shook off the melancholy.

Austin kept close as they exited the park and neared the cemetery. Another couple stood next to a tombstone at the far corner. They placed fresh flowers next to it. Willow didn't want to disturb them and hoped they wouldn't think it strange she didn't walk to a specific tombstone but instead strolled between the grave sites, noting families and children and some headstones dating back to the 1800s. If JT had survived and made this trip to Wyoming, he would no doubt have come here too.

That much she could be sure of. But the rest of this was utterly unpredictable. Instead of JT here with her now, Austin McKade, of all people, walked the cemetary with her.

She turned. Austin had stopped a few yards behind her, his features disturbed. She backtracked, gently touched his arm, and glanced down at the tombstone.

McKade tombstones lined the space. Logan McKade. He died four years ago? Next to him must be Austin's mother, Catherine McKade. Dead twenty years. Then grandparents. Wyatt and Elsie McKade.

"I'm sorry, Austin. It was insensitive of me. I didn't even—"

"It's okay."

But the turmoil in his gaze told her otherwise. Deep pain was etched on his face. More than she would expect to see from someone looking at family members long buried. And because of the look of regret, the myriad of dark emotions rippling over his features, she finally understood why he didn't want to talk about his life here. What had happened that still tormented him?

At this moment, she had no idea what to say or do. Should she stay and comfort him, though she didn't know where his anxiety stemmed from? It obviously went much deeper than the loss that came with death, and that alone was profound.

She sensed Austin didn't want comfort from her.

"I'll give you some space." *And kick myself repeatedly as I walk the cemetery.*

Though she strolled, she didn't read the tombstones. Her mind far from there, she didn't even truly see them. Even if she focused on them, tears blurred her vision. The pain in this life could overwhelm. She needed hope. Something to hang on to.

God, help us find Jamie Mason. For Katelyn's sake, and for the girl, if she's in danger, as well as for Austin and me. We need your help. We need something to grab on to in this.

She thought she was tougher than this. But maybe the turmoil of the last few days and weeks could strip even the strongest person, reducing them to rubble.

A child screamed. Willow's heart jumped, her attention drawn to the park. The scream turned to laughter, calming Willow's nerves. She was much too edgy. A father swung his young child around. The sight warmed her heart. She definitely needed more heartwarming moments.

Willow welcomed the interruption to her morbid thoughts. It helped her focus on why they were here. If she could figure this out, then she could end the danger and unite Katelyn with her daughter before it was too late for the woman to say her goodbyes.

That's what mattered.

Glancing over her shoulder, she checked on Austin. Brows wrinkled, he kept his attention on the park as he slowly made his way toward her. She strolled the rest of the cemetery. Might as well complete her walk, despite the fact that the only purpose it had served was to stir up unwanted memories for Austin. Likely those memories had hit him the moment they crossed into Wyoming airspace.

CHAPTER TWENTY-TWO

Austin hoped that by the time they solved this—if they did—he would have overcome his issues.

They had hit him full-on when he stared down at his father's tombstone. It had taken all his willpower to hold himself together and not fall to his knees in anguish. The man shouldn't have died. Austin had been there. He should have stopped the chain of events that led to the tragedy. Could he ever stop blaming himself?

Though he was still chafing at seeing his father's grave, he kept his composure as he approached her.

Willow crouched close to a tombstone and ran her hands over the epitaph and name. Benjamin Haus. 1910–1989. What was she thinking about? She was obviously distracted today. His fault. He'd been the one to distract her with his dark mood. She'd always been hypersensitive to his disposition.

"I had hoped that by coming here we'd run across something to help us. At least that's the way it always seemed to work for JT."

"He trained you well, Willow. We'll find something." Austin hoped, for her sake, if nothing else. Willow couldn't seem to recognize or accept that she had JT's gift, his talent, in addition to all the experience and training he'd given her. Maybe by the time this was over she would see it well enough.

Her bright eyes lifted from the tombstone to peer up at him. Her long, shiny mane hung down just so. What a picture-perfect moment—for a genealogical magazine, that is.

She rose and dusted off her pants.

As they headed back to the Jeep, Austin scanned the area but no longer saw the suspicious vehicle. He almost felt silly. Except there was nothing wrong with being overly cautious if it made the difference in a life. If only he'd believed that before his father had been killed.

Without thinking, Austin took Willow's hand as they walked. She didn't resist, but Austin wasn't sure why he'd done it. Old habits died hard, maybe. It was sure looking that way when it came to Willow. But she was much more than an old habit to him. She obviously meant far more to him than he had a right to feel.

Once they were in the car, they buckled their seat belts and Austin started the ignition.

"What about your brother?" Willow asked.

"What about him?"

"If you haven't seen him in so long, then why not go there now? We're close to Grayback, aren't we?"

He dropped his hands from the steering wheel. Thought about it.

"What are you waiting for?" She peered at the mirror in the visor and pushed aside a few loose strands of hair. "People exit this earth, leaving issues behind. Death doesn't wait for us to resolve our regrets. You need to reconcile broken relationships."

She was right. "Don't you think I know that?"

"I'm sorry. I don't mean to intrude. It's none of my business. But, Austin, I wasn't ready for JT to die. He was so full of life, and if I'd had an inkling that would happen I would have done everything differently."

He backed the Jeep out of the parking lot, still uncertain which direction he would head. "What would you have done differently?"

"I would have been in town for one thing. I'd been traveling too much. I was too busy working, albeit in business with him, but I wasn't deliberate about spending quality time with him. I would have had breakfast with him. Spent the day looking at photo albums. Telling and showing him how much I loved him. And . . . and I wouldn't have let him get on that bike that morning."

Her words impacted him and he steered toward Grayback. "That's just it. We can't know when it's our time."

"So we have to live every day as if it's our last. As if there's no tomorrow."

"Are you doing that now? Are you living this day as if there's no tomorrow? Is this what you really want to be doing?"

He wished he hadn't asked the questions. Because deep down, if this were his last day on earth, he'd want to be with Willow. He sure hoped she didn't ask him the same kind of questions. He didn't want to have to answer.

"Yes. I want to be doing good in the world. Doing what God called me to do. If that means helping a dying woman find her daughter so she can tell her that she loves her, then yes, I'm living to the fullest. But you're missing the point."

"No. I didn't miss it. You're trying to tell me I shouldn't let more time go by without talking to my brothers. Heath is here. Liam is a DEA agent. He works undercover a lot. I don't even know where he is." Shame flooded him.

"But you can start with Heath here and now."

Her voice was entirely too happy. That shouldn't grate against his nerves, but Willow acted as if she were solving his problems. It wasn't that simple.

"You know what?" He steered into the Elkhorn Convenience Store parking lot. He wondered if Jax and Addie still owned and operated it. "I need to call him first. I can't just show up without calling. It wouldn't be considerate."

That wasn't the whole of it. He couldn't face his brother, talk to him for the first time with Willow looking on, especially since he'd gone to so much trouble to hide his past from her and lost her for it. At the time, they'd taken their relationship as far as they could. Willow couldn't go deeper with him, a man who kept too many secrets, she'd said.

He regretted his inability to give her what she'd wanted. They'd spent a lifetime, he and his brothers, hiding their complete dysfunction as a family from the public eye. Another old habit he'd been unable to quit. He'd just kept on hiding.

"While you're calling Heath, I should call Dana and then Katelyn to check in and give them an update. I just wish I had something good to report. We need a break."

He understood all too well about needing a break—that one clue, that one piece of information that could change everything. He hoped this didn't turn out to be a dead end and huge disappointment.

Austin got out of the Jeep, leaned against it, and got out his cell phone.

"I'm going inside to get us something to drink," Willow said.

He nodded and watched the passing cars on the two-lane road between Jackson and Grayback near the Gros Ventre Range, still part of Bridger-Teton National Forest. Funny that he'd come this far but hadn't made it the whole way. Not yet. He might go in and say hello if Jax or Addie was there, depending on how his phone call to Heath went. In the meantime, he watched the door to the store, guarding it from a distance.

He stared at his phone. Now he'd come to the moment he'd successfully avoided since Heath had contacted Emma, asking for Austin's number. He was obviously waiting for Austin to make the next move. Ridiculous.

I'm not ready, Lord. I'm just not ready.

Too much time had already gone by. How much more time would he let go by before seeing his brothers, or at least one of them? They were the only family he had. Would it take another death, and this time the death of one of his brothers?

He missed them. Growing up, they'd been close and leaned on each other through the struggles with their alcoholic father. Their father's brutality had forced them to toughen up in order to survive, and as soon as they'd gotten the chance, they'd each found a way to escape and gone their separate ways. Heath had dreamed of joining the army, but he'd been protective of Austin, the youngest of the three, and had waited until Austin had turned eighteen and gone off to basic training himself. Heath hadn't wanted to leave Austin at home alone to bear the brunt of their father's wrath. Liam, a year and a half younger than Heath and older than Austin, had left as soon as he could. Another McKade to join the ranks of military servicemen.

Heath had become a Green Beret, Austin an air force fighter pilot, and Liam had been navy.

Funny how long ago they couldn't wait for the chance to get away. Now Heath was back, his feet anchored deep in the soil of his birthplace, and Austin had come back too, drawn by some invisible force. Only Austin had no plans to stay.

He'd returned once before since leaving home, and coming back had been the biggest mistake of his life. Somehow, Austin should have done something to prevent his father's death. He knew it. His brothers knew it too. They blamed him. How could they not? Guilt lingered in the recesses of his heart and mind, ready to rush forward and paralyze him. He hadn't wanted to look into Heath's eyes and see the disappointment, the blame there, like he'd seen on the day it happened, and again at the funeral. He couldn't bear to see that in his brother's eyes, so he hadn't come back.

But if he stood here and thought about it too long and hard, he would never call Heath.

If he'd learned anything while working with the Child Abduction Rapid Deployment team, it was that every second of every minute counted. He could apply that to life in general. He'd already wasted too much time. He stared at the number, then mustered the courage and hit the call button. As he waited for the call to connect, a cloud moved over the sun, leaving him in the shadows. Crows gathered on a nearby electrical line, cawing. A bunny dashed across the field next to the Elkhorn.

He glanced at the Elkhorn storefront—the posts made out of knobby lodgepole pine holding up the porch of the older-than-dirt store. Metal cowboy and western-life silhouettes graced the storefront.

Willow still hadn't returned.

Maybe he should check on her, then call Heath back.

"Hello?" Heath answered.

Austin's heart surged to his throat.

"Hello? Austin, that you?"

"It's me," he said. He had to find his voice. The words he planned to say. Except he didn't have any.

"I'm glad you finally called me back. Glad it wasn't an emergency or that I needed to get ahold of you." Heath had an edge to his voice.

Here we go again. Of course Heath would have to jab at him about taking so long. Laying into him like he was a child. The black sheep of the family. He cringed inside, sagging against the vehicle. Heath sounded so much like Dad. It took Austin back to a place he didn't want to go. He almost wished he hadn't called. "Sorry. There's been a lot that's happened."

"Listen." Heath blew out a breath. Austin could picture him pinching his nose. Reconsidering his words. "I'm sorry. I didn't mean to jump down your throat. I know I sounded just like him, didn't I?" Heath released an incredulous laugh.

Austin didn't know what to say. He paced the cracked parking lot long in need of repair. Kicked around a few pebbles.

"I swore I'd never be like him," Heath finally said. "But all that aside, how are you, little brother?"

Now there was the Heath that Austin remembered. And loved. Relief swelled inside.

"I'm here in Wyoming. Stopped at the Elkhorn store."

Now it was Heath's turn to be speechless.

Austin offered a chuckle to dispel the awkward moment. "Surprise, surprise."

Heath sputtered a laugh. "Surprise indeed. So what's keeping you away? Come on home."

Home? Austin didn't want to think of it as home. The house and ranch belonged to Heath. Dad had left his oldest son everything, as if he'd lived in the Dark Ages.

"I have a matter to take care of first, then I'll stop by. I'm not keeping you from anything, am I?"

"Nothing that can't wait until later. Are you in Wyoming on business?"

Austin squinted up at the sky, then glanced once again at the store. "You could say that."

He walked to the end of the vehicle. On the other side of the Elkhorn sat that same SUV he'd seen at the park and twice before.

CHAPTER TWENTY-THREE

Willow leaned against the side of the old log cabin convenience store and spoke to Dana. "How's the age progression going?"

"We should see something in a day or two. The age progression photographs that were created early on and put on milk cartons depict her favoring her mother, though you can still see her resemblance to her father, Cliff."

"Can you send me a picture of both Cliff and Katelyn in their twenties?"

"Sure. I'll text it to you. Do you want me to call her and ask about any relatives in Wyoming?"

"Might as well. I'm going with Austin to meet his brother. Why don't you try to see if you can get ahold of her now?"

"Meet his brother? What on earth for?"

"Austin grew up here and, since he's this close, he wants to see his brother. I'm tagging along." *Is that okay with you?* She didn't want to get into it with Dana. As much as she adored the woman, Willow wished she would let her animosity go.

"I was going to add that you're there on business. He can see his family while you work, but my words will fall on deaf ears, won't they?"

Though Dana's words were true, they grated. Still, she forced a chuckle. "I didn't hear anything you said." From here, she could still see the top portion of Grand Teton. How could anyone not be inspired? Willow took a calming breath. "At least we're here, following this thread that JT would have followed had he lived. I have to believe I'll find what he would have found." Willow had no doubt JT would have found something. The question remained—would she, even with Austin's help?

She ended the call just as Austin appeared around the corner of the building, his demeanor burdened with what could only be described as fury. He strode toward her.

"Willow. Where have you been?"

"Right here."

His shoulders slumped. "When you didn't come out of the store, I got worried. Why didn't you come back to the Jeep?"

"I wanted to give you some privacy while you were talking to your brother. Besides"—she averted her eyes—"I couldn't focus on my conversation with Dana if I was close enough to hear yours. I would have been listening to you instead of Dana. I can't help myself. Sorry."

An SUV pulled out of the parking lot from the other side of the store and headed down the road. Austin watched it with great interest.

"What's going on?" she asked.

"I think that SUV's been following us. I've seen it too many times and now here it is again. I memorized the license plate. I'll call Emma to run it for me. But this time it had to have been parked in the back before we arrived, unless I missed it pulling in, which I doubt." His frown deepened. "I should have been more cautious."

Willow had started to relax, if only a little, believing she was safe in Wyoming—far from the happenings in Seattle.

"I'm thirsty. I meant to get us drinks. Can we get something before we head to your brother's ranch? We *are* going, aren't we?" She waited for his reaction.

Brows furrowed, he nodded. "Sure. Let's get a soda. It's still a few miles to the ranch."

Inside the Elkhorn, Willow got a bottled water instead of soda. Austin paid for his soda and her water. A tall, lanky man well over seventy took his money with a shaky hand. "We got the best well water in the state right here in these parts."

Willow nodded. "That's good." She wasn't sure what he wanted her to do with the information. "I need my water to go though."

He narrowed his eyes, angled his head to study Austin. "You wouldn't happen to be the youngest McKade brother, would you?"

Austin grinned. "That would be me. How're you doin', Jax?"

"Well, I'll be. I thought that was you. It's good to see you back . . ." Jax scratched his head.

"It's Austin. My brother Heath runs the ranch."

"Austin." He snapped his fingers. "My memory ain't so good. And who's this pretty young miss? Your wife?"

Heat suffused her cheeks. Of course the guy would think that. "Oh, no, nothing like that. We're here on business together." She reached over the counter and shook his hand. "I'm Willow Anderson."

The man grinned, revealing crooked and stained teeth, which told his age and of a life well-lived. "Well, you could've fooled me, but I suppose I've said enough and had better keep my mouth shut. Tell that brother of yours I said hello. The other one too."

"Liam."

"Yeah, that's the one. Haven't seen him in years."

"Neither have I." Austin took a swig of his soda. "That guy who drives that black SUV that just pulled out of here. Who is he?"

The man rubbed a hand over his balding head, pressing the few silver wisps of hair flat again. "That'd be Silas Everett. He's the Hoback County sheriff, next county over. This state has too many sheriffs and their deputies, if you ask me. We don't have that much crime to begin with, and they never seem to be around when you need them anyway."

"Oh? What's he doing here in Bridger County?"

"He comes here. Sits back there in his SUV behind the store to drink a beer after seeing his wife, Ellie. He divorced her years ago. I hear tell the daughter got involved with drugs. Ellie's raising the grandkids now." He shook his head. "He comes to see them every so often. Then stops here, like I said, to catch his breath, then heads back. Sad situation all around."

This guy was a wealth of information, albeit some of it gossip. Maybe Willow could get him talking and she'd learn something useful. He'd certainly lived here long enough and was willing to come forth with secrets—at least other people's secrets.

"Thanks, Jax. We're headed out to see Heath now, so I'll be sure to tell him you said hello."

Willow started to object. She wanted to stay and talk to the man, but Austin gently took her arm and ushered her from the store.

"I don't think he's going to believe we're here on business the way you felt comfortable enough to haul me out of there." She tossed him a grin, hoping he'd know she was only teasing, but there was truth in the jest.

He grunted in response as he made his way around the Jeep.

They got in and buckled again. "See, you worry for nothing. The man you thought had followed us was only a sheriff, and that's his pattern. We just happened to cross his path several times today. It's a small region in a sparsely populated state."

"I'll still keep an eye out for his vehicle just the same." Austin drove down the road, heading away from the Teton Range.

"You never said how your call with Heath went."

"No, I didn't." He watched an approaching fork in the road as if he was unsure about where to turn, then hesitantly took the right fork.

Evergreens grew thick among the hills, and last year's snow—glaciers probably—remained on the mountains over the rise. A pristine lake on the left reflected the crystal sky. A sign announced their entrance into the Gros Ventre Wilderness. Another sign, this one a yellow diamond, depicted six different kinds of animals. They passed the sign too fast, so she only had time to recognize half of them. "Did that sign have a bear on it? And moose and elk? What else?"

"Probably antelope. I wasn't paying attention."

"Bears cross the road?"

"Not just any bears. Grizzlies. Watch out the window. You might get lucky and see one through the trees, rooting for berries. You don't want to see one up close and personal though. That could be deadly. As for moose and elk crossing the roads, my brother hit a moose once. He was only sixteen. Had just gotten his license."

"And the moose? Did it survive?"

"No idea. It disappeared into the woods. They're huge, you know. But Heath totaled his truck."

"Are you going to tell me how the call went or not?"

"Better than expected. But grizzly bears, they're dangerous. Keep your distance. Understood?"

"Understood." She understood him all right. He was redirecting the conversation. Didn't want to talk more about Heath.

She definitely should have kept her distance.

If only she didn't need Austin in this with her. There was risk in spending too much time with him—her heart could fall under his spell only to be broken. Again. She should be smart enough, after having her heart broken once, not to go right back to the same man.

"I'm sorry. I didn't mean to push you about the phone call to Heath."

"No need to apologize. I'm the one who should be sorry. I'm

anxious, that's all. The call with Heath went fine. He's looking forward to seeing me. And no, I didn't tell him you're coming."

"I assume he doesn't even know who I am or that you dated me."

"I try to keep pleasure and family separate. So that kind of makes this all the more awkward."

How she understood. She'd wanted to unload her secret, the burden she'd carried for much too long. Maybe she could get things out in the open before they got to the ranch. Seeing Heath again would be like a new start for Austin, she hoped. She wanted to have a fresh start too, in a manner of speaking.

Austin jerked the Jeep to the left.

Into the trees. Willow let a yelp escape, then she realized he'd turned onto a forest service road hidden by thick pines, invisible from the paved road.

As the road grew rougher, the Jeep bounced, climbing over rocks and boulders. No wonder he'd insisted on a four-wheel-drive vehicle. She should have expected this. She equated it to the worst turbulence she'd experienced while flying. "You do remember how to get there, don't you?"

Great. Had she really said that out loud?

When he said nothing in response, she softened her tone. "Is this the driveway?"

"Not yet."

She couldn't tell if the tension rolling off him was because of what she'd said or if he was nervous about seeing his brother. A deep ravine came into view to her left and her heart stuttered. She had to look away.

"Is this even a road anymore?"

"The ranch is out of the way. Makes it hard for fire trucks to get here when something burns."

He spoke of his mother. *And hard for someone to come to your aid when you have an abusive father.* She kept those words to herself. She'd already said too much.

"Hold on. It gets bumpier."

"What?"

"Or we could hike in the rest of the way. But that could take us two hours."

"I didn't dress for a two-hour hike, sorry." Willow held on to the grips with both hands, squeezing them tight. She almost wished she had asked him to drop her off at the courthouse so she could search records. See if she could find a connection between Katelyn Mason and Wyoming from archives that couldn't be found online.

"The views are stunning once you get to the ranch. It'll be worth it."

He turned the Jeep off the road and drove under a large pine arch with the words *Emerald M Ranch* burned into it.

She was running out of time if she wanted to tell him before they got there. "I need to tell you something. I don't know how to say it now without making this more awkward, but I want to move forward. Please forgive me—"

"Just say it, Willow. We're almost there. I promise I won't be mad."

"Okay, here goes. When we dated before, you didn't want to talk about your family, or where you grew up. Your home. Everything that's important to me and why people often hired my grandfather—to find out where they came from, their inheritance."

"Willow, please." Austin yanked the steering wheel left.

Right, she was procrastinating. "I know it was wrong to do this, and again, I'm sorry. I looked into your past myself. I knew you were from Grayback and grew up on this ranch." Waiting for his reaction, she held her breath.

His jaw worked. "I figured as much."

"But in my own defense, people hire private investigators these days before they go too far, you know? I didn't hire anyone. I'm not saying that."

"No need to beat yourself up. What was between us is long

over. You're forgiven and it's forgotten. I couldn't give you what you needed, and you didn't trust me."

Willow's throat grew tight. The controlled hostility edging his tone seemed to say that nothing was forgiven or forgotten. And that he still cared for her.

The Jeep leveled out some as he turned onto an actual driveway. The tires crunched over the gravel and a larger-than-life two-story rustic log cabin with a wraparound porch came into view. On the other side of the cabin, a peaceful lake. Austin's knuckles tightened on the steering wheel. She shouldn't have brought up any of that now. Why did she stink at timing?

He parked the Jeep, then shifted to look at her. "At least I still have a *few* secrets from you."

CHAPTER TWENTY-FOUR

Could he have been more of a jerk?

Austin wished he'd included some warmth with his cold statement to soften the blow, but he hadn't been able to muster that even for Willow. To her credit, she was the one to offer a smile, and she seemed to understand that being this close to his family and his past made him all kinds of crazy.

"Should we get out? I assume that's your brother standing on the porch waiting."

"Uh, yeah, we should." He sent her an apologetic look. "Sorry. I shouldn't have said that about my secrets."

"So you still have secrets from me, huh?" Willow's teasing tone couldn't hide her curiosity as she opened the door and got out.

He did the same. Breathed in the fresh mountain air, the feral beauty of this remote ranch so near the wilderness area. The memories sucked him right back, but he didn't want to go there. He wanted to make new ones. Apparently Heath was trying to do the same. Everything looked different now.

As he hiked toward his brother, he worked to calm his nerves.

Admired the old cabin, which had been transformed with a bigger porch and new logs. Had Heath also renovated the inside?

Much too soon he clomped up the wraparound porch steps and faced his brother. Willow crept up behind him. An old tan-colored cur dog thrust his head under Austin's hand. "Hey there, Timber."

His smile as big as the sky, Heath immediately thrust out his hand. "It's good to see you."

Austin took it, and Heath yanked him into a brotherly hug. His brother held him so hard, he could swear a bear had gotten hold of him. Why had he stayed away so long? When Heath released him, he studied Austin long and hard, his blue eyes wells of emotions like their mother's.

Then his attention slid to Willow.

"And this would be?" He stepped forward and gently took the hand Willow offered, cupping it in his much larger ones.

"Willow Anderson," she said. "I hired Austin to help me on a case."

"Oh?" Heath's eyes snapped to Austin, then back to her. "Case?" A small laugh escaped. "I'm a forensic genealogist."

"A what?" Heath's grin was infectious.

"It might take a while to explain."

"Well, come on inside and you can tell me all about it." To Austin, he said, "This was and is your home too. You're free to come and go as you please. How long are you staying?"

Heath led them through the door into the house as he talked. When Austin stepped inside, he hardly recognized the place. "Initially we were only going to be here for a night, but we might need to stay longer." Another day or two might be necessary. "We have rooms booked in Jackson."

"Rooms in Jackson? You could have stayed here. Can't say I'm not hurt you didn't think of that first, but I'll get over it." Heath grinned. "If you're here on business, then I understand why you didn't. Getting to the ranch isn't an easy haul."

"And we *are* here on business." Austin wanted to make that clear—for his sake, if not for Willow's.

The aroma of pot roast hung in the air. His stomach rumbled. "Everything looks different. And you've turned it into a guest ranch."

Heath chuckled. "Yep. We get families and groups for retreats. Lots of photographers because there's easy access to the wilderness. Business is good. I added cabins and just recently built two more. I want to keep it small, though, so people can feel like they have their own private wilderness retreat."

Willow strolled the great room, looking at photographs. She touched an old saddle and glanced at Austin.

Heath grinned. "That's Pop's old saddle. Dad's is up on the bannister. You die, your saddle will get to come inside the house too."

Austin laughed. Was his old saddle still in the barn? "You've really transformed this place. I can hardly believe it." How had Heath moved past their experiences growing up in this house?

"I've worked day and night to renovate the place." Heath led them to the kitchen. "There's a roast cooking in the Crock-Pot."

"Smells good," Willow said. "We don't want to interrupt if you have work to do."

"I'm usually hands-on with guests most days. Everyone left this morning with our ten guests to head up to the backcountry camp in the wilderness area. They'll be there for two nights. I'm staying here this time. Good thing, too, or I would have missed your call. It'll be suppertime soon. You'll join me, won't you?"

How could they refuse? Austin looked to Willow for that answer.

Her warm and friendly smile said it all. "We'd love to."

"I'm a little leery of your pot roast. I don't remember you being any good at cooking."

Heath's laugh made Austin smile. Relaxed him. Coming here had been the right thing to do. He had the urge to take Willow's hand and squeeze it. She'd encouraged him to come to the ranch when he'd wavered.

"I guess you'll just have to take a chance." Heath opened the Crock-Pot and poked around inside. "I think it's about done. I didn't eat lunch and I'm hungry. Mind if we eat a little early?"

"Of course not," Austin said.

"Is there anything I can do to help?" Willow walked around the counter. "I'd be happy to set the table."

"Thank you, but no. I want you to make yourselves at home. You're my guests here. Have a seat at the table. Be warned it won't be anything fancy."

Austin studied his brother as he prepared the roast and arranged potatoes and carrots on a platter. Gathered the dishes and glasses and offered them drinks. Who was this guy, anyway?

Sure, Austin had looked up to him growing up. Heath had protected Austin any number of times against their father's brutality, then he'd gone into the army and become a Green Beret. *De opressor liber.* The Green Beret motto that meant to free the oppressed. That totally fit Heath, who'd protected Austin.

Now he'd turned into a businessman, somehow freeing their dilapidated old ranch house and property from the shackles of the past and turning it into a vibrant, moneymaking ranch. Heath had renovated himself along with the house.

The table set, Heath took a seat and joined Willow and Austin. "Now let's say grace."

He bowed his head and heartfelt words of thanks escaped his lips. "Amen."

With the food shared and plated, Austin slowly lifted the first forkful to his mouth. It smelled good enough. Both Heath and Willow looked on, waiting for his reaction.

He took a bite and chewed. Nodded his approval. "It'll pass."

"Oh, come on," Willow said. "I'm sure it's as wonderful as it smells."

She took a bite and smiled. When she finished chewing, she said, "My compliments to the chef."

"It's elk."

Willow's eyes widened and she stopped chewing. Austin burst out laughing.

"It's good, bro."

She appeared to accept that she'd just eaten elk, angling her head.

"I've learned a few skills over the years," Heath said around a mouthful of roast. "Some that would even surprise my brothers. But I must confess, I didn't make the roast. I hired a woman I've adopted as my grandmother—Evelyn Miller. She takes care of things here in the house. Cooks and cleans and helps prepare meals for the guests too. I pay her, plus she has her own room in the house. I'd introduce you, but her back's been bothering her. Her son's in town to take her to the doctor, then downstate to visit family. She'll be back tomorrow. That's why I stayed behind today."

"When was the last time you talked to Liam?"

That question might have been the wrong one. Heath pushed his plate away and frowned. "I called him and left a message the same day I called you. Haven't heard back. I know he works undercover. He'll call when he comes up for air. Maybe he'll surprise me like you did and just show up in town."

Austin nodded his understanding. He cast the ridiculous image of a happy reunion for all three of them together here at the ranch out of his mind and steered the conversation to the Emerald M Ranch. "Tell me what all you've done."

"Why don't I show you? In fact . . ." Heath hesitated, then directed his next words at Willow. "I have a proposition. Granted, you're here on business, but why not stay here at the house?"

"No, I couldn't. That would be too much trouble." Willow eyed Austin, pleading for help.

Admittedly, that might be too much for Austin too. He needed to catch his breath before he stayed here in the home where he grew up. Though Austin said nothing, Heath appeared to understand his hesitation.

"All right then. How about this? I have a couple of cabins available. They're newly built and not rented out until next week. You could stay there if you don't want to stay here in the house."

"Oh, we couldn't put you out like that," Willow said. "Besides, we'd have to pay for our room anyway since we'd be canceling so late."

"It's no trouble at all. Where're you staying?"

"Cowboy Village."

"I know the owner personally and can have a word with her so you'll get off without a hitch. They'll have that room rented within the hour this time of year. Just give me the word."

Austin gauged Willow's reaction. Was Heath putting too much pressure on her? Did she want to stay? Behind her long dark lashes, her hazel eyes held the same question for Austin.

He slowly nodded, answering for her. "Okay, but I insist on paying the going rate for renting your cabins."

Of course he had to offer, even knowing Heath would refuse.

"Absolutely not."

Throughout the rest of their conversation, Austin watched Willow as much as he watched Heath. She glanced between Heath and himself as they ate, admiration shining in her eyes for his brother. A sliver of jealousy found its way into Austin's heart, but not because of Willow. Heath had obviously dealt with the troubles of their past, while Austin still struggled.

How had he let go and moved on?

CHAPTER TWENTY-FIVE

Charlie was on a mission.

"Oh, come on, Bronc." The clunker's shocks protested as she steered down the bumpy logging road through the thick pine forest, crossing over the Bridger County line into Hoback County. Another risky move on her part. But she needed to search the old ranch house she'd shared with Momma. The house had been sitting empty for two months since Momma was murdered in cold blood right in front of her.

If she hurried, she might still be able to get to the house and search for answers before it got too dark.

Not like she hadn't tried before. But she had to be careful. Couldn't stay too long or let anyone see her coming or going. He could still be watching and waiting for her—the man who killed Momma wanted to kill Charlie too.

Why, she didn't know. She wanted to find out but on her own terms. Not begging for mercy at the wrong end of a gun. She was determined to find out and hoped to come out on top and alive once she did. She turned onto a two-lane road and headed in the opposite direction of the cabin where she'd hidden in the mountains.

She'd lost track of time when she'd stayed too long training the horses at the ranch—a good, solid job at which nobody had to see her. She'd been riding Amber and gotten lost in her dreams of a life she wanted to live. The job—which her friend Mack had given her—wasn't about the money, but about the freedom to live out in the open and be herself without the fear that someone would find and kill her.

That's why she was on a mission. She suspected she knew the killer, but she had to prove it. There were only so many hours in the day.

She needed to get back into the house and search again. The bills hadn't been paid, so the electricity would be turned off by now. Who knew what manner of vermin had taken up residence in an empty house sitting in a field in the wilds of Wyoming. Momma had made Charlie a co-owner before she died and, looking back at that now, Charlie had to wonder if Momma hadn't had some kind of premonition.

Squeezing the steering wheel, she accelerated, causing the Bronc's loud muffler to rumble. For a moment, she imagined what the truck had looked like in its glory days when some high school motorhead had owned it. She'd gotten it dirt cheap after selling both her and Momma's cars so she would have something to fall back on until this was over. Then she could get back to her regularly scheduled programming, which meant going back to the University of Wyoming and finishing her last year. But honestly, that was the last thing on her mind. Grief and fear crippled her while at the same time empowering her to see her plan through.

With a killer still out there and her life at risk, she laid low but stayed close.

The house would be just over the next hill. She accelerated. With no electricity and nothing but a flashlight, she'd accomplish little if she didn't get there before dark.

If only she hadn't lost track of time.

Poor Rufus. She'd left the German shepherd alone for too long. He'd probably messed on the floor by now. Once she was done searching the house, she'd have to hike the trail back to the off-grid cabin in the dark.

Before she turned off onto the driveway to the house, she glanced in the rearview mirror.

Her palms immediately slicked. What was he doing on this road? Panic took hold. She couldn't afford to have a panic attack while driving, but they came on stronger and fiercer now than before.

Breathe in. Breathe out.

Focus on the road.

The house—her destination before he appeared behind her—passed by on the right.

She couldn't possibly stop there now. Not with Clyde Everett on her tail. Momma's boyfriend. Charlie suspected he had killed her mother. Clyde and her mother had a heated argument that same day. After the funeral, he had followed Charlie. Grabbed her and left bruises. Stalked her. She tried to get a restraining order on Clyde, but Sheriff Silas Everett was not only Clyde's cousin but also his alibi and claimed he was with him during the time someone had shot and killed her mother. Nobody would believe that someone wanted to kill Charlie too. She could only count on herself for protection, and well, maybe a little help from Mack, who had put her up in that off-grid cabin while she worked this out.

The grille on Clyde's truck grew bigger in her rearview mirror.

Please let me get home safe tonight. Let him turn down another road.

And just like that, God answered her prayer—the very first time she could recall. The vehicle slowed and turned off the road.

Into the driveway leading up to Charlie's house.

CHAPTER TWENTY-SIX

Willow picked her way around the biggest sagebrush she'd ever seen. Heath had given them the long tour of the Emerald M Ranch. He'd parked his shiny blue extended cab truck at the back of the permittee property in the Bridger-Teton National Forest and they'd walked from there.

Now Heath and Austin took turns throwing knives at a fence post that had taken a thousand hits in the past. Maybe knife throwing was a required skill living in Wyoming, though she wasn't sure what use it would have since they weren't living in the Wild West anymore. Heath guffawed, and the two men suddenly looked like young boys again, just killing time. Laughing together, they made their way back to Willow. She'd stood a few yards away from the circus act.

"A stay at the Emerald M will get you private cabins. Three meals a day. Canoes, kayaks, hiking, and fishing. Trail rides and a backcountry pack trip into the Gros Ventre Wilderness. Guests can take in views of the Teton and Wind River ranges. The Grayback River headwaters and canyon. And I can manage all this with only a handful of employees."

"You've done well for yourself," Austin said. "Dad made the right decision giving this to you."

Heath stared off into the distance, where a significant barn stood next to a corral. A beautiful black horse and an appaloosa grazed in the meadow. He scraped a hand over his jaw and around his neck. "I sold off a few acres to the west, and from that money I was able to improve the property. I would have sold all of it and shared the proceeds with you and Liam, but you wanted no part of it."

Austin shook his head. "To think, Dad could have done this. Made something of this place. I couldn't be prouder of you."

That put a huge grin on Heath's face. He had dimples like Austin's. "It's good to see you. Don't be such a stranger from now on, okay?"

"Okay."

While the brothers talked about the horse barn and stables, Willow watched them together. It had been right and good to come here. She'd love to come back and visit the region some time when it had nothing at all to do with finding Jamie before her birth mother died. For the moment she allowed the scenery—the evergreens on the mountain peak lifting their arms to praise their creator, the sky and mountain reflecting in the pristine lake, the beautiful horses grazing in the meadow, woodsy cabins nestled in the trees, and majestic mountain ranges in the distance—to whisk her away to another world, and almost another time.

The place was beautiful and dreamy and wild. She sensed some part of that remained in Austin, no matter that he'd chosen to make his life far from Grayback.

JT's voice resounded crisply in her thoughts. *"Willow, we're branches on a tree. We grow in many directions, but we're always connected to our roots, whether we're aware of it or not."*

As much as the brothers were different, they were the same. The Austin she knew was a professional, a former FBI agent, but here with his brother, he morphed into a man who looked like he belonged in the mountains of Wyoming. Why shouldn't he? This had been his home, and no matter how much he wanted to escape his past, this setting stayed with him.

She followed the guys down to the barn, leaving the truck behind. Inside the barn, the musty smell of horses and hay met her. Austin stepped up to an old-looking brown horse in a stall and pressed his hand against the horse's muzzle. "Hey, Jinx. It's been much too long since I've seen you."

Realization slowly dawned.

Austin . . . he was a cowboy. Her heart rate kicked up a few notches and the barn tilted, but she put her hand against a wooden rail to steady her fluttering nerves. This guy she once thought she might have loved . . . who was he?

As if to underscore her slow comprehension, Heath strolled up behind him and placed a tan cowboy hat on Austin's dark-haired head. He startled and stepped away from the horse. Put his hand on the hat. "What?"

"It's yours. Your saddle's back there too."

"You didn't get rid of them?"

"Of course not."

The two brothers shared a look—they had an understanding between them. No matter what, they were always brothers. Heath would never give up on that and neither would Austin. Willow had to look away. Maybe she shouldn't be there. They needed time to reconcile on their own about whatever it was that had driven them apart to begin with. But she was here, so she steadied her runaway emotions while she took in the sight of the brothers.

When it came to appearances, Heath was a slightly older version of Austin. And they were very much alike in other ways. On the surface, Heath appeared to put on a good show. No doubt he had his act together. But she had this uncanny sense that he had the same way of holding it all inside—keeping his secrets close.

What had happened in their family to make them this way?

With darkness approaching, they hiked back to the truck and got in. During the bumpy drive to the cabins, Heath and Austin talked about old times. The breeze filtered through the cracked window, bringing the heavy scent of pines, sagebrush, and horses.

Heath steered up to the first cabin situated twenty-five yards from the next one. "Here you go. These are the two new cabins I mentioned, in addition to the six already on the property. I haven't named them yet. I could call them 'The Austin' and 'The Willow.' How about that?"

Willow laughed. "I'm good with that."

"These are closer together than the other more private cabins in case a group of guests wants to stick close. Take a look and see what you think. I'll bring up fresh towels and sheets."

A new thought hit her, bringing along panic. "What about internet?"

His deep laughter could mean only one thing. "Are you serious? People come out here to unplug."

Shoot. She should have stayed in Jackson. Both Austin and Heath had already climbed from the truck cab, and she slid across the seat and hopped onto the hard ground. She might need to get a pair of boots for this stay.

Heath waited while Austin went ahead to the newly built, rustic-looking cabin. "You can come back to the house if you need internet. I hope that won't be too inconvenient for you."

"Of course not. We won't be staying that long. But I appreciate your hospitality. I'm sure Austin does as well."

"I hope you stay longer than you planned."

He hitched his cheek, revealing a half grin and a knowing look in his blue eyes, and she averted her own before he read the truth. One she knew he already suspected. The man was no fool and had seen through them. Sure they were there on business, but they'd had a relationship before—and now they were both pretending they'd moved on and let go. But their past together hovered over them, closing in on them, threatening to drag them down—and deep. Problem was, she wasn't sure if that was a bad thing.

"I'll be right back in a few minutes with towels and sheets. The kitchen is already stocked with a few dishes and utensils. But it's BYOF—bring your own food. I can grab a few things from the big house for tonight if you need anything."

"That's all right. As long as I can get a glass of water tonight, I'll be fine. We'll figure out something tomorrow."

Supper was good and meeting him was important, but she was growing anxious to get back to the whole reason she'd come to Wyoming. She wanted to call Dana and see if she'd learned anything. Still, she couldn't deny that seeing Austin in his element, getting a glimpse into his past and his life and who he really was meant more to her than she could fully comprehend at the moment.

Heath marched back to his truck and drove off. He ran a big outfit here. One he'd practically built himself. She hoped Austin wasn't jealous of his success. She found him looking out a panoramic window at the dense greenery in which the cedar cabin was nestled. Funny, he hadn't taken off that cowboy hat. She kind of liked it on him. He appeared lost in thought. Had he even noticed her approach?

"And you were so worried about seeing him," she said. "It all worked out, Austin."

Willow didn't know what exactly had caused a rift between them to begin with, or had she misunderstood? Was it all to do with their father? She wanted to ask him. "Whatever differences you had between you, it appears you've put them aside. I'm glad for you."

Now she was talking out of turn.

If he and Heath could move on from whatever dark past haunted them, could she and Austin put their differences aside too and perhaps capture what they'd once had together? No. She wasn't sure they could. She could too easily let the hurt and pain of losing him resurface. She definitely wouldn't risk going through that again.

Somehow she had to resist the current called Austin that threatened to sweep her up in him. They had to focus on their goal. Time to put some space between them.

She stepped back from the window while he remained, staring out into the forest.

"Where are you going?" He snatched her wrist and reeled her in.

Her determination went right through the window and disappeared into the woods. How could one simple touch so easily strip her of her resolve? "Nowhere. Just thought I'd look around the cabin."

He pulled his attention from the window. It landed on her face, traveled down to her neck, then back up to her eyes. Her breath came in short rasps. What was he doing? He lifted a strand of her hair and gently pushed it out of her face. His eyes dropped to her lips.

Oh no. She would have taken another step back, but her feet had betrayed her. The real Austin—the man she'd wanted to know deeply, thoroughly, stared down at her now. She could see the truth in his eyes, and much more that scared her.

"Thank you for encouraging me to come here today. For coming with me." The words came from some deep place in his heart. She could plainly see that. A place she'd longed to see before, but he'd hidden his true self. Why now? Why was he showing her now?

Her pulse edged up.

"Heath comes on strong at times. But don't worry about him."

Heath? Why would she worry about Heath? She was worried about Austin now. Her reaction to him. "Why were you scared to come here to begin with?"

"There's so much you don't know."

Then tell me. I want to know. But she'd made that mistake

before. He'd revealed a portion of himself tonight, even if only in a look. Could she wait on him to share more when he was ready?

She heard Heath's heavy, booted footsteps approaching the cabin. Austin released her, the haunted look returning to his eyes. *What had happened here?*

Heath entered the cabin. "I brought towels and linens. Some for each cabin. And your bags." He set the two duffels on the floor and the sheets and towels on a chair.

"What about the Jeep?"

"It's fine sitting at the main house tonight. I'll bring it up in the morning."

Heath opened a case. He pulled out a large canister. "Bear mace. Just in case." He handed a canister to each of them.

Then he pulled out a handgun. With a glance at Willow, he offered the weapon grip first. "Austin tells me you know how to use one of these. A Sig Sauer P328 .380. You can use this one while you're here if there's a need. It won't kill a bear, but it's for protection in general."

Willow looked from one brother to the other. "I don't understand."

"Don't get me wrong. You should be perfectly safe here. Austin explained you've had some trouble and that he's here to protect you as much as help you investigate."

Austin must have told Heath while they walked to the barn and she wasn't paying attention.

She took the weapon, wishing she hadn't needed the stark reminder of potential danger. "Is it legal for me to have this?"

"Wyoming doesn't require a permit. If you're a law-abiding citizen, you can carry a gun even in the national forest."

"That's good to know." Willow examined the gun. "My grandfather taught me. I lost my weapon in the fire."

Lines creased Heath's forehead, but he didn't ask her about the fire. How much had Austin shared with him?

"All right. You ready to head to your cabin, Austin?"

He crossed his arms. "I'll stay here for a while. I can walk over with my things."

"Not a problem. You know where to find me if you need me." Heath left them alone in the cabin.

Austin pinned her with his eyes—the intensity holding her hostage. "Are you going to be okay?"

"What? You mean alone in a cabin in the woods? I can rough it like the best of them."

That earned her a laugh. "You call this roughing it?"

"Yes. Yes I do."

His dimpled grin beneath that cowboy hat sent tendrils of warmth curling around her heart.

She was in so much trouble.

Her cell rang. Surprised she got a signal, she glanced at the screen, then up at Austin with a smile. "It's Dana."

Willow answered. "Hey. What have you found out?"

"I've called Katelyn. The news isn't good."

"Oh?" Willow eased into the padded maple rocking chair. "What is it?"

"She's in the hospital. Taken a turn for the worse."

Willow lifted her face to Austin. "We're running out of time."

CHAPTER TWENTY-SEVEN

Katelyn Mason stared at the ceiling from her hospital bed, accustomed to this scenario more often than she would have liked. She thought about the phone call from JT's assistant, Dana. She didn't know about family connections in Wyoming. Willow must have been following a rabbit trail. A tear slipped down her cheek. She didn't bother to wipe it away but let the ache in her heart work its way out. She'd wait until the emotions passed, though, before she called her brother-in-law, John, to let him know she was back in the hospital.

She dreaded making that call. He traveled for his job as a consultant and she didn't want to worry him. But he'd be furious with her as it was—more hurt, really—that she hadn't called him already. She couldn't bear to see the pain in his eyes, which only added to the pain she already felt.

Because of his years of experience in oil, he'd been a consultant to her when the wells first came in. He'd been the one to talk her into drilling in the first place.

But the way he looked at her lately, she almost thought he had developed romantic feelings for her. She didn't feel that kind of love for him. But if he proposed, she would consider the proposition. What if Willow found Jamie? Jamie would need a father figure if she died. Someone stable and loyal. Yes. Katelyn would consider his proposal if he offered her one.

Maybe she should even encourage it.

Either way, she wanted this misery to end soon, but not too soon. The nurses tried to keep their expressions bright, but she saw the pity in their eyes all the same. Still, Katelyn had fooled them many times and gone home from the hospital to live another few years before she became sick again. If only she didn't have that deep gut feeling that the end was drawing near for her. The way her back and neck ached. The extreme fatigue weighed her down like never before.

Please let me find my daughter first.

But what if she actually found her? Was she being selfish to want to see her daughter, meet her, hold her in her arms? Her daughter then would lose her mother—a mother she'd never known about. There was always the chance that Jamie had died long ago. She had always believed she had an intuitive sense about such things. Like when Cliff had died. She'd had a feeling something bad was going to happen. But she'd never had that feeling about Jamie.

Instead, she had always sensed that Jamie had survived. That whoever had taken her that day had treasured her. Loved her like only a mother could.

She'd been told that women who took babies in this way were unable to have their own child or adopt, and the deep ache and longing twisted their perspective until, out of desperation, they stole someone else's child. Katelyn's baby was certainly not the first ever stolen. The doubts about her decision to continue searching, even after two decades, weighed on her. As of that moment, nothing in Scripture could help her silence the doubts.

The trouble was, if she called off the search, she'd always wonder, and she couldn't live with that. But what did that matter? She wouldn't live much longer anyway. A fact that only drove her need to know. She'd lived too long with this endless cycle of doubt and determination.

Except she'd also had her doubts about Willow Anderson. She hadn't had the heart to pull out. Not when it seemed to give JT's granddaughter hope on the heels of his loss.

Katelyn felt that loss to her diseased bones as if it were her own. Secretly, she'd harbored an infatuation for the man. He'd been a charmer. She'd thought maybe they could have grown closer. An easy friendship, perhaps, or one last romantic fling before the end. She would have treasured the camaraderie—but then again her death would only have left the man empty. Instead, she was the one left hurting with the news of his loss.

She had to hang on to hope that Jamie would be found.

You're out there somewhere, Jamie, I just know it . . .

CHAPTER TWENTY-EIGHT

This had been a very bad idea.

Darkness closed in on Charlie as the sun finally sank far beyond the horizon, turning the forest almost an inky black in places where the moon didn't shine. Charlie hiked the trail off the beaten path to the off-grid cabin where she lived for now. She'd had to park Bronc up a little ways in the woods on a forest service road. She didn't like to hike in the dark and mostly avoided this scenario. She carried her bear mace and 9mm handgun and hoped she wouldn't be required to use either of them. Half her focus remained on making her way along the nearly two-mile trail to her cabin. The other half on Clyde.

Why had he gone back to the house? Did it have something to do with the argument he'd had with Momma the day she was murdered? Did it involve Momma's last words to him? That is, if Clyde had been the murderer. Despite all her suspicions, she couldn't be positive. But who else?

The forest remained unusually quiet. Her heart raced. A coyote's cacophonous yip from somewhere much too near startled her. She picked up her pace. The cabin barely came into view off the trail nestled between the dense trees. A perfect hideout.

But she still had a haul to get there. Sleeping alone in a secluded cabin in a dark forest didn't scare her. She was accustomed to living out in the sticks with Momma, though this was much more remote. If she stayed at the house—her house now—she wouldn't be able to sleep for fear he would kill her there.

Her dog's bark reached her from the cabin. Was Rufus barking because he sensed her approach? Or had a nocturnal creature, a raccoon or a coyote, disturbed the peace, sending him into a frenzy?

Poor Rufus.

She'd always been good to make it back before dark. Fix dinner. Take Rufus on a walk. Then settle in for a good night's sleep. She didn't like lights on at night. She didn't want to draw unwanted attention to the cabin in case he thought to search for her in these woods.

Maybe she was being paranoid, but she had every reason to be. She crept quietly down the trail, listening for a misstep in the cadence of night sounds. Though Rufus barked incessantly, the critters around the cabin had grown accustomed to him—he was now part of their world.

He'd been given to her as a gift. There was no better security system than a German shepherd guard dog. They'd grown close and she trusted him. But his vicious barks worried her. If something was outside the cabin that had disturbed him, then she'd prefer to be inside with him.

Fear coiled around her. She hurried to the door and fumbled with the key in the darkness, shushing Rufus. "Calm down, boy, I'm coming. I know, I know. You need to go." And likely already had.

She opened the door. Rufus shot past her and into the woods.

"Rufus! Rufus!" Charlie called after him, but she couldn't follow him. The way was much too treacherous, even for a grouchy German shepherd.

She called after him repeatedly. Commanding. Demanding. Pleading.

Aware that every shout was in direct defiance of her plan to keep quiet and stay hidden. Twenty minutes later, Charlie slipped into her dark cabin, bolted the door, and found her way to the cot.

Now what was she supposed to do? Her security system had run off.

CHAPTER TWENTY-NINE

Willow had donned a T-shirt and sweats to sleep in. On the bed in "The Willow" cabin, if Heath followed through with that suggestion, she pulled the cozy comforter up to her chin.

"She's in the hospital. Taken a turn for the worse." Dana's words resounded in her head. Would Katelyn even live long enough for them to complete their investigation? This hunt for Jamie could very well lead them nowhere, and it gnawed at the back of her mind. Pricked at her heart. If she hoped to get any rest, she'd have to shake the enormous pressure to find Jamie in time. Remove it all from her mind, or she'd be worthless tomorrow. She couldn't afford to waste one day.

She hadn't considered today a waste, because they'd come all this way and hoped to hear something from Hank. Why hadn't he already contacted them? But more than that, she'd known Austin had needed this time with his brother. Tomorrow . . . tomorrow she had to get serious in her search for Jamie.

Willow shifted on the comfortable mattress. Heath had spared no expense for his customers who wanted to experience nature. Nothing better than getting a good night's sleep with a top-of-the-line mattress while roughing it. She could almost smile at that. She was a nature girl all right. Enjoyed viewing nature from the safety of a panoramic cabin window. Hiking a trail now and again wasn't too bad, but not too far or for too long.

Her mind refusing to rest, she reached for her cell and pulled up the image of the abductor Dana had sent her a few minutes ago. The forensic artist had taken the grainy image from the hospital security camera and aged the abductor, but she'd taken great liberties since that was a difficult task and she had no other photographs to go by. In the meantime, she continued to work on an image of Jamie, though Willow doubted the forensic artist would come up with an image that looked much different from Katelyn. But one never knew, so that's why they continued with their efforts.

Willow feared that she would fail to resolve JT's last case. He'd solved almost every mystery, every question he'd ever taken on. How utterly surreal that he had died in the middle of this impossible task, leaving it to Willow. If only for that reason alone, she could not fail.

She let her phone screen go dark and set it on the side table next to the weapon Heath had loaned her.

That, too, was surreal. He'd only given it to her as a precaution. Far from Seattle, she should be safe in Wyoming, especially here on the hard-to-reach guest ranch that hosted only a few families and friends. Austin was in the nearby cabin—as close as he'd ever stayed to her, physically, and emotionally, he was getting closer. He'd shared more of himself with her on this trip than he'd ever shared before, and they weren't even romantically involved. What was that about? She couldn't help but think it had everything to do with him coming back to Wyoming and facing what he had left behind.

She also had to consider the very real possibility that JT had, in fact, been thinking of Austin's struggles when he'd called him for assistance. She knew her grandfather—that would be just like him. Her heart smiled at thoughts of JT, then she turned her thoughts to Katelyn and Jamie.

Lord, please let us find the truth for Katelyn. Please let her stay around long enough. Listen to her heart's cry. I know you will. You're good at that.

For the first time in days, Willow relaxed, her mind stopped churning, and sleep finally took hold.

———

Shadows shifted in the darkness. The silhouette of a man approached. A knife glistened.

Willow's eyes opened. Her heart pounded from the dream and her frantic breaths filled her ears.

She lay perfectly still, quieting her breaths enough to listen.

It was only a dream.

Her heart rate slowing to almost normal, she soundlessly sat up in the bed, wishing she'd stocked the fridge with at least a few groceries. A jug of milk. Something.

The cabin was much too quiet. The temperatures dropped at night too much this time of year for singing frogs and insects. A cool breeze brought a woodsy scent and raised goose bumps on her arms. She crept over to the open bedroom door. Across the room she spotted the cause—the window was open. The curtains billowed.

Fear strangled her. Momentarily prevented her mind, her limbs, from reacting.

Her pulse spiked. Was someone in the cabin with her? She couldn't afford to stand there and do nothing.

Something moved in the shadows.

Willow dove for the bed. Her arm outstretched, she reached toward the nightstand. Grabbed the Sig, twisted, and aimed.

A man's form filled the threshold. He was heading for her!

She fired twice, and in the same instant he disappeared.

Oh, great! What now?

Palms sweating, Willow gulped for air. Was it over? Had he left? Had she shot him?

Her position on the bed was far too vulnerable. She slowly rose. He could still be in the cabin. Holding the weapon at the ready, she lifted her phone to call 9–1–1. But given how far out they were, she would do better to call Austin. If she could get a signal.

A stupid signal!

Finally, the call connected. With the phone to her ear, she slowly crept out into the living area. Keeping her back against the wall, she remained ready to shoot the next thing that moved.

Come on, Austin, answer your phone.

The door burst open. Willow fired. The figure lunged to the side.

"Whoa, whoa, whoa! It's me! Willow, it's me, Austin!"

Her limbs went weak with her pulsing heartbeat. She lowered the weapon. "I could have killed you."

Holding his own gun, he rushed to her. "I heard the gunfire. What happened?"

He grabbed her arm and pulled her against him. Willow drew comfort from his warm, strong body. From his presence.

Heart still racing, she grasped for the words. "Someone was here. He was in the cabin. He must have come through the window. I found it open." She fought the need to cover her face and sob. "I don't know!"

Austin stared down at her. "We'll figure it out later. Did you call 9–1–1?"

"I was going to, but I called you. You didn't answer. I tried to call and protect myself at the same time. I could barely get a signal."

"It's okay. You're going to be okay. I didn't answer because I was running to get here."

"I know." She leaned against his chest, hoping she wouldn't collapse.

"The door wasn't locked."

"He must have left that way."

Austin drew her closer to him, rubbing her arms and back. "I want you to call 9–1–1 now." He took a step away.

She pulled him back. "Don't leave me!"

"Okay, okay. I just want to check the cabin, that's all. I need to make sure we're alone. Then I'll check the perimeter. Chances are he's gone." Austin peered at her, but she couldn't see much in the shadows. "Are you good?"

"Yeah. Let's turn some lights on and I'll be better."

"I'd agree with you, but we don't want him able to see into the windows. He could take a shot at you then, if hurting you had been his intention. Tell you what. I'll make sure the windows are closed and the blinds and curtains shut, and then we'll turn on the lights."

"Fine, but I'm coming with you."

"Stay behind me then."

"I still have my gun."

"The way your hand is trembling, not to mention your aim, I'm not sure that will help us."

"Thanks a lot."

"You want honesty, don't you?"

"Sure, lead the way."

Austin held his weapon and cleared the cabin, finding only a couple of windows with curtains open to let dawn filter in. After closing all the curtains, he flipped on the lights, which chased away the shadows. Willow positioned herself to get a signal and called 9–1–1. She spoke to dispatch, relaying the information. While she spoke, Austin examined the open window where the intruder entered but didn't touch anything.

Before she ended the call, light filtered through the blinds on the front windows of the cabin.

"Headlights." He tensed. "Get back from the window."

"Why? What do you think is going to happen?"

"No point in taking chances, Willow."

She moved to stand at the far wall. Austin continued to peer out the window, then his tense shoulders relaxed. He opened the mini blinds so she could see.

Heath's form headed for the cabin. He knocked, then cracked the door. "What's going on in here? I heard gunshots coming from this direction. Everyone okay?"

"No, we're not okay." Austin had kept his weapon ready to use but lowered it. "Come on in."

Heath entered. "Is someone hurt?"

"No," Austin said, "but someone broke into the cabin through this window. Looks like it wasn't locked. Nobody locks up around here, so maybe it was an oversight the intruder was counting on."

Willow choked on unshed tears. "I was sleeping. A dream woke me, but now I think I must have heard a noise in my sleep. It was weird. I realized the window was open and then saw something move, so I ran back to the bed and grabbed the Sig you loaned me. I think it might have saved my life tonight. I shot at him. He fled the cabin."

She shuddered, unable to control her trembling limbs.

"Here, hold this." Austin handed his weapon to Heath. "Stand guard until the law gets here."

He gently removed the Sig Sauer from Willow's trembling grip. Good idea. Then he wrapped his arms around her and cuddled her close. He said nothing at all, seeming to understand that she needed to be held. She pressed her forehead against his sturdy chest, hoping to soak up his courage and strength. Sure, she knew how to use a weapon and to protect herself, to a degree. Facing a real-life attack stripped her confidence and laid her bare. Too many close calls. She wanted to dissolve into the carpet.

"Why does this keep happening? I thought I was safe here, at least for one night."

He rubbed her back, his hand trembling. This had upset him as much as it had her. She moved back from him to give herself room to breathe. "What am I going to do?"

Heath paced the room. "First, you're moving in with me tonight. Both of you. I'm sorry this happened while you were here. And then you're going to tell me what the heck is going on. Maybe I can offer some assistance."

Rubbing her arms, Willow composed herself. "I'm good with that, thanks. I'm just going to gather my things while we wait on the sheriff."

They'd cleared the house. The man was gone. Willow moved toward the bedroom to grab her duffel and pack away her things. She glanced at the closet. He wouldn't be hiding in the closet.

I'm okay. I'm going to be fine.

She placed one foot in front of the other, putting distance between her and Austin and his sturdy brother. Warmth permeated her back. She glanced over her shoulder. Austin followed her. Willow allowed herself a tenuous smile. Of course he would stay close and protect her. She'd never thought she'd need that, though she had a feeling it was equal parts Austin the man and Austin the protector that she needed.

She flipped on the lamp on the nightstand.

A slip of paper rested on the stand. "Austin?"

"What is it?" He stood on the other side of the bed, hands on his hips.

Willow lifted the paper, opened it, and gasped. "It's . . . it's a note. A warning."

Heart pounding, she read it out loud.

STOP THE SEARCH. IT'S A DEAD END.

"The man at my bed with a knife—it wasn't a dream."

CHAPTER *THIRTY*

Muscles tensing, Austin fisted his hands. The man had gotten close enough to her to leave a note? A threatening note, no less. He could have killed her if he'd wanted to. He'd tried in Seattle. Why didn't he kill her here? Austin's throat tightened.

He tugged latex gloves and a small plastic bag from his jeans pocket and then secured the note in the bag. Willow's hazel eyes grew big. He shrugged. "I like to be prepared, I guess. Besides, this is the first big break we've had. An actual piece of evidence."

They weren't hired to find a killer or even the abductor, but all the better if this brought them closer to the truth about Jamie Mason.

Willow pressed her hand to her throat. He knew exactly what she was thinking. "Come here." He held her again, getting much too comfortable with the action.

Austin hadn't told her that she'd grazed him with a bullet. It had ripped through his shirt and scratched his arm. Nothing major. No need to upset her. But that concerned him—he had thought she'd be a much better shot. She should have killed him tonight. He was glad she'd missed. Maybe it had more to do with divine intervention—it wasn't his time to go. His knees still shook at the close call.

Both his and hers.

He never should have left her alone. Even in a cabin next to his. His tense neck and shoulders ached. Headlights shined bright in the distance, moving up and down as the vehicles bumped along the rutted drive to the cabins.

"Why don't you sit. I'll get you a drink of water. Looks like the law has finally arrived."

Willow eased into a chair without a word. She'd drifted into a dazed state. Not good.

Heath moved to the door. "I'll go out and meet them. I suspect Sheriff Haines will have come himself. We're friends, so I'll let him know what's happened."

"Sounds good." Austin headed to the kitchen to get water for both himself and Willow. Their search for a person abducted two decades ago had grown complicated. Now Willow's life was in danger because they were looking for answers. Getting help from the local law in finding whoever had broken into her cabin could help them in their search.

Heath entered, along with the sheriff and one of his deputies. Two other deputies had been dispersed to search the grounds to see if the man remained. Austin hoped they wouldn't trample any additional evidence. Getting in and out of here wasn't easy.

Sheriff Haines propped his hands on his hips, his gun resting in the holster on his belt. A stocky man in his early sixties, he had thick reddish hair layered with gray that looked more yellow than red.

"How's Tanner doing?" Heath asked.

The sheriff's expression turned somber. "That grandson of mine is a real fighter. He's hanging in there. Thanks for asking, Heath."

"You're welcome. I'll keep him in my prayers. I'm going to head outside and look around." Heath exited the cabin.

After introducing himself, Sheriff Haines gestured to the deputy beside him. "And this is Deputy Taggart. Now tell me what's going on here."

He eyed Austin, disapproval etched into his features. Austin had drawn the sheriff's attention four years ago when his father had his accident. He wasn't surprised when the sheriff turned away without acknowledging him.

Sheriff Haines questioned Willow for more details about the break-in and she told him about the attacks in Seattle. Then Austin shared his side of the story.

"And you think this guy followed you here from Seattle?" Sheriff Haines lifted a thick yellow brow.

Willow's features paled. "I hope not, but who else could it be, especially considering the note the guy left?"

"We'll move up to the house with Heath tonight, Sheriff. Heath and I can watch out for her better there."

"I'll take the note with me," the sheriff said. "We'll process for fingerprints and do that for the cabin too. Check for footprints. Considering you're the first person to stay here, like you said, we could get lucky. Then why don't you come in to see me tomorrow and show me what you have so far on the missing girl. If you have pictures or names. Maybe I can help. Maybe not. It's worth a try."

"I have one right now. I can show it to you." Willow swiped her phone and showed it to the sheriff. "It's the abductor."

He examined the image, scrunching up his face.

"It might not be a very good rendering, since it was an age progression done on a grainy photograph," she said.

The sheriff crinkled his forehead. "Email it to me. I'll do what I can to get the word out."

That was certainly more than Austin would have expected. The man had his hands full with law enforcement duties and search and rescues, which could be particularly challenging in these parts. Austin suspected he was only being hands-on because of his relationship with Heath.

Willow's face brightened. "Thank you, Sheriff. I appreciate your help."

When the sheriff and deputy moved outside to search the premises, Heath returned to help Austin and Willow gather and load their things into the truck. He drove them the short distance to the main house at the ranch, his house, and ushered them inside.

"As you can see, I've added on in the renovations. There are four rooms upstairs. Two downstairs. I sleep downstairs. Evelyn stays in a room downstairs too." He sent Willow a wry grin. "I wasn't expecting guests today."

"I'm sure the rooms are fine," Willow said. "Thank you, Heath."

"I just wish you would have stayed here to begin with, then maybe this wouldn't have happened." Heath helped them lug their bags up the stairs and showed them their rooms. "You two get a good night's sleep. I'll watch the house. Me and the dogs."

"Thanks, bro." Austin hoped Heath understood the depth of his gratitude. By the look in his eyes before he headed downstairs, he seemed to.

Willow had already disappeared into the bedroom and closed the door. He'd wanted to talk to her more to make sure she was all right. When the door opened and she stepped out into the hallway, that part of him that couldn't seem to let go of her could have grabbed her up and held her forever. He reined in those crazy, stupid thoughts as she drew near.

Her glistening eyes zeroed in on his shoulder. Soft lines formed around her mouth and eyes. "I'm so sorry that I almost shot you."

Bottom lip quivering, she lifted her hand and touched his shoulder. He resisted wincing, for her sake, and savored the concern pouring from her.

She fingered the torn fabric. "Is this from the bullet? It grazed you?" Her shoulders slumped.

He gently gripped her arms. "It's okay. It's over. I'm alive. Never thought I'd be glad you have terrible aim." He teased, but his attempt

184

at humor fell flat. "Now go get some sleep. No one is going to get by Heath and Timber, old dog that he is. Timber, that is."

Unfortunately, someone almost got by Austin tonight.

"I'm worried about Jamie. Are we putting her life in danger because we're trying to find her? We don't know where she is, so we can't even protect her."

"I don't have an answer." He wondered what she would think if he told her the reason he'd resigned from the FBI. If he shared that on his last assignment, he'd been working to find an abducted child. Was he even up to the task of protecting Willow?

She left him and went back to her room. He returned to his own room, sat at the chair next to the window, and stared into the night. There was so much she didn't know about him. So much he wanted to finally share—but it was pointless now, because they had no future together.

CHAPTER THIRTY-ONE

Something woke Charlie in the middle of the night. From her room she heard Momma's frightened voice speaking in low tones. She slipped out of bed and crept down the hallway to listen.

"No, please don't do this. I'm sorry . . . I made a mistake. I shouldn't have asked for more . . ."

A man wearing a mask fired his weapon point blank at Momma. She dropped to the ground. Before the shock of that moment engulfed Charlie, the man pointed his weapon at her and spoke in a gruff, unnatural tone to disguise his voice. "I'm going to kill you too."

She turned and fled down the hallway. A bullet hit the wall, barely missing her. She ran into her bedroom and slammed the door behind her, knowing it would merely slow him. Not stop him. She climbed through her window and slipped out into the night. She sprinted through the meadow in the back of their two-acre lot and kept running. Momma's screams echoed in her ears. Her body dropping to the floor played through her mind.

Adrenaline propelled Charlie into the Bridger-Teton National Forest, which she knew like the back of her hand.

186

From a distance behind her, the man shouted that he would find and kill her. She appreciated the warning. She would never let that happen.

Charlie shot up in bed, a cold sweat drenching her body. The dreams came less frequently now. Instead, the fear and anguish and deep, aching loss showed up in panic attacks.

I shouldn't have asked for more . . .

More what? More money? More time?

The Hoback County Sheriff's Department investigator, Randall Koonce, had wanted to accuse Charlie of killing her own mother. He claimed there was no evidence anyone else had been in the house except Charlie. She thought maybe he was trying to protect Clyde. Sheriff Everett, to his credit, had put a quick end to the line of thinking that put Charlie as the suspect. But she still couldn't count on him to protect her from Clyde, even if she got a restraining order.

Charlie would remain hidden from the man who threatened to kill her while she tried to figure out what her mother's words had meant when she said she shouldn't have asked for more. Had Momma known the man? It seemed like she'd known who'd come for her and why. It had to have been Clyde. Who else? Part of her feared that Sheriff Everett might bend an ear to Koonce's accusations and decide Charlie was guilty after all. He'd throw her in jail.

That thought alone could bring on the panic attacks. So she'd disappeared. As far as anyone knew—besides Mack—she'd gone back to the University of Wyoming to finish out her last year studying animal science. As soon as she didn't fear for her life anymore, as soon as she found out who had killed her mother and why and that person was behind bars, then she could go back to school. Maybe. It would be hard to get on with her life without her mother, but that's what Momma would have wanted. Charlie didn't want to let her down in this life or the next.

Dawn filtered through the trees and cabin windows, which meant she'd slept late. She rubbed her tired eyes. She needed to figure out why Clyde had driven up the driveway to the house she'd shared with Momma. Charlie's house now.

Yawning, Charlie shrugged out from under the covers and began the task of making her cowboy coffee. She used a Coleman propane stove. Easier than a wood-burning stove. Staying in the cabin was just like camping, except she had stacked logs protecting her at night instead of the thin vinyl sheets of a tent. The coffee would take much too long to heat up though. Last night she'd stayed up late, waiting for Rufus to come back and listening to the lack of night sounds in the cold mountain air. She'd eventually fallen asleep.

Rufus . . .

A sliver of hope drove her to the door. Would she find the German shepherd sitting next to the cabin?

When she opened the door and looked out into the crisp morning, disappointment displaced her small hope.

"Rufus!" she called.

The dog was gone. She'd thought they were friends. She'd figured he would remain loyal to her, though he'd belonged to Mack, who had given him to Charlie for her protection. Rufus had probably gone back to Mack, unless something had happened to the dog.

She closed the door and got dressed. She'd search for him as best she could before heading in to work with the horses. Then she would try once again to stop at the house and look through Momma's things. If she could find out where that trust fund had come from that paid her college tuition, the home renovations, and for a better life, that might give her some answers. Momma never spoke of family—including grandparents or even Charlie's father—other than to say they'd all passed on from this life. She didn't even know who her relatives were. Admittedly, Charlie had never cared much about that until now, when she had no one left. If she had someone else, maybe she could share this burden with them and find her mother's killer.

Charlie had to take it one day at a time. Be careful and methodical.

If she hurried and became careless and allowed someone to recognize her, that mistake could be deadly.

CHAPTER THIRTY-TWO

Willow waited with Austin in the sheriff's office. They'd arrived three hours ago, but the sheriff had been too busy and kept putting them off. At least they'd been able to grab sandwiches from a vending machine.

The sheriff spoke with a deputy just outside his door about an ongoing search and rescue involving a couple of teenage boys who had gotten lost hiking. Her heart went out to the families. While she waited, she'd had time to study the photographs of the sheriff with his department awards as well as with various friends and family members. He had had quite a career. Huffing, Sheriff Haines entered the office, shut the door, and sat at his desk.

"As you might have heard, we got a couple of boys missing, so let's make this quick." He whirled around in his chair to a credenza and pulled papers from a fax machine. Then faced them again and scooted closer to his desk.

He adjusted his reading glasses and stared at the pages. He slapped the sheets face down on the desk as he skimmed each one, then brought his full attention to Willow and Austin. "I want to make this clear up front. I'm helping you for several reasons. One, because I know and respect Heath. He's made himself a pillar in this community. He's like a son to me. I'd do just about anything for friends and family. Two, because you were attacked and the note tells me there's a connection. So while your investigation into the past isn't my investigation, they're connected. The sooner you find what you need the better. After a few phone calls, I confirmed the story and the original picture of the abductor. I put it up on our website and sent the image through law-enforcement channels throughout the state."

"Since the original picture was grainy, I'm not sure how accurate it is," Willow offered.

"That's a problem, to be sure, and this might lead nowhere."

A deputy knocked on the door and stuck his head in. One of the guys she saw at the cabin last night. Deputy Taggart? "Sorry to interrupt, but I thought you might want the information." Without an invitation, he stepped into the office and zeroed in on Willow. "I got a call this morning from someone who claims they might have seen the woman in the picture you sent out. Claims she lived around Clair, a small town one county over in Hoback County."

Willow sucked in a breath. Next to her, Austin tensed as well.

Deputy Taggart looked to his boss, who lifted his chin, letting his deputy know he could continue. "I called the sheriff in Hoback County and spoke directly with him. He wasn't sure about the picture but said if it's who he thinks it is, the woman died two months ago."

His words weighed heavy on Willow. "But . . . what about the daughter?"

"I asked. Sheriff Everett said he didn't pry into people's lives. Said you were barking up the wrong tree. That's all I could get out of him."

"But he gave you a name, right?"

"Marilee Clemmons is the woman who died. But I didn't get the daughter's name, sorry."

"A name, if this is the woman we're looking for, could make all the difference," Austin said.

"Thanks, Taggart. I'll take it from here." Sheriff Haines peered at the deputy, his expression not completely warm.

Taggart nodded. "Yes, Sheriff." He closed the door behind him.

"Well, looks like you have a name now. You can't be sure it's even the right woman, just based on that picture."

"You're right, we can't, but it's a start," Willow said.

"Now, is there anything else I can do for you?"

"I think we're good," Austin said. "Thank you for your time."

Sheriff Haines shoved from his desk and stood. "You're welcome. In the meantime, I'll turn your break-in and the note over to my investigations unit and we'll see what we can find out. But I need you to understand that I have my hands full with not only residents but tourists, and our SAR unit. I'm happy to help if I can, but you two have been hired to do a job. I suggest you do it and head home."

In other words, he wanted them out of his jurisdiction as soon as possible.

Willow and Austin stood as the sheriff opened the door to dismiss them. "We hope to wrap this up soon and appreciate your help," Austin said.

At the door, the sheriff said, "If another crime is committed against you, be sure to call us so we can look for evidence while it's still fresh. Are we clear?" The sheriff's friendly gaze shifted from Willow to Austin and hardened. It was subtle, but Willow hadn't missed the coldness toward Austin.

There must be a story behind that. Something Austin hadn't shared. No surprise there.

Willow and Austin thanked Sheriff Haines and exited the facility.

Sitting in the Jeep, Willow powered up her laptop. Austin used his tablet.

"I'll look at the county appraiser's website for Marilee's property," Austin said.

"Good, I'll search for any articles about her death."

They both worked in silence for a couple of minutes. "Found her. It's an article in the local newspaper," Willow said. "Says here she was . . . killed. Murdered." Unshed tears surged.

"Oh man." Austin leaned back against the seat.

"Bad enough she died, but why didn't the deputy mention that? I think we should march back in there and ask the sheriff about the murder."

"Believe me, he's been very generous with us. But it's not his county, so he might not even know."

"Really? If they haven't found the killer, probably all law enforcement is looking for the suspect. What about the sheriff in the county where she lives? Hoback County. How do we find out more about the murder? I wonder if they solved it."

"One thing at a time." Austin stared at his tablet. "Got the obit here. She worked at Clair Nursing Home. Oddly, it doesn't offer her surviving relatives like . . . her daughter." His eyes met Willow's. "She was a nurse. Let's search her name and see if we can find her daughter. Look for a picture. Maybe we can also gain access to her house and look around."

Willow couldn't remember the last time she'd seen so much excitement in his gray eyes. They brightened almost to a silver-blue.

"If she looks anything at all like a young Katelyn Mason, that will tell us something." But what if she looked nothing like Katelyn? That wouldn't necessarily mean she wasn't her daughter.

"I hope you're right." He peered back at his tablet.

After a few minutes of searching, they both came up empty. No images of Marilee's daughter on the internet. Not even a name. What could that mean? That Marilee was very protective of her daughter's identity?

Willow shut her laptop. "Let's go with what we have. Go to the nursing home and ask questions."

"Let me do the talking, Willow. I know what I'm doing. People aren't that willing to talk to strangers these days. And we definitely don't want to tell them we think she abducted her daughter. That would raise hackles."

Hackles? She loved how he'd morphed back into a guy who'd lived in Wyoming.

"Agreed. Marilee Clemmons might not be Jamie's abductor. We wouldn't want to cast a bad light on her."

Austin put away his tablet before starting the Jeep and steering onto the road that would take them to Hoback County and the small country town of Clair. It wasn't that far but still took time on the curvy mountain roads.

Willow called Dana hoping to find out if she'd learned anything from the genealogical records—if Katelyn had connections to Wyoming. She could ask her to search the records on Marilee Clemmons. Maybe that would turn up information about her daughter—abducted or not. Or other family members who might be willing to share. Willow ended up leaving her a voicemail.

As they headed north, Willow could just make out Grand Teton to her left. She took in the stunning scenery once again, then it disappeared behind another peak as Austin veered right at a fork in the road.

She considered everything they'd learned so far and hoped they weren't barking up the wrong tree, as the sheriff had said. If not, then this was further than anyone had gotten in the investigation—at least according to the files she'd read. Sheriff Haines had given them a lot today. Make that Deputy Taggart.

There'd been something antagonistic in the sheriff's eyes when it came to Austin. Willow wanted to know why. She reined in the questions she had for him. She would only overwhelm him and shut him down again. How did she get this guy to open up?

More to the point—why did she care?

CHAPTER THIRTY-THREE

Austin gripped the steering wheel and focused on the road. He tried to ignore the scenery and the realization that he'd missed this place. He also tried to ignore Willow's citrusy perfume that teased his senses. He could try all day long to overlook the fact that he missed Willow, but his efforts would fail.

"You seem distant," she said.

"I'm thinking about helping you find this woman while keeping you safe." He glanced her way, hoping he'd injected enough humor into his tone. "My brain doesn't work like yours. I can't think on multiple topics, much less talk about them at the same time. I usually zero in on one thing." Usually. But Willow was a huge distraction for him. Willow and the Wyoming setting.

"I get it. You're super-focused."

"Two things don't leave much room for me to make conversation. I'm sorry."

"The sheriff seemed like a nice enough guy, but I got the feeling he didn't like you. Was I reading him wrong?"

Great. "Nope."

Willow sat silently. Austin suspected she was keeping quiet in hopes that he would freely divulge more information without her having to pester him. How long would she wait?

Five minutes later, he chuckled. "I'm impressed."

"About what?"

"You haven't asked me more."

She smacked his arm. "Are you going to tell me or what?"

"I'd prefer not to get into that while we're gearing up to question people at a nursing home, but I will tell you this much. It's wrapped up in my father's accident. The sheriff was close to the family who died along with him."

A few beats of silence from her, then she said, "He seemed to like Heath. He even mentioned he was like a son to him."

"The sheriff blames me." Now why had he said that much? He'd prefer to talk about it later. But that was just it—if it were up to him, he'd procrastinate until it was forgotten.

"Care to share with me why he blames you?"

"Not particularly. But I know you won't stop thinking about it, and you need to focus on the task at hand."

Austin switched on the blinker and took a right toward Clair. He sank lower in the seat. "I had an argument with Dad. He'd been drinking, and I argued with him and let him drive off mad . . ."

He wished Willow hadn't asked. Grief tore at his insides. Why did she always want to pry? She'd poked around at a painful wound that hadn't healed. When would Austin learn? This was exactly what had driven a wedge between them before—his unwillingness to talk. Couldn't she understand he wasn't ready? Still, maybe it was time he tried.

He regretted losing her before.

He'd given her something, at least, but he needed to clarify. "I let him drive off while he was drunk," he repeated. "I didn't *know* he was drunk. It took a lot to get him there because his liver was already toast. But I should have known. I should have seen it. I'll regret my part in that for the rest of my life."

"I don't know what to say."

Now *that* could be a first.

He steered through the town with one stoplight and turned into the Clair Nursing Home parking lot. Found a space and parked. "There's nothing you *can* say."

Without waiting for her response, he climbed out of the Jeep. Together they strode to the building and Austin held the door for her. She scooted by him, leaving that citrusy scent again. He shook it off but wished he hadn't when he followed her in and was met by nursing home smells.

Disinfectant and asparagus.

In the open area, a circle of patients sat in chairs and wheelchairs and tried to throw bean bags to make it inside a hula hoop on the floor. Others hung back from the circle and watched.

Approaching the nurses' station, he introduced himself and Willow to Kim, a tall, lanky nurse with bulging eyes set in a pale face under short black hair.

Taking in her no-nonsense, matter-of-fact expression, Austin decided on a direct approach. "We've been hired by a family member to look into Marilee Clemmons's death." Which was indirectly true. "I was told she worked here."

Nurse Kim's bulging eyes looked them up and down. Would she be friendly and cooperative or unwilling to talk? "Yeah, she worked here. I know her well enough to know she ain't got no family. Least none that showed up at the funeral."

"She has family," Willow said. "She has a daughter."

"Besides her daughter. I doubt *she* hired an investigator."

Oh boy. This was going south and fast. "And why is that?"

One of the elderly men who lingered outside the circle rolled his wheelchair closer as if he had something to say, then seemed to forget where he was going. He stared blankly.

Nurse Kim came around from behind the counter, her fist and a manila folder on her hip. She sighed, then waved them back to a room and shut the door. "What do you want to know? A deputy investigator already asked his questions. I take it he didn't offer you any answers."

"You've already told us she didn't have any family besides her daughter. What about friends?"

"She worked here for a good fifteen years. We were her friends. Outside of this facility, I'm not sure. You'd have to ask Charlie."

"Charlie?"

Kim's eyes bulged even bigger, if that were possible. "I thought you knew her daughter."

"We know her as Charlotte," Willow said.

Great recovery.

"Right." Kim shrugged. "I don't know what I can do to help you. I hope you find her killer. Maybe between you and the sheriff's department, she'll get justice."

Austin offered her his business card. "If you think of anything that can help us, here's my card."

Kim opened the door and exited, leaving them to show themselves out.

"What now?" Willow asked as they walked out of the room and into the hallway.

"We have the daughter's name. We didn't have that before."

Kim headed toward the man in the wheelchair who'd approached earlier. "Can I help you, Mr. Haus?"

He lifted a gnarled hand as if pointing to Willow. "Marilee. I know Marilee."

CHAPTER THIRTY-FOUR

Hope swelled as Willow approached the man. He wanted to talk about Marilee. She shared a look with Austin and saw that same hope surging in his eyes.

The elderly stored a wealth of information, especially when it came to the past. JT always said there was no greater travesty than when a family history died with a family member who never bothered to share stories of the past.

Or when others didn't bother to listen. The result—families forgot where they came from.

Since Mr. Haus wanted to talk to them, this was where Willow would take the lead. With a look at Austin, she lifted her chin, and he gave a subtle nod.

Kim clutched the wheelchair handles, ready to roll Mr. Haus away. When Willow approached, she put on her biggest smile. It was genuine. She loved talking to the elderly. Mr. Haus smiled back, and Kim relented as though realizing he might enjoy the conversation.

Willow crouched to his eye level, keeping her smile in place. "Mr. Haus?"

He slowly lifted his hazy eyes to meet hers and nodded. Wisdom that could only come with age lurked there. "My name is Willow Anderson."

"Do I know you?" His voice gurgled.

"We've never met, no. I came here to talk to someone about Marilee Clemmons. Do you know her?"

A confused expression shadowed his eyes and he slowly shook his head. "Can't say that I do."

Willow could hardly contain the disappointment that gripped her. But she continued. If only she could get him to talk about something, maybe important memories would surface. "I'm a genealogist and visited the cemetery up the road. The Haus name I saw on one of the tombstones was spelled H–A–U–S. Is that how you spell your name?"

He tried to angle his head back at Kim, who remained behind him, as though she would know. Then he reached for his mouth with a trembling hand as if commanding it to speak. "Yes. People don't know how to say my name. Never did. It's pronounced 'hoss,' not 'house.'"

Willow offered a soft laugh. "You're not alone. As someone who has studied genealogy, I know something of family naming conventions. It happens all too often. Tell me about the man in the grave?"

She hoped the topic would get him talking about his family and then back around to remembering that he knew Marilee.

"That's my father in the grave." His voice wavered with uncertainty. Willow sensed he still hadn't decided if he could trust her.

With the deepest respect, she patted his hand. Her heart went out to him. Many people left in nursing homes were lonely. It broke her heart, but often families didn't have the resources to care for their elders themselves.

Mr. Haus started talking about his family just like she had hoped. Arms crossed, watching from a distance, Austin stood against the wall. She shook off the sudden self-consciousness and listened intently to Mr. Haus's story.

"My great-granddaddy worked the cattle drives. But my grandpa never cared for it. Settled in Jackson Hole, working at a mercantile. My daddy worked with hunting outfitters. As for me, I got me a good construction job. And my sons"—he held up two fingers—"I have two of them. Nothing I did was good enough. They hardly come to see me anymore."

"I'm so sorry to hear that, Mr. Haus."

He grinned and winked at her, grabbing her hand. "But you— you can come see me as often as you want."

The man had turned feisty and was flirting with her. Willow giggled. "Oh, I'd love to come as often as I can, but I don't live here."

His expression shifted, surprise evident in every wrinkle. "Oh? What brings you here then?"

Now was the time to bring up Marilee again. "I'm looking into something for a friend who lost someone."

He stared off into the distance, his silver brows pinched. "I lost someone. I lost a friend. She worked here." He twisted around in his wheelchair to stare at Kim for confirmation.

She nodded.

"Was Marilee your friend, Mr. Haus?"

A tear leaked out of the corner of his red-rimmed eye. "She took care of me. No one else is gonna take care of me."

He tried to roll his wheelchair away from Kim.

"Now, that's just not true." Kim clung to the handles, her intention clear. "We're all here to take care of you."

Willow stepped back. She hadn't meant to agitate him.

"Marilee knows my secret," he whispered.

Kim began wheeling him back to his room, speaking in calming tones.

Austin rested his hand on Willow's shoulder. "Come on, let's get out of here."

"No, wait. I want to apologize to Kim."

Austin headed for the door and waited.

Kim's shoes squeaked back down the hallway. She appeared surprised to see that Willow was still there. Just before she headed into another patient's room, Willow called out. Kim frowned, then approached. "Look, I have work to do."

"I wanted to apologize. I didn't mean to upset him."

"I know you didn't. I appreciate that you took time to talk to him. I wish I could have warned you he gets like that. He has dementia. He only has one son, not two." Juggling a clipboard and a banana, she rubbed her cheek against her shoulder.

"Is it okay if we come back and talk to him?"

Kim looked at her clipboard as she walked away. She called over her shoulder. "I suppose that's up to him."

CHAPTER THIRTY-FIVE

When she and Austin approached the Jeep, Willow noticed a slip of paper stuck under the windshield wiper. It flapped in the breeze. They both had spotted it at the same moment and both reached for it, but she was quicker. Before she opened the paper, they both glanced around.

"Let's get in the car first," he said.

Inside the vehicle, Willow opened the note and read it out loud.

"If you keep looking, if you tell anyone, her death will be on your hands. Her life depends on you now."

Willow gasped for breath. She opened the door and bolted from the car and into the parking lot, where she bent over her thighs to suck in air. If she kept going, she was going to get Jamie killed.

"It's not fair!" *You hear that, God?*

The pavement rolled and blurred. Whoever left the note was probably watching her reaction now. The thought that someone had followed them to this nursing home overwhelmed every nerve ending in her body.

Austin's strong arms wrapped around her. "Willow. Willow, calm down, please. I can't stand to see you like this."

She tried to shrug free. "Leave me alone."

"No, I don't want you standing out here in the open. We need to leave. Now." His voice left no room for her to argue, but she tried anyway.

"Just let me catch my breath. I need a moment, okay?" She couldn't get enough air. "What are we going to do?"

He guided her to the vehicle. "Later, we can look at security camera footage to see who left the note, but I have a feeling this person wasn't that careless. But right now, we're going to get back into the Jeep and get out of here."

She climbed inside and shut the door. She'd made a complete fool out of herself. "I'm sorry."

"No need to apologize. It's no less disturbing to me." Austin started the engine and steered the Jeep out of the parking lot.

Maybe more disturbing to him since he was supposed to protect her. "Where are we going?"

"Away from here."

"Whoever left that note has been following us. Who is it?"

He watched the rearview mirror. She'd noted he was always on the lookout, so she couldn't understand why he had missed their tail, but she didn't want to accuse him. Now wasn't the time for that discussion.

On the console, a plastic bag held the note. Everything was evidence to him. He couldn't stop collecting it.

"We have to end the search, Austin. He's going to kill her. And we're so close to finding her. What am I going to tell Katelyn?"

"We have to tell the sheriff. He can contact the local FBI too, who can then decide to reopen the case. And don't worry, we can make it look like we're going to give up on the search while we hand over this information."

Willow hung her head. "That will take time. Too much time."

"Possibly."

"How do we make it look like we're giving up? Do we leave Wyoming?"

"We're close to finding her, Willow. That much is obvious. I need time to think."

"We can't just walk into the sheriff's office and hand over the note. That could also be a death sentence for Jamie. So what do we do next?"

"I'm going to take us back to Heath's. I want you to breathe and relax. We're going to find her, Willow. And I'm going to figure out who has been following us. Maybe he hasn't been following us at all, but because we're going to the right places, he knows where we'll be. This means we're getting closer."

"Doesn't he realize that leaving us notes tells us we're on the right track?"

"He must be desperate."

Would the guy who'd broken into her cabin try again? Would he kill her this time? Chills crawled over her. She rubbed her arms and looked out the window. "Who have we met along the way that we could add to our list of suspects?"

"Let's think this through slowly and methodically."

Willow pressed her head against the seat back and closed her eyes. "So we have a name. What sort of name is Charlie for a girl?"

"Good call coming up with Charlotte in front of Nurse Kim. But the name Charlie. Maybe that's the point. Her name makes it sound like she's a boy."

"I think you're right. I can't believe we're so close to finding her." But what exactly would they find? "There's something else at play here. Mr. Haus said Marilee knows his secret."

"That could be taking us off track," Austin said. "The nurse said he has dementia. It could be nothing at all. Remember, he thinks he has two sons."

"It could be connected, see? We believe Marilee abducted Charlie, and Mr. Haus says Marilee knows his secret." She stared out the window. "But everything has changed now with the note. Anything I do could be construed as continuing the search."

"Right. Everything has changed. But we can't give up on finding Jamie . . . Charlie. I'm just not sure yet how to continue without putting her in danger. But we'll figure it out."

"But will we figure it out in time? Why is someone just leaving notes now when in Seattle someone was trying to kill me?" Someone who succeeded in killing JT. Willow clenched the armrest. She couldn't wait to find this person and make sure justice was served.

"That's a very good question. When we get back to Heath's house, we'll get on the internet and find out as much as we can. Why don't you call Dana and give her an update? Find out what she knows too. Maybe we'll pack up and make it appear that we're leaving tomorrow and hand the note off then."

"If only we could figure out where Charlie is so the sheriff can protect her. We need her picture to go with the name so we can be sure that she is even Katelyn's daughter. Maybe we could get her DNA if we could get into her house and work the case like that."

"One thing at a time, but I think the notes are confirmation that Charlie is the one. We don't want to tip this person off. I'll figure out how to inform the sheriff. Just give me time to think."

Time. Something they were running out of.

"I was watching you back there. You were a whiz with Mr. Haus."

She regarded him. Why was he complimenting her now? Trying to calm her frazzled nerves? Did he think that would work? Hmm . . . "What can I say? I love anyone who can remind me of JT."

Watching the road and the rearview mirror, Austin managed a cute triple-dimpled grin. He must have a clue how that grin affected her. Why else would he brandish it now?

When he looked her way, esteem registered in his gray eyes. She turned her attention to the scenery. Once she and Austin were able to put their past aside, they actually began working well together. Not something she needed to linger on.

The conversation with Mr. Haus still fresh on her mind, Willow thought about JT. If he had lived, would there have ever come a time when he would have stayed in a nursing home? If he had, he would have put a brand-new spin on the old adage "The life of the party."

Mr. Haus seemed like a nice old man. She wished his son would come visit him.

"Marilee knows my secret."

What had Marilee known? Whatever it was, did it get her killed?

FRIDAY, 5:11 P.M.
EMERALD M RANCH

Back at the ranch, Heath met them at the door and introduced Evelyn, his adopted grandmother/housekeeper. Willow warmed to her immediately. Did Heath know what a treasure he'd found in this woman? By the adoration blooming on his face, yes. Yes, he did.

"Can I help you in the kitchen, Evelyn?" she asked.

"Oh, heavens no. You're Heath's guest. If I need help, Heath can help me." Evelyn squeezed Willow's arm. "You go upstairs and freshen up. Supper will be served in half an hour."

"Are you sure? Because I'm happy to help."

Evelyn chuckled and winked. "Maybe next time."

Willow did as she was told. After freshening up for supper, she gathered in the dining room with Heath and Austin. She still hadn't heard back from Dana, except a text saying she would send along an image shortly. Willow's phone buzzed just as Heath carried lasagna into the room and set it in the center of the table.

"Excuse me, I need to look at this." Willow pulled up the image Dana had sent.

Austin hovered over her shoulder. "Is that her?"

"Do you even have to ask?" Willow smiled. "She looks like the image of Katelyn in her twenties. This updated version could help us more than the outdated photos on milk cartons that have been circulating for years. But look, the artist included different hairstyles to help us." She scrolled through the pictures.

Evelyn and Heath stood at the table and waited.

"I don't mean to be rude, but we just got the forensic artist's compilation of what this girl should look like in her twenties." Willow flipped her phone around so they could see the image. "Someone abducted her twenty-one years ago. No one knows where she is."

CHAPTER THIRTY-SIX

Except Heath.

His heart scrambled around in his chest. He knew the girl in the image. He knew *where* she was, and that she was hiding. He'd been the one to help her hide.

He also knew there was going to be trouble. Part of that resided with him.

Because what he didn't know was *who* had hired Austin and Willow to find Charlie—a girl who didn't want to be found.

He needed to redirect their attention while he recovered. Figured out what he should say and what he shouldn't. "Well, why don't we eat before it gets cold, since Evelyn worked so hard. We wouldn't want to disappoint her."

While they plated their food, Heath worked to compose himself, appreciating the training he'd received as a Green Beret. He could almost be grateful for the experience of living under a brutal alcoholic father. Heath had learned to maintain his composure under the worst circumstances.

He'd count this situation among those.

He and Austin were finally reconnecting—heck, he'd go so far as to use the word *reconciling*. But Austin and the genealogist had been hired to find Charlie. Too many questions swirled around her mother's murder. And considering Clyde's relationship with Marilee, and that Clyde was Sheriff Everett's cousin, something smelled like too many dead salmon floating on the Grayback River. Heath had sworn to keep Charlie's secret while she searched for her mother's killer. She stayed in a cabin just under two miles up the trail. Close but not too close.

Heath might never have considered helping Charlie, going to such lengths, if he hadn't already been through a similar tragedy. He'd befriended a young mother at a church he'd attended near Fort Carson, Colorado, where he'd been based. She'd had a restraining order against her ex-husband, but that hadn't been enough. Heath had assisted her in finding a place to stay but had made the mistake of sharing her location with a friend. If only he hadn't.

Her husband found her and almost beat her to death. Heath showed up in time to stop the man, but he blamed himself. He wasn't going to make the same mistake twice—he wouldn't give Charlie up without good reason. He'd die before he'd let anything happen to her.

"How's the food?" Evelyn's question yanked him back to the present.

"Excellent, as always," he lied. The lasagna was probably wonderful, but it tasted like cardboard at the moment. Not her fault. His stomach had soured at the revelation of who his brother and the genealogist had come to find.

Austin and Willow went on about the lasagna, even the elk meat sauce, and thanked Evelyn. Smiling, she sauntered back into the kitchen. Willow claimed she'd hired Austin, but by that hope brewing in Austin's eyes when he looked at her, Heath suspected much more was going on. If Austin had found someone and fallen in love, Heath couldn't be happier for him. Even a little envious. But his inner demons wouldn't let him do the same.

"I hope you're paying her what she's worth." The teasing gleam in his brother's eyes singed his heart. He wanted to be forthright but not yet. He couldn't reveal Charlie's secret. Not until he had all the facts.

Aware that Austin was studying him, he tilted his head to the kitchen. "I can't afford to pay her what she's worth." He paid Evelyn plenty, but she was a priceless gem.

Finally, after he forced down an entire plate of lasagna—Evelyn would worry if he didn't—he figured it was time to dig deeper. For his own peace of mind and for Charlie's safety. "Tell me about the person who hired you to find this girl. What do you know about him?"

He couldn't imagine that Clyde or Sheriff Everett had hired these two—especially since they'd come all the way from Seattle. Made no sense. What was going on?

"Well, I suppose we've already shared with the sheriff," Willow said, "so you might as well know. I don't usually share clients' information. For their privacy's sake, you understand."

Heath set his napkin on his plate, waiting for an explanation.

"A family member has been searching for her a long time. It's . . . complicated." Willow hesitated. "I might as well tell you—her mother has been looking for her."

The lasagna churned in his gut. Her mother was dead—she couldn't have hired them. Heath fought the urge to bolt from the table and pace. To blast these two for taking this assignment. Finding out who had hired them could help solve Marilee's murder, but he had to play this right to prevent them from tipping off the murderer.

"You say her mother has been looking for her."

Austin pushed his plate forward and clasped his hands on the table. "She was abducted from a hospital twenty-one years ago."

This was too much. Heath wanted to run from the table. Instead he eased away. He wanted to rail at them. Instead he said nothing.

This person had lied to them. Had hired them to find Charlie because she'd gone into hiding. Staring out the window at the pristine lake reflecting the mountains, he hoped the view would soothe him but was disappointed.

Why, God? Why is this happening? Heath *wanted* to trust Austin. He *needed* to trust his brother. Except he wasn't sure he could count on Austin to track with him on this. How pathetic was that? He'd wanted this reconciliation with Austin. Hoped to see him around more often—but now he found himself on the opposite side of their search. He never imagined he'd find himself in this kind of jam. He would love to give Austin the benefit of the doubt, but how could he do that without jeopardizing Charlie's safety?

"You all right, Heath?" Austin asked.

Willow had begun to help Evelyn by stacking the dishes. Heath wanted to tell Evelyn he'd do the dishes later so they could have some privacy, but he couldn't do that without hurting her feelings. She didn't want anyone in "her" kitchen anyway.

"I was thinking about the young woman. If she's even still alive, she has a life now. Has friends and hobbies and a family. Why destroy her life with the revelation that her mother isn't her real mother?" He knew that was just a lie—a big fat lie—to fuel the search. Heath turned on them and eyed Willow. Her eyes grew wide from the intensity coming off him. He should tone it down, but he couldn't rein in the confusion and anger. Unfortunately, he wasn't the man he thought he was if he couldn't control this. This so-called mother could be the one who murdered Marilee and wants to find and kill Charlie.

"Have you considered that the woman you're looking for doesn't want to be found?"

CHAPTER THIRTY-SEVEN

She didn't want to be found.

A dense copse of spruce trees kept Charlie hidden as she stood next to the horse. She'd ridden Amber to her house, picking her way through the back trails. She ran her hand over the soft hair of Amber's lightly freckled neck, the familiar scent of evergreen needles and musky horse comforting her. Then she lifted a pair of binoculars to her eyes. Mack hadn't minded that she'd wanted to take Amber for a long trail ride. One day she'd have to pay him back for his generosity and willingness to keep her secret. The man was nothing if not trustworthy and honorable, even if he'd been a little pushy about his religion. She was glad she'd listened to him on that point.

After spotting Clyde driving up to her house, she couldn't afford to park Bronc there and take her time searching. She thought her house would've fallen off his radar by now. That *she* would've fallen off his radar. What had brought him back to the house? Trying to cover his tracks in case someone decided to dig deeper?

She'd wanted to get in there and dig first, but she hadn't wanted anyone to know she'd stuck around. If everyone—including her

214

mother's killer—thought she was long gone from here, then she would be safer. Some might think that disguising herself and staying off-grid was overkill, but they hadn't watched their mother get murdered. Hadn't gotten their own lives threatened. She knew with a piercing certainty that he wanted to find and kill her. She had to find him first.

"No, please don't do this. I'm sorry . . . I made a mistake. I shouldn't have asked for more . . ."

What had her mother meant by those words?

Charlie would get justice. The Hoback County Sheriff's Department had their hands full when the region exploded with tourists. Ongoing search and rescues. The list went on. She didn't know where the state police were on her mother's case, if anywhere. All she knew was that nobody cared as much about finding Momma's killer as she did.

Her vision blurred as the tears came. She swiped furiously at them.

"Oh, Momma, I miss you." Lowering the binoculars, she pressed her face against Amber's pink muzzle. Rubbed the horse's neck. Thought about her mother.

Momma never made much money from her job. But that didn't keep her from talking about the two of them taking a trip to Europe when Charlie graduated college. But Charlie didn't want to travel. All she wanted was to ride horses. She dreamed about them all the time and drove Momma crazy. On Charlie's fifteenth birthday, Momma finally took her to ride a horse. Then three years ago she met Mack and started to work for him on his ranch in the summers.

Pull it together now, girl. *"You were meant for great things."* She could hear Momma's words.

Now . . . now she was all alone in the world.

Mack was the only one she would trust. He'd been her only friend when her world fell apart. Well, Mack and Rufus, until the dog had run back to Mack. A man's best friend, sure. But apparently not a girl's best friend.

"That's okay." She slid her hand along Amber's neck, running her fingers through the coarse hair. "You and I understand each other, don't we?"

The horse chuffed.

Charlie loosely tied Amber's reins around a tree. "You stay here until I get back. I won't be long, I promise."

Riding Amber in was a good plan. She wished she'd thought of it sooner. She could enter through the back of the house. If anyone approached, she would hightail it out the same way, like she'd done the night she'd escaped certain death. She would run for Amber, who would carry her off into over three million acres of Bridger-Teton National Forest.

Charlie kept to the edge of the woods until she had to cross two acres of meadow and then made her way to the back of the house.

God, please keep me safe. Odd that the prayers came more often now. Momma hadn't been much of a churchgoer, and just when Charlie wanted to go to church, she couldn't. Not yet. At least Mack had loaned her a Bible.

Please help me find something tonight.

CHAPTER THIRTY-EIGHT

Growing up, Austin had spent as much time as he could in these woods, pretending he was someone else. Pretending he was safe. As if on a mission, he dragged Willow deeper into the dense forest. The familiar surroundings ignited memories, both good and bad.

Tensions had mounted at supper, given their conversation and Heath's question. His brother's words had disturbed Willow. Austin wanted to get her away from Heath so they could talk. So while Evelyn prepared a special dessert at Austin's request, he'd taken the opportunity to bring Willow to his woods. They always calmed him.

Maybe it had been a bad idea to stay at the house. He'd question Heath about his sudden agitation later. Austin was tired of secrets. Now that he suspected Heath was hiding something, Austin better understood how Willow had felt when he had closed himself off from her.

She tromped behind him. "How much farther?"

"We're here." Austin pointed at the small brook he'd wanted to show her, along with the remnants of a fort he and his brothers had built when they were kids. He was surprised any part of it remained. "Here's where I came to hide when Dad was drinking."

Even though he was much too late, if he was going to open up, now was the time. Would she want to hear it? By the look in her eyes as she took in the crumbling fort, he was making the right decision. He wished he hadn't waited so long.

Willow reached out and touched the rudimentary structure. "I'm sorry your life was so awful you felt you had to hide, but I'm glad you had a place to go."

Leaning against a tree, he felt the bark press into his back. He focused on that pain instead of the prick at his heart. "Before the fire. She left our father."

"Wait. Are you saying your mother left you behind with him?" A deep sadness interlaced her understanding tone.

That could undo him.

"Yes, that's what I'm saying. She couldn't take us with her. She couldn't afford three boys on her own. So she left us."

It felt good to open up, to let himself be vulnerable. To be seen and heard.

Willow drew near. Mosquitoes—the only thing he hated about these woods—buzzed around them, apparently only slightly deterred by the insect repellent they'd put on.

"I lost my parents in a car accident, but it has to hurt even more to know that your mother chose to leave you."

"He was harder on her. She thought we could take it. And we did. We made it through with only a few scars." The emotional scars took the longest to heal. "She came back to try again and the fire took her."

He expected to see pity but instead tenderness shone in Willow's eyes. Austin wanted to pull her close. He wanted to do so much more with her. But he shouldn't. He needed to protect himself. He didn't want to get hurt again. Nor did he want to hurt her. Emotionally, he was damaged goods. Opening up and being vulnerable to her might not have been such a good idea, after all.

"What are you thinking?" she asked.

Could he be that completely honest with anyone? His heart beat erratically at the thought of actually telling her. "I wish I could erase my past and knock down the walls that I built. I wish that you and I could start over."

Oh man. He'd said that out loud. His pulse pinging around inside, he held his breath. Longing poured from her eyes. Longing mixed with indecision. He knew exactly how she felt—he was feeling the same.

He thought he'd gotten over her, grown past his feelings for her, but he'd lied to himself. He leaned in, brushing the top of her head with his thumb, and down her soft cheek, to move her hair behind her ear. She inched her face up ever so slightly, and that was all the invitation he needed. He cupped her cheeks. All conscious thought left his mind.

Eyes closed, his lips touched hers—soft, supple. Needy. He drew in her essence, all that was Willow—a reminder of all he'd lost. All he could have had with her. His mind emptied of even his loss as he savored beautiful Willow, pulling her into his arms and deepening the kiss. Tonight he'd opened up his heart until she'd touched it. And now the world quaked beneath him. He had never kissed her like this.

It thrilled him.

It terrified him.

A low growl rumbled, morphing into a high-pitched, piercing shriek.

Willow startled and stepped away, but he caught her before she stumbled. She pressed into him as though afraid. "What *is* that?"

Austin held her nice and tight. "An elk. The sound of a bull elk bugle."

"A what? It sounded like a Ringwraith from *Lord of the Rings*."
He chuckled.

The elk bugled again, the sound bringing back memories. Willow appeared riveted as they listened. When it ended, she stepped from his arms, looking dazed. Was that from the elk or the kiss?

She put distance between them. Should he apologize? His throat thickened.

The walls were quickly going up around his heart—a defense mechanism, he knew. Should he even be considering a relationship with her again? He wanted to ask her, but maybe now wasn't the time. He feared what she might say. Willow had always been the open one, wanting to talk it out, and now here she stood, holding it all in.

That bewildered him. He never knew confusion could be so painful.

She touched the structure that had barely remained over the years. "You said you'd come here to hide."

"Yeah."

"I keep thinking about what Heath said. What if he's right? What if Charlie doesn't want to be found? What about her rights? If given a choice, would she want to know about her birth mother? What kind of torture would that bring to someone if they'd grown up believing their parents were their real parents? In searching for the truth about ancestry, there've been plenty of times we've come across discrepancies about relationships. It's never pretty. In fact, we learned my grandfather on my father's side fathered a child outside his marriage. So Dad had a half brother. He and Mom were on their way to find him when they died in the car accident."

He wanted to reach for her again. Comfort her. "Did he know they were coming?"

"No. That was a tough decision, but they thought it was best to approach him in person, or at least to try."

"So he still doesn't know?"

"No, and I have to wonder what good it would do for him to find out now. What difference can it make, except when a medical history might play into it? So maybe my uncle doesn't want to be found either. How can we know, Austin?" She looked up into his eyes. "How can we know if we're doing the right thing?"

"A crime was committed. We were hired by the victim's mother, herself a victim, to resolve a cold case. Still, I understand what you're asking. It's a hard question."

"And if we keep going, we could get her killed."

Or you, Willow. There had already been attempts on her life. JT had been murdered to stop the search. He thought about Michael Croft, whom he'd failed to save—of course, the man hadn't wanted his services.

Two women's lives were in danger now, and he wasn't sure how to keep either of them safe.

Then there was his monumental failure at the FBI. He'd made a tough call, and a life had been lost. He could still remember the crushing wails. The sound had reverberated through his being.

A shudder coursed over him.

"I guess we should pray about it and trust that God will lead us down the right path," she said.

Her faith was obviously stronger than his.

In the meantime, he'd talk to Heath and find out what had disturbed him. Suspicion coiled around Austin's gut. Heath was hiding something.

That seemed to be the family curse.

CHAPTER THIRTY-NINE

Darkness descended on the house. Charlie hadn't wanted to use her flashlight, but she had no choice. She flicked it on and continued searching through the rolltop desk. She might not get an opportunity to come back. Not with Clyde searching the house too. She assumed that was why he'd returned here. He could have found what he needed and destroyed it by now. Had he already searched through the desk?

Why had she been such a coward? She should have come back sooner. As it was, she'd forgotten the key to the house. But it was easy enough to get in through the unlocked window.

Think, Charlie, think. Where would Momma have put her bank statements if they weren't in the desk? Momma had told Charlie she had a trust fund from which she received monthly payments, although Momma's will hadn't said anything about her trust fund or named Charlie as the beneficiary. The lawyer didn't know anything either. Until Momma's death, Charlie had never considered it strange her mother would be the beneficiary of a trust fund. Until now, she had never even cared.

Charlie had gained access to Momma's bank account and

222

downloaded the statements from the last couple of years. Nothing unusual there. No money coming from said trust fund even before the date Momma claimed payments to her had stopped. She'd been livid.

And that was about two months before she was murdered.

Charlie wanted to know where the cash had come from—the father her mother never told her about? Some other family member? And why had it stopped? What did Clyde have to do with it?

That her mother's murder had to do with money was a reasonable assumption.

Dusk looming outside, she shut the desk. She still had to ride Amber back. Mack would probably be wondering where she'd gone and would send out a search party of one if he noticed she hadn't returned with the horse and he couldn't get ahold of her.

She pulled out the two-way radio. "Mack, you there?" She waited. Nothing.

She sent him a text. If she caught a signal at some point, the text should go through. Cell signals were spotty in the region, if she could get one at all, but that's why they used the radio. She had a SAT or satellite phone back at the cabin for emergencies only. She wasn't bleeding, so it wasn't an emergency. The phone was expensive and not much better than a cell phone anyway.

She shined the flashlight around the house as she crept to Momma's room. She was alone here, and it felt strange to be sleuthing in her own home.

Momma's bedroom.

The peaceful lavender comforter remained just as it had been when Charlie left and belied the violence that had occurred in this house. How much or how little had the authorities done to find her killer, especially given the sheriff's relationship to Clyde? Not nearly enough.

The closet door hung open. Charlie shined the light on Momma's shoes at the bottom. Momma loved the kind of shoes that she couldn't wear at her job as a nurse, while Charlie loved boots.

Shoes . . .

She dropped to her knees and pulled out the shoe boxes, dumping the pretty sandals and stilettos. No wonder Momma wanted to travel. Get out of town. She wanted to dress up but had no place to go. Charlie had been the reason she'd stayed. In the back corner she found the box that had contained her own favorite boots. Opening the box, she hit pay dirt.

Stacks of bank statements. Charlie hadn't known about this account. There were other boxes. Why hadn't the sheriff's department done more in their investigation? Why hadn't someone already discovered this? Unfortunately, Charlie knew exactly why. They didn't want to find it.

Nausea rolled like waves in her gut. If she had brought Bronc, she could take all the boxes back with her.

Light flashed across the wall from one side of the bedroom to the other.

Someone was coming. Heart pounding, Charlie grabbed a handful of the statements, then moved the boxes back into the corner. Stacked more shoes and boxes on top.

For a moment she thought about making a stand. This was her house after all. But someone had walked into the house and shot Momma. Staying hidden and doing her own investigation was the only way open to her.

She peeked between the mini blinds.

Sheriff Everett?

He trudged toward the house, his chin lifted from left to right as he searched the area. The only reason for him to be at the house was to investigate her mother's murder. Or to make sure any evidence that had been left behind was destroyed.

Some would say Charlie should work with him, but how could she trust him? He would side with Clyde like he'd already done.

Could even be involved. She didn't want Clyde, or anyone, to know she had stayed in the area.

She feared her ragged breaths would give her away as she slipped out the back window. Only trouble was, she couldn't get the window closed. It had jammed. If he looked through the house in the dark, he'd see that someone had been inside.

Please help me, God!

She ran through the dark and across the meadow, just like she had done that night two months ago.

"I'm going to kill you too." The gruff, unnatural voice resounded in her head as if she had just heard it. She stumbled but found her footing. Focus. She had to make it all the way across the field before the sheriff discovered someone had been in the house.

Breathing hard, she found the spot where she'd tied Amber to a tree. But Amber was gone. Had she, in her rush, failed to tie a decent knot? A beam of light flashed across the meadow. The sheriff. How far would he search?

Charlie had to find that horse. She looked behind her and spotted Amber through the trees.

In the meadow!

Not twenty-five yards from the sheriff. He would see her. To make matters worse, Amber trotted in Charlie's direction. The horse knew Charlie was in the woods. She'd simply wandered off to graze. The sheriff's light found the horse.

Charlie couldn't wait for Amber. *Sorry, Mack . . .*

CHAPTER FORTY

Too much was happening too fast. Her head would spin right off if she wasn't deliberate about holding herself together. With her left hand, she fingered the charm on the necklace Austin had given her. In the other hand, she gripped the mug of hot chocolate Heath had offered. He and Austin talked with Evelyn in the kitchen, fussing over the special dessert Evelyn had made.

Cheesecake. Willow's favorite. Austin had obviously told her. Evelyn wouldn't let them eat the cheesecake until it had properly chilled, which meant they'd have to wait until tomorrow, to Willow's way of thinking.

Willow should have been in there with them, talking and laughing. But she'd excused herself to sit on the sofa and watch the sunset—pink and orange clouds bursting around the silhouette of mountains. She drew a measure of peace from the scenery.

Austin's father must have been the worst sort of man. Why else would Austin ever leave such a beautiful place? Now that she was alone for a few moments, she allowed herself to think about his kiss. But she wouldn't think about it too long. Closing her eyes, she rested her head against the sofa and relived

226

the moment he'd drawn near, touched her face. Tingles had crawled over her.

She knew she shouldn't have led him on, but her heart had utterly disagreed with her mind and took charge, inviting his kiss. Willow could hardly believe he'd taken her up on it. Or had he been the one who'd sent the invitation and she'd given her permission? That part was a blur. Regardless, what was she supposed to do now? It had been hard enough working with the guy without thinking about everything she might have had with him, if she hadn't needed to know all his secrets.

And that was just it. Austin had opened up and shared with her. Why now? Why not back then? And what was she supposed to do? Thoughts of him filled her mind and senses. She couldn't afford to get distracted. But later, maybe later, after they found Charlie, she and Austin could explore a relationship. The kiss—had his intention been to let her know he wanted to try again? Willow needed to think about that long and hard, but with her romantic compass spinning, she wasn't sure which path to take.

Her phone buzzed in her pocket.

Dana. "Hey, thanks for calling back."

Phone to her ear, she perused the living room and listened to Dana. "Still looking for a Wyoming connection to Katelyn and Marilee Clemmons. Oh, and I know you didn't ask, but I searched records for Henry Haus to see if he did, in fact, have two sons like he said. After searching online resources and still getting nowhere, I decided to go ahead and create the Haus family tree myself to generate some applicable record hits. Turns out he only has one son. At least as far as I can confirm. So the nurse was right about the dementia. Or I could keep looking."

Willow held back her frustration. Dana likely needed the diversion, and she had only meant to help the poor old man. "We should really focus on finding out why Marilee took Charlie—if there's a link between her and Texas. No rabbit trails, okay?"

"You're right. Maybe the next time you see him, if you do, he'll claim he only had one son. But I'll tell you the interesting part about my search. The son I found isn't a Haus at all. A different name is listed for his father on the birth certificate. But in building the tree, I discovered Henry Haus is named as the great-grandfather of two children through this son who doesn't share his name, so I'm glad I built that family tree myself. Could be the son was adopted by a stepfather."

"Or Mr. Haus had an affair that produced a child." Like Willow's grandfather on her dad's side had done. Maybe that was the secret Marilee had kept for Mr. Haus, but Willow directed the conversation back. "I think we're getting closer to solving Katelyn Mason's mystery. We have to be."

"What am I missing? What more have you learned?"

Willow lowered her voice. "Someone left a note. Someone doesn't want us to find her. He threatened to kill her."

"What are you going to do? Please tell me you've gone to the authorities."

"Not yet. We're going to. But we have to figure out how to do that without the person behind this knowing. And he's watching. He knew I was at the cabin here at this guest ranch. He knew we were at the nursing home. This is making me sick. Katelyn's daughter's life is now in danger because we're searching."

"Don't forget about *your* life, Willow. Maybe I should talk to Austin and remind him to protect you. Sounds like you're still in danger even though you're in Wyoming instead of Washington."

For sure her heart was in danger. "No, please, you don't need to remind him. I know you're doing all you can from there, but please stay safe, Dana. If you're willing to keep working with me through this, that is."

"Of course. I want to get to the bottom of JT's death. We can't let someone get away with what they've done. What would you like me to do?"

"Just keep searching for Wyoming connections to Katelyn, or any other connections you think of—follow every lead, listen to every hunch. As for me, I want to find her and warn her, but I'm afraid to take even one step in that direction."

Headlights flashed up the long drive and bounced. "Looks like someone's coming. I need to go."

"Me too," Dana said. "I have the grandkids tonight. I'm making popcorn and we're going to watch a movie. Willow?"

"Yes?"

"Be careful. I'd much prefer it if you'd turn this over to the police or if the FBI would just open it back up. I want you to be safe."

"I know." Willow ended the call and stuck her phone in her pocket.

Heath and Austin headed out the front door. Through the window she watched them wait for the approaching vehicle. She took in this lovely home—the house Austin had grown up in—though it had been through a fire at some point years ago and more recently a renovation. This was his past, his history, the part that had been missing in their relationship before. She wasn't sure why it was so important to her, but she couldn't have imagined this day would come.

Thick photo albums rested on a shelf. Her heart jumped. Maybe she could get a better look into his family, his childhood. It surprised her that the albums had survived a fire and would be kept at all. Austin had a major aversion to remembering his past and childhood. Maybe things had been loving at first, but then everything changed. Willow wanted to know more. The albums could hold precious pictures of them with their mother. A happy family.

She snatched one from the shelf and flipped through the photographs, wishing she had hours to look through all of them. She wasn't completely certain Austin would want her digging this deep into his life, even though he had opened up to her tonight, throwing her equilibrium completely off balance.

A photograph—something more recent—was jammed in the back of the album. Austin wasn't in the picture. Heath stood next to a horse along with a young girl. An older teenager. Willow removed the photograph and held it near the lamp emitting soft yellow light.

Oh. My.

Apparently Austin wasn't the only McKade brother who kept secrets.

CHAPTER FORTY-ONE

A Hoback County Sheriff's Department SUV towing a short horse trailer crunched along the gravel. Apprehension stirred in Heath's gut. His property was in Bridger County but bordered Hoback. Sheriff Everett stepped out of his vehicle. Heath had never liked the guy before, but he especially didn't now that he knew Charlie's reservations about him. He had a bad feeling about this.

"Sheriff, what can I do for you?"

"You can take your horse off my hands."

"Come again?"

"I don't like bringing the trailer up here. Takes too long." Everett walked around to the horse trailer. Heath and Austin followed the sheriff and watched him open the trailer.

Heath instantly recognized Charlie's favorite horse. He schooled his features, allowing his surprise to show but not his utter panic. Charlie had taken the horse out earlier in the day for a long ride. Heath had tried to call her on her cell when she didn't answer the radio. While Austin was taking that walk with Willow, Heath had wanted to talk to Charlie about why they were here. He hadn't

231

panicked then, because in these mountains, cell service wasn't always a guarantee. But the lack of radio response worried him.

Heath took the reins and ran his hand down Amber's neck, walking her the rest of the way down the ramp.

"Are all your clients accounted for?"

"As far as I know. But I definitely need to check on that."

"You could start with who was riding this horse. I found the mare grazing over on the Clemmons property in the back. That's fifteen miles from here, depending on which route you take. Maybe the trails are faster."

Heath didn't want to lie to the law, but he had too many suspicions about Silas Everett and wouldn't jeopardize Charlie's secret or her life. Everett wasn't in his own county anyway. He only brought the horse back to give him an excuse to ask questions.

"I'm not a horseman, but I think it's highly unlikely the horse would have wandered off on her own to that property."

"You never know," Heath said.

For the life of him, he didn't know what more to say. *Try the truth, Heath?* Except Charlie had trusted him when she couldn't trust the sheriff. If Heath couldn't find her, then he would give the Bridger County sheriff a call. Sheriff Haines. A search and rescue team would be sent out. Charlie would be exposed then.

Another thought accosted him. What if the man who wanted to kill her had found her?

Please, no . . .

He wouldn't let his mind even consider that possibility. Still, it gave rise to the question—was he doing the wrong thing by hiding Charlie? What if she was out there somewhere hurt? Or murdered? He needed to find her. But he didn't need Everett's help.

Best get this sheriff on his way.

"Is there something you want to tell me, McKade?"

Heath shook his head. Charlie didn't want anyone to know she was still in the area. Didn't want her would-be killer to know. But he'd obviously hired professionals to find her—Austin and Willow. They claimed her mother had hired them to find her—well, her mother was dead. Who else had hired them except the person who wanted to find and kill her?

Heath had always considered himself a decisive man and had never been cornered like this. No matter which way he turned, he could see no clear path.

"I have something to tell you." Willow appeared out of nowhere. Heath hadn't noticed her approach. She stepped up and introduced herself.

She shared the story of the missing girl with the sheriff.

Oh, I really wish you hadn't done that.

"You told Sheriff Haines we were barking up the wrong tree, but this note says otherwise." Willow held up a bagged slip of paper.

"Willow. What are you doing?" Austin asked, his brow furrowed.

"I'm sorry, Austin, I don't think we can wait any longer," she said, and directed her next words to the sheriff. "Someone left it on our Jeep today outside of a nursing home. Proof enough that she's alive and well and someone doesn't want us to find her. I'm giving you the note so you can investigate. Sheriff Haines has the other note. We'll turn over all we know and all we've found so far. But you likely know this girl, since her mother was murdered in your county not two months ago. She's in danger. I might be endangering her by telling you now."

"Have you found who murdered Marilee Clemmons?" Austin asked.

Sheriff Everett stared at the bag she held and shook his head. "You think her murder is connected to this person leaving you notes to stop looking for Charlie?"

"Yes," Austin said.

The sheriff's features shifted as though he couldn't decide how to react to the news. Finally, he forced a controlled expression and took the note from her. "Appreciate you letting me know. Are you going to stick around in case I have questions after I look into this?"

"I'm not sure how long we're staying," Willow said. "But since we were hired by her birth mother to find her, that isn't going to stop, despite the notes."

"Even with the threat to her life?" the sheriff asked.

Willow's eyes flicked to Heath, a feral glint in them. What was that about?

"No disrespect to you, but Mrs. Mason hired us because law enforcement let her down. I have to see this through."

Sheriff Everett grimaced but said nothing more. Got in his truck and slowly headed down the driveway. Willow stomped away. Austin stared after her, his face contorted.

Heath didn't have time to think about the growing tension.

I have to find Charlie!

CHAPTER FORTY-TWO

Austin found Willow in her room. She'd stomped off when the sheriff left. Heath had done the same as he led the horse away to the barn. Nobody had eaten the cheesecake, which was probably just as well. Evelyn insisted it wasn't ready. Regardless, he carried a slice up to Willow now that it had had more time to cool. Poor Evelyn had gone to all that work because Austin had given her the special request.

He had no idea why Willow had gone ahead and told the sheriff about their case when Austin had asked her for time to carefully consider their next step. He peered through the half-open door. Willow's duffel bag lay open on the bed. His heart dropped.

He nudged the door all the way open. "What are you doing?"

She peeked around him down the hallway, then drew him inside her room covertly. Like an informant.

"What's going on?" He set the ignored cheesecake on the desk.

"Sh. Keep your voice down." She paced the small room. "I'm packing. I'm leaving."

A chill crept up his spine. "What's happened?"

Unshed tears glistened in her eyes. Austin wanted to reach for

235

her and tell her it was going to be okay. He mentally chained his arms to his sides.

"I don't know how to tell you this." She turned her back to him and walked to the window to peek out, then she shut the mini blinds.

Confusion rolled through him, trying his patience. "How about you tell me, Willow, before you drive me crazy?"

She slowly turned to face him but kept near the window. "Heath has been lying to us."

Dread soured in his gut. "What are you talking about?"

"Please tell me you didn't know."

He fisted his hands. Okay. Now he had to hold in his frustration. "What are you talking about?"

"Heath knows Charlie."

Austin couldn't have heard her right. He stood there a moment, letting her words soak in. The walls of the room pushed out, then closed in. "I don't understand. What do you mean?"

She took a step closer, her expression like a mother coddling a child. "I found a picture of Heath standing next to Charlie and that very same horse the sheriff brought back tonight." The tears spilled over this time.

I don't believe you!

"Please tell me you didn't know. You're always hiding stuff. Nothing's changed. I thought we . . ."

Austin pressed a hand against the wall to hold it up before it came crashing down on him. She was actually accusing him of hiding things again? No. He couldn't think about her accusing him. He had to focus on her accusations regarding Heath. "I need to see the picture. Where is it?"

"What? You don't believe me?"

"It has to be a mistake."

She moved to the duffel and took out the picture. "Here, since you think I'm lying."

"I didn't say you're lying." He yanked the photograph away and stared at it. Sure enough, Heath stood next to a girl who he would recognize without the age progression photos—she looked so much like her mother. "I don't know what to say." Or think.

"Austin," she whispered.

The hurt in her voice said volumes.

He risked a glance at her, angry with himself. Hadn't he warned himself to keep his distance from her when it came to his heart? But she'd wounded him. "How could you even *entertain the idea* that I knew about this?"

She sucked in a breath and seemed to shake off her own pain. Her sorrowful eyes pleaded with him. "I'm sorry, I don't know what to think. What if it's him? What if he only wanted to keep us close so he could keep tabs on us? What if he's leaving the notes?"

"You don't believe that."

"I don't want to believe it. But it kind of makes sense."

"No, it makes no sense whatsoever." Austin thought back to the moment they had received the picture of Charlie and Heath had seen it. He'd definitely reacted. Austin should have caught it then. His training should have told him Heath knew something. Austin thought Heath might have been hiding something. But this hadn't entered his mind. No. Now he was lying to himself. That wasn't it at all. Austin had refused to believe Heath's reaction was related to the girl. He had denied the truth because he wanted the reconciliation he was working through with Heath to succeed.

He handed back the photograph. "I'm going to talk to Heath."

Austin opened the door. With a glance over his shoulder, he spotted the duffel bag again. He thought better of just walking out and instead closed the door. One, then two steps, and he was close to Willow. He thought back to the moment he'd kissed her. That had been the biggest mistake in his recent history. He could never get over the past because he kept making new mistakes.

Still, he wanted to mend the hole in the earth between them that had formed because of Heath's lie.

"Please . . . please, wait for me here. I'm going to talk to Heath. This could all be a misunderstanding. If he knows her, then we could find her tonight before her life is threatened." Austin searched her eyes, her demeanor, hoping to see agreement.

She was marble.

"Look, you don't know my brother like I do. Heath has always been about honor. He always does the right thing. That's why he's been able to build this reputable guest ranch, despite our father's reputation in the area." Her doubt created a painful knot inside his gut. Anger twisted it tighter. Still, he needed her to believe him. She was upset. She couldn't have really meant what she said.

He desperately wanted his words to her to be true. But even if they were true, Heath had lied to them both. He'd hidden that he knew Charlie—a lie of omission.

Austin would save his anger for that conversation, which would likely send them back to where they'd been for the last several years. Estranged.

CHAPTER FORTY-THREE

Willow stared at the door after Austin walked out.

She plopped on the bed. Tossed the duffel across the room. She grabbed her necklace and almost yanked the chain to rip it off but caught herself. Why was she even wearing it? She never should have accepted it. She reached for the clasp, but the kiss—that kiss—thoughts of it flooded her mind.

She dropped her hands, leaving the pendant where it lay against her heart. She couldn't bring herself to remove it.

"What am I going to do?" Her shoulders sagged.

The duffel bag on the floor called to her. A big part of her wanted to pack and move to a hotel in Grayback. Or even as far as Jackson to get away from the brothers and their secrets, especially the former FBI agent brother with whom she'd shared a past. Her feelings for Austin had grown when she hadn't thought she'd watered them. Obviously the root had remained alive and well, deep in the soil of her heart. But those feelings for him could be clouding her judgment about everything. Putting some space between them might help her think clearly. Might help her see what she was missing.

Could she walk out on him? She sighed. Not like that. Somehow she had to find the strength to overcome the vortex of wild emotions swirling around her, threatening to overtake her, to suck her down and keep her there. Sheer exhaustion and a heavy heart weighed on her. All she wanted to do was curl up and sleep. She changed into sweats and a T-shirt, grabbed her laptop, and crawled under the covers. She couldn't waste time sleeping.

It had been all she could do to keep from insisting she go with Austin to face his brother. She wanted to see the look on Heath's face when he learned what she had discovered. But Austin had enough issues with his brother tangled up in this home and their father. Issues they had appeared to be working through. She didn't want to be the one to shatter that.

Would everything Austin had gained by coming here be destroyed when he faced Heath?

God, please, no.

Willow spent a few minutes sending up her heartfelt prayers for the brothers, for Katelyn Mason, and for Katelyn's daughter, whom they now believed was Charlie. She should call the terminally ill woman to see how she was doing. Maybe telling her they were this close would give her enough hope to survive the onslaught of illness that had returned, but, then again, worry and concern for her daughter in danger could do her in. Better to leave Katelyn with the hope that Willow and Austin were making progress and would find her daughter soon.

She thought back through what they knew so far, and what she'd been through. They believed JT had been murdered. The house he'd shared with Willow had been burned down. She could have died in the fire. Arson with intent to kill. Her life remained threatened and now Charlie's life as well.

Who was behind this?

The woman who had been a nurse and had recently worked in a nursing home had walked into that hospital room two decades ago and stolen Katelyn's baby. The FBI and the police had decided it had been a random act, unfortunately common enough, because there had been no ransom note. Nothing to gain by stealing the baby even though Katelyn had been an overnight millionaire.

But if Marilee was that woman—and Willow was reasonably certain she was—then she was gone, murdered two months ago, before the attacks on Willow had even begun. Someone else had been involved. Someone with the means to travel to Seattle and Wyoming. Someone with a motive strong enough to commit murder and willing to risk being discovered by leaving threatening notes. If only she still had the notes, then she could compare them with Heath's writing. There had to be something in this house with his handwriting on it. Still, the very idea of him writing the notes sickened her.

The cheesecake that Austin had brought up rested on the desk. He'd been so thoughtful. Again. But she couldn't eat it now.

Willow hoped these new events would be reason enough for the FBI and other law enforcement entities to reopen the cold case on the Mason baby. But regardless of what direction their investigations took, Willow had to finish this for Katelyn, and for JT, who'd accepted the challenge. Though he was deceased, his business reputation was at stake. Willow couldn't work his last case and fail. Even though he was gone, she'd feel like she was letting him down. Willow had wanted him to be proud of her.

Sheer terror at the thought of failing unfolded inside her. Heart tumbling, she closed her eyes and breathed slowly until the ache in her chest was gone.

What would JT have done under these circumstances? Why had he *really* planned to come to Wyoming?

I'm missing something. It's probably staring me in the face, and I can't see it.

She would never see it unless she could push past the angst brought on by being too emotionally involved with Austin. It was time to get over it and get to work.

She opened her laptop and found Dana's email containing the link and log-in to the genealogy site she had been using to build the Haus family tree. She almost ignored it, but curiosity snagged her. Who was the son who Marilee had kept a secret? If in fact that was the secret to which Mr. Haus had referred.

She pulled up the information, though she struggled to focus. She stared at the computer screen while her mind remained on Austin and Heath. An image of Heath's face when he first saw Charlie's picture continued to play in her mind. She should have suspected it right then, in that moment. But she hadn't wanted to believe it. She had wanted to trust that his sudden coolness had nothing to do with Charlie. That's what happened when one was too close to someone.

Heath and Austin had practice at hiding secrets. Maybe she shouldn't blame Austin—he'd spent a lifetime hiding that his father had been an alcoholic and the brutality he'd experienced at his hands.

Was a drunk father better than no father?

Willow didn't know. She could only imagine.

She fluffed her pillow and sat up taller in bed, blinked her eyes, and stared at the information in front of her.

The Haus family tree. Mr. Henry Haus was linked to great-grandchildren through their grandfather, Silas Everett.

Sheriff Silas Everett was Mr. Haus's biological son?

Definitely a family secret, considering the birth certificate, but was that the secret that Marilee had kept for Mr. Haus? Could she have been murdered for that knowledge? Willow didn't know why that information would warrant murder. To protect an inheritance perhaps? It wouldn't be the first time.

But that could mean the sheriff was mixed up in Marilee's murder somehow. Charlie could be the one to identify her mother's murderer—which was why someone didn't want her to be found.

And Willow had just handed off the note to him.

CHAPTER FORTY-FOUR

Austin marched toward the barn, the house fifty yards behind him. Evelyn sat up in the living room reading *Reader's Digest*. He could see the house from this distance. Willow would be safe for the moment.

The lights were on in the barn and shadows moved inside. When Austin entered the barn, the scent of leather, hay, and wood shavings accosted him. The smells brought an explosion of memories, both good and bad, making this conversation that much more difficult.

Heath had already taken care of Amber. He worked to place a saddle and tack on his feisty dun stallion, Boots. His stern gaze remained on his horse.

Austin swallowed the accusations. He knew better than to approach with his mouth loaded and ready to shoot. He fisted his hands to hold back the anger. "What are you doing?" He barely contained his fury with the question.

"I'm getting ready to take a ride."

"You do that often?"

"What? Ride at night? No."

"Then why are you doing it now?"

Heath narrowed his eyes. "What's with all the questions?"

Regret boiled up inside, born from every mistake he'd ever made. He didn't want to open up the chasm between them when they had only started building a bridge. Their estrangement wasn't Heath's fault. It had never been. That burden lay with Austin.

Still, how did he ask him why he'd hidden the fact that he knew Charlie, the very girl Austin and Willow searched for?

"You have something on your mind, Austin, but I'm sorry, I don't have time to talk right now."

"You lied to us."

Heath dropped his radio, the only sign that Austin's words had affected his brother. Heath picked it up and secured it to his belt, then placed his hands flat on Boots as if the horse would topple over. He hung his head. "What did you say?"

"Willow found the picture that proves you know Charlie. You knew the instant we showed you the picture. Why are you hiding that?" *Please tell me something I can believe and let me see the truth in your eyes.*

Heath continued to hang his head for a good long moment. When he finally looked up, his eyes held a challenge of his own. "I'll answer that question if you'll answer one of mine."

"Go ahead. Shoot." Austin crossed his arms. This was just like old times. When they were boys, they would've found themselves wrestling before too much longer. The situation might even come to that now. He hoped not.

Releasing the horse to stand on its own, Heath faced Austin, though he kept ahold of the reins. "How much do you know about this person who hired you to find her?"

Relief filled Austin's chest. "That's easy. This girl is part of an FBI cold case. Our client, Katelyn Mason, is her birth mother. Charlie was stolen from her hospital room two decades ago. It's not a lie fabricated to find her."

244

"And you're absolutely sure that she's Charlie's mother? Because Charlie has a killer after her. She's hiding from him and doesn't want to be found."

Austin nodded, understanding taking hold. "I can see how that might look. But Katelyn Mason isn't that killer. And someone else doesn't want us to find her." Austin relayed everything that had happened to Willow and her grandfather—the details they'd left out earlier at dinner.

Heath dropped the reins. "It's a shock. This news is . . . I didn't know her mother well, but the girl was loved. I met her mom when she brought her to start riding horses. I just can't believe this is true. It's going to crush her. That girl loved her mother. Still does, though she's gone. It was an awful thing for her to watch her mother brutally murdered. That was hard enough." Heath shook his head. "Nobody can know she's still here. Let them all think she went back to the University of Wyoming to finish out her last two semesters. Do you hear me? Nobody."

"The notes make it sound like the killer knows where she is and is allowing her to live as long as we don't keep searching."

"The guy who killed her mother threatened to kill her too. If he knew where she was, she would already be dead." Heath climbed onto Boots and reined in the lively stallion.

Austin wasn't done with this conversation. "I can understand why you didn't come forward with what you know. Why you didn't tell that sheriff. But don't you think now's the time to give her up so we can protect her from the killer? Let her meet her birth mother?"

Heath sighed. "She won't be easy to convince. She believes she can find out who killed her mother. But you digging into this has stirred up a hornet's nest. She might not realize she's in even more danger."

"Is that where you're going? To find her?"

"Yeah, I'm worried about her. If she's all right, then I'll leave her there, where she's safest. She was riding Amber today. Didn't answer my calls, though getting a signal in the mountains is tricky. But that's what the radio is for."

"And she didn't answer that?"

Heath shook his head. Austin caught the horse's reins. "I'll ride out with you."

"Aren't you on bodyguard duty? I'll be fine, little brother. If I can't find her, then we'll call in search and rescue; if I can, I'll try to convince her to come in. But I'm not going to be the one to tell her about her mother—a woman she adored. That's a hard one to wrap my mind around, and she wasn't even my mother."

"You've always been the one to protect others. You protected me from Dad. Just, please, be careful."

Heath's blue eyes darkened beneath his Stetson. Easy enough to see that the guy was beyond worried about Charlie as he rode off into the night.

Austin decided he'd leave the barn lights on for Heath for when he returned. He trudged back to the house and found Evelyn had already gone to bed. He headed up the stairs, hoping to find Willow awake so he could share what he'd learned from Heath. He paused in front of her doorway. The lights were off. He pressed his forehead against the smooth white finish and listened to her soft snores. At least she'd stayed. Relief blew through him.

He would wait until morning to tell her what he had already known—that Heath was one of the good guys.

CHAPTER FORTY-FIVE

Charlie spotted a quick flash of light in the darkness—moonlight bouncing off a solar panel before it disappeared behind the approaching clouds.

The cabin.

Though her feet and legs ached, she picked up her pace until she could make out the place she'd called home the last few weeks. If she didn't know her way around these mountains, she would have been in serious trouble. She'd had to stay focused with each step so she didn't trip over rocks or gnarled tree roots or fall into a ravine. The small log cabin never looked so good. She unlocked the door, entered, and closed it before sagging against the cedar logs.

That had been a close call.

Her phone buzzed. She read a text from Mack. He'd been trying to reach her, he said.

I'm riding out to meet you. Please answer my text.

When she'd fled the house, she'd left the stupid radio at the bottom of the closet. The sheriff, if he ventured into the house, might find that—and then what?

247

She quickly answered the text, hoping she could stop Mack before he made the trip. He'd have to get a signal in order to receive her text though. She could try the SAT phone. He'd probably tried her on that, considering this an emergency.

If she stood just right in the cabin, she could get one bar on her cell. When his text back to her came through, she breathed a sigh of relief.

Mack texted that they needed to talk. She replied and apologized about Amber and said that she would be at work tomorrow. They could talk then. She was exhausted after her three-hour trek back to the cabin. She'd messed up good this time. Sheriff Everett would call Mack to come retrieve Amber or would return her himself. Either way, how would Mack explain the horse being on that property?

The horse's presence would make Sheriff Everett ask questions. She had utterly exposed herself tonight. But she wouldn't let that be for nothing. She had to be close to finding out who killed her mom. Anxious to look through the bank statements, she would risk using the lamp tonight. Besides, she'd spent several hours walking the trails in the dark when her flashlight gave out. The light would go a long way to boost her spirits.

She set the lamp on the table and stacked the bank statements she'd held on to through the cold night. She thumbed through them and found what she was looking for.

A deposit once a month for three thousand dollars. That wasn't the money Momma had made from her job at the nursing home. It was from the trust fund she had mentioned—Endeavor Holdings. That told Charlie something and nothing. But who was the money from? Almost forty grand a year. And why had the money stopped coming through two months before someone murdered her?

Charlie's feet ached and her shins throbbed. Her head wasn't much better. Exhaustion cut her to the bone. She shouldn't let herself give in to the waves of doubt and regret, grief and sorrow rippling over her. But maybe just this once.

She pressed her head into her arms on the table and sobbed.

CHAPTER FORTY-SIX

Austin gripped his weapon. While he waited for Heath to return, he'd walk the perimeter of the house. Make sure no one was lurking in the shadows. He couldn't trust that their stalker would just leave a note this time. Why had his tactics changed? Add to that, they were in Wyoming now. Not Washington. Different state. Different tactics.

He moved quietly downstairs and checked all the windows. Made sure they were locked. Front door too. The lights were soft on the porch so the ambience of nature wouldn't be disturbed. Still, anyone approaching could be easily spotted.

Austin slipped out the back, where someone could be waiting under the cover of shadow in the forest hugging the cabin. Part of him hoped to find someone. Austin could take him down and get answers. End the threat on Charlie's and Willow's lives.

He stood pressed against the back wall of the house. Waiting. Listening. The night remained still except for a breeze that pushed clouds across the dark sky that would eventually bring rain.

Nothing moved. Not even the forest critters. His sixth sense kicked in—someone was there. He felt it in his bones.

But the person wasn't moving either. He knew Austin waited for him. Would he lose him tonight? Was his presence chasing the man away? He readied his gun.

Where are you?

A noise drew his attention. Someone approached from around the corner of the house. He hoped it wasn't Willow. She could have woken up, knocked on his door, and discovered he'd left. He whipped around the corner, pointed his weapon, and was met by a burst of electricity that coursed violently through his body, forcing his muscles to contract. He gritted his teeth through the loss of control. Rigid, his body fell back. On the ground, Austin fought the pain and stared helplessly at the masked man. But Tasers had AFID—Anti-Felon Identification Tags. With each firing, confetti marked with the device serial number released. Cleaning those up would take time, if the masked man even tried. This guy might have just made his first mistake.

Still, it wouldn't matter if something happened to Willow.

Willow! God, please protect her . . .

The man hovered over him and slammed the butt of a weapon down at him.

Everything went black.

CHAPTER FORTY-SEVEN

A shadowy presence filled her dreams. Tugged at her awareness.

Wake up . . .

The words startled into her mind. Fear squeezed her lungs, forcing out her breath. She gasped for air and opened her eyes. Something pressed over her lips. A masked face filled her vision. Terror raced through her veins. Jerking her head back and forth, she screamed. The tape over her mouth muffled the sound. Nobody would hear her.

Help! Help me! God, please help me!

Heart pounding, she lifted her hands to fight, but stronger hands pinned her wrists with bone-crushing force and placed plastic ties around them. Her strength was no match for him, but she forced space between her wrists as he secured the ties.

His body weight bound her, trapped her beneath him. A knife glistened in the moonlight an instant before she felt the sting at her throat. Was this it then? He would kill her? Then why tie her?

His dark eyes remained on hers. The knife was a warning—the same one she thought she'd dreamed about. Saying nothing, he flipped the blanket off while keeping the knife against her throat.

251

A pinprick of pain lanced her neck. Warm fluid ran down the side. He'd drawn blood. His strategy worked. She couldn't move if she tried to.

She wanted to ask why he was doing this. All manner of law enforcement would be searching for her. That is, as soon as Austin discovered her missing.

Austin. What about Austin? What had the man done with him? Her body trembled as hot tears seared across her temples.

She spotted her duffel bag resting on the chair. That wasn't where she'd left it. The bag appeared packed. *No, no, no.* He was going to make it look like she'd left of her own free will. It would buy him time. No one would look for her if they thought she'd left on her own. If only she hadn't left Austin with the impression that she might leave. In fact, she'd said as much.

Hopelessness gripped her.

He hovered near her, preparing to cover her head with a dark cloth bag.

With her eyes, she pleaded with him—*please don't hurt me. Please don't do this.* What could he possibly hope to gain by taking her? He shoved the bag over her head. Grabbed her and tossed her over his shoulder, marching down the stairs with her in a fireman's carry. What about Evelyn and Austin? Heath? Why hadn't they heard the intruder? Were they okay? *Please, God, let them be okay!*

If Austin was all right, this would not be happening.

She thrashed against the man's shoulder, jabbing him with her elbows. Maybe he would drop her. She wouldn't make this easy for him. But he snatched her before she fell and squeezed her until it hurt, never saying a word. The man walked right out the front door with her. She tried to gauge where they were headed. If she figured correctly, he was putting her in the back of the Jeep. Austin's rental? This guy had the keys? Her heart twisted.

Again, she thrashed. Heath! Where was Heath? His dogs. Why weren't they barking? The man dropped her into the back and closed the hatch. She hit with a thud, the breath rushing from her lungs. She didn't want to be weak. Had never wanted to crumble under the weight of everything that had happened, but if ever there was a moment to fall apart, this was it. Maybe if she got it out of her system, she could think of a way to escape.

Sobs racked and choked her.

Willow let the tears come as the Jeep bounced over the rough drive out of Emerald M Ranch. How could this be happening? Why hadn't the man simply killed her while she was still in bed?

His motivation was obvious. Without Willow, Austin would stop his search for Charlie. He hadn't been hired by Katelyn, after all. Once he figured out Willow had been abducted, then the search would be on for her instead. All eyes would be focused on finding her instead of Charlie.

That gave her hope that Austin might be down but not out. But then nobody would be searching for Charlie. This man was going to kill her.

No, no, no, no . . .

Willow had to escape. She had to find a way out. Get out of these ties. But the Jeep rocked and rolled over boulders, tossing her around in the back. Finally, it stopped, and the man got out. He came around for her. If she remembered correctly, there was a deep ravine—a big drop—along this portion of the drive. Her jaw clenched with utter terror. He was going to throw her off the cliff? She had to get out of this. *How am I going to do this?*

Kick him in the face? That's what she would do. Kick him when he opened the hatch. All she needed was a split second—

The hatch opened, and he yanked her out before she could react, then threw her over his shoulder like she was already dead. But she was still very much alive and would fight. She twisted and kicked.

"No! Please, don't! Why are you doing this?" she yelled. He wouldn't be able to understand her muffled words, but he would know she was pleading with him.

It made no difference. He continued his hike.

Willow wouldn't make this easy for him. She wouldn't let the creep toss her over. Heart pounding, she tried elbowing him in the back. He grunted but never let her go. It was no use. Squeezing her eyes shut, she tried to escape images of the terror that awaited her.

She hoped the fall would kill her quickly and she wouldn't be left to die in pain. His footfalls crunched over the pebbled road as he carried her to meet her death. Her breaths came hard and fast.

He yanked her from his shoulder and dropped her. She expected to freefall but instead hit something hard, pain seizing her back. The smell of stale cigarettes, burning oil, and gasoline accosted her. The slam and latch of a car trunk confirmed that she was once again in the trunk of a vehicle.

In the distance, an engine started. The Jeep?

Trees crashed. Had he sent it over the cliff?

Her gut tensed and she recoiled.

He hadn't tossed her over the cliff. She had a second chance to escape.

The car she was in started. As the vehicle traversed the rocky path, once again, her body lurched and rolled in the space. Eventually, the ride evened out. He had driven them from the ranch driveway to the forest road and finally to the main highway. That much she could tell.

Time to get to work.

First, she had to get out of the ties and then she could free her ankles and remove the bag from her head. She'd been blessed with small hands. The guy had been in too big a hurry when he was tying up her hands to notice she'd spaced out her wrists to give herself room. She hadn't been able to get it done while in the Jeep, but now maybe she would have time. Willow slowly worked her wrists back and forth until the plastic ties slid off. Yes!

Then she ripped the bag off her head and the tape off her

mouth. It was too dark to see anything or look for something to cut the ties from her ankles. She tried to undo the clasp, but it was no use.

But she could feel her way around. There had to be something in this trunk. Maybe tools to change a tire could help her cut the ties. She had to free her legs before she bothered searching for the emergency hatch release, if this car even had one. Opening the hatch would do her no good in the middle of nowhere Wyoming if she couldn't run away.

The drive had smoothed out considerably and the vehicle accelerated. Where was he taking her?

Why, God, why? Panic once again squeezed her chest.

What would JT do? He never would have found himself in this situation, that's what.

When her parents died, she was a child. Their vehicle veered off a bridge and into a river, and she kept asking her grandfather why it had happened. JT shook his head and nudged her gently on the chin, then told her, "It was an accident, Willow. If something like that ever happens to you, remember to breathe and calm your mind. Come up with a plan, but don't take too long. You have to open the window before you hit the water."

"Open the window before you hit the water."

She had to open this trunk before it was too late. The tires screeched. The vehicle swerved. Metal crunched. Momentum slammed her against the side. Her whole body ached from the impact. What had happened?

Quiet. Everything was suddenly still and quiet.

Then a groan . . .

The man grumbled and cursed, spewing unintelligible words except for one—moose. She didn't recognize the voice. But it was too late now. He would come for her, and she still hadn't untied her legs. Her heart raced as the footfalls lumbered to the back of the car.

"Open the window before you hit the water."

Willow positioned herself to greet her abductor feet first.

The latch disengaged.

She kicked out with all her strength, flinging open the trunk. Caught him smack in the jaw. No time to waste. She scrambled from the space to see that he lay sprawled next to a boulder. He must have tripped and fallen over it when she kicked the trunk open and into him. He could be unconscious. Or dead. She wouldn't stay to find out.

She hopped around the car to find the front end smashed. She wouldn't be driving her way out of this, but she reached for the keys. Searched for something—anything—to cut the ties on her ankles, all while watching the man closely to see if he got up and came for her. He appeared injured, his right arm hanging oddly.

She frantically searched the front seat of the car. A knife! Probably the one he'd threatened her with. She grabbed it and cut the ties. She took another quick glance around inside the vehicle and didn't see another weapon but did spot her duffel.

I'll just take that, thank you very much. Along with the knife.

Willow knew she couldn't physically engage the man, even when he was injured. She had to leave before he came to—she'd take her chances in the Wyoming wilderness.

FRIDAY, 11:15 P.M.
GROS VENTRE WILDERNESS

Her breaths came fast as she made her way through the woods, hiding behind the spruce and fir trees in her bare feet. She needed shoes. Had he packed those in her duffel? Even if he had, she didn't have time to search.

Help me, God! Help me get away. Someone has to live to tell the story.

Her poor, tender feet. Pine needles and sticks jabbed her, but she had to keep running. She had to live. She had never wanted to see a grizzly bear in these woods, but she wished for one now and that it would charge the man pursuing her.

A gunshot rang out. Had that been meant for her? She hadn't seen a gun, but he must have had it on him.

Willow jostled her way past the trees, low-lying branches slashing her face and body. Darkness engulfed her. Touching the prickly branches and needles, the bark of trees, she felt her way forward as if in a horror flick. She couldn't see a thing. The good news was her pursuer couldn't see her either. He couldn't follow.

Which way should she head? She was more than lost. But then, getting lost wasn't such a bad thing if it meant she was safely away from her abductor. Right now it was more important to hide and survive the night. She kept moving between the trees and thick undergrowth until she found her rhythm. Her eyes adjusted to the strange, eerie darkness of the forest beneath a thick canopy as brief slivers of moonlight broke through the clouds. If only she could pick up speed, maybe she could lose this freak.

His breathing resounded not far behind.

He was still following her?

And closing in.

Fear clawed at her.

I'm doing the best I can and it's not enough. Jesus, help me!

Willow continued until she couldn't take another step. She leaned against a tree trunk, the rough bark pressing into her back, and caught her breath. She had to keep moving. This was her chance to get free. If she could somehow stop this man, or pull off his mask, then that would solve one mystery—but it was far too dangerous. It was all she could do to make an escape.

So Willow ran. Stumbled and fell.

She picked herself up, ignoring the pain in her knees.

I can do this. If it's the last thing I do, I can do this.

His rasping breaths and curses grew distant as she ran. Light glowed in the forest. He'd finally turned on a flashlight. She had to keep moving. Couldn't let her guard down. But how could she keep up this pace all night?

Chances were the man would keep searching until he found her, if he could. And if he caught her—well, she could be sure he would kill her this time.

What felt like hours later, but was probably no more than twenty minutes, she finally lost the beam of light.

Willow slid down a tree trunk and discovered a hollow. She willed herself partially inside, shoving away images of spiders and creepy, crawling insects. Even though the exertion of her escape had her sweating, the temperature had dropped at nightfall and a chill quickly seeped into her bones.

In the hollow, she waited until her breaths finally slowed. The utter silence of night in the national forest closed in on her. No croaking frogs or chirping insects. Along with darkness and silence, cold had settled in the mountains.

Willow waited and listened. She wasn't sure how far she'd run. He'd followed her for much too long, before the light had disappeared. She hoped he had continued in the wrong direction.

Stumbled over a cliff. She almost laughed at the thought. *Better him than me.*

That fear wedged into her thoughts. She didn't know these mountains and could have easily fallen into a canyon. But she was safe for the moment.

Willow fought the tears.

This was no time to cry or feel sorry for herself. She allowed the fury to fuel her and grabbed the duffel bag. Quietly, she felt for the zipper and opened the bag. No cell phone. No purse. But she did find her hoodie and another pair of sweats. Socks and Crocs. They would have to do. She was unprepared to face off with the wild creatures of the night or the drop in temperature. But if she had to, she could bury herself beneath the pine needles and leaves to keep warm and hide, and try to forget about spiders or ticks. Creepy insects were the least of her worries.

With that man hunting her, she didn't know if she would survive the night.

CHAPTER FORTY-EIGHT

FRIDAY, 11:30 P.M.
EMERALD M RANCH

"Austin!"

That voice. That familiar voice. It raked up his back and grated across his nerves. Who was it?

A wet tongue licked across his face, slobbering all over him. His heart lurched. Austin groaned.

"Austin, wake up."

A serious throb felt as though it would crack open his head. He slowly sat up, his hands grabbing grass. Timber and Rufus whined and licked him.

"Are you okay?" Heath shined the flashlight in his face, igniting more pain.

Temples fracturing, Austin touched his forehead. "No, I'm not okay." Images flashed in his mind. "Willow! We have to find Willow."

"Slow down. You have a golf-ball-size knot on your head like someone pistol-whipped you." Heath assisted Austin to his feet.

The ground moved beneath him. He pressed his hands against the house. "Can you tell me what's going on?"

"I was hoping you could tell me."

"Heath!"

"The dogs found you."

Images flashed. "He was here, Heath. He got the best of me." Grief and shame twisted together in his gut. "He used a Taser on me, then must have coldcocked me. See any confetti? We could track the serial number back to the device's owner." Austin searched his person, then the ground. "Where's my gun?"

Heath flashed his light around. "I don't see markers or your gun. I'm sorry I didn't get back sooner. Charlie texted, so I turned around. It takes a while to get up that trail, especially at night, so I took it slow and easy. I put Boots away, but the dogs took off running. They found you. Otherwise I might not have noticed anything was wrong except for . . . well . . . the Jeep is gone."

"What? The Jeep is gone?"

Willow!

His heart pounded in rhythm with his head. It was too much to grapple with all at once. Willow. She'd had that duffel bag out to pack. He thought he'd heard her snoring, and that she'd given up the idea of leaving. He'd trusted her to wait for an explanation.

Wait. He wasn't thinking clearly. Whoever beat him might have taken her.

Dread rose in his gut, threatening to sink him. "I have to find Willow."

He narrowed his eyes as though the action could dampen the severe pain in his temples as he made his way along the side of the house.

Heath led the way to the back and opened the door. The dogs rushed inside the house. "Willow! Evelyn!" Heath called.

Austin made his way up the stairs, pushing off the walls when they tilted, until he got to her room. He knocked softly, hesitating only a millisecond before cracking it open. Empty. He burst all the way in and flipped on the lights. The bedding was crumpled. Her duffel was gone.

Heath appeared behind him. "Found Evelyn. She's still asleep. Must be those new pills for her back."

"Could I be any worse of a bodyguard?"

"No time to wallow. What do you think happened? Did she leave on her own? Or did he take her?"

Austin frowned. "He was here and got to me first. Whatever happened, we have to find her. I'll call her cell to see if she answers."

"I'll call the sheriff. Even if she left on her own, he needs to know someone attacked you."

"Which one are you going to call? You're on the county line. If he took Willow, they could be headed any direction."

"I'll call Sheriff Haines. He'll likely call other law enforcement. I have no use for Everett."

Austin grabbed his cell and called Willow. It went straight to voicemail. "If he took her, why did he take the Jeep too?"

Heath shrugged. "It's a distraction for one thing. We don't know if she left on her own or not."

Something caught Austin's eye. He leaned closer to the pillow and ran his finger over the small stain. Blood. *No!*

Heath grabbed his arm and pulled him back. "It's a drop or two, Austin. It could be anything."

Regardless, Austin couldn't see straight. Couldn't think straight.

He stumbled down the hallway to the bathroom. Opened the medicine cabinet and found the ibuprofen. He struggled to get the lid off and all the pills spilled to the floor. He dropped to his knees, jarring his head again, and pawed at the floor. He only needed four, but his hands were shaking and he couldn't pick up the pills. His vision blurred. He decided to take advantage of being on his knees and began to pray. Beg.

God, when I'm weak, you are strong. Please, let that be true, because I can't think. I can hardly move knowing Willow is out there and could be in danger because I failed. But I have to move. I have to act. Give me the strength to find her despite my own failings.

He had to pull himself together. The ibuprofen came into focus. Austin grabbed four. Didn't have time to clean up the rest. Willow was out there somewhere because someone had bested him. He grabbed a cup of water, took the pills, and found Heath pacing in the hall. While his brother rattled off the information to the sheriff's department, Austin headed for his room, where he opened his laptop. Finishing the call, Heath followed him and hovered over his shoulder. "What are you doing, man?"

"Remember Ralph, that cur dog we had?"

"Yeah, what's he got to do with anything?"

"Remember how he kept running off and Dad threatened us if we let him run off again, so we went in together and got him chipped?"

"That's only so the dog could be identified if found. You're not telling me you chipped Willow."

"Of course not. There was a time or two when I was with the FBI that I wished everyone had a tracking device." One time in particular that he couldn't let go of, and that's what had driven him in his decision. "I bought Willow a necklace at Wyoming Silversmith and put a tracker on that. Let's hope she's wearing it." The image on the screen glowed with a red dot. "There. She's not headed to Jackson or to the airport."

His gut soured. As much as he hadn't wanted her to leave on her own, that would have been a much better scenario.

"No. I wouldn't imagine her abductor would take her there. But she's deep in the Gros Ventre Wilderness Area. Come on. Looks like he's got a big head start on us."

"Isn't the sheriff on his way?"

"Yeah, but he can meet us there and maybe pick up her abductor at the same time." Heath grabbed Austin, his blue eyes dark and forceful. "We'll get her back, little brother."

With his laptop, tablet, and cell phone in tow, Austin followed Heath out of the house. The only issue would be getting a decent signal out there. But he knew where she was now and that was something.

They climbed into Heath's truck. "Let's go, let's go," Austin said. "We're wasting time."

God, I can't lose her.

Heath started the ignition and peeled away from the place Austin once called home. He steered down the drive and onto the road. "You'll have to tell me which way to go."

"Okay. Let's head northwest once we get to the main highway."

"I know that. I know how to get to the wilderness area along the road, but I'm talking after that."

Right. He hoped the ibuprofen would kick in soon.

"So you tagged your girlfriend." Heath's teasing tone came across loud and clear.

Austin tried to ignore the harassment and the pain in his head. "My girlfriend? You've got it all wrong."

"Tell you what, I'll let you prove that to the both of us as soon as we get her back."

"You're on." He stared at the red dot. "It stopped."

"What? The red dot?"

A knot lodged in Austin's throat. "I just realized. The red dot is not even moving. It hasn't moved since I pulled it up. I don't like this. I'd prefer if he kept going and we caught up with him. But stopping . . ."

"He could have gotten to the place where he plans to hide her. Don't think the worst."

But Austin couldn't help himself. A million scenarios ran through his mind about why an abductor would stop in the middle of nowhere.

None of them good for Willow.

CHAPTER FORTY-NINE

After Willow donned the extra layers of clothing from her duffel bag, she still wasn't warm enough.

Twigs snapped. Leaves rustled.

Her pulse jumped. She hoped she melded with the tree hollow and the dark forest would keep her hidden. Holding her breath, she listened. Blood roared in her ears.

Had he found her?

Grunting sounds met her ears. A musky scent accosted her.

A grizzly bear? *God, please don't let me see a grizzly bear, despite my earlier wish.*

A low growl morphed into a high-pitched scream that echoed musically through the woods. Willow released her breath. An elk. Striking terror in her heart, a bulky silhouette blacked out what little moonlight had broken through the forest canopy. The creature was mere feet from her. Releasing another ear-shattering bugle, the bull elk turned, displaying a large, wide rack of antlers. Was she in danger?

She turned to stone again. *Please don't see me, please don't see me.*

Willow could hardly believe the size of it. The beast continued forward, moving through the forest.

A laugh of pure relief almost escaped. The elk didn't seem to care about her presence. She knew nothing about these animals, but what a moment. She hoped she would be able to share about the experience with Austin.

Should she get up and move again or stay hidden in the hollow? Maybe if she could make it to a high point, she could better see where she was. Yeah right. And stumble off a cliff. Without a sense of direction, she wasn't sure which way to head. She was truly lost. But that was okay as long as her abductor didn't find her.

Had he finally given up so he could go after Charlie?

Oh, Charlie . . .

Again, she thought about what JT would have done in her situation. She pushed herself farther into the tree hollow, packed the duffel bag over her legs, and scooped pine needles over her legs like a blanket. Might as well stay here for the night. Otherwise she could run into the guy out there searching for her.

God, please hide me tonight. Hide me in the shadow of your wings. Help me understand.

Because she didn't understand any of it. Why did JT have to die like that? Why was she on the run now because she'd chosen to find a woman who'd been abducted? And for that matter— why had *she* been abducted? And why was Austin involved in her life again?

Her uncertainty about his presence reminded her of a squirrel flitting back and forth across the road, danger looming with the squirrel's indecision. Yet Willow had no doubt that Austin was an integral part of this search for Charlie. His walking back into her life was by creative design, just like the universe. The forest and creatures around her.

How could she be angry? How could she regret working with

him? If she had the chance to go back in time and change what had happened between them before, would she? Regret over her mistakes overwhelmed her. Could she even walk through one day without making a mistake? God help her, because if it weren't for his grace, where would she be?

Coyotes howled much too close for comfort. But if they were close, that meant *he* was likely far away. Still, she shivered with cold, raw fear.

Something breathed much too loudly, then snorted. Another animal. Definitely not a man. She gripped the knife she'd taken in one hand, but she wanted a weapon in both hands. She reached forward and felt around in the debris for a stick. A rock. Anything. Her fingers brushed up against stone. She dug her fingernails into the loam around the rock and urged it from the earth.

If her abductor found her, at least she was prepared to defend herself.

A memory flickered through her thoughts. She closed her eyes and let her mind drift back to the day she learned her parents had died. JT was with her. His strong arms around her, holding her. He had to have been grieving himself, but as a child, Willow hadn't known that.

She only felt his love for her and heard his whispers in her ear. *"Remember, Willow. The Lord is your rock and your fortress. He's your savior. My God is my rock, in whom I find protection."*

Only near the end of the Scripture did it sound like JT said the words to himself to soothe his own heartfelt grief at the loss of his only daughter. Now JT was with his daughter. And Willow was here alone.

No.

Not alone.

God is my rock.

She held tightly to her weapons, and repeated the words silently to calm her fears. Surreal peace flooded her heart, but she struggled to trust it. She should stay awake, remain on guard, but fatigue weighed her down. At least she was safe, warm, and dry.

Except . . .

Soft raindrops tapped the leaves on their way to the forest floor, the leading notes to a rain shower symphony.

CHAPTER FIFTY

Faint light broke through her lids. Willow shifted uncomfortably beneath the cold, damp leaves and rain-soaked duffel bag, the hard bark of the tree cutting into her side and bringing her back to reality. She didn't want to wake up. Not yet. A painful crick ached across her neck and shoulders.

Footfalls over pine needles and the rustling of foliage drew her fully awake. The light—a beam from a flashlight.

She reached for the knife. Where was it? She found the rock. Panic cinched her throat.

The footfalls grew closer and resounded as if he had no intention of sneaking up on her. Willow pressed herself deeper into the hollow, feeling around for the knife as she gripped the rock. Though her hands trembled, she prepared to fight for her life.

God is my rock.

The beam of light shined in her face, then dropped to the ground. A familiar form moved into her line of sight. Seconds ticked by before her brain registered. Austin crouched down at eye level and looked at her, his concern overwhelming her. A surge of gratitude swept over her, forcing a tsunami of tears down her cheeks.

He reached for her, easing her gently out of the hollow, then lifted her to her feet and wrapped his arms around her. He pressed his face into her neck. "Willow," he said, taking in a deep breath.

It was all she needed.

CHAPTER FIFTY-ONE

Austin held her trembling form. Soothing words escaped his lips. He didn't recognize his own voice. "It's okay. You're going to be okay." *Thank you, God, for letting me find her.*

She was all he cared about.

Heath approached, relief surging in his eyes. He kept his distance, giving Austin a moment alone with Willow. Austin never wanted to let her go. Wouldn't until she was ready.

The rain had stopped, except for latent droplets making their way slowly through the trees. He ran his hand over her cold, wet hair. A new pang hit him in the chest. "We need to get you back. Get you warmed up. Are you . . . are you all right?" What a stupid question. He wished he could absorb the cold from her and take all her pain away.

Willow was the one to step away.

The wild look in her eyes terrified him.

"How did you find me?" Her soft voice cracked.

"I'll explain that later."

Her eyes narrowed and she reached for the knot on his head but stopped before touching it. "What happened?"

He was surprised she could see in the limited lighting.

"Nothing we can't talk about later."

"All that matters right now is that you're okay." Heath stepped up. "We need to head back now. The deputies are looking over the wrecked vehicle. Your abductor could still be here searching for you. There's an injured animal out there somewhere too." His brother gestured at Willow. "She needs to answer questions, see a doctor."

Austin nodded and took her hand. He couldn't help himself and drew her close again. "I'm so, so sorry. This never should have happened to you."

He held her again, wishing they were already somewhere safe and warm where he could hold her without interruption. That is, if she even wanted him near her now. He could hear Michael Croft's voice again. *"You're fired. Get out. I don't need you."*

He'd found her because of the small tracking device on her necklace, but she had been the one to keep herself alive, with God's help, he was sure. Why had he ever let her out of his sight, trusting she was safe in Heath's house? Or for that matter, out of his life to begin with?

"Come on, guys. Let's get out of here." Heath's gruff voice thrust them apart. He grabbed her duffel.

Willow turned and stepped toward Heath, then collapsed. Austin crouched to help her up.

"I'm okay. I'm okay. My legs are stiff from sitting in the tree hollow half the night." Her shaky voice didn't fool him. She was completely drained.

Austin lifted her into his arms. At first she protested but then settled against him. She'd been strong long enough. As he tromped through the woods behind Heath, he imagined the sheer terror she had experienced while fleeing from her abductor.

He wanted to ask her questions. Did she see who it was? Could she describe him? What had been his intention? They'd seen the Jeep at the bottom of the ravine, but thanks to the tracker they knew she wasn't in it. Still, for a few terrifying moments, he had thought the worst.

With her soft form in his arms, the fury subsided, if only a little. He could deal with his failures later, but right now the vibrant, living woman in his arms was all that mattered.

CHAPTER FIFTY-TWO

With Willow safely tucked away in the back seat of Heath's truck after paramedics examined her, Austin watched the tow truck mount the wrecked sedan. Two Hoback County deputies conversed with forest rangers next to their department vehicles, waiting for more law enforcement to launch a search for the abductor in the Gros Ventre Wilderness and Bridger-Teton National Forest, though chances were the man was long gone.

Willow had answered their questions, but they still didn't know who this guy was. The police said the vehicle had been stolen. Willow believed the collision with the moose had left her abductor with a broken arm though. That narrowed the suspects down to men with broken arms.

Had someone helped him get away? Were two different criminals involved—one in Seattle and one in Jackson Hole—and now coming together for a single, final act?

Austin was more than eager to be next to Willow again and get back to Heath's house where he could concentrate on her. Rather than sitting up front, he climbed into the back seat with her. Heath had left the truck running and the heater blasting.

274

It was too hot for comfort, but Willow needed to warm her chilled bones.

"Charlie's in danger." Her still-wet hair hanging down the sides of her face, she stared out the window. Vehicle lights illuminated swaths of the two-lane mountain road.

Heath climbed into the driver's seat and steered onto the road to head back to the ranch.

"Don't you see? Taking me tonight. It was all a distraction. He's going to kill Charlie. He's going after her. We need to get there first. I wanted to tell the deputies that a girl's in danger, but I honestly don't know who to trust anymore. The man after her could be anyone at all. Even the sheriffs I already told."

Heath swerved into the opposite lane, receiving a blaring horn in response, then back to his own lane. He'd obviously been watching Willow through the rearview mirror instead of the road.

"You have some explaining to do, Heath." Willow pulled her attention from the window to stare at the back of Heath's head.

The pulsing throb in Austin's own head increased. Why hadn't he brought ibuprofen with him? The minimal relief he'd gotten from the four he'd taken had already started to wear off.

"I can tell you what you want to know," Austin said. "I had planned to tell you last night, but when I got back you were already asleep." He explained everything that Heath had shared, including why he didn't initially tell them the truth.

"Would you ever have told us if Austin hadn't confronted you?"

Heath glanced to the mirror, then back to the road. "After I talked it out with Charlie, sure. It all happened so fast."

She hung her head and stared at her fidgeting hands. "He tried to warn me away, but I just wouldn't listen. And now he's going to find her."

"Relax, she works on the ranch," Heath said. "She should be at work this morning. We'll talk to her then. You can tell her everything. He won't find her there."

Austin suspected Heath was crazy with worry on the inside and his words were meant for himself. Heath only tried to convince himself that Charlie would be okay.

"Haven't you heard a word I've said? This guy took me tonight to distract you. That has to be the reason. He got all of us off the ranch so he could go after Charlie. He knows she's there. We can't wait for Charlie to just show up at work. We need to go find her now. Can you call her while we're driving? You need to warn her."

She looked to Austin for agreement. "She makes a good point," he said.

"I'll try her on the radio."

While Heath tried to contact Charlie, Austin stared at Willow. He couldn't stop looking at her. She was here in the truck with them. Alive. He had a thousand things he wanted to say to her, but not now. Another, better time. Still, hadn't that been his excuse before? He was always putting things off. Like she had earlier, he stared out the window as leftover droplets of rain slid down the glass. He needed a moment to regain his composure.

He'd finally faced the guy and been bested. It was all he could do to contain his fury and shame. He wanted a rematch. More than that, he should get out of this business altogether. But not yet. He had no right to feel for Willow the way he did, but it wasn't like he could quit now and walk out on her. They were near the end. They would find Charlie and introduce her to her birth mother. Catch the person responsible for too much grief.

"I can't reach her on her radio," Heath said. "Let me try again on the cell. We have SAT phones for backcountry emergencies, but I don't have that with me. Charlie could call 9–1–1 with it, if she needed to." They waited while Heath tried calling. He left a voicemail. Tossed the cell over the back seat to Austin.

"Text her that she's in danger. Let her know we're on the way. The texts often go through when a call won't."

Austin sent the text but got no reply. Were they already too late?

Soft fingers brushed across his hand. "It wasn't your fault."

Her words landed on his heart. If only he agreed. He shook his head, not wanting to discuss his part in her abduction until they were through this. When her fingers wrapped around his hand, his conscience pinged, refusing to relent. It was time to tell her.

"You asked how I found you tonight."

Soft lines grew in her forehead. "Yes."

Austin slowly reached over and found the small chain, lifting it from her neck to expose the western-styled pendant the size of a half dollar. Despite everything, a grin tugged at his cheek. "You kept this on."

She repossessed the pendant from his fingers. "Yes." The look in her eyes suggested she second-guessed her decision.

"It doesn't matter why you did. The truth is that I put a small global tracker on the concave side of the pendant. You'll see it on the back if you look close enough. I'm surprised you didn't find it."

Fire blazed in her eyes. "You what?"

He threw his hands up in surrender. "Just hear me out." He was going to do this. He was really going to tell her, and Heath would hear it too. So much for him keeping his worst nightmares to himself.

"I'm listening."

"Are you sure you feel up to this right now?"

"I'm wide awake. We have to find Charlie. While we're headed that way, just tell me, Austin. Quit putting it off."

Heath turned down the blasting heat. So he could hear every word?

"I'm duly scolded. When you were in the hospital you mentioned wanting to know the story behind why I left the FBI." He drew in a long breath. He didn't want to go there. Didn't want to think about it, but Willow deserved an explanation. "When I was a fighter pilot, I crashed during a small skirmish in the forsaken desert of a forgotten country. Nothing I'm supposed to talk about.

A family hid me until I could get out—their children had been taken by guerrillas. Terrorists. Whatever you want to call them."

"Taken, why?"

"Sex trafficking. I hated seeing their pain. I wanted to do something to help, but I couldn't." He couldn't seem to get enough air and cracked the window. "So when I was honorably discharged, I got my degree so I could join the FBI. I wanted to find missing and exploited children. I worked with the CARD team on several assignments, but on my last one . . ." Austin squeezed his eyes shut to let the images flow freely. Maybe to work up his courage too. The mantra played through his thoughts.

When every minute counts . . .

"A father abducted his son from his ex-wife—the boy's mother. The local authorities contacted the FBI. Various teams were assembled, including the CARD team. We were under great pressure to find them, and we did, twenty-four hours later. The father's green minivan was spotted two states over. We followed protocol. Found the house where he was suspected to be hiding. I was first on the scene, along with two other agents. We heard the boy screaming. We couldn't wait. While one agent announced our presence to attract the father's attention, the other agent and I found a way into the house."

Austin calmed his breathing, slowed his pulse. Prayed his headache wouldn't get the best of him.

"It's okay," she said. "You don't have to do this."

"No, I need to tell you. He was going to kill his son, Willow. I'm told that he didn't want his ex-wife to have the boy. That's a sick, sick man. But he aimed the weapon at his only son. I shot him. I shot the kid's father."

"So you saved him, Austin. You saved the boy."

"I saved him from certain death, but I shot his father right in front of him. There's a certain amount of psychological damage that goes with that. What if we had waited for more backup?

Maybe the man would still be alive and his son wouldn't have had to endure seeing his father killed. The kid saw everything. He wasn't grateful I'd saved him. He blamed me for killing his father."

"I'm so sorry, Austin. For that family. And for you—you can't blame yourself for that. And when the child gets older, he'll be grateful to you."

"I'll never know if it was the right decision. I sure don't feel like it was. Sure, we got the child back in the arms of his mother, but not without a significant loss. Maybe his father could have gotten help. I was so messed up that the OPR—Office of Professional Responsibility—gave me a psychological evaluation and suggested I needed time. So I took a permanent vacation." As a private investigator he could pick and choose his cases. "I can't fail any more children."

What was that look in her eyes? Disappointment? He couldn't read her, and for once he didn't want to.

"Why did you agree to help me with this? To help Katelyn Mason find her child?"

He lifted his eyes to meet hers. "Don't you know?"

For you, Willow. It's always been about you. Had he ever stopped thinking about her?

CHAPTER FIFTY-THREE

Charlie rested in her bed, staring out the window. She hadn't been able to sleep. After the storm clouds had moved out, through a small opening in the tree canopy, she'd watched the night sky roll by. Her favorite part of the show—the blackest night sky revealed the brightest stars.

Beautiful.

But the scenery brought back a memory, and she didn't much feel like reminiscing.

"You're gonna be a star one day, Charlie. I can feel it."

"No, Momma. I just want to ride horses."

Momma smiled. *"I have money to make that happen, honey. We'll build a barn. Get some horses. But you're going to learn how to take care of them first."*

Charlie pulled her attention from the window and the night sky and the memories. *The money, Momma. Who did it come from?*

She'd taken riding lessons and now cared for and trained the horses, under Mack's careful guidance. She and Momma had made plans to build the barn. But Momma had insisted Charlie get a degree first—and then the horses would come. Charlie had to work hard and earn everything because nothing came free in this life. Momma said hard work built character.

She didn't want to think about any of it now. She only wanted to sleep. Exhaustion ached through every bone, every muscle. Once she'd finally flopped on the bed, she should have gone under in ten seconds flat. Instead, her thoughts ramped into overdrive. Images of Sheriff Everett at the house stalked her, along with the deposits in Momma's bank account. Who were they from? How could she find out?

Would Sheriff Everett look into the deposits if she told him she believed they could be connected to her mother's death? Or was he involved?

Huffing, she rolled to her side. Fluffed her cheap feather pillow again. The sky had already started lightening, and she hadn't slept a wink. She wouldn't be worth half what Mack paid her at work today.

Birds chirped, stirring in the early morning, and irritated her, reminding her she needed to get up too. But it was much too cold to get out of bed. She hadn't planned to be at this cabin when the weather started turning.

A new sound drew her attention. Wings flapped as birds dispersed. The woods fell silent except for this new unwelcome sound. She sat up slowly and angled her head to listen as something moved before dawn even broke.

A four-legged creature?

Charlie had never been afraid of staying here alone, though she wished Rufus had remained with her.

A shiver crawled over her.

Now she understood why she wasn't able to sleep. Providence had kept her awake so she could hear *him* creeping toward the cabin. She edged toward the window and peeked out. Twenty-five yards away she caught a glimpse of someone between the trees.

Clyde?

Time for Charlie to run.

CHAPTER FIFTY-FOUR

Willow quickly changed into dry clothes in Evelyn's room so she wouldn't destroy evidence in the room where she was abducted last night. Austin's story had rattled her, but she didn't have time to think about that. Not yet.

Heath had tried to contact Charlie to no avail. Now he was out saddling the horses. They would ride as far as they could up the trail to Charlie's cabin. It was still early for her to be heading in to work, but if she was on her way in, they would meet her coming as they were going. The off-grid cabin was less than two miles from the ranch up a trail deemed too dangerous for guests—the perfect place for her to hide. Austin and Willow insisted on riding with Heath, who had called Sheriff Haines and explained that they believed Charlie was in danger.

Heath duly agonized over betraying Charlie's trust, but with her life in imminent danger, he'd had no choice. Still, they couldn't wait for the sheriff. Heath had been adamant that Charlie remain in hiding, per her request. But the girl needed protecting. All along, she'd claimed the man who killed her mother had also threatened *her* life. Now it seemed he was going to follow through with his threat.

Willow didn't want to waste time thinking about what had happened to her last night. She cared more about finding Charlie before it was too late. After all, she was in danger because Willow was searching for her.

Too late to turn back now. Still . . . *"Have you considered that the woman you're looking for doesn't want to be found?"* Heath's words echoed through her head.

What if telling Charlie the truth would only complicate her life? But Willow couldn't play God and keep the information from her either. She'd been paid to find her. Although, Katelyn hadn't paid Willow to tell Charlie the news, had she? Willow couldn't help it. Everything that could go wrong flitted through her mind.

Even if she found Charlie safe and sound today and told her everything, Charlie could refuse to see Katelyn anyway. Wouldn't that break the woman's heart?

JT, why did you take this on to begin with?

At Anderson Consulting, she had been accustomed to dealing with dead relatives—not those who had a free will and could make choices.

God, please give me direction. Show me what to do. Please help Katelyn and Charlie. You're all about restoration, aren't you?

With that thought, Austin's face came to mind.

That moment in the woods when he had found her hiding in the tree hollow came back to her. She'd never been more glad to see someone, or more glad that Austin had been *that* someone. When he'd carried her in his arms back to Heath's truck, she hadn't wanted to leave his embrace. Willow shook off the unbidden memories. Charlie's life was in danger. She shouldn't be thinking about what Austin meant to her.

Or that he was helping her, working with her to find someone's child. *"I can't fail any more children."*

"No, Austin, you can't. We can't fail Katelyn. We can't fail Charlie," she mumbled, and finished pulling on her dry jeans.

Despite her resolve to see this through—her faith and hope in things unseen—a sense of dread boiled beneath the surface. She left Evelyn's room, strode down the short hallway, and found Austin standing at the front door, wearing a jacket, jeans, and a Stetson. He looked like he belonged here. Like he would always belong here. She couldn't even picture him living in Seattle working as an FBI agent. Coming here had given her a glimpse into the guy he'd been before. A guy he'd hidden from her.

Who are you? She sidled up next to him.

He grinned. "You ready?"

She zipped up her thick fleece hoodie and took the extra jacket he offered. He didn't open the door but stood in her way. Was he having second thoughts? "You don't have to go, Willow. I'd prefer you stay here. You've been through an ordeal. Please, for me, just stay here. We'll get a deputy up here to stay. Or I'll stay with you."

"You have to go with Heath. He's waiting. Charlie is waiting. Now let's go. Katelyn hired me to find her daughter. I'm going to be there when we do. Each minute you spend arguing with me is just wasting time." Willow pushed by him to open the door.

She marched through the door and down to the barn, leaving Austin to follow.

Next to the barn, Austin held the reins as Willow climbed onto Amber, the gentle horse that Sheriff Everett had brought back last night. She didn't consider herself an experienced rider, but she'd ridden a few times in her life. Austin and Heath were experienced riders and could help her when the trail got rough.

Lines etched Heath's features. "With any luck, we'll run into her on her way down to the ranch." Regardless, she should have texted or answered her cell or the radio. Heath was worried about Charlie, but Willow suspected it was more than that. He probably believed he was betraying her confidence.

His blue gaze hung on Willow's. "She trusted me to keep her secret, but to stop the madness, she needs to be restored to her rightful family. I don't like it though. This is going to come as a complete shock to her. She loved her mother. The woman who raised her. Charlie loved her like we all love our mothers." He shook his head and stared at something in the distance. "Who was she? Really?"

It wasn't a question Willow could answer.

He climbed onto Boots and headed out. Willow followed Heath, then Austin behind her as the horses took to the single-file trail. Had she known how steep and rocky the trail would be, she might have opted to stay behind. She tried to remain loose and calm and simply let Amber follow Boots. The horses moved faster than Willow would have liked. What if Amber stumbled on a rock and broke a leg? They would both go down.

Instead of thinking about everything that could go wrong, Willow turned her thoughts and prayers to Charlie.

She pictured the girl in the photograph heading down the trail, surprise on her face at seeing them. But try as she might, she couldn't muster belief that today would unfold that way.

The trail narrowed and bigger rocks slowed the horses down. At some point, Willow knew they would have to walk. She couldn't imagine the trail getting worse.

"I almost forgot to tell you," she called over her shoulder.

"What's that?" Austin asked.

Maybe it was too hard to talk right now, but she needed to share the information. They hadn't had a chance to debrief earlier. "I made a discovery last night while you went to the barn to talk to Heath. It's about Mr. Haus's son."

"You mean that guy at the nursing home?"

"That's the one."

"And his son?"

"Silas Everett. You know, the sheriff who showed up last night with this horse."

He angled his head. "I don't know what that has to do with anything."

"I keep thinking about what Mr. Haus said. That Marilee knew his secret. Maybe that was one of his secrets. Silas Everett is his biological son. I'm not sure who knows that."

"You mean besides Nurse Kim, who told us he has one son. So it's not really a secret, and even if it were, you don't think she was murdered for that secret. People don't care about that kind of thing anymore. It's not motivation for murder."

"There are reasons to keep the information a secret. Like an inheritance. A person could be removed from a will if it were discovered they were not the biological offspring," she said. "It's brutal, I know, but I had one such case, and I had to search for the lost heir. The true heir."

"I think you're getting off track. Someone could have killed Marilee Clemmons to keep her quiet. It's obvious more than one person, more than Marilee, is involved in Charlie's abduction. We know that someone doesn't want you to find Charlie. Maybe Marilee had been paid to abduct the baby and her knowledge was a threat to the person who hired her. What we still don't know is the connection to Katelyn Mason. Why *her* baby?"

Willow pushed a protruding evergreen branch away. "I hope Katelyn isn't in danger now."

Heath slowed, reining in his horse and angling it just enough so that he could look at them, his expression fierce with worry. "I know the notes have warned you away from finding her, and you believe your abduction was a distraction so he could get to her, but what if you're wrong? What if this person doesn't know where Charlie's been hiding, and all we're doing is leading him to her?"

CHAPTER FIFTY-FIVE

"Charlie!" the man called. "I'm not going to hurt you. I'm here to help."

Gasping for breath, Charlie couldn't let herself stop, but she couldn't force her legs to keep moving either. She dropped behind a group of boulders and sucked in the cold morning air, sweat coating her body despite the temperature.

Panic set in, freezing her limbs.

God, I thought I could trust you. Mack said I could.

She'd known better than to trust anyone—not one single soul, except for Mack. And she was glad she'd listened to her instincts. She'd known not to trust Sheriff Everett, but she hadn't expected to see Sheriff Haines here—the Bridger County sheriff.

Why had he shown up at her cabin? He'd come dressed in plain clothes. She only recognized him because she'd seen him with Mack. They were friends.

But a sheriff who wanted to help would've dressed for the part—and given his name. Not slinked up behind trees as he made his way to the cabin. Holding her weapon behind her, she'd slowly

287

opened the door, ready to run, and made the mistake of giving him the chance to explain. He'd put on a smile and inched closer like she was a skittish doe.

When he was about fifteen yards from the door, she'd said, "Hold it right there. What are you doing here?"

"The man who wants to kill you, he's coming for you. I know everything, Charlie. I'm here to protect you."

"Who told you I was here?"

His eyes had flicked to the left, then the right, as if to see if they were alone. Clyde had done the same right before he'd grabbed Charlie after Momma's death. She'd gotten away from him and wouldn't make the mistake of letting a suspicious person get too close again. Add to that, the sheriff had something in his hand that he held to his side as if hiding it. What was it?

"Heath McKade. Who else?"

Wrong answer.

Charlie had dashed outside and around the cabin to run deeper into the national forest. With the sheriff standing in her path, she couldn't make it to the trail that could take her down to the Emerald M Ranch and Mack.

She wouldn't believe it until she heard it from Mack—he would have been there too if Charlie had been in imminent danger. How had the sheriff found her? Mack never would have told anyone where she was.

And now she was in a world of hurt, tired of running. Panic setting in. She couldn't breathe, but she needed to run.

Sucking in a long breath to power her through, she shoved from the boulder. She had to keep moving.

Suddenly, her body buzzed with pain. Electricity surged through her muscles, making them stiff, shutting her down. She fell and hit her head. Everything went black.

Her eyes fluttered open. How long had she been out?

Charlie was hanging upside down over the sheriff's shoulder.

Her body still dazed, her head aching, she wasn't sure if she could move, but she wouldn't let him know she was conscious, at least not yet. She had to get her bearings. Make a plan. Where was he taking her? She could just make out the terrain—the Grayback Canyon loomed down farther. At the bottom of that canyon, the Grayback River.

Not much time for her to strategize.

The rush of the river met her ears. Fear squeezed her throat. *No . . .*

God, please help me! Charlie rammed her knee into the man's gut. He dropped her, and she scrambled away. But too late she realized she was pinned between Sheriff Haines and the Grayback ravine—not yet the deep canyon—but still, tears engulfed her.

"Why are you doing this? I don't understand."

Regret surged in his eyes. "Why couldn't you just have stayed gone?"

"You? You killed my mother?"

"No. You have it wrong. That wasn't me."

"Then explain it to me. What's going on? You're going to kill me, aren't you?"

He inched toward Charlie. He would push her off.

"I want answers. Tell me how you're involved in this."

"Believe me, I'm being merciful. This is for the best. It's better that you don't know the truth, so you can die in peace. The truth would tear you apart."

Angry tears burned her eyes. "What are you talking about? What truth?"

She took in her options—she couldn't escape him by running to the right or left. He could hit her with that Taser again. "Please, just let me go. I promise I'll disappear. You won't have to see me again. I can stay gone, like you said." Whatever that meant. "I won't even go back to school. I'll leave the country."

"I wish you had, honey. And I'm real sorry about this."

Would he use the Taser again or just push her? Heart in her throat, Charlie made a mad dash. *God, if you're there and I can trust you, please don't let the Taser hit me. Help me survive!*

She propelled herself into emptiness.

CHAPTER FIFTY-SIX

"I think it's time to get off the horses, Heath," Austin called up to his brother.

Heath said nothing and continued. They all sensed the urgency of the situation, but Willow was having a harder time with Amber since Heath increased his speed despite the rocky trail. Austin tensed his neck and shoulders and clenched his jaw as though he could keep Willow safe on the horse by doing so.

A few minutes later, the cabin came into view—just barely—behind a copse of fir trees. It was secluded all right. The woods were eerily quiet. It had taken far longer than he had thought it would to reach it.

Heath got off his horse, his features as grim as they'd been at the news of Dad's fatal accident. They hadn't passed Charlie on the trail.

Austin got off his horse. Willow stared at the ground from the saddle, uncertainty in her gaze. Austin reached up. "Here, let me help you."

"I can do it." She slid from the saddle like she'd done it a thousand times.

Austin gently grabbed her waist to steady her, just the same. She didn't resist.

"You're a natural, you know that?"

"What do you mean?"

"On the horse." He wanted to smile at that, but this wasn't the time.

Her attention was drawn to Heath when he pulled a rifle from his saddle scabbard. They tied the horses to some trees. Time to move in and search for Charlie.

"Why don't you wait with the horses?" he asked Willow quietly. "Please."

"I'm coming too. But I'll stay back and give you space to work."

Fair enough. Austin readied the 9mm Glock he'd borrowed from Heath and they slowly crept toward the cabin. Willow was just a few feet behind him.

"Charlie? You in there?" Heath called as he knocked on the door. "I brought friends. You can trust them."

"Your life is in danger, Charlie." Austin held his weapon at low ready. "Willow and I have come to help. We've come with some important news about who killed your mother." Right. They didn't know who killed her. But they knew he was coming for Charlie.

Austin drew up next to Heath and gestured to the door. Time to go in. He hoped she wasn't simply hiding inside—they would scare her with this next move.

Heath prepared to kick open the door. Austin put his hand up to stop Heath and tried the knob. It wasn't locked. He hoped he'd find Charlie inside alone, but he was prepared for the worst. Still, he rushed in with his weapon drawn. "It's empty."

Willow and Heath followed him into the sparse one-room cabin. A propane stove sat in the corner. Papers covered a table. Bank statements? A shelf stacked with canned food—chili, beans, soup.

"I don't like this." His lips in a tight line, Heath shook his head.

Willow moved to the small cot in the corner and sat on the

292

creaky bed. She ran her hand across the rumpled, worn-out quilt, then scrutinized the room. "There's her backpack. Her clothes are still here. That doesn't tell us much."

"You sure there's no other way for her to get to the ranch?" Austin clomped around the cabin.

"Besides this trail? Yes. I'm sure. You saw the ridge. It wouldn't make sense to take any other path."

"Unless she thought she was in danger." Austin stepped outside the cabin and searched the woods for signs of a struggle. The possibility remained that Charlie had been abducted—or worse, murdered. He didn't want to speak the words out loud. Saying them would somehow give them life.

Austin circled the cabin, going wider with each time around. That Charlie had been living in this secluded, off-grid cabin told him a lot. She was terrified and didn't believe anyone could protect her better than herself.

Footprints. Boots. Large, with a deep impression. A man. Austin wanted to take a picture of the prints, but finding Charlie took priority.

"Found something," he called.

Willow appeared around the corner and approached Austin. Heath wasn't far behind. "Look here." Austin gestured to the ground. "Footprints. Someone was here. Someone other than Charlie, unless she wears a men's size 11.

"If it's the same guy who got me last night, he has a Taser and isn't afraid to use it. Let's keep looking. Maybe she's still running or found a place to hide. We can't be that far behind him." Austin didn't have confidence in his words, but they had to keep hoping until all was lost. The question remained—who would they find chasing Charlie?

Austin had made the mistake of getting ahead of himself far too often. He couldn't afford to jump to the wrong conclusions now. That could get Charlie killed.

Despite the clouds in the sky and the chilly morning, sweat poured down his back. Images of the mission gone wrong accosted him. Regardless, he would see this through to the end. And he wouldn't fail.

He couldn't.

"What now?" Willow asked. "Where do we look for her?"

Heath looked through the scope on his rifle. "She's smart. She's always on alert. If he got here before us, she got away. I hope that's what happened. We can figure out the trajectory of these footprints. Which direction she ran. Then we can head that way. I'll try to call her again if by some magic I can get a signal."

Austin and Heath spanned out, searching the ground.

"Come on," Austin whispered to Willow.

The dark circles under her eyes told of her harried night. Austin blamed himself, but he wouldn't think about that until they had Charlie back. Until they found the man who had abducted Willow and was intent on harming Charlie.

"There," Heath said. "These footprints lead deeper into the woods away from the trail. If she kept going in that direction, it would take her to the river."

Austin squeezed the grip of his Glock. He hoped he wouldn't have to use it today.

"Should we call out to her?" Willow asked. "Let her know we're coming and that we're friendly. We want to help?"

Heath lifted a finger to his lips and crept forward on the pine needles.

Austin tugged Willow close and whispered in her ear, "I don't want you going into this. It's dangerous. I'm supposed to protect you. Please stay here. Stay back."

"Then protect me, but I have a weapon too, so I'm not completely helpless." Willow pushed beyond him to follow Heath.

He wanted to kick himself. He hadn't thought they'd be walking into this kind of situation. Hadn't believed it. Heath moved quickly and quietly like he was still a Green Beret on a covert military mission as he followed the tracks. Austin followed behind Willow and Heath, looking for clues to lead them to Charlie.

The way grew steep in places, more hazardous. The trees denser. Even the forest appeared darker.

A man hiked between the trees toward them. Tension corded Austin's neck. "Look."

Heath paused and peered through the evergreens.

The man picked up speed, covering the distance quickly. Sheriff Haines breathed hard. "Got here as soon as I heard."

"Glad you made it." Heath peered through the scope. "We could use the help." He explained what they'd found at the cabin.

Sheriff Haines worked to catch his breath. "No need to put more people in danger than necessary. Why don't you take Miss Anderson back to the horses, McKade? Your brother and I will continue the search."

Austin frowned.

"Now wait a minute. I'm here to find her. Someone hired me." Willow lifted her chin. Defiant to the end.

"He's right." Austin gently took her arm.

She protested.

"It's the sheriff telling you to go back, Willow." He guided her back toward the horses.

She leaned in to whisper. "Something's off about this. I don't think we should leave Heath there alone."

Willow tried to turn back. He caught her and urged her down the trail. "I agree. That's exactly why I don't want you there. Please, just trust me for once in your life." She must have heard the urgency in his voice because she complied.

Beyond the cabin, they made it to the horses. Willow turned to look back. "Did Heath ever tell anyone where Charlie was hiding?"

"No. Not even the sheriff. He told Haines to meet us at the

ranch but never said where exactly we were headed. And even if he had, no way could Sheriff Haines have beaten us here."

"Go, Austin. You have to do something. You shouldn't have left Heath back there alone just to protect me."

Austin paced. He never wanted to leave Willow again. He should keep her at his side to protect her. Forever, if the deepest place in his heart had its way. But what about Heath? Did he realize the danger? Did he recognize it?

Determination shivered in her hazel eyes, making them look more green, like the forest around her. "It isn't him, Austin. He's not the masked man who abducted me."

"How can you know?"

"Sheriff Haines isn't as big as the guy from last night. Plus, he doesn't appear injured. His arm isn't broken."

"Doesn't mean he's not involved."

"Let's go back. We'll follow at a distance in case Heath needs us." She gripped her weapon and chambered a round.

A shot rang out.

Heath!

CHAPTER FIFTY-SEVEN

Heart pumping much too hard, Willow sprinted behind Austin, rushing between trees and thick underbrush, over rocks and fallen branches.

"Heath!" he called. "Heath, are you all right?"

Austin should approach quietly, to her way of thinking, but what did she know? A pang throbbed in her chest on Austin's behalf. For his brother. The desperation in his voice nearly undid her. Gasping for breath, Willow wanted to fall to her knees. She simply couldn't keep up. Austin slowed and glanced back at her, his eyes dark with worry.

"Go. I'll catch up," she said.

"No." He shook his head. "No. I'm not ever leaving you again."

"Not even . . . ?" She let the words trail off. A lump formed in her throat. *Not even for your brother?*

"Not even for Heath. He's a big boy. Can take care of himself." Fear surged in his eyes.

"Let's go then." They had wasted time talking, but it gave her a chance to catch her breath. That he would stay behind with her when Heath could be shot and dying sliced open a chunk of her heart. She didn't know how to process the raw emotion coursing through her.

"No," he mumbled, then sprinted forward. "Heath!"

He slid down an incline. Willow followed him down without sliding and Heath came into view. His form was slumped against a boulder.

"Heath! What happened?" Austin dropped to his knees next to his brother.

"I'm okay," he said, but his voice said otherwise.

"You're not okay." Desperation echoed in Austin's tone. "You're bleeding. He shot you?"

"Go. Go find Charlie. That jerk must have her somewhere. I don't know if she's already dead."

"You're going to die if you don't get help," Austin said.

"I'm putting pressure on the wound. I know what to do, and there's time before it's too late. Hurry, you're Charlie's only hope. But be careful, he'll know you're coming."

Austin gripped the collar of his brother's shirt. "Don't die on me, Heath."

"Go get her." Sweat beaded on Heath's brow. "I'm too stubborn to die. You know that."

"Stay here." Austin directed the words to Willow, the silent message in his eyes. *Stay with my brother and take care of him.* Then to Heath, he said, "Watch out for her."

Heath lifted his chin, gesturing deeper into the woods. "He headed southeast. Just be careful. You know he'll shoot you if you give him the chance. But I know you can handle yourself, little brother."

Austin took Heath's rifle and ran in that direction.

Willow dropped to her knees next to Heath, despair etching her soul. Austin had said he wouldn't leave her, not even for his brother, but circumstances had changed. She wouldn't have him stay here. She wouldn't have it any other way. Still, disappointment pinged in her heart that he'd had to leave her, despite his reassurances. Ridiculous. She wouldn't leave Heath here alone, even if Austin hadn't asked. "What happened? Why did he shoot you?"

"It hit me that he wasn't wearing his uniform. He came from the wrong direction. I hadn't"—he grimaced—"I told him the ranch."

Apprehension overwhelmed her. "What can I do to make you comfortable?"

His face morphed into an intense frown. Oh no. He had wanted Austin to go after Charlie, so he hadn't let on how much pain he was in. Moisture bloomed on her palms. Heath could bleed to death right here in front of her, and there was nothing she knew to do to help him. Nothing she *could* do.

Grimacing, he handed over his radio and tossed her his cell. "Evelyn might not hear the radio, but try that. If not, then see if you can get a signal. Call 9-1-1. Emergency services. Call Deputy Taggart. Someone. Or the Hoback County Sheriff's Department. The county line runs through these parts."

Her vision blurred, but she forced back the tears. Any help that might come would take far too long. "Are you sure there isn't anything else I can do?"

Heath didn't respond. Had he even heard her?

Willow's slippery fingers interfered with her use of the radio and search for a cell signal. Regardless, she couldn't find one. No one answered the radio. She pushed to stand. Teetering, she leaned on a wide evergreen. She walked around to continue her search for the signal, feeling completely useless.

Nothing. She refused to fall into this trap of helplessness. "Maybe I can get you to the horses, or better, bring one here to you, Heath. I don't want to leave you, but I don't think you can wait as long as you led Austin to believe." Her eyes followed the path they'd taken, which disappeared between the thick trees.

"It hurts like heck, I won't lie. But most of the pain is coming from the pressure I'm putting on it to keep it from bleeding. That's the danger. Loss of blood." His words came out between gasps and grunts.

Heath hadn't come across as the sort of man who couldn't handle pain—and it hadn't been that long since he'd served as a Green Beret. Nausea boiled like lava in her gut. "Tell me what to do."

"Back on the horses, there's gunshot wound powder."

Austin had asked her to stay with him. "Why didn't you tell Austin?"

"You know why. He'd waste time. Charlie . . ." Heath grunted.

"Just like I am now." Willow started to take off.

"Wait."

"What is it?" She didn't need to waste more time.

"I need to tell you something. You tell Austin in case . . . in case . . ."

Oh, don't say those words!

"Before he took off, Haines told me . . . he told me Dad wasn't drunk. The accident wasn't his fault. Tell Austin I'm sorry for being disappointed in him. I hope he can forgive me. Tell him . . . tell him that I'm proud of him."

"He'll be glad to hear it when you tell him yourself." Willow left him and climbed up the incline she'd carefully maneuvered down earlier. That must be what had caused the rift between them. Heath had to live so they could work it out. He could be the one to tell Austin. If Heath died while she was gone, Austin would never forgive her. However, he would never forgive her if she failed to do the one thing she could do to save Heath.

Austin would save Charlie.

Willow would save Heath.

She had to believe it would work out or she would crumple under the weight of it.

What a strange twist of events.

She hurried, climbing over tree trunks and around boulders, through the undergrowth as fast as she could. The cabin came into view to Willow's right. They'd left the horses tied off to trees a few yards up the trail. Willow made her way to where the horses should be.

But . . . where were they? Had she gotten turned around? Was this the wrong place? She turned in a circle. No. They had left the horses here. The animals' droppings proved it.

Willow leaned over her thighs to catch her breath. *Now what do I do?* Without the gunshot wound powder, Heath might die. Without the horses, how could she take him to get help?

A twig snapped. She stiffened. Before she could turn, a hand covered her mouth. Pain ignited as the muzzle of a gun thrust against her rib cage.

CHAPTER FIFTY-EIGHT

Austin still couldn't wrap his mind around Sheriff Haines's involvement.

He'd picked up Charlie's trail as she'd run from the sheriff. Austin crept to the edge of the bluff, his heart sliding up into his throat. The Grayback River Canyon. Here, it wasn't so steep, but up farther he would get dizzy if he stood too close. He remembered that much from his childhood.

He crouched to study the ground. The sheriff had been cutting through the woods quickly and left a trail, whether he wanted to or not. He'd caught up with Charlie too. They'd been here all right. He couldn't be sure, but the footprints suggested someone had gone into the river. What he didn't know was if the sheriff had shot her first. Or stunned her.

He rose slowly, watching the swift current and the white water. If she remained conscious, uninjured, could she survive the river?

Failure wrapped around his chest and squeezed. He scraped a hand down his face. Lifted the rifle and peered through the scope, searching downriver, but the river curved and twisted out of sight.

302

He couldn't follow the river and catch up to her. Either she made it on her own or she was already dead. He could make it back to Heath and save his brother.

Twisting on his heel, he stomped back into the woods, following the same path in reverse. Realization hit him. He pressed his back against a tree—the same path the sheriff had taken, according to Heath. Why hadn't he run into the guy? Had Charlie already gone into the river when they met up with Haines? Whatever the timeline, Haines wasn't here and Charlie was gone. A measure of fear corded his neck. Heath and Willow were back there. He'd left them.

He'd left her when he'd said he never would.

God, why are my choices not choices at all?

The faintest sound drew his attention. He remained pressed against the tree, then slowly peeked around it. Movement in the forest caught his eye. The forms were distant, but he could make out two people. He peered through his scope.

The sheriff had someone. Charlie?

No . . .

Terror fisted around his heart and squeezed. Sheriff Haines had taken Willow.

What had happened to Heath?

Anguish engulfed him. He had to take this guy down once and for all. Watching them through the scope, he hoped he had the opportunity. As if sensing he was being surveilled, the sheriff turned his head in Austin's direction, then tugged Willow close. Using her as a human shield?

His finger trembled against the trigger. Could he do it? Could he pull the trigger? And if he did, would he save Willow's life or end it?

The forest thickened and the two disappeared. The window of opportunity had closed. Just as well.

Austin understood the sheriff's plan. He would draw Austin

to him. He'd already killed Heath, or so he thought, and now he would eliminate everyone who knew Charlie's true identity. He must have some plan to explain this. He was the sheriff—he could make it look any way he wanted.

The scent of fear and desperation wafted up to him—his own. *Please, God, give me a plan.*

CHAPTER FIFTY-NINE

Stones in the river bottom had pressed hard against Charlie's feet as she'd made her way to safety, the pain nothing compared to the sheer terror she'd endured. She'd fought to keep her head above the river as the swift current had carried her out of the canyon. Eventually, she'd found a shallow eddy and a way out.

Still, her jump into the river could have killed her just as easily as the sheriff could have.

Why would Sheriff Haines want her dead? The same reasons he'd killed her mother? The masked man that night—it had to have been him. He claimed he hadn't killed Momma, but any man who could murder someone could lie about it.

He hadn't been willing to answer her questions. Just wanted her death to look like an accident. But she'd been smarter and faster.

At least she'd survived the river, and then she'd dragged one foot after another, making her way out of the water. She'd dropped to the pebbled riverbank, her fingers digging into the gray silt and rocks. She'd closed her eyes and succumbed to sheer exhaustion. She had no idea how long she'd rested, but

305

she wished she hadn't stopped. Because he wouldn't. He would never stop looking for her.

All she'd wanted was answers. Now she had more questions.

Somehow Charlie had to make it back to civilization and get help. She wasn't sure who would believe her. Her word against Sheriff Haines's?

But Mack. He would come looking for her when she didn't show this morning. He was probably already on his way, which would put him in danger. He wouldn't suspect Sheriff Haines.

She'd been so wrong about everything. Queasiness roiled inside her. She curled into a ball until it passed. Pushing to her knees, she drew on an inner strength she hadn't known existed inside her.

She had to make it back. She had to find and warn Mack.

Charlie took in her surroundings. She'd run far enough from the sheriff that when she'd jumped in the river, it carried her back down, closer to where she wanted to head.

She could thank the river for that. No, maybe it was like Mack always tried to tell her—she should thank God. She didn't much feel like thanking him right now, if he even cared about her. If he did, why was she in this mess at all?

Tears burned her eyes. Every part of her body ached from lack of sleep, and the tumble into the river, and fighting the current. Her soul ached—if that was even possible. Still, she could give prayer another try.

God, thank you. Thank you for letting the river save me instead of taking me down and under. Now . . . can you help me make it back? Please, let good win this time.

Because evil had won when it killed her mother.

Charlie forced herself to keep going as she hiked along the riverbank until she could head east, away from the river. She had to make her way through the forest until she found the trail that would take her past the cabin and back down the mountain toward the Emerald M Ranch. Mack no longer used the trail for the guest ranch for horseback riding because it got too steep and rocky in places, and a twelve-year-old girl had gotten hurt. For a while, Charlie had felt like she'd had her very own trail. She loved working with the horses and living in the wilderness, and wished it hadn't been under the direst of circumstances.

As she shoved through underbrush, over boulders, and between trees to make her way back to the trail, she kept her senses attuned to the nature around her—and to the fact that the sheriff might be hunting her.

After more hiking, in the distance, she caught a glimpse of a portion of the trail. Farther down, she'd find the cabin. She would steer good and clear of it and keep on the lookout for the sheriff. He wanted her dead. Pressing her back against a tree, she squeezed her eyes shut and sent up a prayer for protection. It helped, actually, believing that she wasn't alone. That Someone was listening to and watching over her.

Charlie stepped over a fallen branch but didn't quite clear it. She tumbled forward, slamming one kneecap into a rock. Pain stabbed through her knee. She pulled it to her chest, waiting for the pain to subside.

What would happen if she just waited here? Would anyone come for her? Would anyone besides the person who wanted her dead find her?

Charlie couldn't wait. She was more concerned about the help she knew she could count on—Mack. Using the branch she'd fallen over, she climbed to her feet and spotted a form resting up against a rock. His head lolled to the side. And blood. So much blood.

Mack!

CHAPTER SIXTY

Sweating and out of breath, Sheriff Haines paced the cave. He watched the opening. Fisted and refisted his free hand, the other gripping an oversized pistol.

"Why couldn't you heed the warnings?" he asked. "It didn't have to come to this. I didn't want to hurt Charlie. She was doing just fine lost to the world. All you had to do was stop. Didn't you think about her life? Now look what you've done."

Her hands bound with plastic ties again, Willow pushed herself into the shadows and against the rocky wall as though a secret passage would open up behind her and she would simply fall through. She received pain as her reward when the wall denied her entrance. She couldn't watch him anymore and turned her face. Where light illuminated, faded petroglyphs could be seen on the walls. Was this cave so secluded that no one had discovered it yet? He'd gone out of his way to find this hiding place.

Another guy was in the cave too. A bruise on his head, he was out cold. Sheriff Haines kept fidgeting with that Taser. She hoped he wouldn't use it on her.

She hadn't thought she'd find herself in this position again so soon after her experience last night, when she was freezing in the wilderness, left to face off with all manner of wild creatures. Still, that would have been better than facing off with a wild man.

One thing she knew. Sheriff Haines hadn't been the one to carry her last night. He didn't have a broken arm. Nor did he appear injured, even if she'd been wrong about the arm. Then who else was involved?

She just didn't get it. Why didn't he just kill her and be done with it?

Finished with his anguished discourse, he edged to the cave opening, stood in the shadows, and waited. All she could see from here was his silhouette. He had to be waiting for Austin to come for her. The sheriff had seen that she meant something to him. And now she wished she hadn't allowed Austin to protect her or care for her. He probably thought he'd failed again, which would crush him after what he'd been through. But she understood—his brother had been dying. Nor did she blame him for going after Charlie.

His options had been limited.

Willow loathed tears. How she hated them, but she couldn't stop them from streaming down her cheeks. She wanted to growl in anger, to force the tears back. But she didn't want to draw the sheriff's attention.

She knew Austin would be here soon and put himself in danger for her. He would follow the tracks to the hidden cave in search of her. She still wore the necklace, but he would need a signal to find her. Maybe she could do something to save herself. If she could find a rock, maybe she could approach the sheriff from behind and use it. Lift her tied hands. But the sheriff was taller than she was by several inches. He'd gotten the upper hand with Heath, a former Green Beret. What did she think *she* could do?

Heath . . .

God, please help Heath. Send someone to find him. Her heart said the prayer, but she struggled to believe anyone would find Heath in time to save him. He'd sacrificed himself for Charlie. Charlie! What had happened to her? Had the sheriff already disposed of her? She had to believe, to keep holding on to hope, that Charlie was okay. That they would all make it out of this alive.

Except, JT hadn't made it out alive.

If he had lived, what would he tell her now? She struggled to recall his wise words, but they didn't come to her. Nor did any direction from God surface in her heart.

If you could just show me a way out. Help Austin.

That's exactly what needed to happen. Austin needed to find and save her, like he did last night. But he needed time to do that, so maybe she could help him along a little by hounding the sheriff with questions.

She swallowed the sudden lump in her throat. "Why did you take Charlie all those years ago?"

His intimidating form shifted at the cave entrance, then he stomped back toward her. "I told you to keep quiet."

"I deserve answers. And who is that guy? Just someone who got in your way?"

The sheriff crouched down to eye level, his presence formidable. Maybe she shouldn't have asked. "You have it all wrong. I didn't take her."

"Then what's this all about? If you aren't behind Charlie's abduction when she was a baby, then who is? Did you kill Marilee?"

"Enough with the questions. You thought you were some kind of investigator. Well, you got it all wrong." Deep frown lines, coupled with overwhelming regret in his bloodshot eyes, made him appear ten years older. He shook his head and headed back to the cave entrance without giving her any answers.

Willow stared straight ahead. He was right. She'd failed miserably. JT never would have found himself in this situation if he had lived to come to Wyoming to follow through with finding Charlie.

The consummate puzzle solver, JT loved to fix things. Her thoughts went back to his response after one of her rage-filled moments six months after her parents had died. *"If I could fix this for you, I would."* He was that kind of grandfather.

"You owe me an explanation," she said. "My grandfather was killed because of this. He was everything to me."

Sheriff Haines slowly turned to look back at her—the hurt and pain in his eyes more than evident. Could it be?

"I'd do just about anything for friends and family." The sheriff's words came back to her.

Only in this case, Heath hadn't rated as friend or family. JT would have fixed whatever was broken in Willow's life, if he could have. "That's it, isn't it? You're doing this for someone you love. For a child, or a grandchild."

The truth registered in his eyes, but he said nothing.

"Give it up, Haines," Austin shouted from outside the cave. "I know what you're up to. You can't get away with it."

Willow's heart leapt with joy, but fear for Austin anchored it to the ground. "Austin, I'm inside and okay."

Maybe her outcry had been exactly what the sheriff had wanted—otherwise he would have gagged her in addition to tying her up.

"If Heath dies because of you," Austin said, "or if you hurt Willow, there isn't any place on this earth where you can hide. Let her go."

"I'll trade her for you."

"No! Austin, no!" she screamed. "You must know it's a trap. He's only going to kill us all." Willow had no idea how Austin could get them out of this. The sheriff had the upper hand and he knew it.

She had to help. Somehow, she had to do something. Then Austin stepped into view, his hands lifted. The sheriff pointed his weapon at Austin as he entered the cave.

"What . . . what are you doing? Are you crazy?" She stared at

Austin. His walking in there to give himself up was not the heroic act she had expected.

He grinned. Really? Something was funny? "I came for you. I'd think you'd show a little more gratitude."

"He's going to kill us," she said.

"Shut up, both of you."

"You can let her go now," Austin said. "That was our deal. A trade. Remember?"

"I can't let her go," the sheriff said.

Austin didn't seem to register the sheriff's words. They hadn't surprised him. He took in the guy still unconscious on the cave floor. "What? Are we going to wait for him to wake up before you kill us?"

"What do you mean?" Willow looked at the guy, who groaned. If what Austin said was true, they had a few precious moments and that was it.

"You're smart," the sheriff said. "I'll give you that."

"He wants it to look like this poor soul kidnapped and tried to kill us. You probably had intended that for Charlie, but she got away."

Could it be true? That would mean Charlie was still alive.

"Even if she survived the river, if she's out there somewhere, it'll be her word against mine."

"See, it was this guy all along, he wants the world to think." Austin directed his words to Willow but kept his eyes on the sheriff. What was Austin planning? "This guy killed Marilee and tried to find and kill Charlie, but we got in the way. Once we're all dead, there's nobody to say it happened differently. But what I don't get is why."

"I think I do. I think someone was paying him to keep an eye on Charlie. If someone was close to learning the truth and finding her, then he was supposed to kill her," Willow said. "He said he'd tried to warn us away, so he was the one who left the notes. In that way, he had hoped to save Charlie, but we didn't heed the warnings. All this because someone he loves is in trouble. He needs money to save them."

"I don't owe you an explanation, but I didn't kill Marilee. I'm sorry it had to come to this. I never intended for it to go this far, but now that it has, I have to protect my family."

Now that was something Willow could relate to. "So you *are* a family man. Kids? Grandkids? What do you think they'll think about their grandfather once they find out?"

His eyes glistened. "They won't find out. I have to do this for them."

"Surely no amount of money is worth murder. And Heath, he was your friend. You said he was like a son to you."

"Desperation can make you do things you can't imagine. Money means survival. Multiple organ transplants for a sick child when insurance has maxed out. People die waiting for their turn on the list. I would do anything for my grandson. I didn't set out to kill anyone. I didn't kill Charlie's mother. I tried to warn you away from finding Charlie. Why didn't you listen?"

"How'd you even find her?"

He scoffed. "Find her? I never lost her. I've been watching her for years. This is all on you. Now I'm in too deep, and have no choice but to follow through. Tanner will be taken care of now. He'll have his whole life ahead of him."

The weight of his words pressed against her heart. She sank to the ground. "Someone paid you. Someone is paying you to do this. Who is it? I want to know before I die."

Hurt flickered in Austin's eyes. She read the message there. *Have a little faith.*

Seriously. He would get them out of this?

"So what's the plan?" Austin asked. "It'll have to look like there was a struggle between me and that guy to explain the knot on his head and his concussion. Maybe I hit him and then he shoots me and I bleed out?"

Why was Austin giving the sheriff ideas about how to kill him? Willow stayed where she was on the ground. She had no idea what he was doing. He'd lost it. Really lost it. Maybe it had everything to do with the fact that he'd failed that last assignment with the FBI and it was messing with his mind now.

She couldn't stand to watch. Couldn't stand to see him losing his mind right before her eyes.

"He's a good man, Willow. He'd be good for you."

Austin had come with baggage. At the time, JT had seen past all that. What would he say if he could see them now?

"You think you're some kind of hotshot, don't you? That you're going to somehow save the day."

"I do."

Suddenly Austin flicked out a knife and threw it at the sheriff, who fired his weapon. The knife stuck in his chest, in his heart, and he fell backward, dropping the gun.

Austin fell to the ground and Willow crawled to him. Grimacing, he sucked in a breath.

She cupped his face and peered into his eyes, hoping and praying he was still with her. "Austin, please, are you okay?"

"Yes," he croaked out. "I wore a vest. Figured I would end up standing between you and danger."

He crawled over to the sheriff. The man's expression was dazed and pale, his eyes glazing over. Deputy Taggart rushed into the cave holding Heath's rifle. "Glad I gave you my vest," he said.

"My kids . . . my grandson," Sheriff Haines pleaded. "Please help him get the money. I did it for him."

"If you didn't kill Marilee, then who did?" Austin asked.

He shrugged. "Charlie . . . didn't have to die. If you had never found her, she could have lived."

His eyes unfocused. He was gone. Willow shut her eyes. They still hadn't found the connection. She'd completely missed Sheriff Haines as a possible suspect.

314

While Deputy Taggart used his radio to call for help, Austin cut the ties on her hands and feet and helped her stand up. He wrapped his arms around her. How many times would she end up in his arms under these kinds of circumstances? She longed for the day, for the moment, when she could be in his arms because . . . because they were meant to be. She pressed her face into his chest but only felt the hard vest that had protected him. She stepped back and looked into his eyes. "Are you sure you're okay?"

"It hurts a bit." He took off his shirt and removed the vest.

The man at the back of the cave stirred. His voice was gruff. "Oh man, you killed the sheriff? I would have liked to have made him suffer before he died."

Willow eyed the guy. Had he been pretending to be unconscious? "Are you okay? And who are you, anyway?"

"Clyde. Clyde Everett. I loved Marilee. I wanted to marry her, only she had a thing for some other guy who wasn't even from here. But all these years and she couldn't get over him." Clyde wobbled as he stood and reached for the wall, his voice cracking with anger. "He'd come back to town. She was going to go see him. Meet him at a motel. But someone killed her instead. And this guy, a sheriff for crying out loud, he grabbed me at my house and shocked me with that Taser, tied me up to bring me to the cave. Knocked me out again. My head is killing me now."

"Who?" Austin asked. "Who was she going to see?"

"I don't know his name. But if he loved her like she thought he did, he wouldn't have left her. But if you can believe this jerk sheriff, it wasn't him who killed her. I think he was lying."

"I need to get back to my brother to make sure he's okay." Austin turned his attention to Willow. "I went looking for Charlie."

She nodded. "But you found me."

He weaved his hands through her hair, raw emotion pouring from his eyes. Her heart stumbled around inside—she was dizzy with what she felt for him.

"Willow, we need—"

"To find Heath." She stepped back, fearing what he might say. "Let's go get your brother."

"You go on," Deputy Taggart said. "I've called for emergency services and law enforcement. I'll stay here with the sheriff's body."

"Come on, then." Austin took her hand. "Let's get back to Heath. We have to stay alert. Don't forget that Charlie's still in danger. The sheriff wasn't the one running this show. He didn't do this alone."

She hated saying the words, but Austin needed to know. "Heath was alive when I left him to get gunshot wound powder," she said. "He didn't tell you how bad he was. I never made it back with the powder."

Was he already dead? Would Austin blame her?

CHAPTER SIXTY-ONE

The distant whir of a helicopter gave Austin hope as they exited the cave. He needed to get to Heath as fast as possible. He turned to Willow and Clyde. "Are you okay to keep up?"

Clyde grabbed his head. "No, man. I can't make it. My head is killing me. I'll wait with the deputy."

Austin could relate to that pain.

Willow nodded. "I'm right behind you." The determination in her eyes convinced him. Admiration pinged in his heart, but he had no time to ponder matters of the heart when his brother's life was on the line.

If it wasn't already too late.

Austin grabbed her hand and pushed forward through the thick vegetation, leading them back to Heath. This would take far too long, if what Willow said was true—that Heath had been in worse condition than he'd let on. He'd risked his life for Charlie, but that was no surprise. Heath had always been a protector. He'd always put others first. Why had Austin let anything come between them? Why had he stayed away so long?

His anguish-filled heart cried out to God as he pushed himself to make it back to Heath. *God, please . . . help him! I can't lose him too. Do you hear me? I can't lose him too!*

He'd thought he'd made the right decision by leaving his brother and Willow, but getting Heath to safety would have been the better choice. Charlie had escaped on her own.

Though he couldn't have known that, guilt threatened to take him down and under.

"Do you hear the helicopter? We're getting closer." Hope surged in Willow's voice. "Do you think help came for Heath?"

"I hope so."

"I was never able to connect or make a call. I don't know how they would have known."

"Taggart. Deputy Taggart said Charlie had called him. She's with Heath." The deputy had come across Austin in the woods, having followed the same tracks. Charlie had called him, he said, but Heath had already lost a lot of blood. The deputy explained that he'd become suspicious of the sheriff when he hadn't followed through with the investigation of the break-in at the cabin. Then the note that Austin had bagged had disappeared from the evidence room. Taggart had loaned his vest to Austin when the decision was made for him to go into the cave with Haines to save Willow.

Austin pushed faster, pulling harder on her hand. Minutes later, he could hear the helicopter growing distant. No. Austin released Willow's hand and ran. Her footfalls were right behind him.

"Hey!" He waved his hands up in the air like an idiot. No one could see them through the canopy.

Willow tugged on his sleeve. "Look."

Park rangers and deputies, along with search and rescue volunteers combed the area.

"Someone's coming."

Sheriff Everett jogged toward them. "Charlie called me on her SAT phone. I think she contacted everyone in two counties. Wyoming Highway Patrol brought in the helicopter to lift your brother out and get him to the hospital as fast as possible. We got him." The guy's expression remained grim, discouraging Austin from asking questions. He didn't want to hear anything else. He only wanted to hold on to hope.

"Sheriff Haines is in the cave," Austin said. "He's dead. Deputy Taggart is with him. Just head toward the canyon southeast or contact Taggart, who's waiting for help."

"Charlie told me what happened. She thinks he killed her mother," Sheriff Everett said.

"No. Someone else is involved," Willow said. "But Sheriff Haines wanted it to look like it was Clyde Everett. Is Clyde related to you?"

The sheriff pursed his lips. "Why that—"

"Heath." Austin said his brother's name, demanding information with one word. He'd changed his mind. He did want to know more, and he didn't have time to talk about Sheriff Haines, someone whose troubles in this life were over.

"He's going to make it, don't you worry," Sheriff Everett said. "He's strong. But he's in a bad way."

"Where's Charlie?" Willow asked.

"A deputy took her to the hospital to see Heath and to get her statement. I'll let the others know where we can find Taggart and Haines."

"And Clyde. He's there in the cave. The sheriff hit him on the head. He's conscious and seems okay," Willow said.

Willow studied Austin, her eyes filled with grief. "Austin, there's something I need to tell you. Heath told me that Haines said your father wasn't drunk. That the accident wasn't his fault, after all." Her voice trembled. "And something else . . . Heath hoped you could forgive him for being disappointed. He . . . he wanted you to know how proud he is of you."

Those could be the last words of a dying man. Austin stumbled. Willow reached for him and moved in close. He hugged her to him, his heart in turmoil.

Austin hung his head. He never should have left Heath or Willow.

CHAPTER SIXTY-TWO

Austin and Willow got out of the deputy's vehicle. Austin thanked the Bridger County deputy who had brought them to the small county hospital in Grayback.

Willow squeezed his hand. "Let's go see your brother."

As much as he wanted to check on Heath, he hesitated. "Wait. You realize that Charlie is probably in the waiting room. We've never met her. This is it, Willow. This will likely be the end of our search. Are you ready to tell her?"

Her eyes welled with tears, but she blinked them away. "I don't know yet. Let's check on Heath. Let me think and pray. I'll call Katelyn first, just to be sure she wants me to tell her."

"Fair enough. We won't say anything until we know what Katelyn wants." He lifted her hand to his lips and kissed her soft skin.

His action put color back into her cheeks. His heart so open and raw at the moment, he didn't have the composure to hold back. Bad timing all around, but he'd made more mistakes than anyone had a right to make—losing Willow again wouldn't be one of them. Not if he could help it. But first, he had to make sure Heath was going to be all right.

320

"Let's go," he said, leading her to the hospital entrance.

The hospital doors whooshed open. At the information desk, a silver-haired, weathered woman with kind eyes smiled up at them. "May I help you?"

"I'm Austin McKade—here to check on my brother Heath. They should have brought him in already."

Her eyes brightened as if she knew Heath personally. "He's in surgery now, but you go on down and wait for him. I'll be praying for him. That brother of yours is a good man."

I know. Heath had been Austin's hero. As they walked the long corridor, he thought about Heath.

Funny, they had reconciled without so much as a conversation about what had kept them apart. But there was no need. The understanding had passed between them—they were brothers. That's all that mattered. All was forgiven.

For Austin's part, he should never have let anything come between them, especially his inability to accept Heath's disappointment in him. He hadn't wanted to come back just to face his brother's disappointment, or the reminders of their cruel childhood. He hadn't wanted to return just to be reminded of the role he'd played in Dad's fatal accident. But if Haines could be believed, it sounded like Austin wasn't to blame. Dad hadn't been drunk, like they had been informed.

And maybe he could never make Dad proud before he'd died, but he could make his older brother, Heath, proud instead. Heath had always been there for him.

God, please let him live.

In the small space with carpet and chairs deemed the waiting area, Austin slowed his pace. Willow sidled next to him. "I could use some coffee. How about you?"

He reached into his pocket for his wallet.

"I got it," a soft voice said.

Willow and Austin turned to see Charlie standing next to

a coffee machine. Austin would recognize her anywhere, even though her hair was now blonde and spiked. She looked like a younger version of her mother. "I've seen you two coming and going at the ranch while I worked with the horses. I know you're Mack's brother."

"Mack?"

"That's what I call Heath. He's like a big brother to me." She angled her head, looking like a bashful schoolgirl for a moment. "I'm sorry. Where are my manners?" She thrust out her hand. "I'm Charlotte Clemmons."

Austin and Willow introduced themselves.

"You can call me Charlie. It's what my mom used to call me." Charlie's hands trembled as she inserted coins into the machine.

Used to. As in not anymore. After everything she'd been through, she had the resilience to offer to buy them coffee.

"What'll it be?" she asked.

"Two coffees, please." The look in Willow's eyes reflected some of what Austin was feeling. Out of all the imaginings of this moment—facing Charlie—he never envisioned her buying them coffee.

Austin had agreed with Willow that they wouldn't tell Charlie the truth. Not yet. But to continue talking to her like this without revealing who they were and what they wanted wouldn't buy them any points later. How should they handle it? He frowned and looked down the hallway toward the doors, eager for news on Heath.

"I need to find out about my brother," he said.

"They told me he would be fine. All we can do is wait now."

"Thank you for saving his life," Austin said. "Sheriff Everett told me you made the call for help."

"I found the horses too and something I could use to stop the bleeding. I don't think help would have made it in time otherwise. Not to pat myself on the back, but I want you to know it was serious. I tried to come back and warn him not to trust Sheriff Haines.

All he cared about was you two. He wanted to know if you were all right. I see now that you are."

How much did Charlie know about what had happened? And what exactly had transpired between her and the sheriff?

Coffee in hand, Austin motioned for them to have a seat in the waiting area. "You look like you've been through a rough day." His smile was broad for Charlie's benefit, but deep inside he knew Willow's news was about to shatter her world again. News of the crime her mother committed would come as a genuine shock to her, as well as the fact that she could still be in danger.

So could Willow. He reached for her, but she stepped away. "If you'll excuse me, can I borrow your phone?" she asked.

Austin handed it over and she headed down the hallway. He trusted she wouldn't go too far. They weren't out of this yet.

He purchased pretzels, chips, and cookies from the vending machines to go with their coffee. Charlie ate up the snacks like she hadn't eaten in far too long.

"It feels so good to be free. Finally free. It's a long story, but usually I don't talk to anyone except, well, Mack. He was the only one who knew I was here."

"Is that right?"

"I don't know what he told you, but I've been hiding, trying to find out who killed my mom. I still don't know why she was killed. All along I thought Clyde had done it, and that his cousin, Sheriff Everett, had protected him. But it turns out Sheriff Haines was responsible. I have bank statements back at the house. They have something to do with it." She covered her mouth, her face turning several shades of crimson. "I should tell this to someone official. The deputy who brought me was supposed to take my statement, but he had to rush away."

"Someone should be here soon to take our statements about what happened. I don't know if they told you, but Sheriff Haines is dead."

She nodded slowly. "I heard talk on the radio. It should be a relief, except I don't understand why. Why would he kill her?" Tears choked her voice. "He said he didn't kill her, but he tried to kill me. Why should I believe a liar? He kept talking about the truth. The truth would tear me apart. What truth could hurt me more than watching my mother murdered in cold blood?"

"I'm sorry about your mother."

She swiped at her eyes. "At least it's over now. At least he got what he deserved. I wanted answers. Now all I have are questions, memories, and the house. She and I owned the house together, but I don't want to go back there. Not without her. I tried, but I hear her voice like an echo. I miss her so much."

Charlie broke down and cried. Austin pursed his lips. Willow lingered in the hallway, watching, a look of turmoil on her face.

CHAPTER SIXTY-THREE

Willow moved down the hall with Austin's phone to her ear. She hadn't connected the call to Katelyn yet because Charlie's anguish ricocheted through her heart. But it was time. Still, she hesitated. Katelyn had hired Willow to find her daughter. But Charlie loved Marilee as deeply as any daughter should. She loved the woman who raised her.

The woman who abducted her.

It was painfully obvious that Marilee had loved Charlie in return. Still, Willow suspected that someone had paid her to take the baby. Had she so desperately wanted her own child and then all the pieces had fallen into place? Clyde had mentioned a man she'd loved for years. A man who wasn't from here. She thought back to his words.

"He'd come back to town. She was going to go see him. Meet him at a motel. But someone killed her instead." Was the man she loved and couldn't get over somehow connected to the abduction? Or to Marilee's murder? Regardless of the answers to those questions, Charlie was the one who had to deal with all of this now.

How could Willow shatter the young woman's world once again? Bottom line? It wasn't up to her.

She pressed the call button and waited for Katelyn to answer.

Part of her hoped she wouldn't. Willow drew in a breath. She had to see this through.

Lord, help me to do what's right. I don't even know what that is.

"Hello?" Katelyn answered the phone.

"Hi, Katelyn, it's Willow. How are you? Are you still in the hospital?"

"I'm home for the time being. My white blood cell count is up. I keep fooling them by living. Never mind about me. What is it? Do you have news?"

Willow squeezed her eyes shut. *Lord* . . . "We found her."

Silence.

She listened intently. "Katelyn? Are you all right?"

"Yes." She sniffled. "Yes. I just . . . I can't believe it. I can hardly believe it." The woman's laugh was sheer joy.

Now Willow would have to bring her back down to reality. "I haven't told her anything."

"Why on earth not?"

Willow squeezed her eyes shut. How would she explain the situation? "She's been through so much. She loved the mother who raised her. It was heartbreaking listening to her talk about her. Jamie witnessed someone kill her mother two months ago, and she's been afraid for her life. She's been hiding. I thought you would want to know about that. I thought that, given the circumstances, you might even change your mind about telling her. It would just be that much more for her to deal with."

Katelyn hesitated, then sniffled again. "I don't want to hurt her or make this hard for her, but I'm desperate to see her. Maybe if you tell her about me, that will be the good news she needs to hear. That her biological mother is still alive for the time being. Jamie has a second chance, in a manner of speaking."

"It's Charlie."

"Pardon?"

"Her name is Charlotte Clemmons. She goes by Charlie."

"Would you please tell her I'm coming? Where are you exactly?"

"At the moment, we're in the hospital. My friend's brother was wounded. It's complicated." Willow wasn't sure she had the energy to tell Katelyn the whole story.

"Do we know who abducted her?"

"We have a few leads. Someone who was involved was killed, though, so we can't get all the answers yet."

"Well, of course, we want the person responsible brought to justice, but right now I'm making plans to come and see my daughter. She needs the support of family now. Willow, can you do this or not?"

"Yes. I can." Willow wouldn't leave it to anyone else. Charlie definitely needed to be warned her birth mother was coming. "But there's just one thing. What if she doesn't want to see you?"

"Not want to see her mother? Let's hope that's not the case. I haven't been searching all these years to be rejected now."

No. I wouldn't think so.

Footfalls in the hall drew her head up. Charlie and Austin headed her way. They must have news about Heath.

She needed to go. Willow hesitated, then asked, "Are you well enough to travel?"

"I've been released from the hospital, Willow. This news does more for my health, my well-being, than anything. Now please tell me where I can meet you."

"Fly into Jackson, Wyoming. Call me when you get there. I'll tell her you're coming." Willow ended the call and handed the phone back to Austin. "Is it Heath?"

"Yes," he said. "He's out of surgery. They're letting me see him. You're coming too. I won't leave you alone. Not until this is over, and maybe not even then." He turned his attention to Charlie. "You either. You stick close to us. This isn't over yet."

"What do you mean?"

"The real killer is still out there."

Charlie narrowed her eyes as if unsure she could believe Austin. Willow followed Austin and Charlie down several hallways. How would she break this news to Charlie? How would she tell her about the heinous deed committed by the woman who raised her?

Austin pushed open the door to Heath's room and entered quietly. Willow and Charlie followed. "Mack—" Charlie rushed to the edge of the bed and acted as if she would put a hand on his arm but decided against it. Tears formed in her eyes.

Willow hung back in the corner, watching the scene. Monitors beeped and IV lines connected Heath with clear bags of meds. Austin stood near the bed, his features brooding at the sight of his unconscious brother.

A nurse bustled into the room, unsurprised by their presence. "He's going to be just fine. I want to see some smiles now for when he wakes up." She disappeared in the same way she'd rushed in.

"I'm going out into the hall to make another call," Willow said. "All right if I use your phone again?"

"Of course." His eyes dark with emotion, he lifted his chin with a clear warning in his eyes. *Stay close.*

"I'll be just right there."

He handed her his phone. "Leave the door open."

Willow did as he asked, but she didn't want anyone hearing her call to Dana. The woman's panicked voice probably echoed down the hallway.

"Sh. I'm okay. Keep your voice down. I think everyone can hear you. It's been a long night. An impossibly long night."

"I've left dozens of messages on your voicemail."

"Unfortunately, I lost my phone. It's a long story—one I can't go into right now." Willow whispered her next words. "But I wanted you to know . . . we found her."

Dana's exuberance exploded over the phone.

328

"I've contacted Katelyn and she's on her way here. But it's not all good. I haven't told Charlie yet. And the person who doesn't want Charlie found is still out there. She could still be in danger. Maybe I've had it all wrong. Maybe whoever did this isn't connected to Katelyn through Wyoming."

Dana's sigh was heavy. "I know what you're thinking, Willow— that you don't have JT's gift for following hunches, but remember he led you there. So don't give up, and please, be careful. I'll keep searching on my end. I'm sorry I haven't found anything yet."

"There's no need to apologize. You're good at what you do. I trust you. Just let me know once you've found something."

Willow turned to see Charlie standing there.

"What's going on? What haven't you told me?"

CHAPTER SIXTY-FOUR

Willow ended the call and tucked the phone away. "We need to talk."

"What's this about?" Charlie narrowed her eyes again. She'd been suspicious for so long, it had probably become second nature.

Austin appeared in the doorway. "I talked to Heath. Just briefly. But he's going to be okay. I just needed to see him. I'm going to let him rest now."

Willow wanted to go to Austin. Feel his arms around her. Comfort him after everything they'd been through. But she remained where she stood—Charlie between them.

"Charlie needs answers."

His lips flattened as he gave a subtle nod. "We should go somewhere private."

"Wait. You're scaring me. I don't know if I should leave Mack."

"Charlie." Heath's ragged voice barely registered. "Charlie . . ."

She answered his call, entering the room, Willow and Austin behind her.

"Go with them. You can trust them. They'll protect you. And you need to listen to what they have to say."

Charlie's eyes widened. Her bottom lip trembled.

Willow had thought she was setting out to do good when she'd accepted this assignment. JT had believed the same. But right now, she didn't know. She really didn't know. "It's okay, Charlie. We know what happened to your mother. Why someone killed her. That's what you want to know, isn't it?" Or at least they had their suspicions. Willow had some ideas, and after this hard conversation, she would chase down another clue.

"Yes. I don't understand. How could you know?"

"Maybe you should tell her here in the room," Heath said. "I can't keep my eyes open. But I'm listening. Charlie, have a seat."

This would put a strain on Heath, but then again, maybe he'd be more worried about Charlie if she left with them. She slowly eased into the chair. "Tell me. Why did the sheriff kill her?"

"He claimed he didn't kill her, but he knew who did." Willow glanced at Austin. "We're still working on the who, but we came here to find you. We've been searching for you, Charlie, before we knew anything about your mother's death."

Her face paled. "Go on."

Willow didn't know how to continue, except to start at the beginning. "A woman named Katelyn Mason hired us to find her daughter. Her baby who was abducted from a hospital room twenty-one years ago."

Silence filled the room. Charlie shifted in the seat. "What does that have to do with me?"

Willow edged closer and crouched in front of Charlie. *Help me, Jesus.* "It's you, Charlie. You're the girl."

Charlie's expression morphed into unbelief and she forced herself as far back into the chair as she could, like a little girl afraid of a monster. "What? What are you saying? Are you saying my mother isn't my mother? That's crazy. Mack, you can't believe them."

Tears surged in Willow's eyes. If only Katelyn could see how much this hurt Charlie. She'd been through so much already. "We can do a DNA test if you'd like, but considering someone has gone to a lot of trouble to keep us from finding you and to try to stop the truth from coming out—even murdering your mother for what she knew—we're pretty sure." Willow wouldn't be there saying the words if she didn't know for certain she was looking at Katelyn Mason's daughter.

Tears streamed down Charlie's cheeks. "My mother. She's my mother, not this stranger who hired you."

Austin fiddled with his phone, then held it up to Charlie. "Here's a picture of Katelyn Mason at twenty-one."

Charlie took in the woman in the image. "She looks like me. So what? That doesn't mean she's my mother." Charlie pressed her face into her hands and sobbed.

"I'm so sorry about all of this. Katelyn . . . your mother . . . she has leukemia. She's gone in and out of remission, and now she only has a couple of months to live. She might not have much time. She wanted to find her daughter. She wanted to see you, have a chance to speak to you before she dies." Acid erupted in her throat. Willow hated the words. Hated feeling like she was guilting Charlie into seeing Katelyn.

"The good news is that you still have time to see her and get to know her before it's too late." Austin crossed his arms. "Just give her a chance."

"There's something else you should know." Willow wasn't sure Charlie, who continued to sob, was listening anymore. "She's coming here to Jackson. Katelyn Mason will be here in the next few hours. No later than tomorrow morning."

"Yeah. Well, what if I don't want to see her?"

"Try to understand. She lost you once years ago, and she's longed to find you and see you. She's spent a lot of money paying private investigators over the years. Could you bear to break her heart? Please. Just give her a chance." She echoed Austin's words.

"I think Charlie needs a few minutes, guys." Heath's words were garbled.

Willow agreed. Heath knew her better. He could talk to her.

The news might have been better coming from him to begin with. She and Austin left Charlie in the room with Heath, or Mack, as she preferred. They stood in a shadowed corner of the waiting area outside this section of rooms. The killer was still out there and Charlie wouldn't be safe until they found out who was behind this. Down the hall, Deputy Taggart marched in their direction.

"We need to go back to the nursing home," she whispered to Austin. She needed to speak to Mr. Haus again.

"I think you're right."

That surprised her. She hadn't thought he would agree. She assumed he would tell her they had found Charlie, which was all they had been hired to do. But like her, he knew Charlie wasn't safe until the person behind her abduction was found. Besides, Willow wouldn't give up until she found justice for JT and Marilee. She and Austin—they were in this together. It should have been JT, but instead it was Austin. Willow thought she just might have finally accepted that fact.

Deputy Taggart hung near Heath's door and eyed them from across the hall, a question in his eyes. Then he crossed the space and approached them. "Well, how is he?"

"He's strong. I think he's going to be okay."

"I need to talk to Charlie. Then I need to hear from you two. We have a sheriff down. I think I understand all the facts, but I still have to do the hardest part of my job as acting sheriff now. I have to deliver the news of his death to his widow."

CHAPTER SIXTY-FIVE

Deputy Taggart had delivered Austin, Willow, and Charlie to the ranch after taking their statements and was leaving two deputies there to watch over Charlie. He was taking the threat seriously or at least didn't want to take any chances that Sheriff Haines hadn't been working alone.

"Is it all right if Willow and I go visit Mr. Haus at the nursing home?" Austin asked.

Deputy Taggart angled his head. "Why would you want to do that at a time like this? That girl needs you."

Evelyn set down a tray with mugs of steaming coffee. "She's sleeping soundly, and she knows and trusts me. I can take care of her if these two have something they need to do."

"Does it have anything to do with this investigation?" Deputy Taggart asked.

"Maybe," Austin said.

"This is a police matter now. I don't want you interfering with the investigation or putting yourselves in more danger."

"We were hired to investigate too, Deputy Taggart." Willow stared at her computer, looking beat. She was working on some-

334

thing and was determined to see this case through. Austin knew just how she felt.

They'd been hired to find Charlie, which they'd done. But she was still in danger until her abductor was brought to justice. Willow was likely still in danger as well. Besides, Austin wanted justice for JT as much as Willow did. "We're only going to question Mr. Haus, an elderly man in a nursing home. If we learn anything from him, we'll share that information with you. He's in Clair though, so Sheriff Everett will want to know what we find out too."

Deputy Taggart nodded. Many law enforcement entities would be involved before this ended, what with a cold case abduction victim found and the person they believed was behind Marilee's murder and the abduction still out there. Austin didn't have time to waste as they waited for others to get up to speed.

"I can't exactly tell you not to talk to Mr. Haus, but humor me. Come right back here. I want to keep track of everyone in case I have more questions, especially if a killer is still out there. Mind if I ask about his connection?"

"I'm not sure," Willow said. "Call it a hunch. He knew Marilee, Charlie's mother, who was murdered. I'm trying to find a link back to Texas and that hospital in Houston where Charlie was taken from."

Mr. Haus said Marilee knew his secret. Maybe he knew some of hers too. Maybe Mr. Haus knew the man she planned to meet the night she was murdered. Austin kept that part to himself. It was a long shot anyway.

"Fair enough." Taggart headed for the door. "Then come straight back to the ranch. Agreed?"

"Agreed," Austin said.

"Keep her safe, McKade."

To my last breath . . . Austin appreciated that Taggart trusted him to do just that. More than anything, he wanted this to be over so he could hold Willow. Kiss her. Tell her the emotions bursting through the cracks in his heart. Working through this with her had brought them closer than they had ever been.

———

Austin drove Heath's truck to the nursing home in Clair. Willow was quiet on the drive, but he understood. So much had happened within a short time that his mind had to catch up. Had to comprehend and internalize. Maybe he could see clearly what they had been missing all along.

Someone had paid Sheriff Haines to do his business. Had Marilee also been paid to abduct Charlie? What was this person's connection to the sheriff and Katelyn Mason? Why had law enforcement not found that connection early on but instead deemed the abduction random?

"You're sure quiet. What are you thinking?" he asked.

"I hope we aren't barking up the wrong tree, as Sheriff Everett put it."

"Well, he was wrong about that, wasn't he? We found her."

"Dead wrong. But we almost got her killed in the search too. Sheriff Haines had been warning us away."

"Since there's another person out there involved—the person who killed Marilee, if the sheriff can be believed—we don't know if Charlie would have been safe if we had left her alone to hide. The truth needed to come out."

"Needs to come out. We're not done here yet."

"I'm with you all the way. I need to know who was behind the abduction too, Willow. And for what it's worth, I think you're on the right track. It's a hunch JT would have followed. It's a thread. So we follow the threads." Would they finally find the right needle?

"You make an excellent investigator. You should apply to work for the FBI."

"I think I'm good right where I am."

"I'm glad you realize that." He hadn't been sure she would keep the business going with JT gone, but maybe now she would have the confidence to do so.

Once they arrived at the nursing home, he followed Willow in, letting her lead the way. She'd been wonderful with Mr. Haus before, forming a loose but warm friendship. He was certain the man would want to see her again—that is, if he remembered her. Dementia often had the unwanted effect of wiping the memory slate clean—short-term and long-term.

At the counter, they met another nurse, Bob. A thirty-something lanky guy with dark hair and glasses.

"We're here to see Mr. Haus."

"You family?"

"Friends. We came by a couple of days ago, and I told him I'd come back to see him," Willow said.

"I'm sorry to have to tell you this, but he passed away."

The news turned Austin's insides to stone.

Willow stumbled back a little. "I'm so sorry to hear that. When?"

"Last night."

Willow swayed. Austin grabbed her elbow. "What about Kim? Can we speak with her?"

"She's in Mr. Haus's room, clearing things out for his son." Bob ushered them past the circle of elderly patients in wheelchairs playing a game involving bubbles and down the long hallway to the farthest room on the left. "Here you go." He peeked his head into the room. "Kim, some people came to see Henry. Claim they knew him. I'll let you deal with it." To them, he said, "Go right in."

Austin ushered a shaky Willow into the room. Antiseptic and asparagus again. Kim eyed them. "Y'all are too late."

Pain etched Willow's face. "What happened?"

"What do you mean? The guy was ninety-two years old."

Willow roamed the room, eyeing the few knickknacks and photographs that sat out.

"He's been here so long, I didn't have the heart to take his stuff out to make room for the next person. He's been here longer than I have. Usually people don't stay so long. Insurance won't let them, or they die. But Mr. Haus beat the statistics."

Austin peered at the photographs along with Willow. She lifted one particular photograph. A man stood next to . . . was that . . . was that Sheriff Haines? Albeit a much younger man—a deputy at the time.

Willow showed it to Austin, then she asked Kim, "Who is this man?"

Kim pointed at the man standing next to Haines. "Mr. Haus's son. And that's his friend. He's the sheriff the next county over now, I hear. Sheriff Haines. I told you he only had one son."

Willow held Austin's gaze.

The man in the picture wasn't Silas Everett. Interesting. Then Kim didn't know that Mr. Haus was Sheriff Everett's biological father. Nor did she know that Mr. Haus had two sons, after all, just like he had said. Who knew? Marilee? Did Sheriff Everett even know his real father had died last night?

"That isn't true." A uniformed man filled the door frame, startling them. Sheriff Everett. He stepped all the way into the room, his law enforcement presence intimidating in the small space.

His features contorted. "He could never openly recognize me. After all, he'd had an affair with my mother that destroyed his family. Could have destroyed mine, except no one knew about it. Not even the man who raised me as his own knew Henry Haus was my real father." He picked up the picture of Haines standing next to Mr. Haus's other son. "Marilee brought him to meet me a couple of times a year for the last ten years or so."

"You're the secret, then. Mr. Haus said that Marilee knew his secret." Willow eyed Kim. "He told us he had two sons, but apparently only Marilee knew about that."

Regret filled his eyes as he shook his head. Then he angled it, suspicion shoving aside the regret. "Why are you two here?"

"We had hoped to ask Mr. Haus if he knew anything about a man Marilee was supposedly in love with. That's what Clyde told us."

Everett shook his head. "My cousin was insanely jealous. You can't listen to anything he says. That's why Marilee fought with him. She wanted out of the relationship. But I knew he couldn't kill anyone. I knew he hadn't killed her. He was with me."

"Sheriff, do you know anything about your half brother?" Austin asked.

"Nothing more than his name. He knew about me, before I knew the truth, and never contacted me. I figured he didn't want to meet me. I didn't know for the better part of my life that old Mr. Haus here was my father."

"He was here last night," Kim said. "He got to say goodbye before his father died."

Sheriff Everett narrowed his eyes. "How often did he come?"

"Usually once a year. Mr. Haus was surprised to see him."

"And he showed up last night? Why?" Willow asked.

"I couldn't say." Kim pursed her lips.

"What's his name?" Willow asked.

"Jay," Kim said.

"Jay . . . ?"

"Jay Haus, what else? After he left, we had to call him to let him know his father had died. At least Mr. Haus got to see his son one last time, only moments before he died."

Could Jay have killed his father because of the secrets he knew— the secrets Mr. Haus claimed Marilee had kept for him? If so, it wouldn't be a stretch if Jay had killed them both.

They had come to ask Mr. Haus if he knew who Marilee was supposed to meet at the motel the night she died. Had that man murdered her? Had Marilee kept her relationship with this man a secret even from Charlie?

But without Mr. Haus to answer their questions, it was another dead end.

Still. Maybe not. Jay Haus had been friends with Sheriff Haines. The sheriff had been working with someone.

Austin studied the contents of the box Kim had been filling with Mr. Haus's belongings. A flash of silver beneath a few shirts caught his attention. He tugged it out without asking permission. Willow looked over his shoulder. An elaborate western belt buckle.

Handcrafted by the Wyoming Silversmith Company.

"It's the same company that made Marilee's necklace," she said.

They'd never connected with Hank at the silversmith company, but there was no need now.

"Do either of you know where Jay Haus lives now?" Austin asked.

"Why are you asking?" Sheriff Everett studied Austin. "I can find out if you give me a reason to look."

"Marilee was the woman who abducted Charlie years ago. We know that Sheriff Haines was working with someone too. Someone who abducted Willow last night."

"Why would you suspect Jay?"

Austin rubbed his jaw. This was another thread. A very loose thread. Sheriff Everett didn't like his questions, but he pressed on. "Marilee kept your secret about Mr. Haus being your father. Did she ever say anything to you about a relationship with Jay?"

"No."

"I think she was good at keeping secrets," Willow said. "If Jay was behind Charlie's abduction and Marilee's murder, there could be a connection to Katelyn somehow. Something that was missed before," she said.

Maybe. But the sheriff wanted a solid reason to look into his half brother. Austin couldn't give him that.

"Was there anything unusual about him?" Willow asked.

Kim frowned. "I'm not sure what you mean. Like what?"

"Did he appear injured?"

Good question, Willow.

She shook her head. "No, he seemed fine."

Austin saw where she was going with the question, but if Jay was their man, he would have come here to see his father hours before he abducted Willow and hit the moose.

Willow faced the Sheriff. "Jay could have been the one to partner with Sheriff Haines in Charlie's abduction. Obviously they were friends."

Sheriff Everett didn't appear convinced.

"Did he bring his father any gifts last night?" Austin asked.

"He had a sack, yes," Kim said.

Austin peered into the garbage can. He pulled out his latex gloves and dug around in the can, then pulled out a package with a big State of Texas sticker on the front. "Pralines from Texas."

CHAPTER SIXTY-SIX

Willow took a long, hot shower. She'd left Austin to speak on his cell with Deputy Taggart about what they had learned. Sheriff Everett was already on it.

The investigation crossed county lines, and they would work together with the state police as well. But all the better—together they would find Mr. Haus's son. He was a "person of interest," as the sheriff had put it. Good thing the elderly man had already passed from this life. Finding out the crimes his son had committed likely would have hurt him dreadfully.

While she dressed, her cell phone rang. She'd been waiting for a call from Dana. Willow couldn't wait to tell her what they'd learned. "I think we found the guy who abducted me last night. I believe he could be the one behind Charlie's abduction. They'll bring him in for questioning once they find him."

"Wait, you were abducted? Why didn't you tell me?"

"That doesn't matter anymore. What matters is that he might be the person behind Marilee's murder and Charlie's abduction." Willow explained everything to Dana.

"Jay Haus's birth certificate didn't come up when I searched for

342

Mr. Haus's son, remember? I found Silas Everett. I'm sorry about that. Not to sound negative, but it all sounds like circumstantial evidence. You know it might not be him. And . . . I'm so sorry to hear Mr. Haus died."

"It's pronounced hoss, not house. He went on and on about how people mispronounced his name. Wait—" Haus. House. "Oh, Dana, maybe this is the connection. Katelyn's sister-in-law's last name was Houser, if I'm remembering correctly."

"She died years ago. I don't see how that—"

"I'm looking for a man. Her husband is still alive." Willow snapped her fingers. "John. His name is John Houser. See what you can find on him. I'm going to look too." Willow abruptly ended the call. She hoped the internet speed out there wouldn't be too slow.

Making the jump from Haus to House was a long shot. It could possibly take a lot of digging and referencing multiple sources to make a connection, if there even was one, but she had a good, strong feeling about this.

A hunch worthy of her grandfather.

She logged into professional software and plugged in *Jay Haus*, using *Houser* as an alternate name, then placed his residence in both Texas and Wyoming and waited for records to start popping up.

―――――

When Willow came out of her room, she was eager to find Austin, but Charlie sat at the table with Evelyn. The older woman patted Charlie's hand. Willow couldn't blame the girl for being distraught, especially after everything she had been through. Willow wasn't sure how she would react at hearing such news.

Willow descended the stairs slowly, gauging Charlie's reaction to her.

She glanced up at Willow, her eyes red, and offered a soft smile. "One of the deputies got my stuff for me from the cabin. I have the bank statements in my bag. Someone kept depositing money in Momma's bank account—one I didn't share with her. One I didn't know she had. We shared everything. Even the house was in both our names. That's what the money was for, wasn't it? He was paying her to raise me, wasn't he?"

Willow's eyes burned. "Whatever transpired before or whatever was going on, she loved you, Charlie. I've come to realize that truth. We can't know the circumstances—at least not yet—under which she was led to believe she should care for you. Maybe she had been told your mother was dying and you would need a mother. I don't know." *Please, Lord, help me to soften the blow. Give me the right words.* "So hang on to that one thing, okay? Marilee Clemmons was a woman who fiercely loved her daughter."

Charlie nodded, biting her trembling lip. "Yeah, okay. I know it's true. I know she loved me."

Willow snatched up her cell when it rang. She was still waiting to hear when Katelyn's flight would arrive. Would it be tonight or tomorrow? "Willow. I'm in Jackson, on the way to Grayback. I talked to Dana and learned you would be at that ranch. I wanted . . . I wanted to surprise her. But I thought I'd better call."

"What? You're already here and on your way?" Willow watched Charlie's expression. Would the girl hold up under all this?

"Yes. I don't want to waste time. You understand. You've done excellent work, Willow. I'm so thrilled, and I know your grandfather would be as well." Willow wasn't so certain anymore.

"Okay. We'll be waiting."

She ended the call.

Charlie's eyes widened. "This is it, then. She's coming here and I'm going to meet a stranger. She's my mother, but she's a stranger."

Evelyn reached for Charlie's hand and squeezed. "Now don't you fret. It's going to be just fine. All you're doing is meeting her. You can stay here at the Emerald M as long as you like. Remember that."

Charlie nodded. "Thank you. It means so much to me. Mack putting me up in the cabin meant everything. I owe him big-time."

"Something else you should know is that Katelyn has a big ranch with horses in Texas. She had always wanted horses. You train them here for Mack—I mean, Heath. It runs in your blood, I guess. I hear you are really gifted with them."

"I think so, yes. I was getting my degree in animal science with an equestrian minor. But it's so much. Too much to take in. I'm . . . scared."

"Take a deep breath," Willow said. "Take it all slowly. God has a hope and a future for you. No one is rushing you into this." Willow couldn't speak for Katelyn, though, who might definitely rush Charlie. "Meet Katelyn Mason. You can always visit her and her ranch later."

Charlie toyed with her mug. "Okay, sure." At least she had relaxed.

Austin hung back in the kitchen, taking it all in. She couldn't wait to give him the news, but Charlie had to come first. She studied his expression as he watched her. Admiration lingered in his eyes. Willow's breath caught at the attention he gave her.

She wanted to be in his arms. But she concentrated on Charlie. The next few moments and hours would be telling. She hoped and prayed both Charlie and Katelyn would be understanding and patient and neither would hurt the other. She left Charlie with Evelyn and moved to stand by Austin.

"Any news about Heath?"

He shook his head. "He's in the best place he can be right now. I'll go see him after Charlie meets Katelyn. We'll see this through, Willow. Together."

The sound of that warmed her heart. She couldn't help it and leaned in his direction. He took her hand and squeezed. Longing coursed through her. She had so much to say to this man. But she feared that once this was over they would go their separate ways again.

"I found it, Austin. I found the connection to Katelyn. John Houser, Katelyn's brother-in-law. He was married to her husband's sister. Jay Haus *is* John Houser."

Austin blinked, his surprise evident.

She continued. "Jay Haus moved to Texas with his mother. At some point decades ago, he started using the name John Houser. It became his legal name, though he never changed it on his birth certificate. But he was born Jay Edgar Haus in Wyoming. I found the name change in a public record search. I needed his original name, along with Wyoming and Texas to make that connection. He's the connection to Katelyn and Wyoming we've been looking for. The man behind Charlie's abduction twenty-one years ago is Jay Haus *and* Katelyn's brother-in-law."

CHAPTER SIXTY-SEVEN

Austin spent the next hour talking to the deputies. He'd informed them of what Willow had discovered about Jay Haus, and they relayed the news. He feared, too, that Katelyn Mason could also be in real danger. Good thing she was already on her way.

One deputy walked the perimeter of the property. Once they had their man, Charlie and Willow would both be safe. He thought that moment would never come.

A vehicle made its way up the driveway. A big blue Suburban. "Showtime, ladies."

Austin moved to the kitchen. He wanted to stand back and observe, protect. But mostly he wanted to be out of the way of the emotional tidal wave that was about to hit.

Charlie stood. Swiped her hands down her jeans. Footsteps clomped on the porch. Willow put on a smile and opened the door. Katelyn appeared pale but nonetheless healthy.

"May we come in?" she asked.

We? Austin pushed from the wall.

"Of course, please." Willow stepped aside and allowed Katelyn and a man into the house.

Austin's muscles tensed.

"Willow, I'd like you to meet my fiancé, John Houser."

———

Avoiding using his broken arm, he smiled and pulled Katelyn close. He was big enough that he could easily break her. "We've known each other for years. I've loved her for years, then finally she said yes."

"We want to make a family for Jamie," Katelyn added, making her reasons for the union clear. "John is a pilot with his own Cessna, and he got us here as fast as he could."

John's expression darkened. Willow took a few steps back and almost stumbled, but Austin caught her. "Watch it there," he said gently.

Act normal. Everything is normal. Don't let him know you're on to him. Not here.

But he was absolutely certain he wouldn't let Charlie leave with them.

Katelyn's blue eyes teared up as she took a shaky step toward Charlie. "Jamie?"

Charlie blinked and looked to Willow and Austin for reassurance. "I'm . . . I don't guess they told you. My name is Charlie."

Katelyn shuddered as though slapped and appeared to reconsider her approach. Regained her composure. "Charlie, then. I'm Katelyn Mason, your . . ." Her mouth quivered.

She raised her arms, wanting to hug the child she'd spent a lifetime searching for, then dropped them. Austin kept his eyes on John Houser, hoping the deputy outside was calling for backup. Surely Everett had already issued an alert for law enforcement to be on the lookout for Houser. The deputy should have stopped him at the door, though. Still, Houser wouldn't do anything here while people he cared deeply about were around. Better to get Houser alone.

"Um, why don't we talk over there?" Charlie offered a weak grin and another glance at Willow, then Evelyn. "Just so we can have some privacy."

"Sounds like a good idea." John made a move to join them, but Katelyn flashed her eyes at him. "No, John, just Charlie. I want a few minutes alone with the daughter I haven't seen for two decades."

"John, you can join us over here at the table," Willow said. "Would you like coffee? Something else to drink?"

Anger and something much more disturbing shone on his face. Possessiveness. "I'll take coffee. Black."

He yanked a chair out and eased into it. The man was far from relaxed. Austin remained against the wall, his hand slowly inching down toward his weapon. *Lord, please don't let it come to that.* He would check with the deputy in a few minutes if he got the chance, but he couldn't leave the women alone with this man.

Evelyn and Willow brought mugs out filled with coffee. Austin caught Evelyn on her way back into the kitchen and whispered, "Stay in there."

She smiled and laughed as though he'd said something funny. Smart woman.

Willow sat across from John at the table. *Not so close, Willow. Not so close.*

She eyed John over the brim of her cup. Then she set the mug slowly on the table. "I want to give you my condolences. I was sorry to hear about your father."

Oh, Willow, you didn't!

John frowned and nodded. "Thank you."

Suddenly, he lifted his chin, suspicion erupting in his expression.

Willow smiled. "That's right. I knew Mr. Haus."

John Houser said nothing, but Austin could see he was calculating what he would do next. Austin remained completely still, wishing his hand was already on his weapon.

"It hit me hard, but he lived a good, long life." So he would play it casual then.

In the living area, Charlie and Katelyn hugged. Austin could hardly believe they had made that much progress. Together they approached the table, wearing tearful but joyful expressions.

"Did John tell you he grew up in Wyoming, Katelyn?" Willow asked.

"What?" Katelyn took a step closer, her arm around Charlie— a cherished loved one. "You never told me that."

"It wasn't important."

Katelyn glanced to Willow. "And I told Dana I didn't have any connections to . . ." Her expression changed as she worked through the implications. "John?"

He rose from the chair, jamming his hand in his pocket. Austin pushed from the wall, reaching for his gun at his back. "Charlie, why don't you take Katelyn and Willow to see the horses? I'll show John the property."

Katelyn led Charlie to the door, opened it, then gently shoved her out. "Go, sweetheart. Go out there. Talk to that deputy and be safe."

"But—"

Katelyn shut the door. Uh-oh. She was as determined as Willow to face off with the man who had hurt her. "Why did you do it, John? Why did you take Jamie?"

He stepped back, his face reddening. "How could you think I would do such a thing?"

Her eyes boiled with fury as tears threatened to spill from them. "Don't lie to me. All this time, and I never saw it. I never saw you for what you really are. And now we're engaged!" She spewed the words. "At least I didn't marry you."

"I love you. I've always loved you. You should have been mine. You should have married me to begin with instead of him."

"Oh, I see how it is—and has always been. You are a sad, sad man, John Houser. I remember vividly how you comforted me when Jamie was taken. Tried to get me to marry you even then when you should have still been mourning Jennifer. It wasn't me you wanted. It was my money."

"It was never about the money, Katelyn. Now, please calm down. You're sick. You're not thinking straight. So what if I grew up here? So what if my dad was in a nursing home here? It has nothing to do with us. I've been in love with you for as long as I've known you. This, our engagement, our future marriage, it was always meant to be."

Fury blazed in Katelyn's eyes, mingling with betrayal. "You took my baby. I've been searching for a lifetime. Her lifetime."

"I've hired numerous investigators over the years to find her," he said. "Why would I do that if I took her?"

"You did all that but didn't want them to find her. You knew they couldn't. Not until I hired Anderson Consulting. Like me, you knew JT Anderson, or his granddaughter, had a real chance of finding her." Katelyn pressed her hands over her face. She looked like she might pass out. "It's all so clear now."

"No, no, no. I'm going to be the father Charlie never had. We're going to be a family now, just like you wanted."

"Get out of my sight!" Katelyn collapsed as though she'd fainted.

Was she unconscious? Austin's gut tensed. This had all been too much for the ailing woman. Willow, acting instinctively, rushed to assist Katelyn. John snatched Willow's hair, yanking her toward him. He pulled her up against him and pointed a gun at her head, using his broken arm as best he could.

Austin's heart jumped to his throat.

Focus. Save her. Take him down if it's the last thing you do.

"You couldn't leave it alone, could you?" Houser asked.

Willow's face contorted with pain. Houser's arm must be hurting him, too, to hold her like that.

"You and Marilee," she croaked out. "You grew up together. She must have had a crush on you and you took advantage of that, even in your early teens, then your mother moved you to Texas. You must have kept up that relationship when you came back to visit your father. You knew Marilee would do anything for you, including raise someone else's baby. As long as you made a few trips back every year to keep her happy and sent her money every month. Years later, Marilee was your father's nurse, so she could watch out for him too. Why didn't you just come back and marry her?"

"I didn't marry Marilee because I fell in love with Katelyn. Beautiful, sweet Katelyn. But she married my best friend, Cliff. We were all still friends then. I married Cliff's sister, Jennifer. That way I could always be part of the family and near Katelyn. We were one big happy family."

"Then she struck it rich. Are you sure that didn't have anything to do with it?" Willow asked.

"It wasn't fair. Mom moved us to Texas when I was only thirteen. I met Katelyn in eighth grade and fell in love with her. I waited for her this long. In the meantime, I worked hard in the oil field in Texas. Tried to make a better life for me and Mom, after what my dad did to us, cheating on her like that. His betrayal crushed her. Then Katelyn . . . she becomes an overnight millionaire? That should have been mine. I was the one to pour blood, sweat, and tears into the oil field. Not her." Again he pulled Willow's hair, forcing out a whimper. "I've come too far to let you ruin this for me. It's taken me a lifetime to finally get what I deserve."

Katelyn finally stirred. Had she heard any of this? She remained on the floor and scooted against the wall and out of the way. Good.

John dragged Willow toward the door. Austin tried to close the distance.

"Don't even think about it. I'll blow her head off if you take another step. I can see what that would do to you. It would destroy you. Just like me losing Katelyn will destroy me. So, we have an understanding. We're both going to lose everything today."

Austin nodded. "Please don't hurt her." *I love her. It's true, I love her.*

He had to keep him talking. Buy them some time. "So, Katelyn should have been your wife. I get that."

"Things took a turn for the better when her husband died. We were friends, sure, but Katelyn had always been mine. I think she knew that all along. Isn't that right, honey? But when he died, that was my chance. Except Katelyn was pregnant with *his* baby, and then she got sick. I came so close to losing her." Tears choked his voice. "But she was focused on that baby. I know she was glad I was there to support her, but everything was slipping from my fingers. Katelyn—I wanted her to love me, but then all she talked about was the baby. The baby this and the baby that."

"And Marilee wanted a baby." Willow locked eyes with Austin.

He read the message in her eyes. *Do it. Just shoot him.*

Not until he could do that without hurting her.

John's hand shook as he fingered the trigger, pointing the weapon at Willow one second, then at Austin the next. Sweat beaded on his temple.

They were running out of time. This wasn't going to end well. Austin couldn't see any way to survive this. Per usual, he had no good options.

Save one. At least Willow and the others would survive. If he could draw the man's gunfire away from Willow, then he could take him down. There was only one way to do that. If only he had a knife.

"Yes. When I went to visit Dad, I'd see Marilee too. She wanted to have my baby. I got an idea. Abduct Katelyn's baby and give it to Marilee. Both problems solved. Then Katelyn would have no more distractions. She could focus on me. She would marry me before she died. I would lose her, but her money would be with me, so she would always be with me. Except she recovered and didn't marry me. Still, I worked with her in the oil business. Managed the money. We were happy together. A deep, abiding friendship that would one day lead to marriage. If only Marilee hadn't gotten greedy and demanded more money. She threatened to destroy it all. She got what she deserved."

A man confessing all had no intention of leaving witnesses.

"I was back where I started. Katelyn sick again. Close to dying. And all she could think about was her daughter. Finding her Jamie. And I tried to stop it. I tried to stop you."

"You killed my grandfather!" Willow yelled. "How could you kill an old man like that? He was the best thing in my life!"

Hold it together, Willow. Don't force him to shoot you.

"He was the only one who could find Jamie. And you, his granddaughter. But you just wouldn't stop." He smiled then. A sick smile. "It doesn't matter. This time she agreed to marry me. Jamie needs a father. Or she would have, if she hadn't died today along with the rest of you."

"She's your fiancé, John. She agreed to marry you. You don't have to lose everything," Austin said.

"There's no way to fix this." John's wild eyes flashed. "I'm so sorry, Katelyn."

Austin had hoped it wouldn't come to this.

"So, you're going to kill me first, right?" Austin said. "Then you can make it look like I killed them and then killed myself, but the only way that is going to happen is if you shoot me first."

"Exactly. I can't let you interfere." He aimed the weapon at Austin and pulled the trigger.

CHAPTER SIXTY-EIGHT

Willow screamed. John released her and dropped to the ground. Austin had shot him. She checked his pulse. He was dead. The deputy keeping watch outside burst through the door. Willow ran to Austin, who remained on the ground. He sucked in a ragged breath.

"Oh, Austin, I didn't think we would make it through this."

He glanced at her but didn't say anything.

"Are you hit? You wore the vest, didn't you?"

He shook his head. "No. No vest."

Fear coiled around her heart. "You're shot! Help, we need help!"

The deputy knelt next to Austin. He radioed for an ambulance and more deputies. "Here, put pressure on the wound."

Evelyn rushed from the kitchen and pressed towels against his side. Willow palmed Austin's cheeks and brought her face close to his. His lids fluttered. "Oh, no you don't. You listen to me, Austin McKade. You are going to live. You are not going to die on me. Heath would never forgive you! Do you hear me?" She pressed her forehead against his and sobbed. "Please, please, God, please."

"I don't know if you want me," she sobbed out the words. "I don't know if you love me. I don't know if it will help, but I have to say this. I love you, Austin. Please don't die on me."

The next few minutes moved by in a slow daze for Willow. Paramedics arrived. They took Austin in a helicopter—the fastest way to get him to the hospital. And they removed John Houser's body. Willow was numb all over. She couldn't lose Austin too.

JT and then Austin. What would she do?

On the porch, watching the helicopter fly away, Katelyn and Charlie held on to each other. Their kinship and the kindred spirit between them helped them connect quickly.

Evelyn held Willow. "You hold on to your faith now. You keep praying. It's a rough day when two McKade men are in the hospital. Both of them put their lives in danger to save others. Both are heroes, if you ask me. Let's get in Heath's truck. I'll drive you down to the hospital."

Willow didn't remember the long, rough drive down from Emerald M or the miles of highway to Grayback and the county hospital. She didn't remember being ushered into the hospital or sitting in the waiting room. Katelyn, Charlie, and Evelyn stayed with her to comfort and reassure her. Willow wasn't the only one in pain. Katelyn still had to work through John's betrayal, but she had Charlie with her now, and she wouldn't throw that away to mourn for the man who had betrayed her.

Though Willow's mind and heart were numb—the only way she could survive the pain—one thought kept swirling in her head. Why had she let Austin go? Why had she given him up before?

"Willow," a soft voice said. "Willow, honey. You can go in and see Austin now."

"What?" She peered up at Evelyn's lined features.

"He's awake and asking for you."

Evelyn helped Willow to her feet and led her down the hallway, accompanied by a nurse. She took her into the postoperative room where Austin was recovering before he was moved into Heath's

room. Dark shadows circled his eyes. His handsome face was unusually pale. Willow drew near to him, unsure of what to do or say. He wasn't even awake. How could he have asked for her?

She sat in a chair and leaned against the bed, as near his face as she could get. Then, finally, gave up the chair and sat on the edge of the bed and leaned forward until she was near his ear.

"I don't know if you can hear me."

"Stop talking," he mumbled.

Willow edged back to look at him. "What did you say?"

His gunmetal-gray eyes blinked at her. "I said stop talking."

She wasn't sure what he wanted from her and started to move away.

"Just kiss me, Willow." His eyes were clear, so it wasn't the drugs, she didn't think. "You're all I've thought about. So, please, just kiss me."

Her heart tumbled around inside her rib cage. His words brought too much joy and shocked her system after what she'd just been through. She leaned closer and gently pressed her lips against his. His hand came up and grabbed the back of her head, weaving his fingers through her hair and pressing her closer with more strength than she would have expected. She let herself get lost in Austin—his essence, everything she loved about him. He'd risked his life for her twice in one day. She wasn't about to leave him.

She eased away, but only a little.

"Every minute in this life counts. I want you, Willow. I love everything about you. I want to spend the rest of my life with you. I've put it all out there for you this time. No more secrets. I hope it's enough. Willow, will you marry me?"

Willow leaned closer. "I don't want to waste one more second without you. There's nothing I want more on this earth than to belong to you. I think JT knew all along that I still loved you, Austin. That I never stopped."

He grinned. "I suspect that's the real reason he called me. He'd planned to head to Wyoming. He had a flimsy thread at best but wanted me to follow it with him."

"Because by following that thread, he would force you to face your past."

"Face myself. He knew I had to do that before you and I could finally be together. I wish I could thank him."

He closed his eyes. The conversation was probably draining him.

She pressed her forehead gently against Austin's. *I love you so much.*

She couldn't have been more wrong in thinking she and Austin were over. But JT had never let go of believing they were meant to be together.

"If I could fix this for you, I would," he'd said about her parents' death. He hadn't been able to fix that, but that's why he'd tried so hard to fix what was broken between her and Austin.

Thank you, JT.

AUTHOR'S NOTE

Thank you for joining me on Willow and Austin's adventure. I hope you enjoyed their search for justice as they rediscover their love. I set this story (and the series) in the Jackson Hole region of Wyoming—one of my favorite places. Though I grew up in Texas, we spent many family vacations in Jackson Hole and the nearby parks. Then, wouldn't you know it, I married a guy who grew up in the region and has family there, and it's also one of his favorite places! So, of course, we had to spend anniversaries there. With the splendor of Grand Teton overlooking the valley of Jackson Hole, and the nearby, awe-inspiring super volcano in Yellowstone National Park to explore, I just knew you would enjoy the stunning setting. I also know that words alone could never adequately depict the spectacular landscape.

If you're familiar with the area, you'll see counties and towns in this book that don't exist, along with those that do. I took artistic license in creating two fictional counties as well as a couple of towns. Bridger County is a fictional county set in the real Bridger-Teton National Forest. Grayback, the Grayback Canyon, and the Grayback River are fictional places. Hoback (or Hoback Junction) is an actual census designated place within the real Teton County and is named after John Hoback, an early mountain man, trapper, and guide and is not connected to my fictional Hoback County, which is also named after him. Clair is a fictional town within Hoback County. Jackson is a real town within Teton County.

I wanted the freedom to write about two sheriffs and their deputies without stepping on the toes of the amazing men and women of the existing sheriff's departments and law enforcement in the region. I modeled the counties, towns, and even Emerald M Guest Ranch after real entities so the story would flow smoothly.

I hope you enjoyed *Never Let Go* and are looking forward to reading the second book in the series—Heath's story is coming next!

ACKNOWLEDGMENTS

Thank you to those who've walked with me on this journey, sustaining me, encouraging me, and putting up with me!

My family of genealogists—my parents, my grandmother, and Aunt Elaine. Admittedly, I wasn't that interested in our family history until recently, but I always loved hearing the incredible stories you unearthed and learning about heroes in our ancestry.

My inspiration—my oil-man brother Jeff and his wife, Tina. Thanks for your behind-the-scenes look at the oil business, striking oil, and for the inspiration behind this story.

My writing friends—I have so many who deserve my thanks, but a special note to these. Susan Sleeman, thank you for your encouragement, friendship, and amazingly knowledgeable writing advice. I don't know what I would have done without you as my daily sounding board. Lisa Harris, we started out in that critique group years ago and just kept going. I'm so thankful for your friendship, prayers, and encouragement. Shannon McNear, what a dear friend you've been to me through the good, the bad, and the ugly. God is with us, Shannon. Sharon Hinck, I thank God for my brief time in Minneapolis. I know he put me there just so I could spend time with you. You are precious to me.

My editors—Sharon Hinck (you get two mentions! Ha!). I don't think I could have even sent my proposal without your sharp eye and gentle prods to up my game. Ellen Tarver, thanks for helping me smooth out the rough places so I could feel confident when turning in the manuscript. Lonnie Hull DuPont, a *very* special thank you for seeing something in my story that you wanted for Revell and for giving me this opportunity. There are no words to adequately express my gratitude.

My agent—Steve Laube, you're one of a kind. Thank you for helping me realize my dream.

My experts—Kimberli Buffalo, genealogist extraordinaire. I appreciate all the time you put into reading the story and helping me get things right. Your insight has been invaluable. If I made mistakes, well, that's all on me. Steven Brown, for answering my questions about private investigators.

To the Revell team—thank you for making my book the best it can be.

My husband and children—Dan, thank you for believing in me and encouraging me to write when I could have been doing so many other things. Rachel, Christopher, Jonathan, and Andrew, you're my inspiration. I love you!

And to my Lord and Savior, Jesus, who opens the doors and leads me through them—you put the joy of writing stories for you into my heart. All the glory is yours.

Elizabeth Goddard is the award-winning author of more than thirty romance novels and counting, including the romantic mystery *The Camera Never Lies*—a 2011 Carol Award winner. She is a Daphne Du Maurier Award for Excellence in Mystery and Suspense finalist for her Mountain Cove series—*Buried, Backfire,* and *Deception*—and a Carol Award finalist for *Submerged.* When she's not writing, she loves spending time with her family, traveling to find inspiration for her next book, and serving with her husband in ministry. For more information about her books, visit her website at www.ElizabethGoddard.com.

LOOK OUT FOR

ELIZABETH GODDARD'S

NEXT

UNCOMMON JUSTICE

Novel

COMING FALL 2019